SEASON OF ADVENTURE

Other books by George Lamming

George Lamming

SEASON
OF
ADVENTURE

Ann Arbor Paperbacks

THE UNIVERSITY OF MICHIGAN PRESS

Copyright © by George Lamming 1960, 1979, 1999
Published by the University of Michigan Press 1999
Published by Allison and Busby Limited 1979
Originally published in Great Britain by M. Joseph 1960
All rights reserved
Published in the United States of America by
The University of Michigan Press
Manufactured in the United States of America
♾ Printed on acid-free paper

2002   2001   2000   1999   4   3   2   1

A CIP catalog record for this book is available from the British Library.

Library of Congress Cataloging-in-Publication data applied for
ISBN: 0-472-09655-9 (hardcover)
0-472-06655-2 (pbk.)

especially for
Neville Dawes
whose secret is clean in this adventure
joining his wishes to my deep gratitude
for the State of Ghana during my stay
with
Sophia, Mary Manful, Vick Merz and Suhame
Sonny, Freda and the African families at Technology
Claud Ennin, Katsina and Ado Kufour
Abdul Atta and Alex Boyo
Four Fingers Bertie Opoku
Good Ol' Jo Reindorph and the C.P.P. youth on Kingsway
weekends in Kumasi

SEASON OF ADVENTURE

CHAPTER I

Beyond the horizon of the trees it was too black to see the sky. But the music was there, loud as gospel to a believer's ears. It was the music of Steel Drums, hard, strident and clear: a muscled current of sound swept high over the *tonelle*. The women's voices followed, chanting a chorus of faiths that would soon astonish the night. They sang in order to resurrect the dead.

'So I put it to you.'

'It's late,' said Crim, 'the ceremony begin.'

Powell wasn't drunk. His step was accurate, though a little slow; but an evening of local gin had aroused his wits. Wind broke like three false notes of a bugle from his behind. For the tenth time he had said: 'So I put it to you.'

'Fartin' may be your national anthem,' said Crim, 'but it late.'

'Take it easy, man, take it easy.'

'But the ceremony go finish before we reach,' said Crim.

'My point will come clear after proper example,' Powell begged. 'I put it to you.'

Irritable and impatient, Crim walked ahead, sorting obscenities in his mind. A nut burst its shell in the red blaze of charcoal at the foot of the hill. The brazier was roasting under a pale hood of smoke. Crim stopped and parried with his hands in the dark, urging his friend to listen.

'Hear that tune, Powell, hear it!'

The women's voices fell to a hush, and the solitary cry of a tenor drum rose sudden as daybreak over the *tonelle*: a soft, funereal chime of steel casing its echo into the street. It whistled like sea wind felling the dark, green fingers of the willow trees. Crim felt the cry of the tenor drum, near and intimate as a feather probing the channels of his ears. Powell had recognised it too.

'Is Gort tenor drum what talkin' now,' said Crim.

'Real great,' said Powell, shaking his head, 'Gort great. He come good whenever he touch that drum.'

'Only got to blow his breathin' 'pon it,' said Crim.

'He come good, good, good,' Powell repeated, hooking his arm round Crim's.

They climbed over the first obstacles of the hill.

'Gort playin' like he was a high priest for the dead.'

'Like independence mornin',' said Crim, 'every note exact like his calypso for Deliverance Day.'

Powell had stopped.

'Is why I put it to you,' he said, as though no interval of silence had passed between them.

'All right, all right,' said Crim, and disengaged his arm. His anger returned, but the drums had tamed his mood. 'All right, is why you say the woman couldn't talk.'

And Powell started again on his slow, remorseless traffic of words towards an argument.

'Not woman, Crim, is lady she was,' he said, 'sort what let you see it when she walk, steppin' quick an' clean like a cat, legs keepin' close-close as if it had a hot boil egg lay twixt her crutch. Education in every part o' her make-up, head, brain, belly an' all. But is only after she done lose him for a husban' that she talk.'

'An' him?' Crim asked.

'Same thing only opposite,' said Powell, 'same class o' people. Sort what makes you feel marriage done order them to meet. So I put it to you how she goin' out with him, not doin' nothin' to lose her value, 'cause pussy is a piece o' property you can't play with in that sort o' meetin'. Things got to happen slow, an' like you didn't know it happen till it done happen.'

He paused to make water by the side of the road, but he didn't stop talking. His urine dribbled like a broken hose over the couple below, but Powell didn't hear what happened.

'This week Mr gentleman try to feel up her fingers,' he said. 'An' she give them like they belong to her sister's hand. Next week was a little kissin' an' so, not free an' easy, but nothin' to make a man feel bad. But is so he decide she was correct. She wasn't cheap,

12

Crim, like the old whores you bash in before you catch their name.'

A gale lifted Powell's urine over his shirt. He staggered back and clapped his hands dry. Walking towards the tree where Crim was waiting, he smelt his hands and closed his fly as he continued.

'The lady correct,' he said, 'kind o' ready-made wife, steady an' so. But now is time something happen.'

'I say to myself he playin' cripple,' said Crim.

'It have things you ain't understan',' said Powell. 'Mr gentleman ain't no cripple, but he waitin' 'cause it always have a limit to that kind o' holding back. Time come an' everything clear, a man expect what is common knowledge. So he decide to take the bull by the horns. An' she ready too.'

Powell rubbed his hands, and soothed his brow, and timed the arrival of his point.

'He know she ready,' said Powell. 'So it had the night he make his move. They position on the Sea Walk face to face an' belly to belly. Scene done set, an' he pressin' her to him an' thing. Start to kiss an' so. But she won't open up, Crim. Lady mouth won't open at all.'

'But what he waitin' for?' Crim asked, 'gentleman or man he ought to know where he store his tools.'

Crim seemed impatient with the man's delay.

'But he don't mind,' said Powell, ''cause is gentleman he is, so he nosin' round her ear like you see some dogs do, making suck-suck noise like he born again. Now he let his hand drop to bottom line, an' he manœuvrin' her in. When sudden so, Crim, sudden so she break away.'

'Is what business she playin' at all?' Crim asked.

'I put it to you how she break away,' said Powell, quickening his step, 'an' run, my Christ, Crim, is run she run like he threaten to murder her.'

Crim paused to consider the lady's escape.

'Was virgin pussy in middle age,' he said.

'It have things you don' understan',' said Powell.

'But is why she run?' Crim raged. He tried to see himself in the gentleman's place.

'Like you, his conclusion was wrong,' said Powell, changing his tone to regret. 'He think she was playin' extra hard to get, so decide there an' then he not wastin' time.'

'But was more than time things start to happen,' Crim argued.

'For weeks she never look him in the face again,' said Powell, closing his hands like a priest in prayer. 'Couldn't look him in the face, but only make believe she didn't want to. An' that was that. Like a man let down he aint make no further move 'cause he say if that's what she want, then that is that. Was only long after he done marry elsewhere she had the guts to say what happen that night. Was shame won't let her talk.'

'But is what in that to shame she so?' Crim insisted. He decided the man must have been diseased.

'Shame make her pride rise up,' said Powell. 'Happen so, when Mr gentleman was pressin' her from down below, lo an' behold, his hand burst open a boil she had 'pon her bottom. Simple as that.'

'But be Jesus Christ,' Crim started, and paused to see Powell's face in the dark.

'An' look what it cost her,' Powell said in a voice grievously dispossessed, 'she never get to be a widow. Never.'

Crim tripped over a stone in his haste to be near where Powell had halted.

'But, but . . . is what wont let she bawl?' he stammered.

'Shame,' said Powell. He could feel the weight of Crim's attention. 'Was shame come 'bout all through her pride.'

Crim always gave way to Powell's opinions, but the woman's shame had confounded him. He scratched his groin, dragging himself slowly up the hill. He was a man of very rough temper, honest and passionate in his actions; but there was no variety to his way of seeing. Either things were clear before his eyes or wholly absent from his mind. A man of clear conscience, he would say, explaining his judgement on himself. Crim saw and acted, making thought and action equal in his habit of directness; until his mind was arrested by some result he hadn't bargained for. A good part of his life had been spent in prison, but his conscience was clear. Powell understood.

14

'So I put it to you.'

'Don't put it no more,' said Crim, 'I go reach it all my own.'

'Can't do,' said Powell, eager for an argument. 'Contradiction done set 'pon what you say.'

Crim broke his habit of directness, and decided to meet Powell's challenge.

'What contradict where?'

'When I put it to you . . .'

'I says I go reach it all my own.'

'Is there contradiction set in,' said Powell like a man gathering his winnings. ' "My" wont take care o' all, an' "all" cover what you can never own.'

Powell laughed, and his wind bugled again, creaking loudly up his spine. The noise passed without comment like a breeze. Powell was the leader of a Steel Drum band, restless and proud in speech, relentless in arguing his point, often perplexed by the curious paradoxes which confused his thinking. He was Crim's habitual partner in crime, but his mind was more alert. He avoided danger until he saw his chance to create an event. Now he was pleased with Crim's response. He heard the tenor drum call again from the near summit of the hill; but he was coming to his point.

'So I put it to you as one man to a next.'

'Who say I's a man?' And Crim's voice meant what he had asked.

'Is you self say so.'

'When?'

'The very day you born.'

'But I couldn't make a note with words that day,' Crim argued.

'Is words make a note with you,' said Powell, 'like how you beat your drum till it shape a tune, words beat your brain till it language your tongue.'

'Is what that got to do with man?'

'Every everything. Till then you aint nothin' but a beast.'

'Some beasts does talk.'

'But talk aint nothin' till it ask,' said Powell. 'Man is a question the beast ask itself.'

'All right, I's a man.'

Crim was weary. The women's chant had joined the dark refrain of the drums as they approached a wide mud bank that swung like a river bed round the *tonelle*.

'So I can put it to you?'

'Put it,' said Crim, 'put it.'

There was a long pause while Crim waited. Powell's mouth gave off a sound like hiccoughs. His tongue tripped over disconnected syllables. Crim was waiting. Meek and resigned, he was giving way to Powell's point.

'But be Jesus Christ!'

'What happen?' Crim asked.

Powell broke into a stammer that grew less audible with each effort to begin.

'Crim!'

'What happen, Powell?'

'I forget. Be Jesus Christ I forget what I go put to you.'

Powell was drilling his thumb into the muscles of his jaw.

'Be Jesus, Crim.'

'It go come back,' said Crim, 'just take it easy.'

Crim would have liked to come to his aid. Powell always seemed to panic under the threat of his own failure.

'But how it is my words waitin',' he cried, 'waitin' right there for me to put my point, an' easy so, easy so I forget.'

'Is like the island where you born,' said Crim. 'It don't know how to find where it begin.'

Powell buried his hands in his pocket and quickened his step. He was perplexed by his lapse of memory.

'But is plain contradition, Crim, is plain contradiction that.'

'Perhaps contradiction help,' said Crim, 'but is the way you forget. Is not simple forget, is forget to remember. I hear it say a same thing happen to old Judge Benedict what reach the height o' law here in San Cristobal. When the butler one time announce that his black-sheep brother was waitin' downstairs to pay a visit, he say there was some mistake. The butler explain that wasn't no mistake, an' Benedict say: perhaps the young man did come to see his mother.'

Powell stopped sudden, trying to unravel Crim's meaning. He

seemed more perplexed than Crim under the spell of the woman's shame.

'You mean he forget the connection between the same woman two sons?' he asked, reaching to touch Crim's arm.

'You can call it forget,' said Crim, 'was a complete wipin' out from his memory. Is like how education wipe out everythin' San Cristobal got except the ceremony an' the bands. To teacher an' all who well-to-do it happen. Everythin' wipe out, leavin' only what they learn.'

Powell reflected on the harmony of Gort's tenor drum. Soft and sure, it seemed to open the pulse of every voice chanting a miracle of faith in the *tonelle*. Perhaps it was Gort's illiterate instinct that helped the dumb power of his drum. Gort's music seemed the answer to his lapse of memory.

'Is bad that wipin' out,' he said, his voice grown feeble with contrition. 'Is murder an' confusion when it happen. It kill everything. Now an' then an' all what is to come it confuse.'

'Was like your woman what let a nat'ral boil tie up she tongue,' said Crim.

'A man must got somethin' that he can't let go,' said Powell, 'like how Gort hold that drum.'

The drum dipped its sound; then surfaced through the air, calling like a human voice from the *tonelle*. The women's voices grew suddenly loud, exulting in the chorus which started to summon their dead. Crim pondered the gradual retreat of the tenor drum.

'I was thinkin',' he said, 'how the Independence would change all that wipin' out, change everythin' that confuse.'

Powell's pride had been aroused. His voice came loud and fretful.

'Change my arse,' he shouted, 'is Independence what it is? One day in July you say you want to be that there thing, an' one day in a next July the law say all right, from now you's what you askin' for. What change that can change? Might as well call your dog a cat an' hope to hear him mew. Is only words an' names what don' signify nothin'.'

The politics of freedom had always haunted Powell's imagination. Day after day he would punish his friends with argument in the

Forest Reserve. He would relate the news as though it were domestic rumour he alone had heard.

'Independence aint nothin' till it free,' he said. 'An' it don' have two freedoms any place. Is how I see it, Crim, clear an' straight like you beat your drum.'

Crim was more docile. He could never understand why Powell should suspect any gift he had been offered. Powell's pride was like the woman's shame whenever he had to receive.

'I say it was a real freedom happen when the tourist army went away,' Crim said. 'It look a real freedom they give San Cristobal.'

'It don't have that kind o' givin',' said Powell, trying to restrain his anger. 'Is wrong to say that, 'cause free is free an' it don't have no givin'. Free is how you is from the start, an' when it look different you got to move, just move, an' when you movin' say that is a natural freedom make you move. You can't move to freedom, Crim, 'cause freedom is what you is, an' where you start, an' where you always got to stand. I put it to you, suppose your little boy come up one day an' say: "Pa, you free to call me son," what you go say?'

Crim hesitated as though the question failed to make sense. Then he turned to face Powell.

'I free to call him son?' he asked. 'Well, be Jesus Christ, I'd slap him down. Before he blink twice I'd have slap him down.'

'I wasn't thinkin' that much violent,' Powell said. 'But is what I mean. Free is free, an' it don't have givin' an' it don't have takin'.'

'But is still free we is in name,' said Crim, remembering the morning two years ago when the Forest band celebrated Independence Day.

'It aint,' said Powell, feeling a spasm of anger burn dry inside his mouth, ''cause Raymond, an' Piggott an' Partride, Lady Carol an' all the powers that now be, the whole kiss-me-arse lot o' them is like the tourist army that give them freedom to bully you an' me. They harsh an' cruel 'cause they think that freedom is a gift they can't afford to lose. Is bad that thinkin', is the nearest any man come to killin' what he is. Take it from me, Crim, you can take it from me. If ever I give you freedom, Crim, then all your future is

18

mine, 'cause whatever you do in freedom name is what I make happen. Seein' that way is a blindness from the start.'

'I don't know 'cause everything confuse,' said Crim. 'Like with the Coca Cola. The children still drinkin' so much o' that overseas water that their piss start to look like a rainbow. Rainbows runnin' down every tree in Forest Reserve these days.' *Setting*

Powell was talking to himself, a soft, reflective mutter of words dribbled slowly beyond Crim's hearing: 'all your future is mine, all my future . . .' 'Tonight I remember uncle Titon,' he said.

'Is that uncle haunt you from a child,' said Crim.

Powell seemed uneasy as they came into the first flush of light. They saw the heads of the crowd vaguely emerge from the *tonelle*. Shovelling huge beads of sweat from his brow, Powell had pushed his hat askew. The light showed a coin of soot under his eye. Crim searched for an opening through the ragged edges of the crowd gathered on the mud banks of the *tonelle*.

'You lookin' wicked,' said Crim, 'like you done dead.'

Powell was nervous.

'How many corpse comin' up tonight?' he asked.

'It have two,' said Crim. 'Papa Guru . . .'

'Guru?' Powell whispered.

'Guru self,' said Crim. 'You scared he go tell what Titon do?'

'An' who next?' Powell asked, avoiding talk about his uncle.

'Guru comin' first,' said Crim, 'then it have a boy what had some bad loss. He follow next.'

Crim stood tiptoe, trying to see Gort's hands above the crowd. The music stirred his memory. He could see the women convulsed with dancing.

'Is like now so when I see Gort,' said Crim, 'I remember Jack o' Lantern. Remember Jack o' Lantern from Half Moon Bay?'

'Best genius the bands ever discover,' Powell said quietly.

The music had swept his voice away. It seemed this music had always been there, immortal as the origin of water swinging new soundings up from the sea's dark tomb of noise. And the women's voices chanted the resurrection of two souls from the ocean's deep chapel of skulls. The white skeletons had heard the call of the drums. The women grew hysterical with song. Each chant was an errand

19

chased by the drums' stern clap of steel. They knew the gods would come; yet danced as though their faith had been forgotten. The voices were tired, but the drums came to their aid, swelling each pulse with a loud refrain, feeding new energy to the night. Then the hard, clear rhythms of steel stooped to a hush, waiting for the anguished whisper of the chant; and the two were still, voice and drum, caught in an equal pause of quiet, making an equal partnership like the harmony of flesh wrapped round the bone. A stranger might have thought the music had stopped: the way their passion shrank and grew dim like the mortal end of breathing. But the drums rose again, ordering the chant to repeat its prayer, and the voices raced away, wading a fearful cry under the muscular stride of the drums.

Nostalgia throbbed like a pain in every pulse of Crim's heartbeat.

'Remember when the police confiscate Jack o' Lantern tenor drum?' he said.

'Was like takin' the air he breathe,' said Powell. 'Was a terrible shame what happen when he murder that constable man.'

'Was terrible to hang,' said Crim, 'but he didn't regret nothin'. I remember the mornin' they pass death sentence, an' the same Judge Benedict ask if he had any last words to say.'

'No Steel Drum boy ever forget his voice,' said Powell.

'I can hear it even now in Gort tenor drum,' said Crim. 'Your Honour, he said, Your Honour I don't care who make the country's laws if they let me make the country's music.'

'Is what those drums sayin' now,' said Powell.

The noise grew louder than ever. The harmonies were dispersed, as the music battled over the *tonelle*, impatient to embrace the sky. The drums had dismantled the darkness; the music started delirium in the women's eyes. They saw the leaves dance fatally down to their shuddering crust of roots. Rocks quivered, and every puddle of water froze like glass. The air was tight as steel around their throats; eyes gazed at the firmament that happened everywhere. Neither resurrection nor descent could name its course. But the firmament was there: a presence arriving in answer to the earth. All the elements had obeyed. And the drums rode their message through the night, moving deeper and deeper in dialogue with the dead. It seemed this music had always been there: a sermon of rhythms in revolt over the *tonelle*.

'I don't care who make the country's laws,' said Crim, 'if they let me make the country's music.'

Powell was weeping his freedom tears.

CHAPTER II

They had forced a passage through the crowd. The reputation of the Forest band made it easy for them to gain a place up front. Powell was the leader; Crim played the second tenor drum. But they weren't keen to perform at the ceremony of the souls. Gort had been put in charge.

'Is what my eyes seein'?' Powell said. 'Over there, first row.'

They both looked at the girl whose elegance was no less conspicuous than the solitary white face beside her.

'Is the stranger man who bring her,' Crim said, 'or else she won't be here.'

'Look at her good,' said Powell, 'education an' class just twist that girl mouth right out o' shape. Like all the rest she learn fast how to talk two ways.' — *dualism*.

Crim couldn't resist admiring the novelty which her presence had created in the *tonelle*.

'Is great she look,' he said, 'almost as great as Gort.'

'She got open-air talk an' inside talk,' said Powell. 'Like tonight she go talk great with the stranger man. Grammar an' clause, where do turn into doos, plural an' singular in correct formation, an' all that. But inside, like between you an' me, she tongue make the same rat-trap noise. Then she talk real an' sentences come tumblin' down like a one-foot man. Is how them all is.' — *authentically, language based*

The girl seemed startled by the fury of the women's dance around the bamboo pole. The *tonelle* was an ordinary meeting place, a clean perimeter of earth partitioned by the night. The pole rose from the centre of the yard, climbing through seven feet of shaven joints, dry as bone, to make a funnel through the ceiling:

21

this was the mythical stairs down which the invisible gods would soon descend. A thick, white line of maize marked a circle round the pole, leaving an area of ground untouched by the women who danced around it. No one could trespass within the circle until the gods had arrived.

In the far corner of the *tonelle*, beyond the yellow arc of light, a tent rose briefly from the dust like a tower whose walls leaned near to collapse. The flambeaux were blown about like hair. Mounted on the wind, they rushed a blaze up to the ceiling; then fell with a downward pull of the air, scattering red jets of flame like a fountain flogged by fire. There were rows of benches on every side; a tumult of feet squeezed close along the corridors of dust. Behind the last row of benches, the space was choked by the crowd which stood, gazing towards the bamboo pole.

'Are you all right?' Charlot asked.

Fola couldn't afford the luxury of complaint. She was a stranger within her own forgotten gates.

'I wonder why you brought me here?' she said.

'They say the dead will soon arrive,' he answered.

Charlot was cautious. He tried to smother her meaning by drawing attention to the traditional purpose of the ceremony. When the dancing came to an end, the gods would enter their chosen priest with a power that gave him full command over the dead. Two souls, whose habitation after life had been the sea, would return to make confession of their past, talk to the living through their priest, then journey from this purgatory of ocean into some other kingdom of space. It was a necessary stage towards their eternity.

'You haven't answered me,' Fola said.

'Somehow I guessed you'd never seen a ceremony of the souls,' Charlot said.

'You know I've never been here before,' she said.

'I felt it my duty that you should,' Charlot said.

He had hoped he could obscure his motives by relating them to his work. Charlot was a teacher of history at the most exclusive girls' college in San Cristobal. Until six months ago Fola had been his pupil. Her career had been an unusual succession of distinctions.

It had caused endless argument among those girls who conceded her gifts; yet sulked at any mention of the privileges these had brought her. But she was popular where it really mattered.

Among the staff there were two opposing views about her character. Some thought she was withdrawn out of conceit; others analysed it as a modest symptom of success. No one could be sure since she had made very few disclosures about herself. Charlot had always avoided a judgment on this pupil. She had great beauty for her age, he had thought; meaning, at the time, that her figure had already achieved the certainty of its promise. That was three years ago.

He had first noticed her sea bathing at the Morant bay. It was a Sunday afternoon. The harbour was empty. Now and again the flying fish would leap and stagger tail upwards through a blue haze of sunlight, then disappear into the water. The tide was slow and quiet as it broke over an arm paddling out to sea. But its temper changed nearer the shore.

The heat was more intense; the beach became a crowd of noises: the loud, lascivious laughter of men gone mad from the music of Steel Drums; women were screaming to be rescued from the spray of foam blown over the petticoats which they used for swim suits. The boys heaped sand over their heads until the drums disturbed their balance.

The voices spoke in a raw and vivid dialect which Charlot could barely understand. He walked through the noise, closing his ears with his hands, hearing the resonant, sea-borne rhythm of the drums behind him. He continued up the wide stretch of sand towards the lighthouse. It was quiet where he paused staring towards the south end of the beach. It seemed unreal that anyone could be alone on a beach so densely crowded in one place. He turned and followed the track behind the lighthouse.

The sound of the drums was no more than an echo now. Here the beach was strewn with pebbles; the waves grew high, crashing far out to sea. From the secluded caves of grape-vine, someone was laughing. Then he saw the party not far away.

These were the families he had met during his first year of welcome in San Cristobal. The faces were always the same. He watched

23

them from afar, trying not to lose sight of Fola on the beach. They had just come in from a swim. The women were busy passing round huge cellophane parcels of cold ham. The men talked and swallowed and looked remorseful whenever they were rebuked. Curious and attentive in every detail, they had managed to be elegant in their greed. The atmosphere was quiet and gay: a closely-guarded suburb of prosperities brought into the open air.

Fola was still laughing. The wind had lifted her hair up from her neck. She caught the ends, pulling two wide, wet bands across her eyes. The drums were rolling quietly up from the south end of the beach. Fola danced her toes under the sand, kicked a hot, black branch of grape-vine over her head, and wrestled her body round to the quickening rhythm of the drums. The music faded away and she was quiet, until a wave broke over her feet.

She had run down the slope of the beach, breasting the pipe-line in a reckless dive into the sea. Two boys chased after her. When she came up, her hair was dripping clean and straight as a horse's mane down her shoulders. Her bikini had acquired the colour of salmon where she stood. The light played daggers over the muscles of her naked torso. The drums were rolling over the trees again. Her mouth was open; and the soft, pink lips lifted widely up to the sun as she danced.

It was this lack of self-regard which Charlot had admired. It gave authority to everything she did. Watching her dance, he was reminded of the crowd at the other end of the beach. She hadn't lost their rhythm—sensual, vigorous, innocent in her sense of physical delight. Charlot was sure there was some hidden parallel of feeling between the girl he met three years ago and the coarse exuberant faces of the crowd which had suddenly grown hysterical in the *tonelle*. Social refinement had become Fola's natural atmosphere, yet she had kept the raw, unbridled certainty of instinct which tossed those women through their dance around the bamboo pole.

Fola was ready to challenge his opinions. She wanted to ask why it was necessary for her to see the ceremony, but she was doubtful where Charlot's answer might have led her. Also, the atmosphere of the *tonelle* had increased in its effect upon her. There was something intimidating about the women. The dance had become more feverish. Fola recognised what they were doing, but there was too much tension in their bodies. She expected something to collapse inside them. Fola had lived in the shadow of two terrors: hypnosis and the sight of rats. She thought of both and the dancing made her shudder.

'What will they do next?' she asked, trying to discredit the importance of her interest.

'They'll make the *ververs* next,' said Charlot.

'What *ververs*?'

'You'll see,' he said, 'it's the source of all the visual arts in San Cristobal. Just shapes of fish, fowl and whatever the gods favour.'

It was warm, yet the wind had set a chill over Fola's arms. She felt a trickle like water drip out of her hair into the crevice of her ears. She started to lift her arm; then glanced at Charlot, and decided against any movement that might attract attention to herself.

No sign of a god was there, but the *ververs* were coming to life around the bamboo pole. Fola watched the women dribble the grains of maize through their fingers. The shapes grew slowly over the dust within the circle: signs and codes and the animals of the spirits that were being summoned.

An untutored perfection guided the women's hands as the earth breathed and struggled into shape. The heart of an animal, emptied in flight, had soon transformed the dust. Fish paused in a fixed astonishment of space. Charlot saw a spear multiply its head many times. Fola was considering the accuracy of lines that showed the skeleton of each remembered creature. The atmosphere boiled with a passion that could derange her mind. The chant had become a monotony which compelled.

The *tonelle* was gradually filling up. The benches couldn't hold any more, but the crowd had collected where a real partition would have walled them out. A child was suddenly awake. She disentangled her arms from two enormous pillows of breast and slid her body down the woman's knees. The flambeaux burnt all awareness from her glance. Awake at last, she rubbed her eyes and joined the women dancing round the pole.

The gods were on their way. The women could hear it from the exultation of their own voices. Blind with fear, articulate in joy, they applauded the frenzied dancing of the child. Charlot believed but could not share the vision which had engulfed those eyes gazing their recognition on the ground. They were about to see their wish come true. The gods would soon arrive, followed by their chosen dead.

'Sometimes I'm a little ashamed the way I feel about this place,' Charlot said; and Fola seemed to take some comfort from his admission.

'But why?' she asked.

'Because it's not the island I like,' he said, 'it isn't the dance or the drums that I really love.'

'Then what are you doing here among these peope?' Fola said. 'How many in your position would bother to come into this shanty town? And it's not the first time you've been.'

'I come because there are things that remind me of myself,' he said.

His reason had given her some assurance against the frenzy of the crowd.

'What's wrong with that?' Fola asked, 'with liking things that remind you of yourself? Everyone I know does the same.'

'But I'm not everyone,' said Charlot.

Fola waited until the noise died down. They could barely hear their voices through the boisterous applause which came from the crowd. The gods were on their way.

'But what's it about the island to remind you of yourself?' she asked.

She had seen Charlot as a part of her own world, yet different from that other world which danced before them now. The division was simple and complete, like the separate cubicles of pleasure that happened on Sundays at the Morant beach.

'You know my background?' Charlot said.

Perhaps this was the last time he would witness a ceremony of the souls; he would soon be leaving San Cristobal. The thought of his departure made him more open. He was inclined to share some private confidence with Fola.

'My father was a Spanish Jew,' he said, 'my mother some part Chinese and half French. I was born by chance in West Africa, but learnt all that I know in England.'

Charlot had left England at the age of twenty-nine: self-exile chosen in the vain hope that he could re-form his tastes by notions of adventure in a foreign place. Life had become a form of speculation for him. Curious and resourceful, he was a young man who had decided to obey all his enthusiasms: a romantic in his pursuit of some other place whose style of living might help to change the habits he had formed.

He had wanted to undermine the monotonous strength of his own inheritance. Europe had become the name of some erratic growth of moss or weed which totally imprisoned all his hopes. But San Cristobal had put an end to all his notions of adventure. Fola seemed a perfect example of his own displacement.

'What does it matter about all those mixtures,' she said, 'you're still you.'

'I'm all these,' said Charlot, 'just as you're a part of those women there.'

Fola was reluctant to answer. She glanced at the women, then quickly turned to see Charlot's face.

'It's not the same thing, you know, unless you want to suggest . . .' Fola stopped sudden. She had that self-protective nerve which can pick up the slightest particle of danger. There was going to be trouble in the turn their talk had taken.

'You want to suggest that I believe in all "that," ' she said. Her voice was low, distant, closing on a note of quiet disdain.

'But I've seen you dance, Fola.'

'What's that got to do . . .'

Charlot wouldn't let her finish.

'It's the same rhythm,' he said. 'And the music of the Steel Drums. You yourself have said no music makes you feel the same way.'

'But what's that got to do with holding ceremonies?' she challenged, 'and talking to the dead?'

'There wouldn't be any music without the ceremonies,' said Charlot. 'You couldn't do your dancing without those women.

It's from being so near to them that you learnt how to move your body.'

Fola felt a sudden resentment towards him. Her triumph would have to be as large as the families whom she was about to defend; for the civilised honour of the whole republic was now in danger.

'Near?' she said, curtly.

'In feeling you are,' said Charlot, 'you can deny them anything except the way you feel when the same rhythm holds you.'

Fola was quiet. She glanced at the child and thought with bitterness: 'so that's how he sees me. The college where he teaches, the way I live: all this means nothing compared with what he *thinks I am*. He thinks I should be like those women. Perhaps he even thinks I was once like that child.'

Fola reflected on the vagueness of her memory. She hadn't forgotten her childhood, but it didn't seem to offer any experience so tarnished as that child's. She wanted to say something that would offend Charlot; but her confidence was badly shaken.

'If you could dance,' she said. 'If only you could dance! Wouldn't it be the same?'

'Never,' said Charlot. 'I could never be held that way. However much I'd like to feel like you, I know now that I can't.'

For a moment Charlot seemed to regret his candour. He had sensed Fola's discomfort. He guessed how she was thinking, and he tried to distract attention from what he had said. But Charlot had some private contract with a truth he couldn't deceive. He refused to change the subject altogether.

'You remember our discussions at college,' he said, 'about having a sense of one's past, the need to know what happened. Not every niggling detail, but the *large* events.'

Fola was thinking about the origin of the ceremony as she had heard him discuss it. Fragments of information came slowly together in her mind. *Vodum* was an African word for spirit. This ceremony was a religious manifestation based on a serpent cult that originated on the slave coast of West Africa. It had first reached San Cristobal during the despatch of slaves in the sixteenth century. After three hundred years of distance, it must have undergone all sorts of change.

But the music seemed to preserve the total spirit of this cult. The facts were unreal until she looked again at the faces of the women. They had lost control over their passions. The bodies seemed to stretch beyond this moment of the dance. Perhaps the gods were there, waiting for the dance to prove their presence in the *tonelle*. The child's eyes revealed some terrible future. Body and spirit had entered equally into what the women and one child had seen. The dance was a kind of prophecy. Fola knew that something was about to happen, something her imagination could not tell. She felt again that old dread of hypnosis and her childhood fear of rats.

The child was wide awake. It seemed she had seen everyone and everything inside the *tonelle*. The dance was an instinct which her feet had learnt. She gave all her attention to the *ververs* dribbled on the ground. She avoided the line that enclosed the pole, knowing it would be an error to touch the circle of maize which guarded the *ververs*.

The women's chant was broken by applause. The child heard the voices competing in her praise. She became hysterical; wild, light as air and other than human, like the night clouding her eyes. Her voice had cried out: 'Hair, hair! Give all, all, all, hair.' And she clapped until there was no feeling in her hands.

And the voices came nearer than her skin: 'Dance, Liza, dance! Dance! Dance! Liza, Liza, Liza, dance! Dance, Liza! Dance, Liza, dance.'

That was all she recognised of meaning in her ears: but she felt the hands pushing her forward now; first a jerk which soon tailed off into the play of fingers down her back. Gently after each jerk, the hands were moving her forward like a pawn; forward to the forbidden circle of maize; forward, forward to the *ververs* that would burst her toes.

Fire of spirits in her eyes, and no longer a child as she watched the shadows strangled by her wish for hair blazing from the summit of the bamboo pole! She trampled upon the circle of maize, exploding shapes like toys under her feet, dancing the dust away. For the gods were descending to the call of voices: 'Come! Come! in O! In O spirit of water come! Come!'

Now: gently, stage after gentle stage and feather-wise as if now

29

orphaned of all sound, the voices were dying, second by full measure of second; then died on the gentlest of all sounds, 'come, come, in O spirit of water come, come, come . . .'

They raised the child like a corpse and bore her, mortal in look and scarcely breathing, back on her mother's bosom. The music was softer now; nervous and shrill as though the spirits had throttled its sound as the tenor drum died, wading slowly and far away like a patter of birds' feet on the roof.

His eyes now bright with magic from Gort's ten fingers on that tenor drum, Crim turned and whispered: 'Great. Great Gort!'

Now, without drums, his fear had come back.

'Maybe a bad night, tonight,' he said.

'Is what make you say so?' Powell asked.

Crim polished the smooth segments of a drum as he watched an old woman who waited near the tent. Her face was dry. Her left hand grew a huge carbuncle, hard as bone over her knuckles.

'I hear it say Aunt Jane an' the *Houngan* had some row,' said Crim. 'She didn't like lettin' them two come in the *tonelle*.'

'But the white stranger man been plenty times before,' said Powell.

'It have plenty times he come,' said Crim, 'but is different at ceremony o' the souls. Only who belong to the dead got any right inside.'

Powell had a natural resentment towards strangers. In the Forest Reserve where all the bands in the Republic met for practice, he would never allow strangers to intrude. But the *tonelle* was not his affair.

'A next thing is,' said Crim, 'that dead boy what spend all his life lookin' for what he lose.'

'What Aunt Jane got to do with that?' Powell asked. He couldn't concentrate for fear of what he might hear about his uncle.

'Aunt Jane aint business with the dead boy,' said Crim, 'but the woman what make him lose all his life-time lookin' aint here.'

'O Jesus an' all spirits,' Powell cried, 'keep that dead quiet tonight. Hold down that dead.'

'Is against all custom for those what guilty to stay away,' said Crim. 'Christ knows I don't feel it safe so near the tent.'

Charlot was leaning forward to watch a procession of women walking into the light. The *Houngan* poured a small libation in the dust, then gargled with a mouthful of the local gin, as he passed forward. The women walked behind, coming abruptly to a halt whenever he paused, offering the bottle to any worshipper nearest his hand.

The women paced gravely through the dust in a white tomb of sheets that clothed their bodies to the ground. Each faith, drinking in its power from the *Houngan's* gin, had poured a libation; then swallowed a mouthful of the gin.

It seemed there was no order to his giving. Fola could feel the pimples swelling over her arms. She studied the faces of those who had drunk from the bottle of gin, so that she might detect some order in the *Houngan's* benediction. But a sweat broke under her eyes as she heard the swoon of a woman's voice behind her. She wanted to ask Charlot what he would do if the *Houngan* ordered them to drink. But the woman's voice was reaching cold and sticky as a hand into her skull. Her breath blew a staleness of gin odour round Fola's ears. Fola's attention was divided between the crippled swoon of the woman's voice and the progress which the procession was making towards the bamboo pole.

Would Charlot drink of the gin? And what would happen if she refused? Was the woman behind her going to be sick? It was the sound of a voice in some near stage of asphyxia, crying: 'Spirit, ride! Spirit! ride! ride! An' come, come, come sister, come, hold sister, hold and let it come, inside O! Spirit, let it, inside O spirit come! An' kind let it O O O come, come.'

Fola noticed Charlot put his fingers to his ears. She looked towards the tent where the procession was waiting. Two of the women lay prostrate on the ground, their heads raised high on smooth, rectangular pillows of stone. The bodies looked like a bridge of corpses leading into the tent. The old woman had stooped to spread a large white sheet over their bodies. Fola hadn't noticed his arrival, yet the *Houngan* now stood an arm's embrace between her and the broken arc of maize near the bamboo pole.

He was a short, black man, narrow around the waist, almost fragile in the spareness of his arms. He wore a pair of snake-

31

skin sandals. The straps parted and crawled in a bright black radiance lapping round his toes. The smell of cemeteries rotted his hands. His eyes were the colour of burnt hay. Delirious in their gaze, they sparkled and cracked into splinters of light like glass. He carried an axe in his right hand, a bracelet of black bones was swinging freely round his wrist when he waved the axe in worship above his head. The gods resided in every tooth of point and blade. Invisible by choice, their absence had made the night more nervous.

'Go on, Fola, take it,' Charlot whispered, 'you'll have to take it.' The bottle slipped but stayed secure, as she passed it back to the *Houngan*. Fola hadn't swallowed, but she could feel the sting of the gin at the edge of her tongue. It made knives in her mouth, slitting the tubes of her throat with each inch of breathing.

Powell and Crim had been watching her all evening. They knew the old woman was watching too. Crim didn't trust the knowledge in Aunt Jane's eyes. He grew more nervous each time she glanced up at Fola.

'Stranger man playin' he not notice nothin',' said Crim, 'but that girl go panic.'

'Let she panic,' said Powell, and spat between his legs in the dust. 'You would panic same way inside where she live. Never see her house? It got more room than the prison she father send we to.'

'She go panic!' Crim kept saying, 'that girl go panic!'

'If the stranger man what bring she don't notice,' said Powell, 'let she panic.'

'But who know what happen next if that girl go panic in here,' said Crim. 'That girl father done swear he go crush these bands out of existence. Is not ordinary police you playin' with, Powell, is Chief Commissioner o' police in question. He could crush these bands like that!'

Crim snapped his fingers and turned away considering the swoon of the woman's voice on the other side. He was afraid for the future of the bands. But Powell's resentment had got the better of his reason.

'Till they get crush,' said Powell, 'let she panic!' His voice was like the blade of the *Houngan's* axe.

The *Houngan* had entered the tent alone. The old woman sat on a box guarding the sheets with a candle in her hand. She had seen Fola. She watched her until she noticed the look of agitation in her eyes. It increased with each fit of the voice swooning behind Fola's head. Charlot hugged his jaws and blocked his ears as he stared, unseeing, at the ground.

Every voice, spirit-obeying and servile as dust, soon fell humbly into a silence which spread over the *tonelle*. Fola wanted to run away. But her departure might have seemed an act of blasphemy against the still reverence of the crowd gazing towards the tent. The silence persuaded her to feel that she was being spied upon. She was haunted by the look of knowledge in the old woman's eyes. Fola would have liked to see her own face in a mirror. It would have helped her to obscure any visible signs of her fear. But the woman's swoon had returned. Other voices were coming to her aid in a million nightmares of general weeping.

'Last night, last night, night, it stretch me out, his spirit stretch me out!'

'It stretch beside her whole again. Spirit! collec' his bones! Feel, I feel it fit him! In every part! Fit him spirit, fit him whole . . . come, come, come inside O! Spirit, come! Come, Guru, come, come . . .'

'Let it ride you, sister, let it clim' you slow, let it, let it . . .'

'Spirit give her good, give her spirit, give her good . . . good. Give!'

'Clim' sister, clim' your mountain, clim' it slow, slow, slow. Ride it, spirit, ride her kind.'

'Clim', clim' her spirit, belly to back an' under clim' her good. Hold, hold, sister, let Guru come, come clean an' ride, ride in his white bones home, inside! Inside the sister spirit make his home. Come, Guru, come! Come!'

The voices were all raised in prayer, answering to the grave supplications of the priest. Fola looked to see if there was movement in the tent; but her glance was intercepted by the old woman who still watched her. Was the old woman's glance an accident? The voices had wrought a gradual contamination of Fola's senses. Was she becoming a part of their belief? Would they really hear the sound of dead voices in the tent? Her questions were other than an interest to examine. She became aware of their contagion in her mind. The prayers were a conspiracy against her doubt. The voices grew loud and louder in their prayers, each prayer like a furious bargain for her faith.

She wanted to leave the *tonelle*. Each moment of her stay seemed to increase the fear that she might not be able to escape the conversion of their prayers. She saw the old woman glance at her again. She was ashamed that Charlot might have guessed what she was thinking. Perhaps this was what he meant by his accusation: she had denied some bond of feeling with the women who danced around the bamboo pole. But it wasn't true. She knew it wasn't true. Yet their prayers couldn't touch Charlot. They couldn't arouse the slightest fear in him. He wasn't near to anything they felt. She reflected on the difference between herself and Charlot. She resented his safety. She wanted Charlot to take her away; but she dared not move while the old woman's eyes blazed upon her, old and sure and purposeful in their scrutiny. If she tried to move, they would have thought their prayers had worked. Her fear was already a concession to their power.

But it was too late to move, too late to talk, too late to stop the slow, hot, slow tautness of muscle under her thigh. Her muscles were giving way to a slow, hot trickle of water sliding down her legs. She was wetting her pants. Drip by drip, then free as a drizzle, her urine was making a noiseless puddle under the bench.

The pimples hardened on Fola's arms. The old woman was snuffing the candle out as the voices faded into the silence of the tent. The wind stirred a noise like water tunnelling dead leaves through the dark; but the noise didn't pass. It seized its echo in one place, repeating a tremor that circled within the orbit of the tent.

'You don't believe it, Charlot?' Anchored to her honour, Fola cried: 'Do you?'

'There's no one else in the tent,' Charlot said dryly. Yet they could hear two voices: the *Houngan* speaking softly to identify one known dead presence in the tent. The details were ordinary as the names of streets. Then the other voice rose, barely audible at first, choked in a struggle to link its syllables; and that noise of the wind came down, nearer, more tremulous, like the suffocation of a tide breaking fretfully over firm sand, and the woman swooning behind Fola in all her guilt for being the dead man's sister.

The dead voice was bringing one stage of its accusation to an end. The entire *tonelle* had heard her slip to hell. The dead man's sister was weeping her atonement, possessed by the need to be reconciled with the voice thrust in mockery under her skull. Her hands clutched at the wind as her voice dribbled its odour of stale gin into Fola's ears.

'Tell it! Tell it!' she cried, 'help him, *Houngan*, help him tell it all. Is a last time his soul see water. Spirit pour! Pour it out! Wash me through from hole to hole, in an' out let it run! All over! Bring me! Bring! Bring me to his sea-wet water. Ride me spirit! An' comin' I comin'! With it! Comin' wide open with it! All! All! All o' me comin' wide open comin' in a hot night-time water, O spirit is come I comin'! Sea cool O spirit clim' me an' I come, done come! Cool, cool, sea-wet cool all in an' out, cool, I done come, cool, cool, cool . . .'

Her body slumped forward. The dead presence was still. Fragments of the episode passed from voice to voice along the benches. Powell's hands shook when he heard the *Houngan* whispering prayers for the soul's release from the water.

'So it was the diamonds,' Crim said. 'What Titon do that for? Why Titon put his knowledge to such evil purpose?'

'Money, money,' said Powell, 'is money make him do it. . . .'

'But is what the sister an' Titon want so much money for?'

'Just 'cause they want it. Is worse, worse kin' o' wantin' to possess you,' Powell observed as he waited for the *tonelle* to recover from the memory of Guru's voice returning his sister and the long exiled Titon to their treachery.

The episode was fresh in Powell's memory; fresh and mysterious. When Titon disappeared with the small iron casket in which the diamond fortune had resided, no one knew until tonight why Titon was now living destitute and far from home. After a month of effort, he had forced open the small iron casket. The lid had been soldered with molten lead, the bottom panelled with expensive and rare velvet cloth like a coffin. Inside, Titon's eyes had beheld, in wonder, the moss green fragments of Guru's false teeth, and not a trace of his diamond future. Like the stars on fire with man's luck, too far and hot to touch; these small grains of fortune had disappeared again.

The *Houngan's* voice hadn't changed its tone. He was making supplications for another soul. Voices answered from the back with similar prayers. Then an interval of quiet when nothing was heard but the dark, tense quiver of the wind moving slowly over the tent. The last soul had surfaced. And soon, sooner than lightning, its sound had bolted with shivers through the old woman's body. But Charlot didn't see when she was hoisted like a bird from the bench, and laid flat out on the ground. And with what power of spirit in every particle of dust feeding her tongue!

Preoccupied with his own past, it seemed he had forgotten that Fola was still there. Charlot was reflecting on his absent friends alive, and without effort could guess where they would be now: almost midnight in London, and the habitual, false voices were over with giving and refusing the very last round of drinks, each manhood proved for the night. Yet the couple from Hampstead would still be parked outside the publican's gate, unsure of shelter, exploiting intellect until the unjust but necessary offer had been made: where are you going to stay? and the prompt refusal to sleep indoors because the state must be blackmailed; the girl, beautiful and most blind as she considers the revolt of her hair and the generous truth that the world will be rescued by a boy on the lunatic fringe; but 'outside' becomes more real as midnight freezes its mattress of heath under each lovering head: the hour for their despising everyone and themselves.

Like the petulant souls in this tent, most of his London friends would be charting through dead lakes of coffee the origin and end of every well-known failure.

Was this a reason for bartering his future to a childish notion of adventure? Was it because the only England he had known was a kind of corpse in future argument with itself, a dead voice bearing witness to its own achievement, passionate in incest with its past? Yes, yes, yes, he said, and heard twenty-nine years of proof for each resounding yes.

But this live corpse of England was a powerful visitation, for it

36

had fathered two aspects of contemporary life. The politics of this corpse had evolved into a kind of pantomime where teams, no less resourceful on either side, performed a bitter conflict of opposing interests. They were flawless in their roles of hateful intensities, whether argument turned on brutal murders in remote possessions, or the rumoured neglect of the nation's kittens.

Their passion knew only shades of emphasis, and Charlot felt hurt in every nerve as the ceremony returned him to the origin of its serpent cult on that slave coast, simmering this very moment with dangerous emergencies. Dangerous and emergent beyond the corpse of England's feeling; for those men alive at the heart and edge of that disfigured continent are ripe, forgetful and ripe with intentions that are too loud to hear a liberal, dead whisper from afar.

In this moment, Charlot was thinking: those Africans will walk the land like adults who are too busy to remember the senile details of arrangements made in their childhood. Hurt in every nerve! Charlot was hurt; for rebel and outsider as he claimed to be, he believed in the very belly of his pride that this could have been his country's finest claim: the hour when eye could have looked into eye with true achievement, and read each other's darkness and misgiving without any loss of face. Yet here he was, using one girl's predicament to test a tragedy that might be waiting for her too.

And in this atmosphere of argument, his own live corpse, his own England, was still speaking with a tongue which knew only shades of emphasis. Time and the skill of poets had forged their language into the finest instrument of speech he could imagine. One word to release an image that returned your meaning perfectly balanced by an infinity of lucid shades. Without this grace of language given, the corpse might have been betrayed. But the language helped. The most monstrous implications of a difference between political enemies could not disturb the general ground of their agreement. If those voices in debate, so gracious and so involved, were not human and alive, history could have recorded a miracle of the dead in a dialogue of judgment on the living.

The second achievement of England's corpse was the effect of

37

the pantomime on his generation. They were angry. But it was not the potent anger of a man unfairly dispossessed, a man whose silence might contain a dangerous future. The anger of Charlot's generation had no precise details. It was not about poverty or hunger or waste. Yet they talked about these things because silence, like the political usage of peace, was regarded as a malady. They shared this lack of emphasis with their seniors in the pantomime. Hunger and poverty and waste had equal urgency with the general activity they called the Arts. Literature among the more attentive was an organism with all its parts complete. They could dissect it like a knee, and put it up again. They checked its pulse, charted the course of its veins, and listened for the mortal pause of its heart, like a patient far gone in cancer. Their anger was an atmosphere in which they moved; a burning faith which showed their futures raped. In anger every one, because they had been deceived, not simply by parents and teachers. They had been deceived by the very assumptions which had once made their country great. They were angry and bitter, made impotent with private grief, because they knew they had to reject the life which the senile wisdom of England's corpse had inherited for them. Intelligence would have blackmailed any sign of their acceptance: and yet they did not feel, in the private sanctions of the heart, they did not feel that the life of the corpse was truly unliveable. Their declarations of refusal were honest. Charlot could swear to that. But honesty was not enough to reach the depths of their original calm. Moreover (and this was the time he packed his bags) their anger had started to pay off.

As he reflected on the name and circumstance of each, Charlot kept arguing with himself that it was not their fault. It was not their fault that many like Charlot had been born poor. There were no hidden calculations in their anger. No one had foreseen that anger could bestow on poverty a new and attractive pedigree. It was useless to deny what had happened. Perhaps they were not looking when the plebeian afflictions of their childhoods turned overnight into an aristocratic necessity.

They couldn't help their anger; for there, effortless and unaided before their eyes, all their intentions had assumed a different role.

Without any change of attitude, without betrayal of the heart, they had suddenly won the approval of their enemies. It was the bloodiest bitch of a thing that could happen to men whose exclusive business was to look. But the corpse had done its work on his generation.

The dormant wisdom of England's old men now found completion in the anger of England's young. Secret and beautiful as a snake, the corpse had crawled into their lives, turning each passion into a circus of abuse, harmless and truculent as birds. Guilt was their last privilege. Their sole atonement became a daily exercise in the rebellious posture.

This was his main interest in the ceremony of souls. It helped him return to the facts of his own inheritance. He wanted to punish Fola for walking blindly into the hell he could not now escape. Ashamed of his own self-pity, Charlot started to feel sorry for her.

Fola was almost frantic with fear beside him. The crowd had taken fright and fled the benches for a while. But she dared not move. The old woman had risen to her full height, thrusting her weak, black hands above her head. She bent her head level to her knees, clutching her fingers in the ground. Tumbled in the dust, she rose again, her hands spread wide, snatching at the air. There was a feel of general turbulence in the *tonelle* as the crowd watched the old woman's body grow more tense. Her hands were erect and stiff. Her head tottered like a sponge from side to side. She was foaming profusely at the mouth.

Charlot whispered, trying to calm Fola's fears. 'It's all right, it's only a possession, but she's got it bad.'

'Please, please can we go?' she begged.

'What was it about the dead boy and his mother?' Charlot asked, as he recalled the wail of a voice from the tent.

'Please, please, I want to go,' Fola cried.

Charlot was scared by the frenzied shake of her hands. Charlot would have left, but the crowd had thickened round the benches. They had pressed forward to see the old woman possessed. They waited until the *Houngan* showed signs of leaving the tent.

The *Houngan* had had a bad time with the last soul. Fola could still hear the echoes of that dead voice wailing for its mother. It was the first experience anyone had known of a soul denying the *Houngan's* power. The dead boy had precipitated rebellion against the gods. The soul had tried to free itself before the *Houngan* could authorise its release. It had driven the old woman to her possession.

Now two men walked out of the crowd towards the tent. Fola believed that they had gone to the old woman's rescue. Her body was still writhing with the seizure which had locked her muscles. But the men paid her no attention. They lifted the sheets, walking in reverse towards the centre of the *tonelle*.

The women raised their heads from the pillows of stone and stood, dazed by the suddenness of the light, waiting for the men to make a carpet with the sheets. The sheets were spread narrowly over the track of dust where the women had to walk on their procession back.

The spirits had cleansed their feet; and custom forbade any contact with the ground until the *Houngan* had given his word. The women stepped carefully over the sheets, pausing whenever the ground appeared. Then the men would find fresh cover for the dust.

There was no stir among the crowd until the women were out of sight. The *Houngan* had left the tent. He glanced at the old woman and walked away as though her seizure were a natural interval of dancing. Her body had relaxed a little, but no one paid attention to her progress. The spirits had mounted her and would soon pass away. It was simple as waiting for the rain to stop. The *Houngan* was coming towards Charlot.

'Is what *Houngan* make so much fuss 'bout them two for?' Powell asked in irritation.

'Is perhaps he feel they make things easy with the police,' said Crim.

'One day he go overstep his power,' said Powell.

He resented the strangers.

Fola had heard the *Houngan's* voice, but she couldn't reply. She was standing like someone in a trance, wondering what the old woman had felt during that wild possession which tumbled her in the dust. If Fola had been sure of her strength she would have run away; but fear had made her weak. If she tried to move, they would think their prayers had worked. Her departure would have been proof of her failure to deny what they had seen.

The *Houngan* was shaking hands with Charlot. He was expressing his wish to show Fola round the room where the sacraments were kept. Fola wanted to refuse, but the slightest sound would have given her new identity away. Her body had lost resistance when she felt the *Houngan's* hand leading her on. She walked beside him like someone in a trance. The earth stirred like water under her feet. Through a cloud of shadows in the door she saw the candles burn pale faces under a black tomb of bamboo. She thought she could hear the last dead voice wailing through tears for the woman who was his mother. Again she felt her dread of hypnosis and the look of rats.

Charlot waited. His body was warm with sweat. He wiped his hands as he walked towards a group of men assembled round an iron pot. The next stage of the ceremony would be the sacrifice. He could see a man caressing two white cockerels in the dark. Charlot had never visited the secret chambers of the *tonelle;* but he had no fears for Fola's safety. On all his visits to the *tonelle,* the *Houngan* had always shown him great respect. His humility in the presence of Charlot was in perplexing contrast with the power he commanded over the *tonelle.*

Perhaps it had to do with the strange contradiction in their beliefs! Perhaps it was not contradiction; for tomorrow, Charlot reflected, they would be part of another vision. Dawn would break over the *Houngan* arriving for Mass in the Catholic church. Perhaps it wasn't a contradiction after all! Like the poetry of his own language their faith was, perhaps, a ground of being which balanced every variation of belief. He joined the men standing round the iron pot. Aunt Jane had survived her seizure. She looked a little dazed; but she seemed to remember every detail of the dead boy's talk in the tent.

'Was never so bad,' she said, resting on Powell's arm, 'in all my time holdin' first watch outside the tent, I never know it so bad. Never know any dead soul argue to break out o' that water till the spirits give *Houngan* power to let it go.'

'I say *Houngan* losin' his knowledge how to handle the dead,' said Crim, 'was like the poor boy carry his madness even after the grave.'

'Was the mother whoever she be what drive him so,' the old woman said. 'Was the mother what drive him so.'

'No wonder she couldn't face what he say from his grave,' Powell said.

'Was the mother what drive him so,' Aunt Jane repeated, glancing slyly up at Powell.

Powell read the question in her glance. They looked towards Charlot who stood alone near the iron pot. Water was boiling thick clouds of steam that ringed his face.

'Where the girl?' Powell asked, glancing suspiciously round the *tonelle*.

'Is where *Houngan?*' the old woman asked, as though she had some doubt about him. 'Papa Bois waitin' with the cocks.'

Powell was still searching the crowd for Fola while the old woman glanced from the iron pot towards the sacred chamber of the *tonelle*. Crim watched Charlot, trying to read the secret of his presence in the *tonelle*.

'What it is he waitin' for?' Crim asked.

'You don't think *Houngan* showin' her 'bout the place?' Powell asked.

He was resentful and suspicious. The old woman looked at him in astonishment. Her hands started to shake again.

'Go ask him, Crim,' she said, pointing towards the iron pot. They pushed through the crowd towards Charlot. But Aunt Jane stood still, gazing towards the sacred corner of the *tonelle*.

The *Houngan* was uneasy in his own sanctuary. Fola watched the candles wriggle their tails like white rats over his back. The wet flames were nibbling at the *Houngan's* hands. 'Will it happen here, will it happen here?' Her words came without sound. 'Does it drive you mad? will it happen here, to me here with him right there?' In a frenzy of thinking Fola recalled the mad voice wailing from the tent.

Her eyes moved swift and restless as the tails of flame over the *Houngan's* back. She glanced from the floor towards the dark corners of the room. The shadows were collecting dead faces in her hands.

She looked round the room to make sure no one was standing behind her. The faces continued moving round the room, a wheel of shadows spinning out of their picture frames to touch her hands.

She felt imprisoned by the nearness of the furniture closing round her body. It was old and simple: a tall bamboo chair and a table with three legs propped fast against an iron bed no wider than the *Houngan's* body. The small chamber was less than half the size of an ordinary bedroom, meek as a stable waiting for birth.

Above two brief alcoves of candle flame, white pots of clay were crowded on the shelf. Spirits were alive in the two earthen jars where the *Houngan* had knelt to appease the revolt of the last dead voice. The African goddess, Erzulie, resided in the left alcove. She stared across a cubicle of space at a picture of the Virgin Mary on the other side. The saints of Congo and Senegal were observing them from the far corner of the room. The saints of the Church were in easy alliance with the gods of the *tonelle*. But the *Houngan* looked troubled. Was it for himself or Fola? He seemed uncertain of the orders he should give the girl kneeling behind him.

Would it happen to her? Fola was shaking with fright from the wail of the voice over the tent. She had heard it. Was it real or illusive? Was it the *Houngan's* voice doing a ventriloquist act? But the crowd had fled when the wail broke from the voice above the tent. There was no illusion about their fright. She had seen the old woman go stiff as wood; and suddenly the threat of hypnosis came upon Fola.

Was it some mixture in the gin? Perhaps it was the gin which had enfeebled her limbs. She got the feeling it was useless to resist. She couldn't hold out any longer. An unfamiliar weight of bone was drilling her body into the ground. Her muscles grew hard; the veins were going to split open her hands.

There was a look of terror in the *Houngan's* eyes as he turned. Fola wanted to scream, but something warned her to be still. If she uttered a sound she would be lost! It was some mixture in the gin! She was sure the gin had worked this gradual stupor on her senses. She parted her lips to smile, but questioned the shape her mouth was making. Fola believed her face was deceiving her. It

43

wasn't her smile which the *Houngan* saw. He had seen something else. Perhaps it was the grin on the old woman's face in the last stages of her possession, when the muscles of every limb had contracted.

Was it going to happen to her? What was he going to do? Fola saw the *Houngan* approach, but she couldn't tell what he was demanding of her. It was impossible to read any meaning in his face. He had taken the axe from the table. He held it out so that the point came near her chin. The flames burnt like spears over the blade. He wanted her to take the axe, but she was slow to understand his gesture. Fola proffered her hand, and something horrible and more solid than gin was opening her throat. Fola watched her hand; yet saw that it wasn't hers; and could not recall where she had seen that hand; from what ancient or forgotten kingdom of time past had she seen that hand! But this foreign hand emerging from her body was in her memory. It was real; yet totally beyond her recollection of any recent time. That hand! The *Houngan* nodded to Fola. He kept nodding until she had read his meaning. It was the wrong hand. Then she understood; took the axe with her left hand and watched him signal her to stand.

Fola was relieved by the strength of her legs. They were firm and steady. The *Houngan* had reached for the bottle of gin. He took a large mouthful, but he didn't swallow. He passed the bottle to Fola, and instinctively she made a small libation on the floor as she had seen the women do. She sipped the gin quickly and returned the bottle to the *Houngan*. But the gin was still in his mouth. Fola could see it weigh in his jaws like a swelling. Why didn't he swallow? She read his signal and lifted her left hand to his face. He held it firmly, polishing the socket above her elbow with his fingers. Why didn't he swallow? But suddenly his lips parted and the gin was spurted like an acid through his teeth in a sharp, stinging spray over her arm. In the same second, Fola had seen the movement of his hand. Now everything turned dark. She could feel the pain where he was pommelling her with his fist on the gin-wet socket of her arm.

It burnt and stung and pushed like an acid into her body. There was a stiffness in her tongue; a noise like water was running out of

44

her ears. Fear had turned her to stone. She was too weak to cry. She could hear nothing but the remembered echo of the mad voice wailing above the tent. The rats of candle flame wriggled round her eyes as she tried to call her mother's name. But no sound came. She could feel nothing but the touch of the *Houngan's* hand, leading her slowly back to the *tonelle*.

'Is this way, lady,' the *Houngan* said.

In the sudden discovery of the crowd she had failed to recognise the *Houngan's* voice. Charlot was not there; yet every glance was Charlot coming to her rescue. Forgetful of complexions, she had seen Charlot in every face. She rubbed her eyes as she leaned on the *Houngan's* shoulder.

Charlot saw them emerge from the secret chamber. The flambeaux were waving like a hand across her face. Fola looked weary, more weary than afraid, he thought. The *Houngan* was making a way through the noise and the crowd, arguing about the confession of the lost soul in the tent. They danced and chanted near the iron pot. The drums had aroused Fola from her stupor. She walked beside the *Houngan*, smoothing the pleats of her skirt as she approached Charlot.

'My brother from afar,' the *Houngan* said and shook Charlot's hands.

'Please, please . . .' Fola was saying. But Charlot had interrupted.

'I'm afraid we must go now,' he said, smiling and squeezing the *Houngan's* hands.

Charlot was impatient to take Fola away, yet careful to look apologetic as he pressed his hands round the *Houngan's* arm.

'Please, please,' Fola was saying as she looked up at the *Houngan's* face. Fola's eyes still showed her frenzy. She hadn't moved when Charlot turned to go. She seemed curious about the mad voice wailing from the tent.

'Did you know the mother?' Fola asked. 'Is she alive?'

'What are you asking?' Charlot laughed, astonished by her show of interest. But her frenzy had caught the *Houngan's* notice.

The *Houngan* didn't answer. He was smiling: a slow, nervous shadow which opened in silence, then quickly closed over the sparkle of his teeth. They saw his hand gradually lose strength among the crowd as he waved good-bye. The drums were pounding, slowly, heavily, crushing all other sound into the night.

Dancing had begun in the *tonelle*. The crowd were warming to the celebration of the drums over the release of the Souls. Crim had decided not to speak with Charlot. The old woman's seizure had threatened to return. They had taken her to a quiet corner behind the tent. Her hands were steadier now, and her voice gained strength with every effort to explain what had happened to that mad voice wailing from the tent.

'His poor brain take a proper blastin',' said Powell. 'In his best years, as Aunt Jane say, his head was a furnace what scorch all sense out o' his mind.'

'Was the mother what cause it,' Aunt Jane said. 'In his best years he never taste what sweetness woman is. Was one sweetness he never know!'

'It rush to his head,' said Powell, 'but he was a good boy. To hold himself in check, not wantin' to contaminate what he touch. You know what it is to hold your manhood back, 'cause you don't want to make no woman sick? Was a proper, good feeling.'

Aunt Jane had pulled herself up from the stone. Her hands shook quietly against Powell's arm. The hard knot of carbuncle started to ache her knuckles. She breathed deeply and waited for her words to gather sound.

'But what use is good feelin' if it live by what aint nat'ral?' Aunt Jane asked. 'Tell me Powell. You tell me, Crim. What use that? The boy was good all right, but nature never get a chance to work itself out o' him, an' that is bad. It stunt him. It cut down whatever size he might have. Was bad, bad, that! A man lose whatever size he be if nature turn off what come nat'ral. If nature can't work itself out, then it work itself in. It turn inside an' stunt what you is. Like the sickness he think he had, it stunt him till his brain burst.'

'But perhaps he didn't even had that sickness,' Crim said.

Aunt Jane was coughing.

'It make no difference,' she said, 'have and not have is equal if your feelin' be the same.'

Crim thought of the lady shamed into dumbness by her boil.

He remembered Powell's lapse of memory, and he was no less perplexed by the dead man's waste of energy.

'Even if it true she give him the sickness,' Crim said, 'would have been a help to own up she was his mother. Was she who drive him so.'

There was bitterness in Crim's voice as he reflected on the mother's crime. The dead man's father had contracted syphilis from her. Shamed by the nature of her disease, the mother had abandoned her son in infancy. She had fled in secret from Forest Reserve to the remote county of Half Moon Bay. Long after the father's death the boy had carried on his search. But it was useless. His mother had become nomadic.

'Not to own she birth him,' Crim said, and spat. 'To turn in hidin' whenever he appear, asking, asking who might know his mother. Was crime, downright crime, I say.'

Aunt Jane moved nearer towards Crim, soothing his head with her weak, dry hand.

'Was crime as you say,' she said, taking Crim's arm between her hands, 'was all he was askin', just to know who she is. Nothin' more he ask, not even touch maybe, but only to see with his own eyes, hear with his own ears from the woman who carry him in her guts . . . only to hear from the one woman who nature open up to let him into life, that and no more might have save him from the blastin' his poor brain take.'

'My Jesus, Jesus, spirit,' Crim cried, 'is the biggest, nat'ral thing any man want to know. Who work on who to give you life? Which man you can call father however it happen, which woman you can call mother whatever her past position. Is the biggest nat'ral thing.'

'Is what the boy keep sayin',' Aunt Jane said, 'In that madness that make him want to break from the water before his time, he just keep sayin': 'who is the woman I could call mother, 'cause she just keep hiding from me, and on purpose!' Over an' over he say it.'

Powell sniffed into his sleeve.

'It make the deadest conscience wake up,' he said.

'Crime, crime, crime!' cried Crim.

'Easy Crim, take it easy,' said Powell, steadying Crim's hands.

He was pounding his fists against his stomach. The old woman patted the back of Crim's neck as the drums made a harsh, dry call above their heads.

'No time for sorrowin',' the old woman said, trying to comfort Crim. 'The dead leave his spirit-water an' only peace with him ever. But we who alive got to look here and now, 'cause you never know who in this night self got the same tribulation. Stop your tongue 'bout what done happen. Stop an' let your own doin' talk.'

'I go play,' said Powell. 'Come let we play.'

'Is time you let the drums give praise and say what is,' the old woman said.

'As you say,' said Crim.

She felt Crim's hands slip from hers as he turned away. Powell walked beside him towards the centre of the *tonelle*. They passed the iron pot where the dust was scarlet with the blood of the two cockerels. A pile of wet feathers clung over the *Houngan's* sandals. But the old woman didn't move.

'What I know I know,' she said, reflecting on the two strangers who had no place in the kingdom of the dead souls telling their past.

The night had given them privacy: yet Charlot couldn't decide whether he should take Fola's hand. It wasn't so simple now as talking about the ceremony of the Souls. Was it because he had known her in circumstances which made such a gesture seem improper? The impact of the ceremony had given him his chance. He couldn't see Fola in the dark, yet he could tell from her silence that her agitation was great. Contact would have been a natural way of showing his affection.

But this relation of teacher and pupil had come back to mock his feeling. It was more enduring than he had thought. He rebuked himself for yielding to the folly of these conventions; but it didn't work. He started to think that any show of intimacy would have been a gross indifference to the way she was feeling. Instinctively he had returned to his former role.

Some aspect of Fola's certainty had been badly shaken. Was it the novelty of the ceremony? Or a feeling of guilt about the distance which her style of living had put between her and the women who danced round the bamboo pole? Charlot didn't want to press her with questions until she had recovered from the ordeal of the last few hours. Without any distortion of the truth, he wanted to restore her calm.

'I was hoping that Chiki would be there,' he said. 'I wanted you to meet him.'

Fola made no reply.

'It's Chiki who helped me understand how the ceremony is every man's *backward glance*,' Charlot said. 'Only the dead can do it, Chiki says, and the living who are free.'

Fola was silent.

Charlot realised that she wasn't going to speak. She showed no interest in the name, although she had always been curious about his friends.

'I remember a similar ceremony,' Charlot continued. 'Chiki had come in to make sketches of a dance. He worked like a lunatic. Then he stopped. I'd never seen such an expression on his face, angry, I thought. Then he turned to me and said: 'It aint enough to understand what they are doing, and it aint enough to change it either.' Then he tore the sheets up and walked out.'

Fola's mind lingered only on the unknown name, and that phrase: *the backward glance*. But she didn't speak.

A warm wind rose bending the trees at the crossing. They heard an engine stall, and the headlights of a car slowly grew dim. The night had been torn open where they stopped, waiting for the car to pass. But the lights had failed, and the folds of the darkness closed again.

Charlot's talk had lost its effort. It made no difference to Fola's silence. She walked beside him like a prisoner, grateful for his patience, yet firm in her intention not to make known what was happening in her head. She wanted to escape. Charlot had a feeling of acute dissatisfaction with himself. He was thinking like a teacher again. He should have been able to penetrate her silence. He wanted to tell her that he would not be staying much longer in San Cristobal; but that might have seemed a way of bribing her into speech. Fola was no longer his pupil, not in the context of their life at

49

college, or in the sudden discovery that he had to cope with a girl whose secrecy denied all the advantages of his knowledge. His failure was an accident which had now made them equal. But it was too late to take her hand. Charlot saw the marble columns of the house emerge; and he knew that time had cheated him. This arrival was too soon.

They walked under the pale domes of light which guided the track of gravel up to her house. Charlot was reluctant to say goodbye. He had seen his pupil in both her worlds. And which was truly hers? he wondered, as they climbed the steps on to the porch. He got the feeling it was the last time he would be seeing Fola. He could have bartered a new future only to hear her speak, to learn what had really happened during that fearful encounter with her forgotten self. But she stood in silence on the porch, shaking his hand.

'It's different for a boy,' she said.

Her words were a relief beyond all his expectations. Charlot's voice had found a new enthusiasm.

'What's different?' he asked, trying at last to find her hand in the dark, 'what do you mean by different for a boy?'

Fola was going to speak; she needed to speak; but a lack of confidence guarded her secrecy.

'Good night,' she said, and turned away.

The conventions of respect had been lifted for ever from this pupil's restraint. She didn't even wait to hear what Charlot would say. A breath of jasmine blew up from the garden, and lingered where he turned in retreat from the silent columns of white marble.

The earth breathed with insect noises. The familiar rhythm of steel had pursued them through the wide, black spaces of the night. The rhythms of steel were riding in triumph over the *tonelle* as Charlot walked under cover of darkness, and watched the sky open upon a skeleton of stars dancing to the ceremony of the drums.

CHAPTER III

In an afternoon of milder weather the rhythms of the *tonelle* are still. Gort sits alone polishing the segments of his tenor drum. The music is asleep, but he can awake it at the slightest whisper of a finger nail. Today he seems more careful to avoid any damage. A single bruise on the polished radiance of this steel is like poison entering his wound. The universe is asleep under his hands, dreaming some harmony which will perfect tomorrow's drumming.

His hands come gently to a rest as his eyes lift their glance towards the Forest Reserve. As he would guide a blind man across the street, so these eyes guide his touch: a simple vigilance of love which guards the beauty of his drum. And when a guide decides to halt, the blind too must wait. So hands and eyes are equal comrades in any labour which Gort's tenor drum attracts.

He ponders the landscape of the Reserve, almost identical in features with the nature he has seen grow like a tree from Chiki's paint. Gort knows nothing about the art of copying things, conserving their likeness on canvas or door or drum; yet the painter is the only man in the whole Reserve whom Gort understands. Crim evokes his admiration; Powell he deeply respects and fears; but Chiki is his comrade, Chiki and the children and the blind.

He shares a total darkness with the blind whenever his eyes see words on paper. He lives the mystery which comes and goes like a season in the children's eyes. And Chiki! It is Chiki's hand that guides him as he watches a distance of colour climbing from the tree-tops to the sky. Today the lake is empty; one thick, red arm of an immortelle tree has fallen into decay. The sky looks like dirt.

Like Chiki's brush emerging from its paint, his eyes now put them together in that order: three different items that are an equal part of the same ruined kingdom. The earth has an unhappily familiar carriage, not prostrate and not erect; but slope-wise and full of an unpromising effort, as though the world has found its rest in a state of convalescence that will not end. But the valley is different where the children wait, learning the filthy language of three women fretting from the street. It seems the valley stands

51

outside its own vegetation, like the children's ears that are no part of the obscenities they hear.

The painter's hand now guides his stare back to the lake, the ravaged arm of the immortelle, and the sky mixing its dirt with splinters of colour that drip like water from the sun. And the valley becomes more isolated, more on the outside of its own surroundings, and more alive because the children are within it. He feels in the children some unfamiliar force, some power of life is now at work, rehearsing in secrecy for some important danger.

This valley is blind; it has no name but that which nature and the law have given it. Music has brought it to the world's attention: a squalid village of communal huts encrusted in this forest. Fathers have often disappeared; mothers grow more dubious about what happened. But the children are confident because they do not care. This is the Forest Reserve where male adults are referred to as the Boys. Fruitful in offspring, or avid ever in their wish to bear, the women are simply women. The children are born by chance; and so they die, escaping always the result of any man's statistics for the valley.

Gort hears the unforgivable voices of the women, and sees the children listen, and cries out to their future to come down and take its refuge in the cradle of his drum. He covers the drum complete within its sack, and decides to take the children out of reach and far away from the ancient obstacle of those women's voices. At the centre of his tenor drum, delicate with lines like a human navel, Chiki has made a hole which doesn't tear the steel, yet opens like a womb under each line. Caught in the illusion of the painted lines, Gort pauses to reflect on his likeness to the blind and the mystery he lives like a season in the children's eyes.

He takes a slip of paper from his pocket and begs his eyes to guide some sense into the words. They look like broken hooks where the first begins, m; the next makes awkward somersaults like a kite, y; and the third is a circle whose perfect line has been brutalised, s; why should an ordinary stick require a tail, he asks, as his eyes disclose a mark that stands erect, t.

He's seen the rest somewhere before; but nothing has come to change their lack of meaning. It's Chiki who has written these marks at his request. He hears the women's voices and recalls the day his eyes watched Chiki's hands arrange those marks to spell a fact which has no place on paper for his unlettered mind; a word that can't explain what he has lived and sometimes seen. He remembers Chiki's question: 'Why won't you ever eat sugar, Gort, taste it in your tea like the others do?' Then his reply: 'A mystery, Chik, a mystery.' And Chiki, loving and always lovable Chiki, writing that word as though it were the first time his hand had learnt it: mystery.

When men, erudite and ordinary throughout the world, discover an answer in that word, they mean those marks on paper; but here Gort follows Chiki's hands disclose a lack of sense in every line whose face on paper pulls a total darkness down his eyes; returns him to the centre of that noise: mystery, Chick, a mystery.

The children had gathered around him now like rival beggars under an arm of Santa Claus. Gort stared over their heads while he was waiting to hear them speak. Perhaps he was reminding them where they should not have been. He glanced over Liza's head towards the huts where the women's voices had stumbled over the trees, stumbled and fallen dead with echoes like the leaves. But the children knew that something would happen soon: something like peppermint, or liquorice, or a three-minute beat on the tenor drum.

Apart from his phobia about sugar, this was the strangest thing about Gort. Neither Powell, nor Crim could touch Gort's drum except to explain a note while they rehearsed; and Chiki who, it seemed, understood why that was so, never asked Gort to let him play the drum. But Gort would sometimes offer the children a three-minute beat as a reward for silence or good conduct. He would lasso the drum round his neck, crouch under their hands and show them where to strike the small wooden baton that made the noise. The three-minute beat was the most precious of all rewards; for with it went the liquorice or peppermint as well.

The children couldn't hear the women's obscenities from the street; but they remembered what the quarrel was about. For Unice, Mathilda and Flo were bitter enemies. Their common hatred was the oldest fact of knowledge in the Forest Reserve; and not

53

only in the Forest Reserve, but Half Moon Bay as well, Saragasso, Chacachare and Belle View, Christ Church Row, the Cockpit country, Sulphur Springs, Essequibo and Potaro: in every village where there were Steel Drum bands and local gin shops. For Unice, Flo and Mathilda were separate and independent agents of a chain of these local gin shops which also sold sugar, cooked crab backs, liquorice and peppermint balls.

Each had tried at one time or another to set fire to the other's shops. Once Unice and Mathilda had formed a brief alliance to destroy Flo; but a similar arrangement soon followed with Unice as the victim. In the end each seemed to agree to work on her own. But the war went on. If Flo gave charity to the blind, Unice would refuse or double the sum; while Flo would arrange some intrigue with the children to prove that she was the queen of kindness itself. Neither God nor man could heal their malice; but they went their way, sometimes without notice, sometimes remembered like hurricane or flood. Except in Half Moon Bay where old Jack o' Lantern had lived. Unice was the cause of Jack o' Lantern's murdering the constable who seized his drum. The Half Moon, as the Bay was called, remembered her like a hurricane or a flood.

'Is why Gort won't ever eat sugar,' Liza said, glancing from Gort to her rivals.

'Why Gort won't eat sugar?'

'Yes, why? Gort never tell a soul in Forest Reserve why he won't eat sugar, but you want to play you know.'

'Yes, why? Is why you won't say if you play you know?'

Liza recalled the women's voices, and decided to imitate their nerve.

'All you like flies what make the same noise,' said Liza.

Her adversaries were ready, ready and full of war like Mathilda or Flo; but the war had been put off. Gort lowered his head from the trees, staring like an astonished lunatic at every face around him. In a matter of seconds they had flocked together like mice, silent and glad to be forgiven.

'Is because Unice tongue so dirty,' Liza said, 'is why Gort won't taste sugar. Is so it is, no, Gort? 'Cause what they say dirty the sugar too.'

Gort smiled as though he had agreed; but the girls were vigilant. No one liked yielding to the other; and certainly not all to Liza.

'Is not sugar they quarrel 'bout last night.'

'It aint sugar as she Liza keep sayin'.'

'I know it aint sugar,' said Liza.

'Then why you say sugar?'

'Is why you say so if you know?'

Liza had lost her chance to say what she knew.

'Is 'bout some strange thief walking round the reserve last night,' one of the girls said.

'Is what it is,' her comrade added.

'Flo believe Unice invitin' some strange thief what not live round here to rob her shop.'

'Is what it is.'

Liza was relieved when Gort intervened; but the others were still fresh from their triumph, for Gort knew nothing about the women's quarrel.

As he considered their willingness, the obedience which came with every pause in their rivalry, Gort would try in secret to count their heads like a school awaiting orders.

'Any of you see Chiki yesterday?' Gort asked.

'I see the strange man yesterday,' said Liza, 'when he come to say bye bye.'

'Is what that got to do with what Gort ask?'

'Is not the stranger man she thinkin' 'bout,' another added.

'Is the stranger man lady what wait outside when he came to say bye bye.'

'An' you wasn't there Liza, you was asleep when the stranger man lady was waitin' outside. Is we what tell you she wait outside.'

Liza had been cornered. She gave her attention to the four blades of grass which she was plaiting into the pigtail she had seen on the lady's head. She hadn't seen the lady last night, but she had seen the lady's head somewhere before.

But the *tonelle* was too anxious, the crowd too large for Liza to say whether it was the night she had danced for Guru's soul. But the lady was somewhere in the dance which tossed Liza until she could not stand.

Her eyes had grown dizzy when the drums shook the bamboo pole like hair falling from the lady's head. Liza had seen the bamboo wave and stiffen, twisting its knots like a long black plait that sprouted up from the *ververs;* growing its huge black orchard of curls like the forest come down in silence with its leaves over the night. The lady's hair was filling her eyes. Thrown like a rope from the bamboo pole, it had swung her by the throat right out of the *tonelle* and up to the sky that frightened with its noise. But the drums burst from the ground, and snapped the rope around her neck, and she had lost the lady's hair.

The *ververs* were dead as rags under Liza's feet; but the women's voices had returned, bellowing with her praise. Her body was working hard, furious and strong like the drums; and she heard the women's voices applauding her feet that danced for a reward they could not give. Liza had wished the lady's hair on her own head. But the flambeaux blinded her eyes when the gods came riding on the drums like fearful black horses in her dreams at night. Her legs had grown dizzy with the dance, and a cold wind sprang up from the sea and closed her eyes against the lady's hair which had just flown away.

'The strange man didn't find Chiki what he really come to see,' said Liza.

'Why Chiki never here when the strange man come?'

' 'Cause he workin'. Is in Moon Glow he work all night.'

'He don't,' said Liza, 'Chiki don't work at night 'cause he say it have too much dark to see what the colours make.'

'I see Chiki work at night.'

'Where?'

'One time when he draw something on Gort tenor drum.'

'Maybe, but he don't work like tonight, an' tomorrow night,' said Liza, 'an' one after the next like what he work every day when the light show what colours the paint brush make.'

'You always know everything.'

'I not say so,' said Liza, 'but is what I see how he don't work at night. Is why he never paint the strange man face 'cause he an' the strange man work sort o' upside down. The strange man teach school in the daytime, an' Chiki refuse to watch his face at night.'

'Is not why Chiki not paint him.'

'Is what if you always know?' Liza asked.

'I hear Chiki say is bad to watch anything white in the dark. White face at night Chiki say don't make for clear lookin'. You ought to wait till it come up in the light.'

'Is not only face,' said Liza, 'I hear Chiki say you ought to wait let everything come up in the light.'

'Not only wait. Is why you say only wait. Like how I see him paint at night. I hear Chiki say you got to bring everything what in the dark up to the light.'

'He aint only say that,' Liza argued, 'is why you never say all what Chiki say. I hear Chiki say sometimes it have a thing what bring itself in the light but it still not clear. Like how the stranger man always walk an' talk like he aint never know where dark is. The strange man don't hide nothing, Chiki say. He keep in the light all time, but his face still don't come clear. Ask Gort. Is why Chiki never here when the strange man come.'

The others glanced at Gort for confirmation.

'Is why Chiki never come when the strange man here?' Gort asked.

''Cause Chiki say he don't like no people changin' dark time for light time,' said Liza. 'Chiki say the stranger man leave his own dark where he sail from to walk free in Forest Reserve light, an' is bad Chiki say, 'cause everybody got his own dark an' his own light, an' nobody aint got no right swapping his own for a next. Is what Chiki say 'bout the stranger man.'

'Is what you say 'bout the stranger man?' Gort asked, thrusting his finger out at Liza.

Liza hesitated. She looked up at Gort and then at the wide billow of the trees clapping their leaves down to the grass over the pond. She was cautious not to say too much.

'I don't know,' she said shyly, 'is like why you never eat sugar.'

'Is what you mean, don't know,' Gort rebuked her. 'I hear you say 'bout me, 'bout Crim, 'bout Chiki, Powell, everybody, an' is why you can't say now?'

Liza played with the pigtail of grass over her hands.

'She 'fraid o' the stranger man.'

'I not 'fraid o' no stranger man,' Liza shouted. 'I not 'fraid o' you neither.'

'None of that,' Gort said, and frowned. 'Nobody 'fraid of nobody round here. Now talk, you, Miss Liza whatever you call yourself, is what you say 'bout the stranger man?'

Liza burnt her skin sore as she twisted the grass round her fingers.

'Is what I say 'bout the stranger man?' she asked, glancing from Gort to the others and back, as she tightened the grass. 'I'd like to look like the stranger man lady.'

The girls screamed in mockery.

'But hear she! Not even tall as the table an' say she want to be big man lady. She want to court woman-fashion with the stranger man.'

'I aint say that,' Liza shouted. 'I aint say that. Nasty liar, I aint say that.'

Liza hiccoughed and felt her hand tremble in Gort's. He was squeezing her. She was going to cry when Gort took a crust of peppermint from his pocket and promised to reward them for silence and good conduct.

'Tell her I aint say that,' said Liza.

'She never say that,' Gort said.

'You hear, you hear for yourself now,' Liza said in triumph. 'I say I'd like to be like, is like I say, like the stranger man lady.'

The girls were humbled to silence.

'Is where she come from that they make so much hair?' Liza asked.

'From America,' one girl shouted, mocking Liza's question with greater triumph in her eyes.

Liza was ready to attack, but the girls had seen Gort fall backwards in a fit of hysterics. His voice rolled like the tenor drum; and the crutch of his trousers split open when he fell back. Gort become suddenly circumspect, as though he had suddenly remembered his age, scolding the girls' silence with his hands.

'Is what we do, Gort?' Liza asked, perplexed.

Determined to conceal the a...ident that would expose his backside to their ridicule, Gort sat erect as a teacher, eager to punish their ignorance.

'She not from America,' Gort said sternly.

'And that hair?' Liza asked, 'nobody here aint got that so much hair. Would take everybody in the Reserve to save up all their hair for more than a year to get that much on one head.'

The girls wavered between the truth of Gort's answer and the possible effort which Liza seemed willing to undertake. Liza was going to make a suggestion when the fear took shape in her mind: 'Ma would burst in my backside with that tamarind rod if she see me just touch she scissors.' She was suddenly aware that Gort might have heard, and instinctively she raised one finger to her mouth. The girls thought she was asking them to obey Gort's order for silence; and a calm, strange and without meaning, came over them. Their silence was no less abrupt than Gort's words.

'It never have a good thing come,' said Gort, meditating on the blindness of the clouds, 'never a good thing come that a bad don't send it. An' the better the thing what come, the bigger the bad what send it. Like when Chiki an' the rest sail to America.'

Now the girls could understand the reason for Gort's change. At first it was abrupt, obscure. Gort had started the same confusion which they had learnt to read in the teacher's eyes at school. When words did not connect with what they were doing, they knew it was a warning that trouble was near.

But America was the secret which opened and expelled all the obscurities of Gort's talk. It was a universe like heaven above their heads, too far to touch; yet real since Chiki and the rest were there. When Chiki and the others had left for America, it seemed that sorrow had run straight up from hell like a witch around the *tonelle*. The drums made music every day, but the sound was not the same. Even Gort's tenor drum, distinct and flawless in every note, had changed its tune. It had begun to talk like a woman who couldn't restrain her tears; and the children would wonder whether Gort was going mad.

But soon they understood. Gort wasn't really paying attention to the steel. They'd notice his hands falter and knock against the rim; but he wouldn't stop to soothe his knuckles. They knew Gort's hands hurt badly, but he didn't stop. The drum never lost its tenor voice, but its cry was sad, and sometimes it seemed that Gort had forgotten the tune. Gort's errors would make the women pause to glance from the window, the way they always do when clouds darken with a warning of rain. But Gort was not losing his skill. It was simply that he couldn't pay attention to his hands. He wouldn't keep his eyes on the segments of the drum, as though he needed them to prove that someone would soon appear and wave where he was looking up at the sky.

The women worried very much that he might go mad; but the children then seemed to believe that there was reason in Gort's glance. Perhaps they would awake one morning and hear Gort's tenor drum like magic calling out for Chiki and Crim, Powell and the rest who were walking and dancing over that ridge of cloud under the sky.

O America! America! O Lord, let America come out of hiding from behind that cloud, just once, not more than once come out in hill and valley, forest and water as we have here in San Cristobal, at least let Chiki come, if only Chiki, but better all America in light and darkness, moon and sky, let come only to show Great Gort his friends are alive and there in answer to the broken music of his drum.

Sometimes they thought Gort's heart would fall out of his body, flutter like a bird, then die like *ververs* before the gods arrived. Night after night they would recall the punishment of that day. No one seemed to care, not even heaven that was always near when the drums rejoiced. God or devil, no one simply cared, for the weather was like a festival when the crowd met at the pier to wish their friends good-bye.

That ever there should be war, good God! How could you not hear the tonelle cry there is no evil like a war; men are not wicked like the war they carry to corners of a heart they do not know; not wicked, good God, we agree, no wickeder than the drums that now must die for what is happening this day; and is it true that no one cares? that the vision of any heart can stop where the eye no longer sees? Prove, prove, good God it isn't true; for the devil is waiting here to win. His sermon tells the facts, explains with a simple glance at that big ship waiting there why Chiki and Powell and all the rest must go. America has sent her own men to war elsewhere which is not fair on any love they leave behind. Crowding to war, America's boys like Crim and Chiki, Powell and all the rest, have heard an order say to leave the farm lands bare. So Crim and Chiki and Powell and all the rest, obeying the need San Cristobal knows, must fill the places of America's Boys now purchased for a war elsewhere. Crim will hold a fork, and Chiki his plough, and Powell will drive an engine over roads whose signs he cannot read. And no one cares for this day when the sun is a carnival all over the sea; the waves laugh like drums, and one man's separation from all his friends looks plain and simple as his spit dying in the sand. All, all are going; but the Boys from the tonelle are the last to leave for Great Gort's hand can't reach across the sea when they have sailed.

Great Gort! only Gort remained because he could not read! Great Gort! Because he could not read! Yet not a word but it made mystery on his tongue that day. To each, but one, he said the same: 'What we *will*, will be.' And the waves cried when Crim came, embraced like an infant in Gort's arms: 'Crim, what we *will*, will be.' Then Powell, never in all his manhood made so humble: 'Pow . . . Pow . . . *will*, will be, will be.' What else could happen here as eye saw eye, reading the secret of each man's tongue; for neither Gort nor Chiki spoke that day. But fist in fist, the moment those hands met, the children saw the sea like dumb rain falling out of Chiki's head. The children saw but could not tell what happened there, as though the earth had recovered its very first tear.

Those children on the pier that day had now grown taller; some had died and others multiplied. For it was that war when six million of another race had cooked in stoves especially made for their dying. But this brood surrounding Gort though not alive that day, were eager to learn, could even see that afternoon, near and fresh as daybreak in Gort's face. Their heads looked like a congregation in prayer as they tried to see Gort on that day. His eyes were chapels of endless Sundays burning with prayers, and his tongue was the first and only gospel of what had happened.

Some of them could now remember what had happened after Chiki and Crim, Powell and the rest had gone. The law had decided to destroy the bands; first, on the pretext that they made too much noise. This was in the colonial days when arrangements were more subtle. But a foreign wisdom knew that noise was a poor excuse in a country where nothing else had ever happened since the discovery of its name. So the reasons changed; and the cause now turned on property.

The Forest was on Crown lands which would be put up for sale. Where could Gort and the remnants of the Boys collect that money? Or the women who were left behind? And this was how America happened: a miracle, ordinary and yet eternal as man's need of bread.

'But it don't have numbers what count that much money,' said Liza. 'Is like the lady hair.'

'Would be more than the hair,' one of her rivals said, 'if it same total Gort say, it would take all the hair grain after grain 'pon every head in San Cristobal to reach that amount.'

'An' who can count all those grains?' another added, crushing Liza's logic to dust. 'Would be a miracle.'

'But it happen,' said Gort, 'it happen.'

'Where Chiki get all that money, Gort?' the children asked.

Gort searched the cave of his wisdom tooth for a crust of crab meat.

'As I say,' he said, following the blind movement of the clouds, 'it never have a good thing come but a bad one send it. An' the better the good, the bigger the bad what send it. Is there me an' your mother an' all you when you come grown size got to make up your mind. 'Cause like we here in the valley, everybody live twixt those two, the good thing what comin' better an' better, and the bad thing what send it growin' badder an' badder. Is there your heart make every war it know.'

The girls saw Liza shorten the grass into a knot and stick it under one of her pygmy plaits. But they had no time for Liza and her plaits when Gort was talking about money as though it were nothing more than Christmas paper, or bits of copper falling off the old frying pans in Forest Reserve.

'Is what part of America Chiki make all that money?' Liza asked.

'My head never hold that part,' said Gort, 'but it got a name like the Virgin Mary. Was there Chiki went with his crazy make-believe, like sometimes how I see the lines gone wild on his canvas, as though they not hearin' what the paint and the brush want to say. Must be so Chiki was that time in the pentecostal church.'

'Is God give the money?' Liza asked.

'God or the devil is anybody guess,' said Gort, ' 'cause I don't know. But Chiki never been no place other than this Reserve an' that place with a name like the Virgin Mary; yet Chiki tell those people in the name, the holy name o' their blessed Saviour, that he fight in the war before near Egypt. Is what Chiki tell them. An' there in Egypt land Chiki say he catch his vision after a straight face to face meetin' with Jesus Christ Himself. An' the vision was that those same people now listenin' to Chiki like you here listen to me, but with oceans of tears running out their eyes, Chiki vision say they should get baptise with the true river water their own Saviour wash in. Is what Chiki tell them, an' all the faces turn to joy, like when you see a promise come fact in front your eyes, 'cause Chiki tell them he had that river water right there with him. He follow Jesus order an' bring it back by the ton from the Jordan river to this place with the name like the Virgin Mary. An' belief? Chiki say he never know belief an' faith so great as when he start to baptise them with that water. First it begin as a little sprinkle an' they only pay a little token like in thanks. Same as how here some people pay for the red sip in those church cups near Maraval hills. Was a token first. Then the numbers come faster than Sunday itself.

'Chiki nearly get dismiss from the farm 'cause he baptisin' day in an' day out with that Jordan water. An' is what make him ask for more token givin', till askin' an' askin' turn it into price. Chiki now fix his price like Flo an' Unice with their sugar, 'cause along with the sprinkle that baptise, Chiki start to parcel little bottles o' the Jordan water which they take away. An' the people just multiply day by day. An' then in the night as well, 'cause Chiki get Powell an' Crim to beat salvation hymn tunes on their drums. Was a hell of a thing Crim say the way those God fearin' black folks work up their backside in Jesus face. An' the more they dance an' sing, the more Chiki hand getting tired with the price his Jordan water bringing in. . . .'

Gort wiped his brow as he watched the clouds and paused for answer to this paradox: was it God or Satan working the magic in Crim's and Powell's drums at night. But a fountain of life, once free, now promised a greater freedom to those black voices in a

chiki charging people to baptise of them w/ supposed water in which Jesus bathed in - collected money to save them from being sold chorus of praise throughout the black length and wholly black breadth of Virginia state. Money flowed from their hands like the true river of Jordan itself.

'An' Chiki was so tired,' Gort continued, as the cloud dissolved, 'his hand get so tired with sprinklin' from head to head, that he had to hit on a new sort o' baptisin'. So he make them all collec', all who had it an' lose it, or never had it at all, Chiki make them collec' in one place. Crim say how it was a fearful moment with him holdin' up the big oil drum, an' Powell keepin' the hose pipe off the ground, an' Chiki sprayin' those faces with his Jordan water, people coughin' an' clappin' like if sickness was fun, 'cause the river where Jesus wash himself was the Jordan runnin' from that same hose pipe in Chiki hands. Crim say an' Powell too say how it was a fearful moment, a fearful, fearful moment. But every penny to meet the price o' Forest Reserve was ready, every penny plus a few cents over was right down ready.'

And so America remained in their memory. America that was no royal land of hope and glory, but a miracle of money and bread! America which would always be felt under their feet like the stride of the drums over the *tonelle* each night!

The Reserve was quiet now, as though Unice and her rivals were all asleep. The children had turned away from Gort as they saw Aunt Jane making towards them. She was sucking cooked crab backs from a paper bag as she approached Gort and his school of children.

'You not see Chiki?' Aunt Jane asked.

'He wasn't here when the strange man come to say bye-bye,' said Liza.

'Aunt Jane ask 'bout Chiki,' Liza's rivals said.

'Was night before that was,' said Aunt Jane, sucking the crab backs as she scratched her ears.

'I aint see him,' said Gort, as though he understood Aunt Jane's misgiving.

' 'Cause Mathilda an' those two at it again,' said Aunt Jane. 'Some new thief they didn't recognise was crawlin' 'bout here last night. An' you know Chiki! Me an' you know Chiki can be up to some funny tricks.'

The children saw what Aunt Jane meant in the story Gort had told. But they didn't talk; for they never risked an opinion when Aunt Jane was near. Gort watched the clouds slowly dissolve into a drizzle, as the school dispersed towards the huts. Aunt Jane had questioned him again about the women and the thief. But Gort knew nothing.

Last night every hut was startled by the street lamps which had stayed on very late. But the Forest went to bed as usual. Alone and in the disguise of a boy, Fola was touring the outskirts of the Reserve.

CHAPTER IV

Lightning burnt a crack over the pane of glass, and a wind whipped the trees into a storm of leaves falling heavily outside her window. The rain hadn't stopped. The fever boiled upwards through her veins and spread across her forehead. Her throat coughed a weak dry sound like shells.

'So he's going,' Fola thought, trying to keep her balance on the floor. 'After all these years he still couldn't feel like one of us. He was just a spy, that's what Charlot was, a cold, detached, self-centred spy. Curiosity was only his excuse.' Yet he had taught her how to look upon her past. She wanted to hate herself for being so vulnerable to his influence.

In the afternoon Fola had waited outside the Saragasso cemetery until the hearses rode away. The mourners, soon settled in their grief, had followed the sun back to their homes. She had loitered in the drizzle, walking among the graves, shocked by the age and number of the dead. The dates looked false. They seemed to avoid any calculation she could make about her own age.

Rain had disfigured the letters. Like the angels carved in marble, she had stared in disbelief at the age of the world she knew. Time was like ever and always from the meaning of those years chipped in foreign numerals above the farewells that heavened each corpse away. Once she had paused to reflect that it was more than a decade since she was seven. But she couldn't recognise her name among the tombstones which were honoured with epitaphs for the dead. She had returned home in a heaving, black shower that lasted all night.

Fola brought the picture close to her eyes and watched the handsome, sunburnt face. Charlot's skin was once the colour of cheese, pale cream and thick with razor bumps; but the sun had grilled it to a smooth, dark tan. The eyes were wide, soft and clear, two dazzling balls of colour perfectly set under his fine, black crop of lashes.

'But he's a spy,' she thought. 'I should have known he was a spy.' She was in love with Charlot, yet struggled to disown any memory of their acquaintance. The fever had shaken the picture from her hands. She tried to stoop, and felt the sudden thrust of pain twisting like a chisel through her skull. The frame lay empty at her feet. Yesterday a similar thing had happened. She had dropped a large plate-glass tray which was her mother's birthday gift from the Vice-President of San Cristobal. Fola couldn't trust anything to the safety of her hands. She raised one leg over the pile of broken glass, and let her body fall quietly on to the bed.

'He's a spy,' she kept thinking. 'I know now he's a spy.'

Fola expected the worst to happen during any illness. When the sweat broke, dripping like rain into her mouth, she started to imagine the taste of blood. She had kept up a violent coughing as she looked for colour in the clouds of breath fading over the mirror. Then she thought of Charlot and decided that she had to live. She thought she saw his face rise in mockery from the broken frame, and her illness seemed a betrayal. Death would have been a kind of revenge against the search which she had started three days ago.

'But he's a spy,' she thought, 'even Therese could tell he was a spy.' Through the thin flush of candlelight she saw an outline of the servant's face in a family group. The chin tilted at an angle above her mother's shoulder. A second before the camera clicked, Therese must have lifted her head. She was slim as wire. Her skin was charcoal black, sharply pointed with bone all over her face. The small, dark eyes betrayed no hint of her cunning.

Fola thought of the child in the *tonelle* as she reflected on the servant's loyalty. Therese had a son who must have been Liza's age. Fola had never seen the boy, yet he existed like a rumour in the

house. 'Would like him grow up like Miss Fola,' Therese would
say, arriving with the six o'clock coffee that always startled her
from sleep. It was the servant's way of concluding praise. 'But
watch the foreign man,' she would advise as she turned to go, 'is
what them sort comin' with, you never know, Miss Fola. You
watch him good.'

Fola tried to smile as she looked again for the servant's face.
The light grew dim, but she could read a chronicle of these mornings on the wall: Therese in starched blue apron and a stiff, white
cap, fretful about her neighbours near the *tonelle*, austere with
strangers, a little servile in crisis, contemptuous of subordinates and
guests who weren't of equal status with her employers. She had
lived at the centre of every secret in the house.

It was Therese who had persuaded Fola's mother to dismiss the
chauffeur. James had been threatening ever since to murder her.
It seemed they had both agreed to ask for an increase of wages.
In spite of her relation to the family Therese thought it necessary
to consult with James. She was sure it would be easier if she were
allowed to make their request; but James argued to take the lead.
He was a week-end preacher, it was true, yet he thought that any
man would have demanded to do the talking. He prepared an
arrogant, little speech, worked himself up to an unspeakable rage,
and surprised Fola's mother one morning on the porch.

'What is it, James?'

'Mrs Piggott,' he stammered again, 'I been meanin' to say it a
long, long time, is a long time I been meanin' to let you know . . .'

'Know what?' she asked, astonished by his coarseness.

James was timing his assault.

'That I want more money or . . . or . . . or . . . by Jesus an' the
Saints.'

His voice grew louder and louder until Fola's mother was
terrified by the violence which had now turned into a threat.

'Or what, James?' she said, catching for breath.

There was an awful silence. Then James rested his idiot eyes on the
porch and turned to go.

'Or what?' she shouted, regaining her control.

'Or I'll work for the same thing, miss,' said James.

67

Next morning Therese confronted them with a simple choice. If James didn't go, she was sorry to say that she couldn't stay. And James was sent.

The pain had shifted to the left side of Fola's head. A pulse rose and fell behind her ear. The rain stopped a while, and she heard a thin refrain of drums coming up from the valley. When the echo of steel lifted again, she thought of the child dancing in the *tonelle*. Would Liza have known Therese's son? She would have liked Therese to bring him to the house one day.

'But it's so different for a boy,' she thought, 'it's always different for a boy.'

The candle sputtered its light up the square of glass which hung above the servant's head. It seemed an improbable journey across that dark margin of space between these two photographs. Fola's past was framed upon these walls: neighbours and friends, the standard families of San Cristobal charting their futures in the private talk of committee rooms, or gathered under the festooned arches of the lawn to celebrate success. Vice-President Raymond, short and stout, with fat like a goitre dripping from his neck, was bending over a silver pyramid of cake. Blind with champagne, he had fought in vain to put out the sixty candles that told his age. The flames ran like white mice up his sleeves: a night which came near to ruin before he ordered an hour's adjournment for a change into fresh evening wear. His guests honoured the interval with praise, while the last two candles waited for his return.

Beside this episode another picture showed Fola and the Vice-President's daughter. Veronica was taller, with sandy complexion and a solitary plait which coiled like a pig's tail out of her neck. They were the guardians of an exclusive caste at college. But Veronica hadn't changed very much, still confident and aloof towards everyone except Fola. She had retained the habit of taking bits of food to bed. She collected crumbs, parcelled unfinished sticks of liquorice which she devoured in the dark. She relished the feel of eating, alone and unseen, as though the nights bestowed a greater kinship with her appetite. It was Veronica who supplied the earliest memories of Fola's childhood.

'So he's going,' she thought, 'after all these years, he still couldn't feel like one of us.' Fola raised her head to see the picture on the floor. The pain spread deeper, blinding her eyes. But she could hear the wash of the sea at Morant Bay, and the drums stealing through the trees. That day she had seen Charlot emerge from behind a huge black trunk of rock. The families thought it their duty to welcome strangers. They did it, so to speak, on behalf of the young Republic. But intimacy was a privilege which the stranger had to win. Fola knew they suspected him, but they were cautious. They had the power to decide his future in San Cristobal, yet their fears were no less active. Obsessed with a need for perfection, they would allow the stranger a natural superiority of judgment. It was a derisive gesture. But they were nervous lest he should detect the slightest error in their own lack of breeding.

Charlot's face had pursued her from the pile of glass on the floor. But she was becoming more resistant to his influence. She could still see Liza dancing in the flames that leaned like a knife, slitting through the servant's throat. These different worlds of time changed without warning, changing their own emphasis of meaning. The light made an edge of shadow that reached to the broken frame of memories from Morant Bay.

Lady Carol Baden-Semper was among that group. Lady Carol's voice seemed to increase Fola's freedom towards the past. It was shrill and slow. After her long campaign against a stammer, the voice had won. Charlot was talking to Lady Carol about his childhood, and Fola watched Veronica who was anxiously watching Lady Carol. For she was a kind of seer to Fola's generation. She had bright, red freckles that made a nest of fireflies over her fishhooked nose, just a narrow ridge of bone with razor slits for nostrils.

The girls wondered how much Charlot had known about her. She had married late to an ex-sailor in the merchant navy. Her huge plantation house in the Maraval hills was the finest example of colonial architecture in San Cristobal. It was a meeting place for Fola and Veronica and the whole college caste whom Lady Carol instructed. She was an excellent pianist, but elocution was the course she emphasised in her curriculum for gracious living.

She had a fund of stories about her husband who had seen active service in the First World War. These were always introduced with the phrase: seen active service in the war; and the way she said 'seen' often made people wonder whether her husband had actually fought. An event could have its origin before or after, but Lady Carol's memory was firmly anchored to the First World War.

She was listening to Charlot with that seer-like patience the girls knew very well. It made you feel that every word you uttered was God's given truth. The girls were anxious for Lady Carol; the way she listened as though her tongue had deserted her. Then they saw her eyebrow lift like polished black scimitars raised in defence.

'And I was as poor as they come,' Charlot had said.

'But you make such a fuss 'bout being born poor,' Lady Carol said. 'You show it off like the medals my half-blind husband get for seeing active service in the First World War. Maybe it's all right being born poor, but what a strange kind o' thinking that let you see it as some sort o' privilege!'

Charlot tried desperately to explain, but Lady Carol was irrepressible.

'I go tell you 'bout a similar case,' Lady Carol said, vernacular slipping like a traitor over her tongue. 'It had a colonial secretary out here, his wife was the Red Cross matron, last lot before Independence, an' she use to talk that same kind o' talk till a natural crisis show what it worth. Fola there will tell you 'bout the Red Cross dance.'

At this point Charlot complained about the heat, and asked whether there was any ice around. But Lady Carol was determined not to give him time to rehearse his answers. She was an old hand at this manœuvre, exploiting diarrhœa and a stammer in her own time. She had continued at incredible speed to describe what had happened during the interval of the Red Cross dance. Her conflict with the colonial secretary's wife had amazed everyone who waited in the long queue outside the ladies' lavatory.

'What natural is natural,' said Lady Carol, glancing from Charlot's head down to his groins. 'I want to pee an' she want to pee.' Now Lady Carol's hand went up like a flag. 'Her pee an' my pee behave the same as your pee, not meanin' no rudeness to you, sir.' Here the hand came down like a flag. 'An' our pee behave the same way as the pee waitin' to pour out the stupid little typist girl she start to insult. You should hear her when the girl refuse to give up her place at the top o' that queue. "Do you know who I am," she ask, "you realise what your refusal can mean," she say, an' each time she stop her face gettin' redder than Semper tomatoes which he paint up for sale. "What this can mean, the colonial secretary's wife being refused by a . . . a," an' now it was comin', I see native or some other word start with 'n' on her tongue, an' I, me, myself, Elizabeth Carol Baden-Semper (an' don' ask where the name come from), I leave the queue to tell her: "Look, whoever you be is your own business, but it don't have no such thing as a priority pee." '

The families were hysterical with laughter while Fola watched Charlot, pretending to be amused. Slapping Charlot on his shoulder, Lady Carol had finished: 'My elocution never let me down so bad, but it worked, 'cause where she disappear I couldn't tell you to this day.'

Charlot tried again to explain what he was getting at by his talk of roots, but Lady Carol had her own methods of argument. She promptly asked to be excused on the pretext of looking for her husband whose sight she didn't trust. Charlot was deeply hurt. Fola watched the Raymonds and her mother prolong their laughter about the priority pee. And it was at that moment, hearing the mockery in their voices, that she had taken Charlot's side against the families.

As Charlot turned to go, Fola had glanced at her mother and the Raymonds, then walked towards him, smoothing her hair out. She lowered her head, trying to hide her naked torso with her hands. The families were astonished by the humility which had come into her voice.

'Please, sir.'

Charlot stopped, but he didn't turn to acknowledge the deference in his pupil's voice. Her relation to the college had forged a convention of speech which seemed irrelevant to his feeling on the Morant beach.

'Please, sir,' Fola said again as she came up beside him. 'I'd like to apologise for what Lady Carol did.'

She felt a tautness like wire strung through her veins. Charlot had rested his hand on her shoulder as the Raymonds or her mother might have done. But the tautness was there. It made a shudder around her knees.

'You needn't apologise,' said Charlot.

'But I must, sir.'

'But why?' he asked, letting his hand slip from her shoulder. They were walking side by side over an edge of grape-vine.

'She didn't mean it that way, sir,' Fola said.

'But I think she was right,' said Charlot. 'If the typist was afraid, then somebody had to put the other woman in her place.'

Fola had lost the thread of her reasoning about Lady Carol's rudeness. The tautness of skin and muscle was still there. She couldn't understand his approval of Lady Carol's behaviour: the way he had withdrawn completely from the circumstances in which the story had been told. Here she was, eager and worried to protect him against Lady Carol, while he was taking sides with Lady Carol against someone else. She couldn't believe that he had failed to see Lady Carol's intention.

And suddenly she felt an immense admiration for Charlot. Admiration and the tautness which had started a nervous falsetto in her voice. She was afraid to speak now. It would have been terribly improper to betray her feeling. This was the first time she had known what Veronica meant by being in love. She was afraid that Charlot might have noticed something. He was making a swizzle with his eyelashes between his fingers.

'Tell me something about yourself, sir,' she said like a child trying to bribe a Christmas tree with friendship.

The drums were coming much louder over the trees. She could almost hear him listening, and she smiled, pleased with his own pleasure in the music.

'Do you like them?' she asked, widening her smile and digging her nails into the back of her thighs.

'Very much,' said Charlot as he leaned his head towards the trees. 'And you?' He didn't look at her now.

72

'Do I?' she s : i, 'no other music can move me like that.'

Charlot had lowered his body on to the grape-vine. Fola sat beside him, choosing an angle that would make it easy to avoid his glance. She looked towards the sea as she listened to the drums.

'Will you stay very long here, sir?' she asked, and heard the question reverberate with a different echo in her head: Let him say yes, for God's sake, let him say yes.

'I think I will,' said Charlot.

'And your friends in Europe?' Fola said. 'Would they like it too?'

And Fola felt the tautness come loose and cool with every stage of Charlot's talk about his friends. She relaxed her body over the grape-vine and listened to him describe this passion for discovery which he had noticed in some of his friends.

How they would often go in search of monuments, cathedrals, important graves; the whole kingdom of names and faces which had been kept alive by the architecture of their history. They would rummage through their reading in order to pay homage to streets, rooms, restaurants, which had survived the men who made them famous. Even before their arrival in a new place, their responses were, in a way, determined by their sense of expectation; as though they had chosen without evidence to be wholly identified with what was not yet known.

Fola had pushed herself up from the grape-vine, considering the near echo of steel which topped the trees. There was only one question which she wanted to ask, just one. She wanted to ask if there were any girls among them. But she couldn't trust his look of innocence. Perhaps he would detect her meaning.

'Were they all young?' she asked.

'They were Americans,' Charlot said.

And the way he said it made her feel she had been caught. But he was laughing and she laughed too. They sat near the large trunk of rock where she had first seen him. He was throwing pebbles at the rock, slowly, idly, one by one. And Fola watched his back turned to her, hungering for the touch of his head against her mouth. The sand burnt like fire under her hands. The water had devoured the families who had gone out for a swim. She watched his arm

73

aim at the target of black rock and thought: there's only the beach and the trees, and the lingering echo of steel in the trees, and you and me, and you're older and in charge, and it would be all right if you did it first because you're older and in charge and it wouldn't matter anyway, and what after all is a kiss, and you could always say you didn't mean any harm, and they'd believe because you're older and in charge, and what could it matter while you're in charge to give me one, just one hard kiss!

'Tell me,' said Charlot, throwing the last pebble over the rock, 'what would you like best, something you could have here right now.'

Fola was ashamed. 'He's seen through me,' she thought, resting her head flat on the grape-vine, 'he's seen; so what does it matter since he's seen?'

She had sat up again and said with obvious challenge in her eyes: 'You tell me first. What would you like best, that you can have here and now?'

Charlot considered the rock, glanced over his shoulder at the trees; and then it seemed the lines had changed under his chin. Fola knew that he was serious, that he would answer.

'Would you have it with me?' Charlot said.

And the tautness came again, but the wires now burnt her veins, and she was sure there was water in her eyes. She was nodding her head to let Charlot know she would.

'Let's go down to the other end of the beach,' he said.

'Which beach?' Her voice returned the question like sand blown into her mouth.

'This same beach,' said Charlot, 'where they're playing the drums.'

They didn't move until an hour later when she heard Lady Carol inviting him to supper.

The moisture had increased under Fola's eyes. She scooped the water from her nose and dried her face. So he's going, she thought, feeling less inclination to disown his memory. Perhaps he didn't see. I hope he didn't know that I was. She was reluctant to say in love. She glanced at the floor where his face had crumbled into shadows over the broken glass. His eyes had lost their mockery.

She felt imprisoned by the childhood which his influence had forced her to explore. But she felt a little free of Charlot now. She didn't reflect on the past to satisfy his curiosity. It was the terrible birth of the child's dance in the *tonelle* which worked a deeper influence on her memory. Liza was the seed from which another world beyond these picture frames had sprung.

In the sputter of candlelight that ringed Lady Carol's face, she could see Liza in a frenzy of rhythm that tossed her round the bamboo pole. The ceremony could not distort her senses here. The dead voice wailing for its mother from the tent had lost its power to deceive. But the child was real. The ceremony was a soil from which the child would grow, natural and sure as plants. When she's my age, Fola thought, Liza might feel no need to argue with the dead.

The child haunted her memory as she tried to summon her past from the world beyond the pictures on the wall. Fola felt the moisture slide down her face, but she couldn't distinguish between the touch of tears and the sweat that broke with a sting of fever under her eyes. She had returned to the centre of a world which had reduced her years to Liza's age, a world that was beyond Charlot's scrutiny.

Was she five or six? Was it a year later or two years before? The difference seemed unimportant beside the weight of that memory which Liza had imposed upon her.

An avenue of poui and immortelle trees had opened into the night. Dead petals were crushed to a wet pulp under her feet. She could hear her mother's voice talking in whispers to a strange man who walked beside her. Little Fola walked ahead, dreaming about boats that could probably sail to the stars. She would try to guess the length of her little finger, then the distance which her longest finger showed above it; the length of her body, and the distance which the altitude of the trees showed above her head.

Stage by stage, she had laboured through an impossible crowd of digits, climbing new rungs of figures to reach that height from which the stars looked down. But each time her arithmetic had failed, and the numbers toppled like a ladder. Then she would hear her mother's voice ordering her to walk a little faster. The voice would return abruptly to a whisper until it rose again, ordering her not to walk so fast. Fola wasn't interested in what they were saying, but the whisper always suggested secrecy, and any secret was a child's temptation to disobey.

Indifferent to what their secret was, feeling no interest in who the strange man was, Fola would glance over her shoulder to make sure the secret had not fled. And for some reason, her glance would remind her that the strange man was not touching her mother. Innocent of motive, she would think how some secret had brought her mother and the strange man very close, but did not let them touch.

But the secret had put a strain on the man's temper. Fola heard her mother's voice break through the whisper to rebuke the man. 'But what you want me to do,' her mother was saying, 'I can't leave my child alone. Put yourself in my place and be reasonable, Piggy, think how the child would feel all by herself in a house that size.' Her mother's voice would gain sound each time she replied to the strange man's argument. It made Fola think there was really no secret in their whispering. The strange man seemed indifferent to how a child would feel if left alone at night.

And gradually Fola seemed to nurse a secret enmity against the man. She took her mother's side, laughing as she recalled the name her mother had given him. 'Piggy' was an insult to any man as tall and strong as the strange man looked. 'All right, Piggy,' her mother went on, 'if it's how you feel, then don't come back.' Her mother was talking like the bishop chasing his pigs from the kitchen door.

The avenue rose in a flood of light that blazed over the Governor's gardens. Fola had forgotten her mother's voice as she watched the people gathered over the Governor's lawn. The Governor was celebrating his daughter's coming of age. Fola wondered what she would be like at twenty-one. The music made her ecstatic. The night was like a dream as she watched the people dancing on the lawn. Now she was filled with gratitude for the strange man who had made it possible for her to see such luxury. He was a constable stationed at the Governor's mansion. Next day she would return to school, feeling like the ladies who danced under the light. She would talk like the ladies to her friends, boasting of her unique excursion to the Governor's party. She wanted to kiss the strange man. She wanted to rush from behind the trees where they stood in hiding and shake the Governor's hand.

But her mother had started a quarrel again. The voice had returned to a whisper as she rebuked the strange man. Instinctively Fola had taken the strange man's side. She agreed with him that her mother was always making some false excuse. She had always wanted to tell her mother what the strange man had just said. Whenever Fola asked for chocolates, liquorice or peppermint balls, her mother would start some excuse about sugar rotting a little girl's teeth. Fola was glad the strange man had found her mother out. And even after what he had done, getting them into the Governor's garden to see what splendour there was among the best people in San Cristobal, her mother could not resist telling the strange man lies.

She felt ashamed for her mother. She wished the man wouldn't stop talking until her mother cried or said that she was sorry. 'Always the same excuse,' the man was saying, 'when it aint wrong because the child may not be asleep, is something else. At midnight when the worst criminal aint awake you'll still tell me nonsense 'bout perhaps the child not asleep. Or you aint sure the bishop didn't see me come in, an' if he know he'll say you aint fit to raise a child. Is always some excuse, Agnes.'

Fola was furious. Her mother was not only a liar, but also ungrateful. And always using me, she thought, to make her lies sound real. The strange man's words seemed perfectly fair. Fola was not afraid. The gardens were deserted where they stood, watching the Governor's party. In any case, the strange man was a constable, and there were hundreds of police outside guarding the Governor's mansion. She wanted to intervene and say that the Governor's party was enough to make her forget that they had gone.

The strange man was still arguing with perfect sense that the child could wait alone. But her mother could not resist making some false excuse. The voice made her furious. 'When it aint me she use,' Fola thought, 'is other people what help make up her excuse. And could she expect anyone to believe what she was asking,' Fola whispered, 'talking as though she an' the Governor's friends was all friends together.' She could never understand her mother's obstinacy. It seemed her mother wanted to insult the strange man after all he had done. 'You think those people dancing there,' her mother was saying, 'you think they would sugges' that sort o' thing. You think they do what they have to do in the bush? Look them, Piggy, look them good. You always say you go be like that one day. But how you think it go happen with your sort o' feelin' 'bout life? You think his Excellency ever sugges' to Lady Lloyd that she go makin' bed in the bush? An' a chil' well within breathin' reach? Is how you want to graduate to the sort o' life you always talkin' 'bout? You is guardian o' the law, but you aint have no pride. An' is what I born with, Piggy, I born with pride.'

Fola thought the man had run away. It was strange and sad. She wanted to cry for the hurt which the strange man's dumbness now made her feel. There was no sound at all until her mother said: 'Now please take me an' my chil' out o' the Governor's place.'

It was not a question or a favour, the way children asked for sweets or talked at school. Her mother's voice was like an order coming from the pulpit on Good Friday. Fola was horrified by the strange man's silence as he walked all the way behind them, like a servant or a pig.

Emerging from that buried night of voices and music in the Governor's garden, Fola reflected on the pictures which showed the families at Morant Bay. And where was Lady Carol at that time, Lady Carol and her two daughters?

The worlds fused and collided in her head. She felt a momentary admiration for Lady Carol. Would her own mother have spoken to Charlot or the English wife that way? Her mind was preoccupied with arguments for and against her mother. The comparisons multiplied. Lady Carol and her mother, Mrs Raymond and her mother. She looked towards the picture which showed her mother and Therese in a family group. Even Therese and her mother! Fola was trying to reach the source of that denial which she had always felt towards her mother.

She was still within the world which Liza had evoked; but it seemed her own childhood was now suspended. It had receded for

78

an interval. Then Fola heard the door open in her room. She had already closed her eyes as she listened for the footsteps treading without sound towards her bed. A voice was making tentative whispers near her ear. She had relaxed her body. The sound of her breathing grew deeper as she summoned a look of perfect slumber over her face.

'You asleep, Fola?' her mother asked again. She didn't stir. Nothing could restore her hearing while her mother waited beside the bed. 'Please go, please, please, will she go.' She was afraid the words might betray her by their sound. Her mouth opened to make room for her false snoring.

'She asleep,' her mother said, bending low to kiss her brow. 'I mustn't wake her. However much I'd like to hear how you feel, I mustn't wake her now.' She was talking to herself and Fola at the same time, relieved and disappointed not to find her daughter awake.

'Please, please, let her go now, please go now.' Fola felt the soft dry touch of a mouth kissing her brow, but her body remained very still, immobile as a corpse under the sheets. She struggled in every limb to achieve her mother's absence. 'Please go now, she had enough, let her go now.'

'Exact as she was when a chil',' her mother was whispering. The voice made no more sound than the distant drip of the rain outside. 'Therese take care o' you like she was your own mother, good ol' Therese, an' you feel for her too, I know how you feel for Therese, more even than you feel for me sometimes.'

She lifted Fola's head in her hands, resting it gently to one side. She gathered the ends of the sheets and tucked them fast under the mattress. Fola prayed that she wouldn't notice the broken picture frame on the floor. 'Please, please, why can't she go?'

'Better come back later,' her mother was saying. 'Wouldn't make sense to wake you now. But she lookin' better, you lookin' much better, thank God.'

The footsteps were receding across the room. The door closed, noiseless as a hand over the sheets; and Fola opened her eyes. But it seemed she had been cheated by her own wish. Now she wanted to call out to her mother. She would have liked them to trespass

79

upon the past together. Fola couldn't understand why she should have undermined her own desire by deceiving her mother by this treacherous slumber.

But her mother wasn't there. Fola heard the rain like footsteps striding across the garden. The curtains weren't drawn. A window emerged beyond the reach of candle flame like a square of black stone blocking her view outside. The drums were softer, no more than a spasm of sound dripping with the rain over the valley. Fola wanted to call out to her mother; but she had gone. Her mother had gone!

Where did it start? Fola wondered as she felt the water racing freely down her face. In what forgotten corner of her childhood did this denial start? Fola pondered again the comparison between Lady Carol and her mother. Now she transferred it to Veronica and herself. She had always felt a certain reserve in her relations with Veronica. A picture of Veronica was supplying her with the earliest memories of her own childhood. And the comparisons started again. Her mother and Lady Carol, Veronica and herself!

The drums were climbing softly through the valley of rain. Near the *tonelle* Therese would be closing her windows against the aggressive clamour of steel. But the sound was different here. It came over the garden, lazy and soft as rain drumming on her window. The candle was making a ripple of white roots where the tallow hardened at its base. She thought of Therese's boy. She wondered where Lady Carol's husband lived before he went to sea. Perhaps he was once a neighbour of the drums in the *tonelle*. 'Poor Semper,' she cried, 'poor, good Semper!' He had taught himself nearly everything he knew. He was lively. His wit had warmth and a certain sea roughness. But there were formal difficulties of speech which humbled him before Lady Carol. In recent times he had become less talkative, and on certain occasions he wouldn't talk at all. Everyone knew why Semper was silent in his own house. 'Poor, poor Semper!'

It was his defect of sight which had started Fola on her drift into an evening when the orchard was silent and green with fruit over the bishop's wall, and an old woman emerged from the bishop's gate, waving one hand at the empty street. But she was then no taller than the window which opened on the old woman blinking her eyes against the sun, and waving one hand as she looked up and down and across the street.

Fola had seen the old woman walk out from the bishop's palace. She had paused at the gate, looking up and down the street; then waved her hand as though she were calling for help. A car came up the street and the old woman started to reverse into the gate. The car passed, and the old woman came out and started waving her hand again; but there was no one in the street. Fola had never seen her before, but she thought the old woman was mad the way she waved like the mock hands which the carpenter, Ashton, used to make from wood. Fola left the house and went to ask what she wanted. It was then she realised the old woman could hardly see.

'Right here,' Fola said, 'is this same house.'

Fola led the old woman across the street and up the steps into the house. Climbing up the steps, Fola noticed how the old woman kept one hand buried in her pocket like a person who was ashamed to let you know it had no fingers. There was utter silence when Fola's mother came out and saw her leading the old woman into the house. Immediately the quarrel had started, but Fola couldn't understand what it was about. Fola got angry with her mother who had promptly ordered her inside.

'It's what bring you here?' her mother had asked.

The old woman didn't answer until she had taken a seat. It seemed to anger Fola's mother that the old woman had chosen the best chair in the room.

'I ask what bring you here?' she asked again.

'You know well as the world why I come,' the old woman said.

'I don't ask what I know,' Fola's mother said curtly. 'Now say what bring you here.'

The old woman still kept one hand in her pocket. Fola's mother didn't sit, as though she thought her standing would cut short the old woman's visit.

'I say I would still live to see my wish,' the old woman said, 'an' what it is I now hearin'.'

'Is you do the hearin', not me.'

'Agnes!'

'Don't settle into no confidence talk with me,' Fola's mother said, 'I ask what bring you here.'

'You was always one to hold secret,' the old woman said, 'an' the worst secret o' all you still hold.'

'You must watch your tongue while you here,' Fola's mother said.

It hurt to watch the old woman trying to get an answer.

'But is what I hearin' 'bout you have to put it off?'

'Is my business that.'

'You mean I got to go blin' before I see my wish,' the old woman cried.

'Your sight last long enough to see better than your wish,' Fola's mother said. 'You know who bring you 'cross the street?'

The old woman was silent. Her face twisted and her eyes closed in disgust.

'Why it is you have to put it off?' she asked, 'is what he find out?'

'You mind your business.'

'But is what your constable friend find out?' the old woman insisted.

Fola's mother was still standing. There was hatred in her eyes, and her hands tightened round her waist when she stared down at the old woman's face.

'Six years you don't set eyes on me or my chil',' she said. 'Is what my business now have to do with you?'

'What it is your frien' find out?' the old woman insisted.

'Don't stretch your stay,' Fola's mother said, 'is better you go.'

Fola was watching them from her room. Through the wide slit of jalousies she had seen her mother turn to consider the empty street. Then her mother walked past the bent wood rocking chair and disappeared through a passage which led into the kitchen. Fola felt sorry for the old woman who sat alone, her head propped shakily against one hand. Fola listened for her mother's steps. The passage was still as the line of sweat dripping down her nose. She crept quietly past the door, and nestled beside the bent wood rocking chair.

'Is why she don't want you to stay?' Fola asked.

Her voice seemed to put a shudder through the old woman. She wiped her half-blind eyes and looked towards the street.

'Who you?' the old woman asked, and her voice trembled like a child's trapped by its own lies.

Fola thought the old woman was scared her mother would soon return. She felt the same anger she had known that night in the Governor's garden.

'Is my mother what don't want you to stay,' Fola said. 'But she is always like that.'

The old woman continued looking towards the street. Fola wanted to ask if her eyes could only see one way. She saw the old woman's hand tremble like the time mad Ashton had a fit and collapsed in the street. The old woman was grinding her teeth. There was water in her eyes. If she had whole eyes like other people, Fola thought, you would say that she was crying; but she didn't know that half-blind eyes could also make tears. Slowly the old woman turned her head as though she were afraid to see Fola's face.

'Is why they have to put it off?' she asked.

'What put off?' Fola asked.

She didn't understand what the old woman was talking about. Fola heard her mother approaching from the kitchen. But the old woman had turned friendly. Her face was moving. She was trying to do something with her face, like any old woman who couldn't smile because her lips were too weak to lift above the teeth. Fola thought she heard her mother coming through the passage. It wasn't too late to make her escape, but she was excited to see the hand which the old woman had kept buried away. Fola thought it had no fingers.

The old woman's hand was emerging from her pocket. She had beckoned Fola to come nearer. Fola was thrilled by the touch of the old woman's hand against her chest. The old woman had proffered her hand as though Fola had to guess what was in the box. Then she saw the old woman close her wet, half-blind eyes; and her fingers opened like a cage. And Fola suddenly collapsed, shivering and screaming in a demented voice that brought a crowd of faces in every window on the opposite side of the street.

The rat had whipped past little Fola's throat, locking its fat white tail in the empty hook of her blouse. It lay dead under the crash of her head against the floor. When Fola awoke some hours later, she was aware of nothing but her mother seated at the edge of the bed, wiping a stream of tears from her face.

'She's just a wicked old woman,' her mother kept saying. 'You just forget her, 'cause she's nothin' but a wicked old woman, just plain, devil wicked.'

That was all she had said. She didn't think it safe for Fola to know why her grandmother should have brought the rat to scare her to death.

How was it possible to forget the old woman's face? Nothing had survived that day except the fat, white rat leaping at her throat, and the old woman's crippled hand emerging from her pocket. Her memory had worked a miracle of omission. Even now, more than a decade later, there were huge areas of Fola's memory which seemed a complete black-out. She had often got nervous at the thought that she couldn't trust her memory. It was a kind of impediment like blindness or a stammer. Sometimes Fola would experience the fear that her memory would collapse and scuttle everything that she had learnt; names and places, lectures, dates, even familiar faces would drop out of her memory like the contents of a box. One day she feared her memory would wither and dry up like a tree no soil could ever restore.

Fola now tried to test the memory which had closed a darkness on the old woman's face. And what did she discover?

The rat was always there. The rat and the window from which she had seen the old woman waving to the empty street. The other windows were no different in size or shape. They offered a similar view of the street; yet they belonged to the house. But this was hers.

Sometimes she would sit there alone, and the feeling would come upon her that the ceiling had stooped level with the ground. The house had lost its roof; every door was buried with the rooms under the earth. But her window remained open like a hole from which she watched the world.

It was from her window that little Fola had learnt of the old woman's death. For a moment she had forgotten about the rat. She would have liked to see the old woman again. As she listened to the voice outside her window, she knew she was taking sides with the old woman against her mother's secrecy. From early afternoon a small crowd had collected near the bishop's palace. Fola wasn't sure why they should have assembled there; but she knew from the fragments of her mother's quarrel that the voices were talking about the old woman. Nothing else was clear.

'I remember it like clock time,' the woman was saying, 'like today is Wednesday the two livin' here, same little cottage inside the orchard yard. She an' the daughter, a nice plump thing she was, not a day older than sixteen or seventeen years, with true, bright skin colour, and a pair o' tits like ripe, yellow guavas, same as she got now. Then like tomorrow is Thursday, the daughter disappear, just disappear so, an' never come back till the chil' was a big grown girl. Was the tits what do her for.'

'Was the mother drive her out,' the other woman said, 'an' for what? For bringin' a sweet little thing into the world. Just for that, like it never happen before.'

The women watched the street from end to end as they spoke. Sometimes they would stop to listen for the throb of a car throwing its echo over the houses. It was the same nervous expectant look which Fola had often seen on the faces of men who were waiting for horses to enter a race.

'And when the daughter move back,' the woman said, 'the old witch of a mother change residence for good.'

'Serve the old bitch right that she drop down dead,' a voice said, 'she . . . she . . . never set eyes on the grrraan . . . chil' till that once one tiiiimmme th . . . three weeks gg . . . gone. An' nearly kkk . . . kill her with a rrat.'

Unice was the stout, brown woman who told the news of the old woman's death. She had close-cropped hair and a scar like needlework behind one ear. She was chewing raw grains of rice and probing her ears with a safety-pin while she spoke. Her stammer was loud as an engine and more frequent than her words. It seemed others had got used to waiting during the long pauses of saliva that made lather through her syllables.

85

'They say the father marry in secret an' then went away,' the short man said. 'An' is wherever he end up that he die an' bury.'

'But why she never come out and say straight who he was?' Unice asked.

'It aint everything you can tell,' the man said. 'You know that better than anybody round here.'

'Some people say Ashton know,' one of the women said.

'What use Ashton knowin',' the man said, 'he too mad to remember anything.'

'She was always one to hide she business,' the woman said, 'but she get it at last, whatever it worth she get it an' we know who this one is.'

One man stood out from the crowd. When he opened his mouth to yawn, Fola noticed that he hardly had any teeth. But his hair was long and tangled like a woman's. He had built a small white coffin the size of a rat which he balanced on his head. He stood alone, staring in silence at the house. Flies played in and out of his nostrils, but he didn't stir. The small, white coffin was safely anchored to his hair.

'What you mournin', Ashton?' the woman shouted.

'Is collect now two crabs you can collect big as your head. Only say what you mournin'.'

The women watched him and jeered and put their questions again. But it was useless trying to make him talk.

Fola wasn't interested in what Ashton knew. At intervals of the day, she had even been unfaithful to her window; for the whole house was smelling of fruit cake and flowers. An odour of garlic drifted vaguely up the passage from the voices in the kitchen. The sky came near, still and curved like the cathedral ceiling during prayers. It looked hard as rock, and blue like Veronica's sailor blouse. The parrot next door was crying time.

Fola had heard what was going to happen, but no one had told her what to expect. That morning her mother had left very early. She seemed afraid of what she was about to do. People had been coming and going all night, and her mother looked very tired. But before she left, she had taken Fola into her room and sat her on the bed. She unwrapped a box that showed a new pair of white buckskin shoes. Two small pink handkerchiefs were dabbed with scent and laid out on the pink taffeta dress.

'Now remember what you see me do,' she said, holding one ear of Fola's between her fingers, 'before you get in the water, dab a few drops on your forehead, an' put a good handful in the mole o' your head like you see me do. Is high time you learn to manage for yourself 'cause you won't always have me. Now you remember that?'

'What?' Fola asked, looking up in wonder. She thought her mother was talking about someone dying.

'But why you don't listen, Fola,' her mother shouted, 'why you don't learn to listen?'

'I listen,' said Fola. 'I was listenin'.'

'All right,' her mother said, shepherding her voice back to a whisper. 'Listen. First you sprinkle two, three, four drops on your forehead, then where the mole is in the centre . . .'

Fola was shaking her head like an old woman expressing her bored knowledge of what was being said.

Fola was to take her bath at four o'clock; rest in the small room next to her mother's for an hour, and change into the taffeta dress and white buckskin shoes at half-past five. By six o'clock she should be seated in the bent wood rocking chair which had always been denied her. It was the second privilege the day had brought Fola.

Her mother had made no mention of the wedding. But when she was about to leave the house, she turned and said: 'We'll be back by the time you ready.'

Fola understood 'we' to mean the strange man and her mother. It was the nearest she had come to feeling the curiosity of the crowd outside.

'Is where you say it goin' to happen?' Fola said.

And her mother replied: 'Ask no questions an' you'll be told no lies.'

It had rained all night. The morning was heavy and slow. The wedding had given Fola a holiday from school, but she took no pleasure in her absence. She sat at her window and watched the other girls go by. They envied her this day from school, and Fola pretended that it was right they should.

'She only playin' great,' one girl said, 'like is the first time anybody get marry.'

'Is only 'cause she go have to dress up,' another said.

'Is only that,' a third girl added. 'If it was like Sunday when we all dress up, she couldn't play great. But only 'cause is ordinary Wednesday an' she go get a chance to look better than me in this ol' print rag my aunt pass on.'

Whenever the girls spoke, they all turned to cock their bottoms up at the window where Fola was watching.

'It aint fair,' one girl continued, 'I don't call that fair competition, usin' she Sunday best to match everybody else Wednesday rags.'

'Is only why she can play great,' the other said, 'but wait till Sunday, I go make she look like a ordinary fish woman when I show myself next Sunday.'

In a whisper which deeply wounded Fola because she couldn't hear, the girl was dribbling news into a crowd of ears around her. 'Uncle Boysie bring it home last night,' she said, 'green roun' the waist with high, white neck I hear my aunt name cowl, is cowl neck it is, with bustle catch up at the back, and the pleats fine, fine, and straight, straight, straight like when you cut grass.'

The other girls tittered as each item came up, then tossed their heads and leapt high in dance until the girl had summoned them back. The ears turned and opened like shells under their hands.

'Uncle Boysie say he don't know if he able to get shoes to match,' the girl whispered, 'but even without shoes, Uncle Boysie say even without shoes I go put the Governor's daughter in the shade.'

Then the girls pranced around like lunatics, shouting: 'And your uncle is a tailor, he ought to know.'

There were tears in Fola's eyes. She had closed the window to dry her face. When she opened it again, the girls had relented. The girl who considered herself Fola's rival had come nearer the window. The others followed close.

88

'It aint fair to behave that way,' one girl said, 'it aint she fault the mother gettin' marry, or that they make it Wednesday.'

The rival, softened by reason, was looking up at Fola.

'Where it is your mother gettin' marry?' she asked, smiling and contrite.

Fola flung the window wide open. She poked a finger in her mouth and pouted her jaws.

'Ask no questions . . . an' you'll get tell no lies.'

And the window banged like a gate. Fola had paused like an adult to emphasise her disdain. A moment later the window opened again on the silent, astonished faces of the girls.

'Dirty, black rats,' Fola spat, and the window banged again.

It was her mother's phrase which finished them. Fola had learnt to use it like a sword.

But she resented her ignorance. Fola knelt in a corner and prayed that the girls wouldn't ever guess that she didn't know. It would have been a crushing humiliation for her on their return to school.

The day passed like a punishment until Veronica arrived. It was just after lunch that Fola learnt all she knew about the wedding. Veronica said she was going to be what her father called the bridesmaid. Veronica's father was then a constable like the strange man who was going to marry Fola's mother.

Fola thought it strange, even a little unjust, that her mother should have preferred Veronica to see the wedding. But she hated church, which was a consolation; and the feel of the new shoes had soothed her temper. She spent all her rest hour trying them on. She had spread newspaper and a dirty sheet over the passage. She walked up and down the house, talking to the noises which the new shoes made. She twisted them to the left; she twisted them to the right. She boxed the tips with her fist, and watched to see what would happen. Then she walked over the passage, and there was gramophone music all the way up from her heels to the laced frills of her taffeta skirt.

The sky had turned purple. The smell of fruit cake and flowers gave way to macaroni pie and peppered crabs in a thick vegetable stew. The spray of cold water over frying pans was singing like a hose-pipe throughout the house. The crowd got thicker in the dark. They were angry and impatient with her mother's delay. They felt cheated of their right to see the bride who arrived with the strange man at eight o'clock. It was hell black in every eye outside.

Fola didn't remember Veronica until the guests arrived. Now her resentment grew into a positive hatred of her mother. They had insisted that Veronica should sit at the table like a grown-up guest. Veronica wanted to stay with her in the bent wood rocking chair, but Fola's mother and the Raymonds were adamant that everything should work to plan. And the plan demanded that the party in the church should be the same party at the table.

Fola was served a bowl of vanilla ice-cream and a huge slice of black fruit cake. One of the women from the kitchen had brought it in on a tray. She spread a napkin over Fola's dress and put the tray on her lap. When the woman had gone, Fola spat into the bowl, drilling her spoon like a fork through the frozen cream. The snivel leaked thick from her nose on to the taffeta dress. She curled up in the chair, staining the taffeta dress with her hands. The tears ran into her mouth and out again along her neck.

'After all,' she sobbed, 'is my mother she is, she aint her mother, she's my own mother, not yours.'

She argued as though Veronica were present to defend herself. The cake crumbled like dirt in her hands; and the tears made a flood of brine in her mouth. Her veins rose large and swollen up from her neck. The fitful spasms of her breathing burnt like a furnace in her throat. Her stomach ached with hunger, but she refused to eat.

When the bishop rose to give thanks for what this wedding had done, the silence had revealed Fola's misery. The bishop paused and tried again to finish his words of grace, but her weeping had spread like an illness.

'She'll be all right,' her mother said, coaxing the bishop to go on.

'She think she go lose you,' Mrs Raymond said with a flush of the mother's proprietary feeling.

Then they heard the crash of the tray on the floor, and Fola's mother ran out.

'What wrong with Fola?' Veronica kept asking.

'She think she go lose her mother,' Mrs Raymond said again.

'She'll be all right,' Mr Raymond said, scolding Veronica with his eyes.

But Fola's violence demanded their presence. When her mother stooped to dry her face, she had thrown the melted ice-cream out of the window. The bowl crashed noisily through the pane of glass.

'Children's love can be a terrible thing,' the bishop kept saying. They stood around, imploring her calm in different voices.

'You not go lose your mother,' Mrs Raymond promised.

The bishop was trying to explain once more the tragic bond of a young and unspoken love. But they all stood in silence, terrified by what they had seen. The child's rage was beyond their comprehension. It was no less mysterious than the change which came over Fola when her mother's husband ordered her to bed. Without a trace of protest the child had climbed into his arms, begging his pardon with her slobbering, wet kiss. That night she went to sleep on the strange man's shoulder.

'And it's been the same ever since,' Fola was saying, 'is been the same ever since, is same since, 'is so, same so ever since . . .'

The words seemed to come like the echo of other voices from outside: 'is so, same so . . .' Syllables changed their phrasing; words showed a length that had suffered by the roughness of an accent uttered in haste. Surfacing slowly from the world which had offered Veronica and herself at Liza's age, words seemed uncertain of their alliance. At every stage of awareness she could feel the change, until the rules of college speech gave way completely to the private dialect of her own tongue at home: 'Is same ever since, and it been the same, same so ever since.'

The fever was subsiding, but a chill had spread up from her toes. Fola heard her sweat like thawing cubes of ice drip down her hands, off her shoulders, making a cold tunnel under her back. The sheets were drenched. She thought of the stages of her fever, and multiplied the disasters that could become the ultimate future of this asphyxia which gradually caged her breathing.

For a moment she was terrified by the rumours she had heard of people who were about to die; how they achieved some madness of vision, some lunatic clarity of perception which it was too late to communicate. Fola was scared because it was the first time, at any stage of illness, that she had ever thought her own death possible. She agreed that death was everyone's end, yet saw no contradiction in the instinct which told her with certainty it could not happen to her. She needed her strength in order to discover an argument that would verify this instinct. Eternity was not a reward for any virtue she might possess. This instinct had nothing to do with virtue. Eternity seemed a property of her existence which nothing could deny. She felt it, embraced it, experienced it, with that certainty of intimate knowing: like knowing she was in bed with fever; like knowing what she had been thinking and how it had started; like knowing this incommunicable change of emotion which she now felt towards Charlot.

Fola saw no need to deny her love for Charlot. She had been in love with Charlot, but this return to childhood had changed the proportions of his influence. It seemed to obliterate any sense of loss she might have felt when he had gone. She tried to remember the name of the painter Charlot had mentioned on their way from the *tonelle*, that man for whom the ceremony was an example of *the backward glance*. 'Only the dead can do it,' the painter had said, 'or the living who are free.'

She saw Veronica framed in her past against the wall. And beyond, another world had emerged to dwarf their years to Liza's age. She could see Liza bright with sweat like the dirty, black rats under the window the day her mother married. And Charlot's face haunted her; but there was no mockery in it now. Fola didn't believe Charlot had jeered; but she believed it was impossible for him to understand what she had felt in the *tonelle*. She didn't think Charlot could even understand what he had done. For Charlot too was a victim of all that had happened. Fola could hear his voice uttering its familiar theme about the need for roots; the need for her to return to the world of feeling which the *tonelle* implied. But Charlot's faith seemed dubious in this moment of Fola's thought. She recalled the gentle hint of mischief in his voice when he had spoken of his American friends in Europe. Their return to the past seemed the opposite of her visit to the *tonelle*. Yet Charlot seemed distressed by this green passion for discovery in his American friends.

In spite of the mischief in Charlot's voice, Fola was anchored for ever to this question. 'Why? Why? Why could his American friends return to embrace their world of monuments and important graves?'

The Americans were real like Liza and this fever which seemed to spread with blinding clarity over everything. That rumour about the sight that comes with dying was in her ears again. Question and vision seemed to be part of the same fever which had aroused her thinking. Why could those Americans surrender all identity to that world whose evidence they had only read? What was the secret of that harmony which related them to their past?

Fola was too weak to talk, but she could hear her answer. She could hear it for herself; but it was larger than herself; for it was also Liza's answer. And it was Charlot's too, Charlot's and the Americans'. It was the answer behind the furious rhythms that possessed the entire *tonelle*. Her thought seemed to acquire the substance of a fact, like the women dancing round the bamboo pole. And her reason now emerged harsh and clear as the violent pounding of the drums in the *tonelle*.

It was because, for Liza and herself it was because their relation to the *tonelle* was far more personal than any monument could ever be to an American in his mad pursuit of origins. *Personal and near*. Nearer than any famous grave that lay before Charlot's eyes. Her relation to the *tonelle* was *near* and more personal since the conditions of her life today, the conditions of Liza's life in this very moment, could recall a departure that was near and tangible: the departure of those slaves who had started the serpent cult which the drums in their dumb eloquence had sought to resurrect.

The Americans took pleasure in their past because they were descended from men whose migration was a freely chosen act. They were descended from a history that was recorded, a history which was wholly contained in their own way of looking at the world. 'But my return! The return that might also come to perplex Liza!' This was more personal since it was a commercial deportation which had shaped her relations to the *tonelle*. Question and answer hung there. All vision was balanced on that difference between herself and Charlot. Between herself and Liza! Fola could hear her child's voice, haughty and petulant, wound the girls, the black rats, who stood, crippled with defeat under her window.

And even then, Fola thought, even in that innocence of insult there was already secreted an æsthetic denial of their blackness: an insult she had learnt, an insult which all her infancy had suckled like an udder. And the udder was Charlot's history: the essential history of all Charlot's world.

Fola looked at her own hands brown as sugar in the light, and the words were screaming through her fever: it was not race, I swear it was not race, it was not race, repeat, repeat, not race, it is not race. It was and is the contagious blackmail of slavery working a crime on every skin that comes too thick with colour. Not race, but the blackmail of slavery; and near, *too near in time to be forgotten by the Americans, Charlot, or me.*

History was the udder Charlot had taught her mind to suckle at. Now it was through his tutelage, through a tutelage foreign to San Cristobal, that Fola had returned to the *tonelle.*

Part-product of that world, living still under the shadow of its past disfigurement, all her emotions had sprung from a nervous caution to accept it as her root, her natural gift of legacies. Fear was the honest and ignorant instinct she had felt in the *tonelle.* Her shame, like that of all San Cristobal, was unavoidable.

The fever had subsided. Her body was cool under the sheets. But Fola got that feeling agin: how death was no part of the terms in her own existence. She could not die because it was in the nature of her life to last for ever.

In her bed, no wider than a grave, Fola now lay, idle as the hair on her head. The mirror begged her to stare, but the light couldn't climb beyond its shadow on the wall. Yet the night like a surface of black glass reflected a crowd of faces that were not there. She watched the candle stoop, soft as a sore, bending two veins of tallow down its sides.

She thought of Charlot as she heard the distant call of the drums coming up from the valley. She had heard them on her return from the *tonelle* that night; but the sound was different now. They didn't shout. They seemed to filter up from the valley through the slow drumming of the rain against her window. Perhaps it was the distance and the rain, but their call was different now. The rhythms came soft, more soothing as she slipped deep and deeper into the moisture of the sheets.

Fola felt the stir of the sheets like water under her back. In her sleep the bed wobbled and sank level to the floor; then rose erect and quivering in the night. The sheets clapped like the canvas partitions of a tent securely tethered to the ground. Like the ceremony of souls, her dream was making a harmony of moments at once familiar and improbable. It had combined two different worlds; yet they were real, beyond any logic of contradiction in her mind.

Charlot was sitting beside her in the *tonelle*. The flambeaux burnt red shadows over Veronica's face. Lady Carol was clapping. Her mother sat near the tent, wearing her wedding dress. She held the child, Liza, in her arms. Then the child slid quietly down her knees and joined the women dancing round the bamboo pole. The drums marched their rhythms like feet over the two women who lay under the sheets. Liza was dancing the *ververs* away. The bishop was waving his cross like an axe through Liza's hair.

But the roles of priest and souls had changed. It was the old woman who felt the power of the deities in her hands. Aunt Jane was going to unlock the waters which had imprisoned the *Houngan's* soul. He had grown hysterical. He had threatened again to break free before Aunt Jane could order his release. Fola could hear his voice, clear and distinct, shrieking her mother's name. The *Houngan's* soul was wailing for a daughter it had never seen. The crowd gazed at Fola's mother as the *Houngan* battled with the deities in the tent. The voice had grown like a flood over the *tonelle*: 'to see my daughter . . . to see my daughter, just once to know my daughter . . .' But Fola's mother didn't stir. She sat patient as a stone, enduring the punishment of the *Houngan's* soul: 'to see my daughter, just, once, only, just, to know my daughter . . .'

Soon the flambeaux had split wide open. The island rose like a turtle from its sloth, entirely cuddled in flames, blossoming a weather that cleansed its crust with water and fire. The floods were ready to swallow her up; and every house, hurricane risen to the moon, now sailed in a mad division of roof and walls over the nearest tide.

Charlot's voice was crying out: 'Forgive us this day, forgive us this and no more than this forgive us now.'

And the old woman from the tent replied: 'What done is done.'

Next day the sun came out like a neighbour who had sinned.

CHAPTER V

A sleek, grey bundle of Siamese fur stretched and breathed over the rug. Its switch of tail had started a flicker of signals round the kitchen. The sun gathered little spokes of flame up from the stove, spilling its reflection through the servant's hands. The fur shrank and quivered like a sponge under the light. The stove was singing, and the flames dribbled past the black, burnt rim where the sun's rays crashed and died in the hard, wide sockets of the cat's eyes.

Its calm resembled the patient cunning in Therese's glance. She strained the red entrails of a rabbit through the metal pipe which sucked all refuse from the sink into the steel drum bin outside. Therese and the cat were the only two living creatures in this kitchen. All insects died at birth. Flies were poisoned on arrival. Only the cat had survived that spiteful vigilance which ruled over Therese's work. She wasn't likely to murder the cat, but sometimes his presence seemed like a flaw in her achievement of corpses.

'Is how smart you is I know,' Therese was saying as though in argument with a rival cook.

The cat's eyes had been transformed into a hard, immobile blaze of light, burning the dead carcass of the rabbit in her hands. It was part of her creed that a cat was a cat, and a thief was a thief, and all talk of pedigree was nonsense.

'Jus' test you with a day's starvation,' Therese was saying as she glanced at her audience on the rug. 'An' you show your true colours like any ordinary criminal.'

The cat continued to stare like a blind man whose eyes had never closed. Therese lifted the wet rib of meat level with her head; then lowered it into the sink, watching for the cat to shift its glance. But the cat didn't stir.

'If is patient you playin' patient,' Therese coughed, 'I patient too. Aint the first time I see experienced criminal behave like you. Is blind you playin', but it got plenty criminals do the same. Only difference is you look straight while another class take on a false cross-eye. But criminal is criminal whatever their class. It only necessary to watch them good, and you see how they graduate from the same, identical school.'

Flies buzzed outside the window-pane, and Therese turned sharply, considering what would happen if the glass gave way. She hugged the meat tight between her hands and watched the flies. They circled and went away. But Therese still watched, and soon there was a small regiment of flies marching over the pane of glass. Therese remembered her rival on the rug, but the cat's glance had already shifted to the window-pane. She forgot the flies, and pondered the depth of intrigue in those eyes turned slyly on the sun-glazed corners of the window.

'As if you think I done born stupid,' Therese intoned, hoping to distract the cat. 'Is come they come to catch my attention so you can get on with your thievin' scheme while I plottin' how to make their funeral. An' now while I talk, you lookin' up there like you seein' with your ears. Is deaf you playin' deaf. But all you is the same, thief, cat or fly. I know my creed, an' it tell me don't meddle with any creature what crawl to take food what aint his own. Thief, cat an' fly, same class o' criminal.'

Therese wanted to get rid of the cat; but it was a rule of the house that the animal was never to be whipped, scolded, or refused. Once Therese had been threatened with dismissal for raising her voice to chase the animal away.

The Piggotts had begun to practice a strange kind of ju-jitsu talk about animals and their nerves. Like human beings, Therese was warned, some cats were more easily destroyed than others. She had always thought a little arsenic would have been enough; but the families had now confused her with their talk about degrees of animal suffering. The Raymonds believed it too; and Lady

Carol, who had started a course in something called V.D.P., kept them all frantic with the latest developments in cat sickness.

During supper parties at the Piggotts' house, Therese had to witness the strangest marriage of words like personality and divide, fracture and broken and split. They rattled like the weight of the cutlery in Lady Carol's hands. It made no sense at all to Therese. She vaguely understood personality, because it was the word she used to describe a professional man, like her doctor. But the rest didn't seem to fit her idea of people like Lady Carol. Split, broken and divide were key words in the vocabulary of some sharp card players Therese had known. Fracture, she thought, could easily be the result of cheating. Therese really believed that their talk had to do with gambling and money, or telling fortunes. But there was one point in their favour. At least, it was an observation which sometimes confused her. Therese had watched the families very closely, and in particular the younger generation like Fola and Veronica. And she had noticed a similar delicacy of stride whenever the cat was walking across the lawn up to the porch. There was no doubt about it: no animal in the Forest Reserve could move with the same noiseless grace which she had seen in Piggott's black, Siamese cat. It had what Therese called style.

Food was another source of her envy. She could take what she wanted from the family stores; but the cat's diet was never to be tampered with. An unfortunate coincidence was her passion for boiled rabbit which was ordered exclusively for the cat. She had turned to rail again at the cat when the sound of Piggott's voice interrupted her. The cat had sprawled full length over the rug while Therese waited, anxiously timing the pause that had come into the voices on the other side. She heard Piggott's voice whisper again.

'Where Fola?'

There was no answer, but Piggott wasn't aware of the silence. He was preoccupied with the stubborn knot of the boot laces threaded round his fingers, and the secrets which his afternoon mail had disclosed. His stomach pressed like an animal's pouch over his knees. Fat gave his breathing an uneven sound. He was still waiting for an answer.

'Agnes, I'm speaking to you,' he said, 'where Fola?'

'Speaking to me,' Agnes said, 'since when you speaking to me? You come in here, not even ask if I livin' or dead, an' now talk 'bout speakin' to me. What you take me for?'

There was an unnecessary urgency in their voices; but Piggott had suddenly remembered his question when Agnes chose to reveal her misery.

'What get into you this evening?' he asked, trying to understand her anger.

'Nothin' in me more than is always there,' she shouted. 'You and Fola alike where I concern. You think you can treat me as you please because I got no feelings.'

Piggott laboured with his hands against his knees, and craned his body back into the hollow of the chair. It wasn't often he felt this need to declare his presence in the house.

'Where Fola?' he asked again.

'Fola is her own woman,' Agnes answered, 'she don't have to tell me where she go, an' I don't ask.'

He saw Agnes wipe her eyes, and let her head hang forward in a gesture of indifference. For a moment Piggott wanted to stretch and take her hands; but the weight of his stomach had foiled his intention. And his mood changed.

'But why you such a miserable bitch, Agnes?'

Piggott's voice had a quality of surprise, as though he had made some new discovery which she could help him understand. Agnes was staring at him like an enraged animal caught in a snare.

'I don't care if you speak or not,' she said, 'but when you do, don't let your tongue go too far.'

'Is my house this and I can speak as I please.'

'But you don't live in it by yourself,' Agnes said, clenching her fists in rage, 'an' the day you think 'bout doin' that, just let me know. When you marry me you didn't pick me up. Remember my legs can still walk.'

'You doin' all you can to bring that day near,' Piggott said.

'Then what you waitin' for?' she asked, rising from the sofa. 'All you got to do is say the word. I aint a day less in anything than the day you first meet me.'

'That was a day,' Piggott said. 'I hope they never make two like it.'

Agnes rose from the sofa; she paced from door to door until she had completed her return back to the sofa. Her memory was like the sound of bells as she flagged her finger before Piggott's face.

'Listen, Piggy, just listen good,' she said. 'I never ask you to take me on. You had all your senses when you decide to do what you do. Remember that. An' remember too what happen through all those years. I didn't sit back like one o' those women too lazy to move. I help you wherever it is you get to. An' I didn't help to prove I could help. I help 'cause it was your own ambition eatin' up your brain. Don't forget to remember that the moment you start ridin' your high horse.'

Piggott heard his khaki tunic fall to the floor. He kicked the boots up into his hands, and slowly rose from the chair. Agnes could feel his reluctance to go, the uncertainty of movement in his legs as he stumbled past the chair. Piggott was afraid to speak, temporarily shamed by his own accusations against himself. He had left unsaid something Agnes wanted to know. He paused at the door, swinging his boots by the laces as he waited, wavering between his impatience to retire and the tenderness which her accusations always aroused in him.

'Was me who help you,' she said in a voice that seemed to express contempt for his retreat.

Piggott returned to the chair and let the boots distract his attention until her anger had receded. Whenever Agnes threatened to recall her services as a wife, he knew it was time to relinquish his rights. All argument came abruptly to an end. He was at once intrigued and diminished by this aspect of her power. All his achievement was contained in her doing like a bowl in some huge and reliable hand. Agnes had made him. He could improve on his previous success, but he couldn't exchange its source for anything else. In spite of his own effort, his acceptance of her claim soon made him feel almost servile to her power. He would occupy his attention with the merest trifle, and think: it's her nerves again! But he dare not say that. She would have assaulted him with reasons for her fatigue until she had led him miserably back to her original claims.

Also, there was no noticeable decline in Agnes. She was still the most beautiful woman in San Cristobal. Her body hadn't yielded an inch of its elegant carriage. Her step was quick, and clean and decisive. Her feet knew where she was going. When you saw her walk up the street, or striding across the huge expanse of lawn and garden that rolled up to the house, you got the impression that the distance had already been devoured. After twelve years her walk was the same: fluid and sure, the chin slightly tilted so that you saw the gradual sweep of her neck curving up from her shoulders. Her shoulders were spread backwards, and her bosom, no larger than her daughter's, lifted discreetly under her blouse. There was no sudden thrust, no sharpness of line in the proportions of her breasts. She had the dancer's subtle and athletic thighs. Her hair flew like a forest of black hay above her head. Her eyes were dark amber like her skin. Agnes was what they would call in San Cristobal a cream sugared beauty. She had the soft tanned complexion of the mulatto like Fola, but she was darker.

This was part of the magic which could still subdue Piggott; and she would sometimes hint at it by regretting that her backside was not flat. She hated wearing stays or corsets, anything which hugged a pressure round her skin; but she could seldom find a dress with the looseness of flair that might distract attention from the tangible rhythm moving with her hips down to the severed halves of flesh which pillowed the base of her spine. Rather than yield an inch to Piggott, Agnes would maintain that a flat backside would have spared her most of the trouble she had endured.

Piggott watched her pack a handful of hair under the clasp. She smoothed out wrinkles from the sofa as she rose and stood before the mirror. She was parcelling her hair with both hands, and Piggott could see her eyes reflected in the glass. She looked a little tired for this time of day. Her mouth hadn't yet lost the nervous shudder which happened when she was angry or hurt. But he knew the worst had passed between them. It would only be a matter of indulging her pride in order to be forgiven. After such an exchange she would pretend to barter peace for an apology that wasn't too direct. It would have been useless to say 'sorry' until some hours had passed. Night was the safest bed for that word to rest on. Piggott was always the first to negotiate peace, and he knew the stages of question and answer by heart.

'Where the committee meeting this evening?' he asked.

'Is what you asking,' she said, her head half-turned from the mirror, 'you know well as the world we meeting at Raymond.'

Ever since Independence the Raymonds' house had become a centre for social workers: a whole, new tribe of middle-aged women whose existence no one knew about until political freedom had rescued them. And there were also young women, not much older than Fola and Veronica, who had discovered a passion for making some contribution to the country. Like Lady Carol's phrase, 'seen active service in the war,' this utterance about making the contribution had become a kind of crutch that kept every ambition above ground.

On a simple, ordinary Wednesday morning when the public flags changed colour, and the national anthems changed tunes; the date, August 24, had acquired a miraculous birth. It had struck a mine of patriotic resources in every heart. The committees, voluntary and unwilling, grew larger and more numerous. There was a committee for everything under the sun: cat shows, beauty contests, volume competitions between radiograms, artists' endeavour (the poet who wrote the new anthem got a scholarship to England and never returned), and any activity which attracted public notice in the capital. The most powerful of the lot was the Piggotts' committee for raising the moral tone of the country's name abroad.

'Is about the Vice-President's dance you going to discuss?' Piggott asked, sensing the temperature in her voice.

'Is really 'bout the music,' she said, 'I don't know what you an' Raymond doin' at all.'

'What you mean?' Piggott asked, and saw her turn to face him.

'Well if they use the Steel Bands this time,' she said, 'they go have to use them for the Independence Ball the fortnight later. You can't make excuse that they play bad, 'cause it aint possible with the Forest Reserve Boys.'

'Who say so?' Piggott asked, and felt a fresh note of complaint evoke his interest.

'Is only natural,' Agnes said, 'if they good enough for the Vice-President ball, they good enough for the Independence Ball.'

'But who the hell suggest them again?' Piggott asked.

He knew by the look of disapproval on her face that their angers were now harmonised.

'Is the history teacher man from London,' Agnes said weakly. Then her voice rose on a wave of distrust. 'An' is all right for him 'cause he done gone 'bout his business an' leave it on our hands. Was he tell the Boys a week before he sail that the committee agree to use them. Was true 'bout the agreein', but why he had to tell them if he know he was going?'

Piggott turned his head to avoid any questions about Charlot. He would have liked to say something abusive about foreigners in San Cristobal; but it seemed too great a risk. Agnes would have drifted back into all the agony which Fola had inflicted on her.

'But Piggy,' she said.

He let the boot drop from his hand, and quickly found a target for his anger. His eyes expressed a feeling of disdain which he knew she would be able to share.

'Dirty ruffians the lot o' them,' he said, retrieving the boot with both hands. 'Two years an' it comin' three we get the Independence, an' it don't mean nothin' to them. They still idle an' makin' trouble all over the place.'

'But is only talk all you talk,' Agnes said, 'like you scared o' the Steel Band Boys.'

'Whatever they decide this evening,' Piggott said, 'tell them make it the last time they bring up the bands, 'cause I go clean up the bands and all what go with it. Raymond and me done discuss that, and I thought it was settled.'

His anger was truly impressive, but this talk of the bands was bringing them too near his fear that she might start again on Fola.

'Say hello to Raymond and the family,' he said quickly. 'Is what time you gettin' back?'

''Bout nine,' said Agnes, 'unless those damn social climbers keep hangin' on. Way they people use Independence you'd think it was a horse.'

Piggott was laughing.

She called out to Therese who appeared, swift and noiseless as the cat, from her kitchen. Therese didn't like the atmosphere of secrecy in the room. Agnes gave her orders while Therese nodded her head and flecked particles of dust from the table. She looked up at Agnes and down at the table as though there was explosive in the wood. Therese tried to see Piggott's face, but she dare not betray her lack of attention while Agnes was talking.

It always gave Piggott a shock to hear himself called the master. 'See you put out the clean towels for the master.' Agnes did it with an astonishing ease. She might have been talking on behalf of an absent stranger when she gave her orders for the master's supper. Alone, Piggott could be exacting in the same role; but his wife's gestures were more fluent. There was a natural severity in her tone. It made Piggott feel more assured of the instinct which had chosen Agnes as his wife. He thrilled to the servant's repetitive cry, 'yes ma'am, yes ma'am.' But he never raised his head or looked in her direction while Agnes was speaking.

When the servant had gone, Agnes walked over to the mirror and examined her face. Piggott could see the look of defeat come into her eyes again. He knew the very smell of her moods; the moment her gaiety was about to turn into an equal flood of complaint. And he wasn't very good at hiding secrets from her. He considered his chances of postponing any mention of Charlot's letter until he had spoken with Fola.

'But is what I do her?' Agnes cried, as though the face in the mirror had reflected her grievance. 'I try my best, and Fola always make it look like nothin', like I aint mean nothing to her.'

Piggott grew wary of speech. He felt the double need to defend Fola while he consoled her mother.

'She just growing up,' he said, 'is nothing but the change in growing up.'

'But aint that the time she might talk to me?' Agnes said. 'Tell me little things, how she feeling, what worry her?'

104

Agnes came nearer the chair, looking at Piggott with the familiar plea for sympathy in her eyes.

'Fola will talk with you,' she cried, 'she'll talk with Veronica. She'll talk with this body an' the next. Fola will even talk her secrets with Therese. But always I come last. When I hear what Fola doin' or think to do, is you who tell me, you or somebody else.'

'Don't worry, Agnes, you mustn't worry.'

'But is more than enough to worry 'bout.'

She leaned against the door, losing all interest in her meeting with the committee.

'What wrong with me?' she cried. 'Why Fola can't treat me like other people, like she treat you. It hurt me deep down when I hear you and Fola talking, the way you talk and laugh, and soon as I appear she'll stop. Just stop so, and everything change like a dead walk in. Only because I present and she don't want me share anything. Is what I do her, Piggy?'

'Don't talk like that, Agnes?'

'But is what Fola see wrong with me?'

Piggott offered his hand as he looked up at her. The light was moist and bright in her eyes.

'You mustn't talk like that,' he said. 'You know you never did Fola anything, and she don't feel the way you say.'

'But is how I can know that?' she wept, jerking her hand away.

'I'm telling you,' Piggott said. 'Time and again Fola will talk 'bout you like she never talk 'bout anybody else. With all the gratitude and everything any mother could expect.'

Agnes rubbed her eyes as she watched Piggott trying to console her.

'Then why she can't tell me?' she said. 'If it so why she can't bring herself to let me hear it straight from her own mouth?'

'Is only because she is like that,' Piggott said. 'We not all the same. But I go talk to her. I go have a good, private talk with Fola.'

'And that's what I got to wait for,' Agnes said. 'See what I mean? I must wait till you tell her to do what should come natural. It don't help, Piggy.'

'Then I won't bother,' he said, turning his blank stare on the floor.

'Is much of a muchness whatever you do.'

'Just give her a chance,' Piggott begged, 'she reaching that age when changes set in. It happen to you and me. It happen to everyone. But perhaps it happen more so to Fola.'

Agnes seemed a little relieved. She smoothed the wrinkles from her skirt and dried her eyes and studied the curve of her body up to her bosom and along her stomach and up to her bosom again and thought in words she dare not utter how it might help if she could have another child and how it might free her from this robbery of affection which she felt and how another child if boy or girl might start the love which Fola had denied her.

'And I don't ask very much,' she said, as she made ready to go, 'if Fola ever could show me one half or even less than half the feeling she got for you, I won't be talking like this. Jesus in heaven could swear I won't.'

Piggott tumbled his tunic on the floor as he rose from the chair, moving gently and with a measured kindness to her aid. It wasn't their habit to make parting demonstrations like this; but he had caught her hand as she turned to go. Agnes became docile as a child, wholly dependent on his strength. She offered her mouth and felt the sure, delighted touch of his lips kissing her good-bye.

'And don't let any committee get on your nerves,' he said, waving her out of sight, 'and see you enjoy yourself. And what 'bout supper?'

'I tell Therese I won't be back,' Agnes said, and let the car cruise her slowly into the street.

He had felt a mixture of pleasure and regret when Agnes spoke about himself and Fola in that way. He knew it was true. For as long as he could remember, it had been so; and while Agnes argued or suffered her daughter's denial in silence, Piggott's sense of devotion seemed to increase towards Fola. It was a kind of gratitude which Piggott felt, as though Fola's affection was the ultimate proof that his claims were equal to any a natural father could ever want to make.

Therese came in to collect the Sam Browne belt. Piggott drew her attention to the tunic on the floor; then he asked for a glass of orange squash. It was the weirdest paradox of taste, that Piggott could not bring himself to eat an orange, yet had an enormous appetite for the bottled juice which San Cristobal imported. Therese always thought that the rind from the orange peel would blister his lips, or set an edge to his teeth.

Piggott washed his throat with the orange squash and felt the liquid like a cataract flushing his liver. For a while he was at peace with himself, in the remote and quiet luxury of his surroundings. The living-room had the spacious feel of a ranch. It was wide with tall bay windows and deep blue venetian blinds on the west side of the house. A red curtain was draped across the room. It opened in half, sliding through a canal of brass hooks when the cords at the sides were drawn. It served as a partition which screened the dining table off.

Piggott stretched and brooded on the dead shadows of the plants reflected in the polished margins of floor projecting from the carpet. Then he heard the rattle of cutlery on the table and wondered whether Fola would arrive in time to have supper with him. The letters had suddenly baulked his enthusiasm for the room. In a fit of temper he called out for Therese. He wanted to know why she had set the table for two since Agnes would not be back for supper.

'Any message from Miss Fola?' Piggott asked.

'Is whole day the 'phone no ring,' Therese said, 'like it gone deaf.'

He was pondering Fola's absence at meals during the last few days.

'But is how you know Miss Fola will be in?' he asked, 'she didn't eat in the night before.'

'Is true, sir,' Therese agreed, 'she didn't come in till straight bedtime.'

'An' last night too,' Piggott said, feeling some promise of her arrival, 'you didn't prepare for her. Like you know she wasn't comin'.'

'I didn't know nothin', sir,' said Therese, 'but after the first night it seem a waste to carry on till she turn up.'

107

'So is how you receive no message,' said Piggott, 'yet you set table for two.'

Suddenly Therese remembered that she was talking to the Commissioner of Police for all San Cristobal. Until she came to work for the Piggotts she had had a natural terror of the police; but her nearness to Piggott seemed to place her on terms of intimacy with the law. Therese always reminded her friends that she wasn't employed by any ordinary corporal. So she answered Piggott now in that calm and thoughtful voice as though she had been sharing opinions with an ordinary private.

'Is just so innocent people go to gaol,' she said, 'they do what aint make sense, but is like their feelin' tell them it right. It don't seem right Miss Fola not eating with her family, so I set her place to make it feel like she go come.'

'All right,' Piggott said very brusquely. He had hoped that Therese would have more definite information about Fola.

'Also, you know, sir,' Therese said, turning to go, 'it have sometimes people behave like they got what they know aint possible; and sudden so what aint possible turn up like it was just watching them all the time.'

Retreating from the room as she spoke, Therese had actually finished her sentence in the kitchen. And she was right. The arrangement of knives and forks for Fola made Piggott feel that she would arrive. He would have a bath and shave, change into the white dressing-gown he wore in the evenings, and wait until Fola came.

His clothes were laid out on the bed: fresh cotton underwear, clean handkerchiefs and the dressing-gown. He searched the tunic for the little box which he had bought for Fola. He looked at it, and tried to anticipate what she would say. He had to find a way of timing his gift so that it might seem a natural introduction to his questions about Charlot's letters. He looked at the small box again, resisting the urge to lift the lid. Then he slipped it with the letters into the pocket of his dressing-gown.

Therese heard the taps humming as she walked up and down the living-room. She knew that Piggott would not be ready for half an hour. She slapped the cushions and turned them over, re-arranging their positions for effect. She corrected the angle of a picture which hung from the wall; then her eye caught the tangle of a spider's web in the wire basket of fern that filled the window.

She was meticulous in everything, and not because the Piggotts were particularly kind to her. She wasn't sure that she liked Piggott himself, but she felt a great loyalty to that sense of perfection which their taste had created in her. It gave her the feeling that she too had style; and it made her severe in her choice of friends among the neighbour's servants. She earned less than the servant next door, but she was very critical of the woman's employers who seemed to pay no attention to what the servant did. The servant never wore an apron, which showed up the cheapness of their taste. They had no sense of *style*. Therese would often notice the servant's two children creep up the track which led behind the house to the servants' quarters. There the children would eat the remains of the supper their mother had served that evening. Therese resented this, and often spoke to the Piggotts about it.

Her son would never have dared to come near Piggott's house. She would take food back for him in the evening; and at night she told him what had happened at her work. It was through this habitual instruction that her son got his idea about the way some people lived. It seemed a more dignified way of training him to become someone like Piggott.

Therese tidied the cushions for the last time and walked towards the table. She tried her fingers round the edge, and stooped to smell the wood. She reflected on the envelope which bore Charlot's name. She had held it up to the sun, trying to read its contents before putting it on Piggott's desk. Therese didn't like the feel of that letter. Ever since noon, she had got the feeling that something awkward was going to happen. The atmosphere of the house had grown more and more creepy as the sun crawled towards evening. She had felt it when the wasp flew into her kitchen.

Therese was terrified of wasps. Her sister had died of tetanus thirteen days after a wasp stung her on the left nipple of her tumoured breast. Therese had seen the wasp enter from the porch that morning. It soared through the living-room and alighted for a while on the potted marigolds on the window-sill. Her instinct for omens had been aroused and she was reluctant to attack the wasp. While it stayed in the living-room she could postpone the meaning its flight had brought to the house. But the wasp soon rose, making somersaults and tottered through the door towards the kitchen.

Therese forgot her habit of reading signs. It seemed better to die like her sister than surrender the territory which was entirely her own creation. She held the flit can like a rifle and guarded her fortress. She thought she saw the wasp change colour, but it didn't fall. It buzzed its way into the kitchen. Therese closed the door, shut the windows tight, and pumped the flit heavily against its back. The wasp could not have survived, but it didn't fall. When she scrubbed a wet rag over the ledges the wasp wasn't there. She never saw it again. This omen was more serious than a failure to trace the direction of its flight.

But the second reversal of the day was even more disturbing. Therese had no affection whatsoever for the cat. In fact, her loathing had grown like a patriot's hatred towards a foreign army in his country, or the ripening instinct for murder in a husband who watched his wife conspire against his manhood. But there was one aspect of the animal's behaviour which Therese admired. In spite of its sex, and contrary to all prejudice, she would often think of the cat as a lady. Perhaps, Therese would say, it was the same way with certain criminals; that art of perfecting an angel's face in order to deceive. But she would admit, in all fairness to the cat, that its manners were perfect. Fola and the cat existed in her mind as examples of what Therese called *style*.

But shortly after lunch, Therese had made the most astonishing discovery of her career with the Piggotts. The cat had relieved itself all over the dining table. Therese hadn't quite got over the shock it gave her. She tried to make the most unlikely excuses. Under the bed, Therese thought, or in one of Piggott's hats, or even in a corner of her kitchen. She might have understood this lapse of *style*. But the cat's choice of the dining table surpassed all reason. With shock and horror in every word she uttered, Therese had kept saying to herself: 'But why, why he had to put his load up there?'

Her immediate reaction was a feeling of shame. But Therese

couldn't tell whether she was ashamed for the cat or the family. She pondered her question until this sense of shame emerged as a reflection of something about herself. And this must have been true; for Therese couldn't summon the courage to tell anyone what the cat had done. She cleaned up the mess, and kept the whole episode a secret.

As she stood by the window, pondering these warnings, Therese noticed a shadow reflected on the gravelled path which started at the gate. The shadow lost its outline as the body came into view. This was the most evil of all omens. It could destroy anything the old witch touched with the spirits that polluted her soul. For Aunt Jane was walking up the path towards the house.

Therese shook her fists and hissed insults at the old woman. She unloosed the bands of her white apron and let it drop at her feet. She tumbled the apron on the chair and ran out of the house. She spat in her hands and rubbed them together because it helped to steady her nerves. The old woman continued walking up the track. She raised her head up from the paper bag, and a clod of boiled rice dribbled down her chin.

'You ol' midnight hag,' Therese said, 'how come you so bold face walkin' in decent people place like this? You off your head or what?'

The old woman didn't answer. A lump of rice had slipped un-chewed down her throat. It gave her the feeling that the passage was blocked and it would have been dangerous to talk. She pumped a flood of saliva in her mouth and swallowed hard.

Therese could feel her breath like a fever shrivelling up her nose.

'What you come here for? Bringin' tribulation with your evil eye?'

The old woman felt better.

'If you playin' wild,' Aunt Jane said, 'better know I born wild.'

Therese took a step back as though she feared contamination from the old woman's touch.

'What it is you want?'

'Mistress in?'

'My mistress out,' Therese said sharply. She had a moment of relief.

Aunt Jane searched her gums with one finger.

'She not in?'

'I say she gone out,' Therese insisted.

'One day you go bust like a full up balloon with pride,' the old woman said.

She had seen a head, then a hand growing long dark shadows up the glass. It was enough to make her feel that the servant had lied. She stuffed the paper bag in her bosom, and wiped her hands on the grass.

'Move out my way,' she said, passing Therese on her left side. 'Pity lies doan poison, or yuh mouth would be a grave yard long time.'

'I say she not in,' Therese argued.

Therese didn't care to defend herself against the old woman's charge; but she worried how Piggott would punish her if the old woman went into the house. He would certainly hold her responsible for what had happened. But Therese couldn't block the way because she was afraid of the old woman's touch. She had to change her tactics.

She saw the old woman approach the steps; then stop, staring at the tiled surface of the porch. It looked like broken glass carefully levelled with a spade and painted for some evil purpose. The old woman considered her naked feet, and wondered what madness had driven Piggott to do such a thing. She heard the servant run up behind.

'You got to use boots to cross this thing?' Aunt Jane asked.

Therese was in a panic. She couldn't imagine what would happen if the old woman had decided to enter the door to the living-room. She was afraid Piggott would hear her voice and come out.

'Not this door,' Therese said, showing the old woman round the house.

'Door is door,' the old woman said, 'if it open for you it open for me. It open for whoever walk in.'

Aunt Jane had turned her back to the house. She saw the servant making signs with her hand, persuading her to walk round the other side of the house.

'Tell yuh mistress is Aunt Jane,' the old woman said.

'She not in,' Therese said.

'You lie,' the old woman shouted. 'One time, two time, all time you lie like it come natural.'

'I say she not in,' Therese whispered, trying to pacify her.

'An' who head I see back that glass?' the old woman asked.

Therese didn't answer. She stood, speechless with self-rebuke. Piggott had heard the voices and come out. Therese ran forward, trying to explain; but Piggott waved her away. She collected the apron from the chair and ran into the kitchen.

'May God an' all gods bless you,' Aunt Jane had begun. She was preparing for a speech; but Piggott cut her short.

'Enough,' he said, pointing over the grass to the track where she had walked on her way to the house. 'I goin' lose the whole lot o' you in gaol. You an' your run-away gran'son an' ever loafin' hooligan, man, woman an' child in that Forest Reserve. An' all that ceremony you makin' out there at night. It aint got time these modern days for your kind o' monkey business. Now you go tell those Forest Boys collect their drums beatin' all that noise at night. Is time to learn a new tune. Now go, get goin' . . .'

Piggott walked down the steps shoving her gently on to the grass.

'I not beggin','' she tried to say, 'I not begging . . .'

'You get goin', Aunt Jane,' Piggott said, releasing her arm, 'an' tell that gran'boy not to make trouble in the Forest Reserve. Or we' go put him an' his ungodly paintings where they belong. Go on, you get goin'.'

'Chiki don't mean no harm,' she said. 'He jus' a little crazy. . . .'

Piggott wouldn't let her finish: 'Get goin', get goin' before I call the police,' he said.

'Wasn't you I come to see,' Aunt Jane said, trying to resist his hand. 'Was the mistress.'

'Me an' the mistress same thing,' Piggott said.

'Was personal,' she said, 'was personal to the mistress for her daughter. Was 'bout her daughter. . . .'

Piggott had interrupted her again, but his manner changed. Any mention of Fola was enough to arouse his interest. He let go of the old woman, walking a little ahead of her towards the gate.

'What 'bout my daughter?' Piggott asked.

'The mistress daughter,' the old woman started.

'What 'bout her?' Piggott became impatient.

'Was only to warn if you know she does walk stray at night,' the old woman said. 'Three, four nights I follow she with my own eye lookin' for what she aint put down, roamin' stray an' talkin' with all sort o' strange wild people she know nothin' 'bout. Was only to warn if you know, 'cause children got a habit o' goin' wild like how my Chiki give up all the good education he get! Same college like Miss Fola, yet Chiki turn back into a pig. Was to let you know.'

Piggott had turned away. He didn't want the old woman to see his misgiving. At first he wanted to kick her out of the yard. He was shaken by the suggestion that Fola had taken to the streets at night for the worst of reasons. Then his fury abated and he turned, trying to look as though he hadn't heard a word of what she had said. He was showing her to the gate with the same impatience as when he ordered her off the steps.

'Now go,' he kept saying, 'you get goin'.'

Beyond the gate Aunt Jane turned to see where he had gone; then spat on the paper bag, and threw it into the gutter.

Therese was nervous. She was spying from the kitchen, and it seemed an eternity since she had seen Aunt Jane turn past the gate into the street. Piggott was walking slowly back to the house. Therese counted on her fingers: 'One, two, three, the devil after me,' and listened for Piggott's approach. If she could finish the rhyme before he entered the house; then her luck was with her. 'One, two, three'; and the devil's voice suddenly reminded Therese that it was the nearest she had ever come to betraying Piggott. But she had done it out of loyalty to Fola.

'The devil only know what that old witch, Aunt Jane, got in her mind,' she whispered to herself, 'but time an' again I tell Miss Fola not to meddle with the foreign man.' Her whisper continued like a rival claim through her count: 'one, two, three, one, two, three . . . Is a spy what I say he always was. It have plenty like him what come in the Forest Reserve collectin' people business, countin' your toes to explain why you walk how you walk. All that sort o' low down peepin' I see them foreign people do. Ah! I keep warnin' Miss Fola to watch she step with that soft-voice crab what crawl in she life all 'cause he could teach.'

Therese kept peeping across the hedge, but Piggott wasn't there, and her mouth made its count like a till: 'one, two, three.' And the devil, it seemed, had won. Therese went cold when she heard Piggott's voice charging through her rhyme.

'But Fola!'

'Hello, Piggy,' Fola said, and erased her smile with the napkin that fell over her skirt.

Piggott looked startled. He glanced towards the kitchen in search of Therese. Something warned him she had known; but her secret had little importance since Fola was there. He was glad Agnes had gone. He smiled and drew his chair up to the table.

'But where you been all this time, Fola?'

'Inside,' Fola said, nodding her head sideways to indicate her room. 'I was taking down my pictures.'

Piggott glanced up at her from the plate.

'Which pictures, doo-doo?' This was an affectionate pet name he called Fola whenever he thought she was in need of help.

'The family pictures,' she said, and scraped the fork near the rim of her plate.

'Lady Carol and Veronica too?'

'Yes, them too.'

'And the Morant bay group also?'

'All! All! All!' Fola said, and regretted the sharpness in her voice.

But Piggott was determined to survive any shock. He thought of the letters, and said to himself: 'I love her better than if she was my natural daughter.' He thought, in particular, about Fola's letter which Charlot had returned with his reply.

'Well, it's always good to make a change,' Piggott said aloud, coaxing her to eat. 'Is what I always say myself, give things a new face. So why not the room? Is yours, no?'

Therese had come in on the silence which followed his question.

She glanced over Piggott's head at Fola who nibbled indifferently at a red claw of garlic shrimp. The devil had warned Therese that she had to make it up with Piggott.

'You see the letter I put on your desk, sir?' Therese asked, in a voice grown servile and pitiful.

Fola didn't raise her head to acknowledge Therese's loyalty; and she hadn't seen the nervous flicker in Piggott's eyes as he glanced quickly at her and down to his food. Head bowed, Piggott was waving his knife at Therese, ordering her to leave the room. He watched Fola selecting bits and pieces from her plate, the way cats do. She hardly spoke during the meal; but her presence was enough to satisfy Piggott. He considered the wisdom in Therese's talk about the impossible realising itself in an individual wish.

As he glanced up at Fola and down at his plate and round the domestic peace of these walls, Piggott could feel, in all its old power of embrace, his original wish for paternity. Sometimes it was more than a wish towards Fola, when the teachers reported on her progress at college, or during their holidays with Lady Carol in the lake resort behind the Maraval hills. On these occasions he would feel that momentary pause of revelation and promise come into his thinking; and his wish would enlarge to a claim natural as any father's. He would begin, in that moment, to make arrangements for her future. He would see Fola then as the perfect substitute for all his ambitions. He wanted Fola *to be something*. He had been driven in his time by ambitions which now seemed simple. They were always within reach, like the rewards in Therese's example of waiting. But Piggott didn't seek this for Fola. He wanted Fola *to be something*, something outside his own experience of the possible.

In the anxious solitude of his wish, Piggott was thinking: '*to be something*, not rich, or just famous; but to be different from me or Agnes, different from what my own mind can imagine now. Different from how Agnes now sees me as the man she made.' He tried to imagine a time when people would say: 'there goes Fola, not Piggott's Fola; but Fola, distinct, separate and pure, like the sky.'

But his caution had increased with the change he noticed in Fola.

He had thought, with a father's assumptions of knowledge, that it had to do with growing up. Now he had his misgivings. Fola had become at once more restless and more aloof. Her questions had acquired a certain tone of calculation; and her silences, which were becoming more and more frequent, contained some agonising and unspoken urgency for those who were around. In spite of his experience of people at all ages, it had come to Piggott as a shock that Fola had acquired the troubled look and liberty of a woman in private conflict with herself. He realised, as Agnes did not, that he couldn't reach her with the simple assurance that all would be well. Fola had begun to see him and her mother with a stranger's reservation, as though her knowledge of them was not enough. It was her attitude to what she knew and did not know that made for this change which confounded them.

Piggott decided that in future he would allow her the greatest privacy of feeling. But it made him uneasy; for his claim to be a father might easily be diminished by the restraint which he now felt in her presence. Her silence had come as a great change; yet Piggott was sure that it couldn't last. Ordinarily, he was the person she would turn to for approval or in the hope that he would silence her mother by a more experienced plan or argument.

'God knows why you an' your mother can't get along,' Piggott ventured as he watched her rise from the chair. 'An' it getting worse. Before you'd just complain and criticise, but now it's like two armies in a war.'

Fola was mixing the medicine of rhubarb and salt which he took after each meal. She stood beside him, waiting until he had finished the loud snapping of his lips after each sip. When she offered to take the glass, Piggott returned it to the table himself, and gently closed her hand in his. Fola managed a smile as he guided her out to the porch.

He drew up a chair, treating her like a guest, and asked what she would have to drink. Fola wasn't thirsty. Piggott shook his head, a little sadly, as though he wanted to suggest that she had been unjust. He poured himself some brandy and sat on the deck chair opposite her. His look was still contrived. It said that he didn't mind. He understood how she was feeling. Together there was nothing they couldn't iron out. He had seen her in this kind of mood before. Except for the silence.

When Fola was angry, she always talked, like her mother who regarded silence as a moment of surrender. It was the silence which troubled Piggott. But he knew Fola's weakness. He knew he could always please her with little tokens of surprise. He'd make her gifts of little things which a man was not supposed to remember. Like the time she lost an ear-ring and decided, out of laziness, that another pair was just as good. Piggott searched the jewellers' for days, and surprised her with a new pair that was identical. Fola would feel a double pleasure on these occasions: that he didn't wait until she had asked. More important still, he had been attentive to her taste in clothes. Piggott took care to notice what she liked.

'In few days' time you'll be eighteen,' he said.

He was going to add that she was no longer a child, because that is how he was thinking as he watched her in the chair, her head turned meditatively towards the ground, and her body showing the same proportions of hip and bosom as her mother's. He paused, closing one eye to inspect the bottom of the glass. It gave him time to recover from the folly of the observation he was going to make. It would have been tactless and stupid, he thought. He narrowed his open eye, hoping to discover some foreign particle in his drink.

'Your mother is a good woman,' he said, raising the glass level with his eyes. 'Always been. Excellent woman. One o' the best, whatever you might think.'

Fola raised her head. She was paying attention, and he knew it. He thought he ought to crown his meaning with emphasis by saying, 'yes, listen, I'm telling you'; but her silence was not familiar. It made them almost equal in experience; became a threat to his self-esteem.

'Sure you won't have a drink?' he asked.

Fola shook her head, and rose to pour him another brandy. He held his head back, draining the glass with deliberate greed. This would have been the moment to surprise her with a gift; but the occasion seemed to warn him that her silence would have demanded more. She had sat down again.

'Think we should make this birthday a kind o' coming out

party,' he said. 'Sort of let people know you're on your own, as your mother would say.'

He was thinking of the letters, and timing the moment for his question.

He had spoken very slowly like a man trying to be absolutely sure about something that had happened a long time ago. Then he drew himself up on the deck chair as though he had suddenly recovered the detail which had slipped his memory.

'Of course, that's for you to decide,' he said. 'No question of that. You must say if that's what you want.'

Fola wanted to say that she would not agree to a party of this kind. There wasn't going to be any party at all. She wanted to be left alone. If her mother were sitting in Piggott's place she would have said exactly how she felt. But she understood Piggott's longing, and nothing had changed her affection for him. She was too attached to Piggott to see him hurt; and she knew how hurt he would have been if she had spoken out.

'Let's talk it over another time,' she said. 'Tomorrow.'

Fola knew she was lying, and she glanced up to see whether Piggott had suspected anything. Unlike the times she had deceived her mother, it always made her feel depraved, almost unclean, if she had to answer Piggott with a lie.

The cat slipped like a shadow from behind the door, arched its back under the chair, and purred against her leg. She let the tail curl in and out of her hand; but she really wished the animal would go away. Piggott stared at the animal with a child's astonishment. Its body was the colour of charcoal and curved like wire. Sleek and practised as a fish, the tail dipped and surfaced over Fola's hand. The eyes were green toys of fire set in its black velvet head. The cat was an item of achievement in Piggott's conception of the home: the way Fola seemed to offer her hand, for example. He saw the cat's playful manœuvre round the chair as an act of almost human gratitude for their presence on the porch. It was worth the risk of another glass of brandy.

Fola watched him as he poured the drink, wondering what he was like at her own age. If she could only see Piggott against the background of a school or his home, arguing with his parents, or joined in conflict with his friends. But his origins could not even be called obscure. They had simply never come up for question in her mind. She had always seen Piggott as he was this moment: her mother's husband, always so eager to please, ambitious for her own future.

She thought of the child, Liza, dancing round the bamboo pole, and tried to see him at a ceremony of Dead Souls, waving the *Houngan's* axe, or entering the tent alone to hold mysterious concourse with the dead. Would he have been embarrassed about her interest in his past? She had lived with Piggott as she had done with her own past. Until these last few days she had never known the tendency to make *that backward glance*. The cat continued to exercise its tail; but she had taken her hand away. Piggott was gazing thoughtfully across the hedge to the nearest house.

'Like how a tree always keep growing up out of the earth,' he said, 'you have to look ahead. Always keep looking ahead.'

The extra glass of brandy had made him more expansive than usual. He spoke as though he wanted Fola to share what was most urgent and secret in his heart. He cuddled the cat in his hands and thumbed its ears.

'Old Colonel Carlysle,' he said, 'In the ol' colonial days! Wish he was alive, jus' to know what happen. Wouldn't guess where the boy who come in every mornin' would climb. But it was he who open my eyes. Always look ahead he used to say.'

He paused, reflecting on the childhood vision which had determined his life. He didn't continue because he wasn't sure Fola could appreciate the differences in their fortunes at a similar age. He felt he ought to suppress the details of the comparison he was making. Fola had taken her privilege for granted. She went to college at the age of ten as though it were a perfectly natural thing to do. He was a servant's child, drunk with admiration for those photographs of Colonel Carlysle's ancestry.

They were all military men; and many a morning little Piggott would sit on the colonel's bed, half-listening for the approach of someone who might discover him dreaming himself into the splendour of those uniforms. When the colonel's family went abroad, the boy Piggott would take the liberty of opening cupboards and trunks. He would dress himself up like a real soldier, studying the photographs to make sure that everything was in order. He always had difficulty with the sword which was half his height; but that was not his fault. From the outskirts of the kitchen his mother had learnt what was absolute and right, absorbed a style of living which became his alphabet. The colonel's way of life haunted his nights, summoned the future in his sleep, travelled through all his days until he met Agnes, who finally married him to his wish.

'Times may change,' he said, 'but the old colonel's words still hold a truth.'

The cat had climbed on to his lap. He was stroking its head as he spoke; and the gesture seemed to give authority to his words. He thought that his reminiscence had acquired a certain tone of gravity through these gestures from his hands. The cat had become his ally as he approached the crucial moment of this evening. It would be the moment he ventured to disclose Fola's present of a watch and the substance of Charlot's letter.

Piggott stroked the animal's back as he rummaged through the fragments of his education for a truth that would resolve Fola's silence and his own distrust. 'There's a tide in the affairs of men, which taken at the flood . . .' And as Piggott's voice lingered on the melancholy rhythm of these words, he thought of his fingers as a silent chorus to their meaning. Some strange revelation had startled his eyes as he pondered that movement of his hands over the animal's back. He wondered how he would have occupied his hands if the animal were not there. For a moment, Piggott was confounded by the thought that the cat had given meaning to his hands. Where would he have put his hands in order to obscure this nervousness which Fola's silence had aroused in him?

He was astonished by this fear which Charlot's letter now increased; the fear that his words might have lost their wisdom without the assistance of his hands. He wanted to glance at Fola, but he couldn't tell what his eyes would have betrayed. The cat was still; and it was this pause in movement which seemed to rob his hands of meaning until he saw them move again. But the feel was different. Tossed like a boat on water, his hand had become a slave to the cat's indulgence. What he had accepted as action on his part was really his obedience to the animal's demand. The cat was not an innocent responding to Piggott's wish. It was his hand which the cat had turned into a toy.

This was the fear which now confused him as he thought of Fola and the letters. He kept his glance on the cat's back, postponing the moment he would think it safe to speak with Fola about the letters. But the cat had gone. It leapt over the chair and disappeared behind his back. And Piggott saw his hand deprived of action, pointless and servile on his knee, waiting for words.

He was unprepared. He started to search the corners of his pocket with that hand as though it had been empty. But the box declared its size between his fingers. Edges and surface identified themselves. The lid grew hard as granite where the hinge sprang a hair's breadth coil of wire against his hand, arguing to be lifted from its cage, ashamed of his reluctance to declare what it contained. The watch ticked like a pulse beside the letters. He could hear his heart threaten to resign its rhythm in the little box.

In a feeble voice he was calling out for Therese. The clock was striking six. It was time for Therese to leave, but she was still there. Piggott needed her to answer; but Therese did not hear. This atmosphere of secrecy had increased her fears that something terrible must have happened to Fola. In such moments, Therese could easily forget that her own son was waiting. She had closed the kitchen door to give some private sanctuary to her feeling.

'It don't feel safe,' she cried as she polished the last shining blade of cutlery. 'I know Miss Fola write something what upset that foreign man bad, bad, bad. But what he answer back, I don't know.'

From the door to the kitchen sink and back, Therese watched the blade of the knife like a mirror in her hands, and tried to recall the details of her visit to Charlot's apartment. Her instinct for danger was like prophesy. The devil had told her that day to open Fola's letter; but her loyalty prevailed. The devil had returned this afternoon when she read Charlot's name on Piggott's mail; but one deception had already put a strain on her luck.

'Miss Fola no go see him off,' she whispered in a voice like evidence that was tragic and true, 'but she visit his place the evening

before. Was that same evening some say they see her prowlin'
'bout Forest Reserve. An' now this noonday letter come from him.
But why he aint write it to Miss Fola? He scared o' hidin' from
Piggott. He know Piggott go fin' him wherever he hide.'

Therese felt a stiffness weigh heavy with swelling in her throat.
Her sense of danger had grown like a personal damnation she
couldn't escape. She let the knife fall from hands, and obeyed the
gradual stoop of her knees dragging her slowly down to the floor.
And Therese prayed. Heaven and all the kingdoms where hope and
promise abide could not deny her prayer.

'God God,' she cried, 'or even one o' you devils what authorise
evil behind my back, don't let that foreign bastard breed Miss
Fola. Not in my time I beg 'cause I love Miss Fola like she was my
boy chil'. Once, twice, all time I beg don't punish Miss Fola with no
make-haste baby. Don't, don't ever ever let that happen.'

Gently, weakly, Therese rose, her knees like fists of wind under
her hands as she opened the door. It would have been wrong to
spy on their secret, but she needed to hear someone call.

Piggott was squeezing his hands over the box, saying to his fear
that he had never known such agony of doubt with Fola's mother.
Was this some law of difference he couldn't understand? Was
it a difference of generation, a difference of education? Whatever
it was, he wanted only to maintain his place in Fola's world. He
could have managed if her silence were an invitation for his help.
But there was such certainty in her mood. He called out to Therese
again; but there was no answer, and Piggott used her silence as an
excuse for his momentary absence. He rose without a sound from
the chair and made two strides across the porch into the living-
room. He stood behind the wall, afraid to be seen, feeling a treachery
of ears somewhere behind his reading. But Therese was not there.
And he read the letters again, choosing Fola's to be the first this
time.

'Dear Charlot,

I feel free and unashamed to wish you good-bye. No harm has
been done. I shall find my own way, but in your eyes the *tonelle*
and I must always be alike; for what you need is a lady in the

parlour and a bitch in bed. May the two meet some time in the woman you marry.

Good luck, Fola.'

The cat surprised Piggott, and a fright shook Charlot's letter from his hands. He stooped very quickly to retrieve it, feeling the weight of the paper like a judgment which Fola's talk of bitch and bed had made certain for him. He could barely recognise his name at the top of Charlot's letter. It had opened his mind to some lack of connection between the person he was and the things he could accept. But Fola's reference to a marriage hurried him through the letter in search of some promise from Charlot.

'Dear Mr Piggott,

My best wishes to you and the family. Most grateful for everything that has happened here. Would like to assure you my relations with Fola have always been honourable. Returning her letter in case it might be of use to you. But as she herself says, no harm has ever been done. She was my best student, and I think she will go very far. Feel great pride sometimes to think that any achievement of hers in this direction may be part of my own work here. But she may need you most at this time. Do not conceal anything from her.

I too have been changed by San Cristobal. Wishing you all well.

Charlot Pressoir.'

The cat was still there. It followed Piggott back to the porch and watched him stoop feebly into the chair. He avoided any glance towards Fola; but he noticed the cat staring at him, and he felt undermined. He didn't know what to do with his hands now he had returned the letters to his pocket. He didn't know where to put them. And the cat wouldn't move. Piggott couldn't concentrate on any meaning the letters might hold for him. But he wished Fola would say something. She wasn't aware of the letters, but if she spoke now, he might probably find his way again. Then he could begin to chart some strategy that would help to break his own silence. He was losing his hold on the evening, and finally his strength gave way completely.

'As I say,' Piggott stammered, unsure where he ought to begin. 'If it's in my means,' the voice stumbled on, 'anything you want you can have.'

There was a note of authority now, as though his voice had taken strength from its promise. But he had forgotten his own methods of dealing with Fola. And it was too late to withdraw. She was beyond bribery. Piggott couldn't say what had come over her. But it had started before he spoke. He could feel the tension which closed her fists. The tension seemed to burst every nerve in Fola's body, like the night she knelt in the *tonelle*, petrified with shame by the shock the ceremony had produced on her.

Now she saw Piggott as she had seen herself: in hiding. It seemed the whole world was determined to keep her in hiding, and to hide things from her. She experienced an utter loss of control, a furious release of feelings: doubts, angers, a sense of expectation for ever denying her grasp. Fola felt this blinding urge to drag herself from under the huge accumulation of things that pressed her down, covering her with silence like a grave. Piggott could stand it no longer.

'Whatever it is you still have me,' he cried, 'you have me, Fola.'

The cat had fled in terror. Fola had leapt up from the chair. She stood before Piggott in a rage of lunatic hands and swinging hair. The air seemed to tremble at her touch. Her fingers were splayed over the early haze of the evening: ten points of flesh, ten forces, ten lives possessed with frenzy.

'Don't pamper me like a child, Piggy, don't do it I tell you,' she raved. 'If I still look like a child, I don't feel like a child, don't do it, Piggy, I tell you I am no child. Don't do it.'

Piggott tried to balance his body on the rim of the chair. He could feel his hands clutch the chair and slip away, clutch and slip, clutch and slip. This was the same rage and torture he had first experienced in her nearly twelve years ago. But she was a child then.

'Listen, Fola, listen.'

His voice seemed too weak to fill the pause which had come between them. He balanced his hands and strengthened his hold on the chair.

'Is what I tell myself without your knowing,' Piggott said, 'I feel you here in front me as a woman. I don't say like a woman, Fola, I say *as*. And is as the woman I take you for that I want to talk with you. I don't have advice or quarrel or anything like that in my head. Know that I see you an' listen to you that way.'

Fola was clawing the air as she waited for him to stop. The same note of petulance and defeat rang in her voice.

'Don't try to make me feel good,' she rebuked him again. 'It aint good I want to feel. I had enough of that. Is only knowing I want to feel, Piggy, is only knowing I want to feel. I aint ready for anything now but knowing, just knowing.'

'But is what you have to know?' Piggott asked, his voice soft and insecure as wool.

Fola's calm was like an insane interval of waiting. She closed her hands, opened them out and wrapped her chin for a while. She was staring at Piggott as the cat had done. Her voice was quieter; but its tone of cold and remorseless challenge was still there.

'Is all right for you,' Fola said. 'But you can't feel the way I feel. You see Aggie as your wife. You marry and start fresh whatever happen before. Is easy for you to believe in Aggie, but all that happen before concerns me, Piggy, is me it concerns.

'Not true, Fola,' he said, sitting more erect on the chair. He felt too weak to deny what she had said. 'Anything 'bout the past that would come back to trouble Aggie is trouble for me too.'

Fola's hands kept up their nervous twisting while he spoke.

'Listen, Piggy,' she said, calling a halt with her finger, 'whatever your feeling you can't see it my way. I don't have to wait till anything come back. It with me all the time. Now it seem asleep, then it wake up. But it with me. Listen, man, listen!'

She walked past his chair. She came to a halt. She ambled slowly back where she had stood.

'It ever occur to you?' Fola said, looking at Piggott as he had often looked at criminals ignorant of the evidence against them. 'Is twelve thirteen whatever it is years you marry Aggie. I see you and know you like a father. Don't make no mistake 'bout that. I know you like a father equal to any the rest have.'

Piggott seemed to take some relief from her admission.

'You give me equal and better than any girl my age and class gets,' Fola went on, 'and Aggie, for all her quarrelsome ways, Aggie is the same. But you never hear me call her like children call a mother. It never occur to you that you never hear me call her Ma, or Mummy, or Mother, or the different names children call a mother. First it was Agnes, her real name, than it change to Ag, Aggu, an' now is Aggie. But never Ma or Mummy or that sort a calling.'

Piggott had lowered his head into his hands.

'And is the same with you, Piggy,' she said, noticing the startled look in his eyes, 'You been always Piggy. Not true? You never ever hear me call you daddy. Never. And I ask why? I want to know why? I ask why like I ask for water.'

'But Fola, doo-doo, Fola.'

'Hold on, Piggy, hold on!' There was a jabbing sound in her voice. 'Aggie ever tell you what I call my real father?'

'But Fola,' Piggot cried, terror in his eyes as he tried to look at her, 'we've gone over all that before.'

'All right, you say he's dead,' she shouted, and Piggott felt the treachery of other ears behind him. 'But even the dead used to be. Who was he, Piggy, tell me, Piggy, who was my father?'

Like the shock of her body leaping from the chair, Fola's tears seemed to strike a fatal wound in Piggott. His eyes continued their idiot stare at the empty space where she had stood. His hand trembled in his pocket, crushing the ends of paper and the brittle spring of the box unhinged between his fingers. She had denied him as she strode across the floor. Piggott could still hear her denial striding backwards from her room. 'You're not my father, not you.'

Alone, he sat and watched the early night grow thick with clouds over the garden. His eyes were wet. In the solitude of his last wish, Piggott was surrounded by the sad and familiar regret his life had always known. He was not her father, he was no one's father. His wish had grown dormant. Piggott could feel his last claim, like the weight of some personal inadequacy, painfully dissolve within him.

CHAPTER VI

The taps are still, barren and more still than the glass which reflects Piggott's image. He rests his huge hand on the spliced crown of metal that will unlock the water; but it is tight, hardens under his fingers; it mocks his need like workers who refuse to stir in spite of the obvious waste which shows in their idle hands. Somewhere beyond this house there is a reservoir of water; sea and river are ever generous in their gifts. The rains will soon steal from a season of drought, and swell to an incredible volume of flood, common and boisterous as men who have no breeding but act to prove their abundance.

So nature continues her whims, swarming the needy with their offspring; yet makes no stir within Piggott's loins, denies his wish to bear; shows him each day in Fola's eyes, her hair, her hands and voice; shows him time and again such lustre of fruit which no ambition can provide. Piggott watches his face in the mirror, withdraws his hands from the taps, and lifts the dentures out of his mouth. He studies this face as though it were a stranger's: the thick gross panel of lips that now retreat over the slippery emptiness of his gums, the heavy jaws of skin that billow like curtains into his mouth. It is no less his face than the hand which once looked like a toy rubbing against the artifice of the cat's back fur.

It is his face and it is there, impossible to remove without some fatal robbery to himself. Yet he wishes it were not; this huge, familiar cave that crumples in like melted liquorice over a child's firm hands. It is his face all-right; yet it remains a traitor to the stature of his name. But it is the face he needs tonight; old and original as his need for the fruit that will be a substitute for Fola's absence. He can't reach Fola any more; yet she is kind, has begged his pardon once again; obeys his slightest wish.

Tonight Piggott has stayed behind, denying himself the pleasure of the Vice-President's ball; and contrary to anyone's expectation Fola has agreed to escort her mother. Out of obedience to his wish, Fola has startled the family with her service; partners her mother in that arrival which is most delicate and most noticeable on such a night. And why? Because it is Piggott's wish, yet he experiences triumph where it does not matter. He has brought daughter back to her mother in a possible harmony of kinship. And Agnes is glad. Her secret has not been uttered, but Fola has relented in the urgency of her questions.

Piggott recalls her smile on their departure from the house, the smile of the prodigal child returning to its fold, grateful and contrite in every gesture. But nothing is changed since her voice bled his deepest wound with a denial no daughter confronts a natural father with. A natural father: natural; that is the word which now examines the perfect lines of his new face, for the dentures are returned, sitting like rulers on a throne falsely inherited. This new face can fit the stature of his name at any hour of public crisis; but now it is not right; it is not the other face, the face which comes most natural to his intention. 'There'll never be need to hide my off-spring . . .' he thinks, 'my wish is clean, clean as the law which can unleash this water if my fingers turn that tap.'

But his intention now contradicts his wish; for it is dark, old and dark like that other face which orders him to find an answer to his barrenness. To be a natural father! What evil in his childhood now takes revenge on his cleanest wish; starves with deliberate cruelty his most urgent hunger! It's not for lack of trying, like his foreign predecessor. Through some miracle of restraint, some angel chastity in their breeding, that foreign couple could explain the impossible virtue which always helped them to contain. And yet alive and happy as though they can still hear St Paul in all his celibate wisdom warning those early Christians to contain, contain unless some wicked and illicit need has invited them to burn.

In Piggott's eyes his predecessor seems to be the very opposite of his own greed; for the foreign couple did it, that fertilising and decisive it, the foreign couple did it three times a year: once at Christmas and again on their birthdays. A reason nothing ever happens to their wish. 'But I've worked, God knows how I've worked,' he cries. Calm as a schooner under its sail, or sweating like the stevedores beneath the great weight of logs they pull over the land, Piggott has worked, God knows how he has worked. And Agnes too!

And now he remembers both his faces, the one with the toothless grin, and the face that has learnt to smile lightning across his gums. For a moment these two faces meet, for a moment and a night, a moment that is always night; and in particular those nights when he and Agnes have had some row: the nights which are waiting for apology: when he and Agnes to the chorus of an unspoken regret are working for a brothered fruit, some sistering yield that may soon partner Fola. No secrecy is here, Piggott says to himself, as he leaves the bathroom. And his wish pursues him across the garden, follows him like a child into the Baby Austin car, cries behind him with the public clock which is now striking twelve.

He thinks of those nights as though it is possible to find some compromise between his two faces; as though he may be able to equalise the separate worlds of rumour and experiment where these two faces negotiate. Obeying the whisper of Raymond's unmedical advice, he thinks how many things Agnes and he have tried to make the only and most ultimate *it* work out; to make that unsaid, little word 'sorry,' now buried like a seed under their sheets, spring forth and blossom with a harvest that may soon walk at Fola's side.

On Wednesdays the position of their bodies stays normal since that is the day they married. Each Thursday for a month *it* has to happen upside down. Fridays are darkened by some more devious and abnormal posture; and the weekends which always last until Tuesday are a more expensive interval: seven minutes before and thirteen afterwards they douse the engines with champagne. Champagne at two pound ten a bottle; and one bottle for each admission that the engines are about to stall. Then there are the lunch-time emergencies when Therese looks stupified because she cannot understand her right to this half day. But it has to be; for husbands with obvious success in the field recall the moments they thought the targets had been taken. Lunch-time is one such moment provided the genitals have risen by chance with the midday chiming of the public clock. Piggott will desert any criminal danger facing the republic in order to plant his wish. And Agnes understands. She sees him arrive, and she obeys the urgent call from garden or gossip.

'Is it true that my two faces meet in that compromise?' he asks as he approaches the ribald quarters of the town. Piggott looks up at the stars which have often misled him with their predictions in the daily press; and knows that his two faces disagree. Never in this world or the next will they smile in harmony. Has the old face won? A surprising quiet resides over the Forest Reserve as though evil has decided to go underground. Piggott brings the car to a halt, and looks around. But nothing stirs. The street lamps have closed down; but even now it is not safe to disclose either face. In the time it takes to sneeze, his new, bright face can alert the entire Forest Reserve; set vigilance in every whisper behind closed windows and barred doors. For the law doesn't trespass on the Reserve with friendship.

And the old face? His old and original face now stays under cover. He dare not let its secret out to anyone but Aunt Jane. For Aunt Jane is the author of this night's intention. She is the hand behind that old face which stares at Piggott; orders him now to find an unmedical answer to his barrenness. Either through fear or from the intimacy of their touch, her tongue will hold their secret. Aunt Jane: author of an intention born in his childhood! Once it was fear, now it is fruit: but her magic has remained for his old face. She is the unmedical knowledge which Piggott now seeks. What champagne cannot touch, her secret potions may unlock.

'And it is Fola,' he cries, 'it is Fola who drives me back. Good God, how is it that a girl still child to my own years can drive me back, drive me back into such black infancy? Piggy! Piggy! Piggy! You are going back. You can't go back. Not now, not now, Piggy, you can't go back.'

Piggott turns away. He hears a young man's voice repeat that no one is in the Reserve. Only the children, perhaps! But Aunt Jane and the rest have gone to hear the Boys play at the Vice-President's ball. They have gone because rumour has warned them that the Boys will not be hired for the Independence Ball; that tonight may be their last, big public night. Piggy, Piggy, what would have happened if Aunt was there? What would have happened? he cries, inside and secret as a worm. What? What? But the headlights show no answer; and he continues, driving and driving and driving he knows not where. . . .

It was the time of night when all the novelties of arrival had come to an end. Each face like a victim of its own appearance was finally recognised. New names became a part of average knowledge. The Vice-President had done his official chores. His soft, dark voice knew how to trim its phrases to each listening need; gave welcome a special aura of praise.

The music hadn't changed its mood. Fola could hear it outside the casino, soft and cunning in its effect on those who had come out to watch the sky. Bulbs were wired along the branches of every tree; so that the lights seemed to gaze with a human discreetness from behind the leaves. She had refused her partner's cigarette; but watched with a momentary feeling of triumph how the match trembled in his hand. He tossed the matchstick over his head, and continued, perfect and casual as the night, with his talk of horses and land.

As Fola listened, she was trying to remember his face. Camillon was his name. But it seemed his face had lost all claims for recognition; eyes and mouth, the rawness of bone had all evaporated into an atmosphere of courtesies. That was all she could recall as she tried to see him in the dark. But his graciousness was natural, Fola thought, he was natural. Horses and land fitted into his anecdotes like an alphabet. She thought of Charlot; and Camillon seemed to emerge again as example of her own lack of understanding.

In spite of the horses and the land, Camillon was an excellent dancer to the rhythm of the drums, light and comfortable in his step. Fola's recent habit of introspection had made her cautious, but when her caution gave way to something which she admired, her enthusiasm was complete. She could feel again that ease with which Camillon had helped her find his rhythm. He had adjusted superbly to her own errors; and, like Piggy, he had a perfect way of ignoring her misgivings.

Yet there was one flaw to his grace. Without her experience of Charlot and the *tonelle*, Fola might not have noticed this; but it was there, for Camillon was wearing it. It was in his clothes. His shirt had a clinical whiteness of surface, ironed to a stiffness that seemed almost austere in contrast to his gestures which were gentle as his speech. The lapels of his coat lay like black daggers across his breast. Camillon wore this evening suit like armour; but it could not imprison his graciousness, or the leisurely emphasis that underlined what he was saying.

'It's two things I really admire about those Boys,' he said, turning his head to catch the echo of the drums, 'one is their relation to that music. The way any man is related to his work is at the bottom of everything. The other is that they own the land they live on. The music and the earth are both theirs.'

And Fola thought: 'How I wish Charlot were here! That Charlot should hear this!' She wanted to ask Camillon whether he had ever told the Boys that himself; but it seemed, for the moment, an unnecessary deviation from what he was saying.

'Behind these hills there,' Camillon continued, as his hands emerged through a blue shadow thrown from the trees, 'I'd like to buy a couple hundred acres.'

Fola suddenly hiccoughed and was ashamed.

'Hundred acres!' her voice exclaimed, as though her words had broken faith with what she really had to say.

'It's not much, you know,' Camillon said.

Fola started to redress her notions of space. She thought of her mother's garden, then saw the total acreage of the republic swallow it up. Of course, it wasn't a fantasy to speak of owning a couple hundred acres of land behind the hills.

'If I were going into business I'd think in different figures altogether,' Camillon said.

And it occurred to Fola, who had become excessively critical of her own judgment, that Camillon's figure had surprised her because he was native to San Cristobal. She got the feeling that Charlot would not have startled her in this way if he had quoted a similar figure. Fola was nervous that Camillon might have been thinking the same thing.

'But what would you do with a hundred acres outside of business reasons?' Fola asked.

'Can you ride?' Camillon asked.

His question was like answer and solution to her wonder. And the second thought occurred to Fola; for her mind worked these days like a magnet attracting particles of a similar element. She

133

thought if Camillon's ambition to own that land was his special badge of success, it was still very different from Lady Carol's or the Vice-President's. They would have thought of growing money out of the land, while Camillon was thinking of a pleasure that was no less strenuous and delightful than dancing to the drums. So Fola was abruptly returned to suckle at the udder of Charlot's tutelage.

She started to think of two entirely different groups of people who shared the same range of income; who had a similar power of spending. Lady Carol and Chief Justice Squires would belong to a commercial and professional group which Camillon's talk seemed to despise. For Camillon, who avoided all talk of money, seemed to identify his dignity with the land which he might own. Fola had detected a hint of disdain when he referred to dentists as the human tooth drawers. Camillon had emerged as a wholly new element in the social relations of San Cristobal. His effect on Fola was astonishing. She wanted to ask something about money, and found she had to censor her question.

'Do you know the folk tune the Boys are playing?' Camillon asked.

Fola had heard it, but the music existed without name in her memory. Camillon struck another match, and listened to the sound of the river churned up from below, sailing across a field of lights which shone from sockets in the crevice of the rock.

There was a heavy scent of pimento in the air. Fola could feel it like a moisture oozing slowly out of her pores. It left a taste which puzzled the tongue: was it wild thyme? or spring water in the morning? or the pure, tepid juice of crushed sugar cane? It reminded them that the mountains were near; and then she heard Camillon's voice, a pure, rich baritone humming folk songs. He stopped, then started again with words. Camillon must have been nervous at first for Fola could tell by the fluency which gradually shaped music and words, that the song was familiar. Yet he had kept up that nervous, tentative humming, like a child who withheld his answer until he could judge a reaction that made him sure he was right. Camillon got better as he went on; and Fola became more secure in the discovery that he was shy: the shyness of a man whose

134

breeding made everything he did subdued, almost apologetic in its restraint.

'But you can sing,' she said, and suddenly thought her comment was out of place. 'I mean you have an excellent voice.'

Camillon gave a little chuckle and said, 'That's very nice of you. Thanks.'

'I mean it,' Fola said, 'you really have a beautiful voice.'

She heard Camillon's chuckle again, less nervous, more prolonged. It surprised and delighted Fola the way he responded to her praise. She thought it silly to make such obvious remarks about his singing; yet he could accept such praise as though it carried real authority; cleansed his doubt with further proof of his own distinction. Fola was touched by the humility which could take from any expression of pleasure such fresh encouragement.

'Practice,' said Camillon, 'not enough practice. Trouble is you just can't reach that standard without practice, practice, practice.'

'I'm sure you can't ever have too much practice,' Fola said, 'but admit you're good.'

When Camillon said thanks again, he made it sound impossible for anyone, however crude, to forget this courtesy. 'But there is good and good,' he added. 'It's a question of standards.'

Fola wanted to agree, but there was an emphasis in Camillon's words which made her effort seem insane. Her thought was limited, exposed, even disgraced by the austerity of what Camillon had said. She felt that she could never get beyond the primitive comparisons of good and better, and still better. When Camillon uttered that word, *standards*, Fola thought he had suddenly grown angry with himself. The word did something to his tongue. It had acquired the curative magic of a drug. With a feverish impulse to redeem herself, Fola was searching for some parallel; and suddenly felt blackmailed by the spontaneous emergence of: penicillin. *Standards* were like penicillin, she thought, humiliated by the crudeness of these associations in her mind.

Camillon tried to distract attention from himself. He was talking about singers, dead and alive, of equal renown. The names often seemed obscure; but Fola couldn't be sure that it wasn't her difficulty in recognising the syllables of a foreign name.

135

'Where did you study?' Fola asked.

'Right here in San Cristobal,' Camillon said, 'I started here and finished in America.'

'Won't you give a concert here sometime?'

'No doctor could afford the time,' Camillon said.

'Doctor?' Fola said.

'Yes, Dr Camillon is my name.'

Her stupefaction was complete. The private world which she had been trying to discover was now undermined at every point. It made all questions look so difficult. She started to feel that she would soon make a fool of herself. But her experience of Charlot and the *tonelle* had done one service which was permanent. On such occasions when Fola's ignorance was obvious to everyone, she would say: 'Well, I don't know, so what?' But she was not ashamed. She had accepted that there were things she didn't know, but she believed that there was little she could not understand if it had been thoroughly explained. And she thought of a phrase which had grown during her reflection on her past: *in the light and unashamed.* She believed that any risk was worth a possible emergence into the light.

'Are things really bad for people like the Boys?' she asked. 'I mean at the hospital?'

'There are rumours,' Camillon said, 'but it may be a problem of staff. I wouldn't like to say.'

'You practice there sometimes, don't you?' Fola asked, admiring Camillon's loyalty to his colleagues.

'Oh, yes, I do,' he said, 'but the general wards are not my concern. Surgery is my special drama.'

Fola thought she understood everything except the way he had described his work as drama.

'I don't mean to be rude,' she said, 'but is it that death is more likely under the knife?'

Camillon gave a little chuckle as he blew a wall of smoke over his head. And as he turned to speak, he kept saying to himself: 'the girl has promise, the girl has promise, the girl is acute. She is the kind of girl I can talk with!' And quickly he censored his thinking when he was about to say, 'not like Eva.'

'I'm not too bad with the knife,' he said, 'but what I meant by drama is a little different. Have you ever seen an operation in progress?'

'No, but I'd like to,' Fola said.

'Can be arranged,' said Camillon, 'but it's like theatre, that's what I meant, in particular, classical drama. The central problem is there for everyone to see. To be alive or not to be, that is the question. I am the chief protagonist. Nurses and assistant surgeons my supporting cast. And as in the best tragedy, when it's all at an end, your specimen taken back to its bed, the question still remains: I wonder what happened next?'

'My God!' Fola exclaimed, and laughed aloud in admiration of his skill.

'But sometimes the nurses make a mess of what you've done,' Camillon added, and heard his voice dying slowly with apology for what he had said.

A sound of water rode gently up the cliff and finished like a shadow contracting slowly out of sight. Like the music and the bulbs shadowed by colour and the leaves, it seemed part of some conspiracy of needs which the darkness had arranged on similar nights. Fola could feel it in the pause which now caught Camillon's hand, erect and nervous as it waited, as though an apology had to be made for the risk it was about to make in her direction. Yet she behaved as though this silence were a natural interval between two strangers' talk.

She heard the river and the demented chorus of noises crawling from under the grass. The night was a kind of luxury entering her ears without any effort of attention. It was impossible to be distracted by the echo of the music or the grey tunnels of cigarette smoke which travelled above their heads. Fola didn't notice Camillon's hand clawing feebly over her skirt. The contact was so feeble that it became no part of her feeling for the night. The hand was simply there like the skirt itself, innocent in its impact on her body. Camillon was making an impossible screen of smoke with his cigarette. But Fola had closed her eyes, guided by her indulgence of the night and the change which had come into Camillon's talk.

'Why did I ask you to come out?' he asked.

137

'Is that a question?'

'Yes, partly a question.'

'But if I had refused,' said Fola, 'would you have known my answer?'

'Now, is that a question?'

'It is my answer,' Fola said.

'That's what I never understand about girls,' Camillon said. 'You see men like an occupation army you have to overthrow. A woman catches a man's glance. The moment itself is an accident, yet before a word is spoken, she says she knows his secret. She's on her guard.'

'And then the war begins,' Fola added, her eyes still closed.

'How different if we could just meet?' said Camillon, 'but you all keep thinking what the man is after, until he's forced to play some game. Then he has to lie his way along with compliments. Tell me, does the girl ever really believe him?'

'Sometimes the compliment says what she knows already,' Fola said.

'And then?'

'He can become a bore.'

Camillon jerked his elbow on the bench.

'I think we feel the same way,' he said, 'I mean when a woman refuses even the chance to know who you are.'

'Who are you?' Fola asked.

'Is that a question?'

'Yes, partly a question.'

'I am my father's son,' said Camillon.

Suddenly Fola's eyes were open, startled by the pitch blackness of the night. She raised her head and watched the clouds of smoke disperse over his head.

Swift as her thinking, she had said: 'I'm glad you asked me to come out.' Now she reflected with some misgiving that she really couldn't tell Camillon why she was glad.

Towards the end of that dance, Fola had felt his thumb like a swollen gland pressing softly against her naked armpit. And in the same moment, waiting to rebuke his hand without attracting notice, she had heard him ask her to walk outside. It was like a promise of refuge from the tension which Fola had borne all evening as she sat beside her mother who kept pretending by her frivolous alternation of gossip and praise that nothing was really wrong. Yet it was true that nothing is wrong, Fola thought. There was nothing improper about the way Agnes enjoyed herself. She was always gay on such occasions, but Fola had resented the exuberance which was a natural part of everything her mother did. In Lady Carol or anyone else, Fola would have seen it as a quality to be admired. But it seemed that Agnes was always too near her own way of feeling. Fola could relax with Piggott or Raymond, Lady Carol or Mrs Raymond; risk jokes beyond her age, and hear them do the same while she was present. Yet her mother would always appear very cheap, delinquent and cheap if she risked the conduct that was a natural freedom for Lady Carol and her friends.

Sometimes Veronica would suggest that Fola was jealous of her mother. Fola had heard this said so often that she tried to consider it without prejudice, and was convinced that they were wrong. There was no reason to be jealous. Indeed, she had often helped to contribute to the appearance which they had remarked in her mother. Tonight Agnes was wearing one of Fola's dresses: a bristling, blue nylon with little black tassels that shook like twigs against her knees. She looked beautiful. Fola knew that this would be so; and she was glad. But it was this sense of her mother's nearness to her own way of feeling which embarrassed Fola. She didn't like this feeling which her mother gave of being so near in years and physical attractiveness. Camillon had made her evening, not only with his singing, but through the distance he had put between herself and Agnes. But she couldn't tell him that.

'You'll forgive me if I say something wrong,' Camillon was saying, 'but it's your clothes I noticed first. I mentioned it to Sid, my colleague who came with me, and he agreed. Then we sat back for a moment, and decided whom we should ask to dance.'

'And you chose me,' Fola said with a note of sternness in her voice.

'It isn't so easy as all that,' Camillon said, trying not to cheapen his choice, 'it never is between two friends like me and Sid. But the two of you looked so alike, the way you'd turn like sisters to whisper

139

something. Then I noticed that you never smiled. You never did, even when your friend seemed to want you to. And that meant something I might admire.'

Camillon was now thinking of two *standards:* the elegant and the demure. And Eva had neither.

'So you chose me?' Fola asked again.

'You make it sound so easy,' Camillon tried to explain, 'it's never so easy. Give me time and I could tell you why I preferred you not to smile. But don't make it sound so easy.'

'And what does your friend prefer?'

Camillon chuckled shyly, like a child conscious of carrying tales out of school. He had withdrawn his hand as though to prove his point of difference between Sid and himself.

'I think Sid likes people not to seem too difficult,' he said, 'if you know what I mean. I don't mean cheap or anything like that. But gay, a decent sort of gaiety, so to speak, circumspect, as it were, like how your friend was laughing when she whispered to you sometimes.'

'He preferred my friend,' Fola said dryly, and Camillon was alerted by the note of scepticism in her voice.

'Why do you say it that way?' he asked, 'she isn't your sister by any chance?'

'She is not,' Fola said bluntly, and her voice reminded Camillon of the exact austerity he had noticed earlier in her face.

'You aren't angry?' Camillon asked, crouching nearer to her arm.

'Is that a question?' Fola asked, and the voice had softened.

'Yes, partly a question,' Camillon said, trying to breathe some sound into his smile.

Then Fola laughed, suddenly and with intention: a noise that was inscrutable yet obvious and intimate to her feeling. Perhaps the night had helped this episode on to its completion. If there were light, Camillon might have seen a different meaning into her laugh. But Camillon had suddenly felt a crushing weakness of nerve, as though his advances had been relegated to the level of a joke. He had known this experience before. And Fola was still laughing. It angered him. It came like insult against his feeling. And gradually he felt that it was necessary to obscure his failure, reduce its importance in her eyes, by sharing some secret weakness about himself. He had to sharpen the point of difference between Sid and himself in order to regain his self-esteem. The music had stopped, and the silence suddenly brought Fola to her senses.

Then Camillon asked Fola, partly solicitous and partly in doubt: 'Is it that some people have certain gifts which deny them others? Because surgery comes natural as song to my hands, and Sid is ignorant of both. Yet he succeeded in fixing up a date with your friend tonight.'

And neither could explain the mute seconds which had followed Camillon's voice; followed it like an eternity of night and days and utter darkness!

Camillon didn't see her move; but Fola was standing in front of him, tripping her tongue through an erratic babble of sound. He could hear her breathing like a pump letting the night air up from the earth. Fola had thrust her hand out as though she was about to strike him in his face. He was scared stiff, not by the damage which the blow might inflict, but by the indignity of their situation. He had no capacity for dealing with this sort of emergency. He was sure the other woman was Fola's sister; his gossip was a slander which Fola could not forgive in her sister's absence.

Camillon wanted to apologise; but he would have been shamed by his feebleness to make any sound with his words. He felt a shudder at the base of his chin; but he daren't lift his hand. It was a sign that his dignity was about to collapse. His fingers were plucking at his coat involuntarily, without his control, like the last spasms of a dying fish on land. He couldn't return to the ballroom until he had found a way of making his peace with Fola without conceding any loss of face. He saw her hand fall weakly down her side as she turned to go. He rose from the bench and took a step towards her. Fola didn't move, and Camillon could feel assurance coming back to his defence.

'I am ever so sorry,' he said. 'I didn't mean to distress you. And I am sure my friend never meant it that way. He just told me. Out of courtesy, you might say.'

Fola waited, listening. His voice carried that sincerity of regret that makes the most trivial accusation seem too crude.

'What difference does it make?' said Fola.

Camillon couldn't understand what she was doing. Fola had trampled over the black beds of camellias, running like a lunatic towards the car park. Camillon thought Fola had gone mad. He tried to catch up with her, then slowly reduced his stride as he came into the light.

Couples were standing on the casino porch; but Fola had turned the opposite way. She was making for the street. A cab emerged from under the trees, blocking Camillon's view. Then he saw her hand like a black shadow swimming through the flush of headlights. The car cruised to a halt. Camillon heard the engine cough. He stood gazing until there was nothing left to see but the scarlet twin heads of light, huge as the moon, offering their dubious welcome to the Forest Reserve crowd in the street: High Life in San Cristobal.

He felt relieved and a little foolish to see her go. Fola's departure had saved his dignity. It was an incredible stroke of luck; yet it made him feel like a fool. First he had tried for her co-operation with a lie about her mother's date; then the fear of exposure forced him to transfer this lie to his nearest ally. And to what purpose? He lingered on the grass, waiting for the music to start. More couples were walking out to the porch. Camillon could feel that nervous plucking of his fingers again. Seen from the porch, he might have appeared to be in hiding. It was happening again: this secret summons to prepare the stages of his defence. Dignity was a kind of switch that started warnings against the world's inquisitive glance. Other men might ignore suspicion; but Camillon could not afford anonymous scrutiny. To be held in doubt was to be half-way in error. It soiled the *standard* he had set himself. He was waiting for the music to start; and his fingers repeated that warning spasm. Perhaps the whole casino was also waiting to hear why Fola had gone. But Camillon knew what would happen. He had already made his choice. Quietly, firmly, to himself. His mind was closed to any reason but his fear. He had decided it was too late to think. No one dare deny him the right to be tired now. He wasn't going back inside. He wouldn't return to the casino tonight.

From the centre of the ballroom ceiling, the republic was swinging its reward for beauty. An enormous crown, wide and spacious as a tomb, was jewelled with stars of cellophane. Veronica watched it like a bone escaping from the black and solitary kinship of her appetite. Mrs Raymond had not come; but Lady Carol was there to see that the Vice-President did not stumble through the intricacies of protocol. She was gazing at a row of tables at the back; then her eyes turned with disapproval towards the band; and finally retraced its journey to the tables where Raymond had been paying his compliments to a young regiment of office clerks from the federal building.

It was difficult to distinguish the targets of her contemptuous glance. She thought it right that Raymond should acknowledge the presence of his office staff; but there should be limits to the generosity of his time on an occasion like tonight. Perhaps it was the Boys who angered her; for the interval was unusually long; long, she thought, and deliberate, like a strike.

Agnes had asked to be excused and had remained for what Lady Carol considered overtime in the ladies' toilet. Fola had gone out and not returned. Lady Carol was old enough to know that something was wrong. It seemed the kind of atmosphere where trouble works like a radio. Each detail spread an aura of disorder. Then she saw Raymond hurrying towards the gents' washroom. His face looked pained, and his eyes sharpened with a flash of spite which was familiar. Lady Carol guided her stare back to the tables where the clerks looked suddenly crestfallen. Instinctively she glanced at the dais where two members of the band were talking without the slightest sign of restraint. Lady Carol couldn't say what had happened, but she was sure that things were getting out of hand. And the climax grew stage by stage after Veronica came over to say that Fola had gone home. Lady Carol knew there must be some connection between Fola's going and her mother's long imprisonment in the ladies' toilet. But the band troubled her more; for the Boys now looked angry and fierce as they spoke.

'Who say tune up?' Crim stammered, 'I'd like to tune his arse.'

'Don't get me wrong,' said Gort, 'is only 'cause I see them waiting.'

Crim wanted to spit, but suddenly remembered where he was.

'We go rest them,' he said, 'come daylight an' me an' you aint no more than a worm when we watch them pass.'

'But what hit you so hard, Crim?' Gort asked as he noticed a fragment of broken glass stuck to the back of Crim's hand.

'I live for the day I see those bastards burn,' said Crim. 'Talk 'bout people who think God A'Mighty groom them special. Look them there.'

'What hit you Crim?' Gort asked again, and looked across the floor, hoping that Powell would soon return.

Raymond was returning from the washroom, but he didn't go near Lady Carol's table. He had gone to speak with Agnes who had just ordered a maid to bring her shawl.

'That cross-leg-sun-ov-a-bitch what standin' there,' said Crim, glancing towards the table where Raymond was waiting. 'It seem he want to give those clerk girls, you know the Bartok one from Bruton lane, that lot he want to give a drink, an' it seem he order Little Boy Charlie to bring one bottle o' champagne.'

Crim paused as though he needed to drill every detail into Gort's head.

'You know Little Boy Charlie with the Sunday-school face,' Crim said, crushing his shirt between his hands, 'first time he makin' a work at this sort o' place.'

'What happen?' Gort asked, getting more nervous. He feared the look in Crim's eye and the flake of glass at the back of his hand.

'Great Gort, you know how those champagne bottles screw up,' Crim said, 'you know how they screw up with wire like a submarine net. It hard to open them things. So Little Boy Charlie fightin' there when sudden so the cork say, pop, and cuff him in his eye. Just as I tell you Great Gort, just as I tell you.'

'What happen, Crim? What happen?'

Crim looked as though he would soon cry.

'The champagne rush up, Gort,' he said. Now there were real tears forming Crim's eyes. 'Rush too quick for Little Boy Charlie to shift his position, an' some spatter on the A'Mighty jacket, an' be Jesus Christ, Gort, you'd have think Raymond walk through a flood, the way he behave. I tell you, Gort, not so much champagne as to discommode a louse in Liza's head, an' that sun-ov-a-bitch,

144

look him good, that benighted crab, he won't touch it, Gort. Raymond refuse to touch it, an' those little typist face sluts laughing, just laughing. So Little Boy Charlie in his confusion call the manager.'

'Could Jesus, Crim, what happen to him?'

Gort rubbed his hands over the drum as though it were a sore that itched.

'Is just what happen,' said Crim, 'Little Boy Charlie so 'fraid he lose his first work in this sort o' place, he playin' honest an' straight, an' that Syrian swine of a manager boss, he 'fraid o' Raymond an' that lot, that lump o' Syrian shit out of the devil's arse-hole. Gort, he tell Little Boy Charlie there an' then, was good thing he come, or he would have pack him flyin' next mornin', but that he got to pay for the bottle he open. There an' then, Gort, he order Little Boy Charlie send his partner with a brand-new bottle, and tell the foreman cashier to take out two pound ten from Little Boy Charlie wage.'

'Jesus Christ an' all the Saints,' Gort cried, pounding his thumb against the drum.

'That leprosy lookin' sinner, Gort, that animal, that Syrian vermin what God ought to order eat grass!' Crim halted and dragged his hand like a saw across his face.

'You know what that mean, Crim?'

'If I know what it mean,' Crim shouted, 'Little Boy Charlie gettin' three pound, seven and sixpence a week, Gort, maybe a tip here an' there bring it to four an' a little over. More than half a Little Boy Charlie wage done spend, Great Gort, done spend before he see a cent o' what he workin' for. An' two children, Gort, I don't have to tell you Gort, Little Boy Charlie got two children tall as Liza with the mother goin' pregnant again. I don't have to tell you, Gort.'

Gort knuckled his fist over the drum. It was so rare Gort used foul language, that Crim seemed for a moment taken aback.

'Time to tune up?' Gort whispered as though in judgment on himself, 'the way I feel, Crim, this whole kiss-me-arse dance can stop right now. 'Cause if we say we aint strikin' a next note for the night, it make no difference who wait, this dance done.'

Crim glanced towards the table where Agnes was wrapping the shawl around her neck. Raymond was helping her up from the chair while Lady Carol concentrated on the band.

'Look them good,' said Crim, 'half start from scratch like you an' me. Some thief an' get away, some sell what they never ever own, but one way or a next luck favour them, an' they behave like they don't fart an' shit no more. Their memory just out-out like a fire, Gort. It aint funny, it aint funny how a man can behave like he aint got no memory at all, Gort, it aint funny.'

'He offerin' to take the Piggott woman home,' said Gort as though all comment from him was now impossible.

'Take that one, take she coming out now,' said Crim, 'all these years she been trainin' that daughter to make up for whatever it is she do. She train that daughter like she was a horse studyin' for the Grand National. Only to make up for whatever happen, 'cause nobody know to this day who that girl father is, where or when the mother get that fatal poke what start she an' the daughter in a race no horse can match them in. A race to only Jesus Christ in Heaven knows where, Gort. Let them go, but the day comin', as I stan' here with water like Liza self in my eye, the day comin', it comin'.'

Gort pulled the sack from under his seat and started to put his drum into its bed. Crim turned his back to the dance hall as though he wanted Lady Carol to know that he was sending her a message with his wind. They sat side by side while the other men watched, and waited for Powell. Gort held the drum between his legs and looked towards the tables at the back. He saw Powell stop on his way. Powell couldn't have known what had happened; for he had paused and bowed to Lady Carol, the way he would do to policemen whom he had deceived.

As Powell walked towards the dais, he glanced his smile back to Lady Carol. Crim had nothing more to say; and he was greatly relieved to let Gort tell Powell what had happened. Also, he was afraid. Powell felt more bitterly about these things than anyone in the entire reserve. But he looked ignorant and free as he climbed the dais and raised his drum.

'Is time to tune up,' Powell said.

He hardly noticed their silence for the secret jubilation he was feeling. He was going to give them the details after this dance.

'In a little way,' said Powell, lassoing the drum round his neck. 'In a little way I get my own back. Little Boy Charlie come up to me, ask me advise him 'cause Raymond tell him bring any sort o' drink, any sort for those clerk sluts; an' I advise him, I advise Little Boy Charlie proper. I just tell him, surprise the bastard with champagne, 'cause I know, I know it wasn't no champagne he mean for the office sluts.'

Now Powell noticed his audience.

Neither Gort nor Crim could speak. Each word of Powell's seemed to lengthen like a rope, lengthen and tighten around those three throats. Powell was staring like Ashton from PetionVille. Just staring like Ashton the morning he went stark mad.

'I'll take you home,' says Raymond, 'one of the constables will see to Fola's car.'

His voice is barely audible. He speaks as though each word has suffered a slow and hateful lynching between his teeth. His face is rigid; his eyes look hard and vigilant. He notices the policeman who keeps sentry beside his car. The corporal abruptly smartens his poise as the couple walk from the porch; then feels a stiffness like steel in each arm. But Raymond doesn't acknowledge his salute. He wraps a blue scarf round his hands; and Agnes hears his teeth make a noise like gravel crushed to a powder in his mouth.

'The bastards,' he says; but Agnes makes no enquiry when he continues: 'Slip broken glass inside my pocket!'

Raymond draws the scarf tighter round his wrist. He has checked the flow of blood; but the scarf is wet. He grumbles at his pain as the engine starts.

'I'll get them soon enough,' he whispers, and feels the jolt of the car, as the street opens under its headlights.

He tries to recall the details of every action from the moment the imbecile spilt the champagne over his jacket. He has forgotten the waiter's face; yet he is sure of his target. The pain has stopped; but each beat of his pulse stirs a brief stinging where the scarf rubs against the drying crust of blood.

Agnes is silent. She sits beside Raymond, barely conscious of his anger, anticipates the curves of each street, her memory ticking like a clock that tells the distance to her house. She pulls at the shawl around her neck, and grinds her teeth. Her lips close and open like a purse as she threads the innocent tassels round and round her fingers. They have become a substitute for Fola's throat. She will strangle Fola, her own daughter, first met in pain, for a while remembered with embarrassment. Fola has filled her anger with a murderous need. For there's no excuse, no trace of reason that can forgive what Fola has done tonight. To leave the casino at that hour, without explanation or apology! And with a stranger?

Her hands shake beyond control as she tries to name the crime which reduces her to this indignity. To be left like a servant waiting for news! To chose an occasion so delicate and so noticeable! But that's what Fola has done. It's her own daughter who choses so gracious an occasion to humiliate her mother. Agnes struggles to contain her anger; for there are things which Raymond should not know; even Raymond. She can't explain the meaning of this night without its long and buried history of private grief.

Raymond can feel her tension, the weight and pain of her silence. It makes his own injured hand look like a trifle, a momentary indulgence in anger. He tries to attract her attention to the night; for Raymond also shares in her judgment of what Fola has done. But Agnes will not be touched by any gesture of his sympathy. Raymond exercises his hand, lifting it up from the steering wheel to bend his fingers. He feels the scarf come slack around his wrist. He moves it freely round his hand and wonders what he should do. Perhaps there's a way to soothe her temper. He thinks of Veronica. But he is at a loss for words. For Agnes is not a woman one can bribe with praise of beauty or achievement. She doesn't need it.

Raymond leans on the accelerator and feels the car climb smoothly up the hill. There is no throb of effort in its climb. Cool as water, and with as little sound, this miracle of transport bears them forward. For a moment he wants to take delight in his possession, like a man who looks upon a job which his own hands have made. But nothing will persuade Agnes to share in his triumph. She lifts the shawl up from her back. She hugs it closer to her neck; then startles Raymond with her request.

'Put me down at the gate.'

'But why Agnes?' Raymond tries to complain, but Agnes is indifferent.

'You leave me there. I want to catch my breath before I get into that house.'

'I won't leave you at the gate, Agnes. Not me.'

Agnes relents; but she does not answer.

'I got my trouble with Veronica too,' he says, as the car hums over the track of gravel.

'Veronica is one thing an' Fola is a next.'

'Fola's all right,' he promises.

'All right, Fola all right!' Her words can hardly reach the threat which they contain. 'I'll murder her tonight, Raymond, I'll murder her.'

The car door slams to, and Raymond jumps out, trying to take her hand as she mounts the steps and plunges into the living-room. Nothing can distract her from her purpose now. Her hurt is deep. For a while Raymond stands on the porch, watches her prowl in silence up and down the living-room, and wonders what will happen; then decides that he must leave the rest in Piggott's careful hands.

The car rolls in reverse out of the yard, cautious and quiet as the hands which guide it safely into the street. The headlights make a haze like morning over the trees. He watches the fine drizzle fly slantways through the leaves, and predicts the future of the night. Raymond knows that it will pour with rain: any minute now, like a temper that is beyond control. Soon the clouds will burst and clap with rain over each acre of the republic's soil. He leans his pressure down, and the engine boils with a sound like bees. The road gives way like carpet under his tyres. Alone, he can reflect on the luxury he has achieved; the rest is safely left in Piggott's hands.

The wind rubs his fingers, and Raymond feels a sudden naked-ness around his wound. His wrist is bare. The scarf has slipped some-where from his hands; but it is too late to think of search. For the drizzle has thickened to a shower. His weather sense has proved him right. It seems nothing will ever make a difference to the luxury of this mood as he leans the pressure down, and hears the car ride him at a great and gentle speed into the night.

That final crash of rain had ruled the neighbours out. No one could hear beyond the wide, repetitive hoof of water striding each roof. But Fola had forgotten to care about such things. A passionate resentment had released her from this bond of secrecy with her mother. They confronted each other in a similar state of rage, playing out their wild and spiteful opposition of interest which neither dared to express; which neither could, in fact, explain.

Instead they concentrated on the waste of nylon on the floor. Fola had torn it off her mother's body. She was fighting hard against her wish to cry. She would have liked the rain to free them from this solitude of threats and dead recriminations. She would have liked the neighbours to intervene and give approval, without words for either side, to the urge which persuaded her to hate *this woman!*

'I don't know who the hell send me with you,' Agnes raved. And the distinction between mother and *this woman* became more fixed in Fola's mind. Now she saw her chance to say something that would settle this feeling once and for all. But she daren't speak when she looked at her mother; for *this woman's* tongue was roasting with words.

'You've been more trouble than profit since the day you born.'

And Fola stood rigid, feeling the change from mother to *this woman* give way to a more appropriate description of her rage. 'The bitch,' she thought. And again Fola saw her chance to make her words a final assault on her relation to *this woman*. But her mother never missed the end of any silence. Agnes got up from the chair and walked towards the door, as though she had to test the power of her legs. But she never left the room. She returned to the chair which, in some irrational presence of mind, she had changed for another. She did not sit.

'That I should live to see the day my own child refuse me . . .'

'But I tell you not to touch my things,' Fola shouted, 'don't touch my things.'

'Ungrateful wretch!'

'Don't touch!'

150

'Who helped you get your things?'

'I say don't touch my things. Don't touch my things.'

'Not a year you been workin',' Agnes cried, 'and you come talking about your things.'

'I tell you not to touch my things. Don't touch my things.'

'And all the years before? Eighteen whole years before! How it is your memory can forget how you get your things.'

'I only beg you not to touch my things,' the voice insisted, 'don't ever touch my things.'

Agnes felt some unfamiliar emotion opened by her daughter's words. They were always the same words, uttered with a burning restraint; and left, like dynamite, to do their work. She seemed conscious of the difference between herself and Fola. When Fola spoke, it was as though sound and meaning exploded in her mouth. But Agnes knew her quarrel was only a return to difficulties which were no longer alive. Her desires did not trespass beyond this moment. She wanted, simply, to convert everything she touched into a memory which success had buried alive. She had suffered greatly when Fola was born. Now she saw the girl, other than daughter, stand outside her, in a cruel resistance to her love, a wicked mockery of her own mistakes.

Each time Fola said: 'don't ever touch my things,' some nerve had collapsed within Agnes. Not from the words which, at some other time, might have been a harmless threat. It was Fola's tone: the dry, ripe, bone-clean certainty of her will towards a chosen enemy. Agnes had felt an impulse to force some violence upon this occasion. But Fola's words returned, charged with an authority of intention she could not deny; and Agnes agreed, against her will, that it would have been dangerous to strike Fola.

But this disinclination to strike became a part of her undoing. If she had struck Fola, the girl's retaliation, whatever form it took, might have been the ultimate proof that all her authority was lost; yet her failure to strike came as a warning that she could no longer be sure what future Fola would make her endure. She thought, without conviction, in a general way about children; but Fola was not a child, she reminded herself, and the speculation turned on men. Not this man or that: just men whom her knowledge had discovered as agents of an inevitable doom which it was her duty to postpone for Fola's sake.

In her silence, active and false, Agnes was trying to work herself up into a frenzy of doing, trying to bully things with her hands. She removed a ring from her middle finger, swivelled it like a toy about her small finger before choking the space of it with the knuckle of her thumb. She paced the room, enlarging every detail of disorder, cursing the origin of everything which had shepherded her into this slough of feeling.

'Tell me what I ever do,' Agnes cried out, 'what I do that hell should curse me with . . .'

She had grown cold under that brutal chorus of her daughter's demand:

'Don't touch my things. Don't ever touch my things.'

That voice was not in favour or request; but a noise like doom giving its final warning of an end.

Heaven and hell were begging Agnes to speak, to answer in the name of mother to her child; for Fola's voice was there again like a hammer on her skull: 'Don't touch my things, don't ever touch my things.'

'Tell me what I do,' Agnes cried out again, 'tell me what I ever do that hell should curse me with a slut like you. Tell me, tell me.'

And Fola's eyes grew stars of light as though her latest name was angel.

'Search your own memory for what you know,' Fola screamed. 'Be what you have to be, an' hide whatever you know. But don't *you* touch my things, don't ever *touch* my things.'

Fola saw her mother shiver and wilt, yet watched her as *this woman*. And Fola was grateful for the night and Camillon's discovery. She didn't believe a word of what Camillon had said about her mother and his friend; but the truth held no importance for her now. It made no difference to the fearful certainty which Camillon had established in her mind. This was the way they had *seen* her mother. She existed for them in a certain way; and this way of seeing was now the only truth that mattered.

What difference did it make because Camillon had thought that Agnes was her sister? It was the way *this woman*, who happened

152

to be her mother, had been (seen.) That was the only truth Fola
shared with Camillon and his friend. Fola now saw her mother
through their eyes. She had placed a similar meaning on her
mother's presence; and every recollection of her mother persuaded
Fola to this certainty: her mother was a *whore, a whore, nothing but
a whore.* That's what she wanted to say. She was the child of a
whore. Every item of her mother's presence was enough to show
her that Camillon's guess was right. The clothes Agnes wore, the
way she laughed, the mischievous frivolity of her gossip, the
intimacy of her embrace when she was dancing with Camillon's
friend, the sexuality in every movement of her body offering its
promises to Camillon's friend.

Her mother's gestures were deliberate, provocative like the
sample which such women displayed in public for the stranger's
gaze. Fola got a feeling of terrible separation from the things she
had been taught. She was losing her hold on what she knew: like
the night she felt her reason slip and sink into the improbable
realities of the *tonelle*. Her mother's presence seemed to drag her
back to that experience of the *Houngan's* voice in dialogue with the
dead souls in the tent; drag her back into the accusation of the old
woman's glance.

Condemned to *this woman* by the fact of birth, she felt entirely
severed from her mother by the meaning of her past. Fola could
see no point of contact between the nature of a whore, and the
accident which had entitled *this woman* to call herself a mother.
Fola kicked the nylon dress out of her way, and tottered towards
the porch. Silent and furious, she stood there in the light; and as
her eyes caught the smeared outline of the scarf, one word now
changed the shade of her thinking. Like the wet, blood-barred
scarf now hanging from her hands, Fola saw *this woman* as *that*.
She thought of Agnes simply as *that woman*.

Agnes was crying. She couldn't name the feeling which had
reduced her to this state of absolute impotence. She felt empty and
pointless as the air. She tried to move, but this body was no longer
hers. It had swindled her of feeling, boycotted all her strength.
Her body was a dead heap of rags that covered nothing. It had left
her nothing but water. That was all Agnes could feel inside her:

water making great ripples of sweat down the hollow crags of her arms, water thawing like ice through the hot sockets of her eyes. There was no one near enough. Piggott had not come back; but this water rose like an ocean around her, sweeping Piggott out of her thinking. It left Agnes without aid. There was nothing left, nothing but a noise like icicles dripping, drip, drip, drip inside her head.

But Fola looked crazy as she stood on the porch. Each finger had knocked like a fist on the switches which made light across the garden. She stood on the porch in a great flood of lights: a similar flood of light which had once showed two candles crawling like mice over Raymond's sleeve. But these lights were different; for they were celebrating a moment of dangerous madness in Fola's mind.

Fola tightened the knots she had made in the scarf. She tugged at the ends. The silk was torn open by her nails It seemed she had to conquer things with her hands. Her rage had given her an impossible strength; freed her from any loyalty. She wanted to be a traitor in the name of some original truth. Fola wanted to outstrip the wind in an obstinate pursuit of something she had to know. She wanted to stand with a weight that would make the stones crumble under her feet. She could resist any danger with this passion. She was *beyond* error; she was *beyond* fear; she was *beyond* shame; *beyond, beyond, beyond.*

Fola was mad with the need to do, because she was *beyond;* taken *beyond* this moment by the nameless futures which were knocking in her head. Like the dead souls in the *tonelle,* Fola was *beyond* her past. She was free; dead to the accidents of her past, dead and free. Fola was a freedom which now reached *beyond* the grave, *beyond* the sky. Dead and free on her eighteenth birthday.

CHAPTER VII

Today is Friday; it is the fifth day of Fola's absence from work!

Office hours are at an end, and the dark encroaches lazily outside the federal buildings of the Republic. To the west of Federal Park the residential plains emerge in scarlet bloom: the immortelle trees drip petals the colour of blood; and close by the private mansions of the president and his neighbours, rival fields of poui trees burn yellow as citrus in the sun. The gardens are waving like hair between the hands of women who wear their post-colonial freedom like a skirt. The wives are comparing curtains.

Here is man's most promising experiment in a race of mixtures. San Cristobal is the world's youngest republic; but it is also the world's finest laboratory of different breeds, fused and balanced like scales on the staggering body of the same fish. It is unique; for here the historic labels of prejudice are easily forgotten: alert and gracious wogs half Chinese in their breed with eyes like vanishing slits; emergent coolies introducing new kinks into their curls; the pure, astonished niggers whose legendary grin has changed to a smile of perfect gravity. Gracious and alert, in the meekest or most open interval of public service, alert and gracious, these are the women who wife the needs of a new bureaucracy.

Near the commercial heart of the capital the sun now shines at a quarter to five. As though by habit, it is always the same one hour before the public clock chimes quarter to six. Stores spew their vanity into the streets. A crowd wait on the pavements and wave in vain for taxis: a long procession of engines throbbing black fuel inside their low bright bonnets marked for hire. They tremble and stand still; now attempt a movement, cautious as snails from end to end of the street. This pause is expensive.

It starts a look of danger in the sullen eyes of the drivers who cuff their horns, fretting for space. Cyclists prop a leg against the bumpers; then lose their balance and dismount, startled by the discovery that it is better and even quicker to walk. An evening class of office clerks emerge like a squad of sentries changing guard. They have abandoned the statistics of a day's regulations in the federal buildings. Sorting their company with care, they push without apology through the crowd to the nearest tavern.

The traffic is regular as clockwork at this hour. But the sun has come to a halt opposite the same window. The girl on the fourth floor balcony feels the sun like a tired, red eye that leans from the enormous blue head of sky above her waiting. It spies over the typists' heads in her office; drills wide, red bars like a prison around

155

the sweepers who collect in the courtyard below; distracts the girl's attention from the queue of blind hands soliciting alms in the children's playground opposite. The bigger boys are rummaging for cigarette ends in a steel drum bin. An aged couple sit together on a charitable bench in the public square and suck cooked crab backs out of an obsolete newspaper. The print dissolves in grease, taunts their reading like an absent guardian which will not let them know what happened in the federal buildings they think they dare not enter.

The girl begins to stir on the balcony. She is restless and sad; for the face of the public clock is ordering her to visit the bathroom for the last time. She wants to postpone this last exchange of intimate talk with her colleagues who now stand opposite a new wall of wash basins and share the same lather. Soon they will descend the carpeted stairs of timber in a cheerful chorus of goodbyes; go their different ways for the night. It is this separation which makes the hour seem so sad; it starts childish wishes in this girl's mind. Crawling towards the splash of soap water, she begins to imagine that all the words they typed today may alter their meaning, contradict the orders which the Vice President has dictated; transfer themselves to pages where they don't belong. She hopes for some improbable discovery which will force them all to remain at work until the clock strikes nine.

Her name which is Eva Bartok Turnstyle has unfortunate associations; but she has been rescued by a certain strength of character. She is flippant and agile. She is admired for making the office come alive with her deliberate vulgarities. She can work and talk and notice what goes on outside without the slightest break in concentration. There is no lull in the pace of her energy. And she is thorough, brisk and thorough. Sometimes she may throw tantrums, but this is only her way of inviting her colleagues to share safe confidences about her life. She seems to need proof of their affection; for this office is an atmosphere she can't afford to lose. It gives her the sense of being near and intimate with people she hasn't known before. Work makes her part of a social life where rumour blends with law in the same importance of decisions which rule the republic and its families.

156

She halts at the door and laughs as she rehearses a story about her sister who sells groundnuts in the remote village of Half Moon Bay.

It seems that the sister has a hard dry scab from a wound inflicted by her mother. Breaking the neck off a bottle, the mother slashed a yard of skin down the girl's back. 'Why did she do it?' the sister was asked, and replied: 'Ma was under the *impression* of drink.' Eva is laughing because it is natural in the republic to laugh at error. Yet she thinks her sister has made the occasion more vivid by the accident of a word. She laughs again, secret in her conviction that *impression* tells a greater truth than influence about the power of drink.

Pushing the door open, she sees Veronica making faces in the mirror; and Eva thinks as she erases her laugh: 'Veronica Raymond wouldn't make that sort of mistake. Whatever position you rise to in San Cristobal certain things still count. Like poor old Baden-Semper making that fatal mistake the night Lady Carol and he celebrated their wedding anniversary.'

Veronica. is still busy with her face. Eva aches to repeat the story about Lady Carol's husband, but she is afraid of the question which will not let her answer that she was there, there among Lady Carol's guests in the Maraval hills. This is the difference between Veronica and herself. Eva turns the tap on and laughs into the water. She laughs because words are Baden-Semper's greatest obstacle and his greatest temptation. They are all he needs to give his money its proper authority. Eva imagines Lady Carol rising from her chair to pass some more garlic trout. Lady Carol is saying as she passes the trout that it is her turn to officiate; whereupon Baden-Semper, imitating the pompous fluency of her speech, has plunged a carving knife into the leg of pork, saying that he will, in the circumstances, aporkiate. On every plate gravy can be heard like the noise of thunder.

'Hurry up with the mirror,' Eva said, 'I want to fix my hair when I done wash.'

'See anything wrong with my face?' Veronica asked, lifting a lid of skin up from her cheek. The mirror counted three spots like seeds at the summit of her cheek.

'Where?' Eva asked, ignoring the finger which pointed under Veronica's eyes.

'You blind or what?' Veronica said, 'there. Look there.'

Her finger-nail stuck like a pencil point over a sore rash of skin. Eva laughed and watched the tap trickle slowly over the soap.

'Is nearly five o'clock,' she said, covering her hands with a lather of soap, 'and I want to get out o' this God-forsaken office.'

Eva dipped her head lower, turning the tap on loud.

'Can't see,' she said, wiping a cloud of lather from her eyes, 'but your man won't notice it. You been going too long.'

'Who's talking 'bout any man?' Veronica said.

'You self,' Eva answered, 'who else you fixing up your spotty face to please? I see too much not to know what a bathroom done make for. Some women catch and some lose, but is there everyone prepare the bait.'

Veronica appeared to shrug her shoulders, but she didn't turn her head from the mirror.

'I've other things to think 'bout but men,' she said, and noticed her breath make vanishing faces over the mirror.

'Just what wrong with that mousy, mousy, man o' yours,' Eva said. 'He won't help you do nothing but talk.'

'Only men, men, men you dream 'bout,' Veronica reminded her.

'Not dream, my darling, life too short.'

Eva slapped her face dry with the towel and started to sing: 'Want a brand-new car, to drive afar . . .'

'Suppose you had one day,' she said, making a hood with the towel over her head, 'just one day you could wish whatever you want and get it. What you wish for?'

Veronica stared into the mirror, nursing her rash with a finger of saliva.

'Well, what you wish for?'

'Nothing,' Veronica said abruptly.

Eva continued singing as she stretched the elastic in her under-wear, soothing the curves of her abdomen with both hands. She spun round on her heels, bright black and thin as pencils under her weight. Round and round she spun to the samba movements of her waist.

'Know what I'd wish for?'

'Something to do with a man,' Veronica said curtly, and took a step back from the mirror.

'Thought you'd say that,' said Eva.

She was teasing Veronica with the thought of an alternative wish; and Veronica now looked a little disappointed in her judgment about Eva.

'And what would you wish for?' Veronica asked.

Eva smiled and cavorted round to see her.

'You're right,' she said. 'But he got to be a man plenty years older than me, not any little green-horn sweating and puffing to make you feel what he aint.'

Eva played with the soft, ripe nipple of her breast like a cow's udder between two fingers, as she settled into her creation of the paternal husband.

'My man got to be sure o' himself,' she said, 'sort o' stable, and solid and responsible. Not rich, 'cause that don't excite me, but when we go out he mustn't have to count an' calculate what prices say. Is what I can't stand in these little force-ripe men, the way they stand up outside Castle Grant restaurant studyin' the menu, an' misreading it like how children skip some words they can't spell, an' all the time they translating the food prices, one hand like a thief in their pocket rubbing the edge o' every coin to make sure if it is a penny or a two-shilling piece.'

In secret, and pretending a lack of interest, Veronica was considering her own future. Menus would be the least bother to the man who would be eligible for her in the opinion of the families.

'Twenty, even twenty-five years older,' Eva said, 'it won't matter once he was still active an' know his way about.'

'He'd be old when your children were still infants,' Veronica suggested, as she polished the rash with some face cream.

'Infants in old age,' Eva said dubiously, 'it don't matter to me once they know who the father was.'

'But what about yourself?' Veronica asked, 'you'd still want to dance and be part of things like committees and so on.'

'Not me,' Eva said, discriminating and emphatic, 'the only committee I want is for birth control, 'cause I got a feelin' that when I start, they go roll out o' me like dry peas from their shell. But I like lookin' after something, in particular old people and children.'

Eva noticed the glint, surprise or deception, perhaps, which had sharpened the light in Veronica's eyes. _Looking after things_ was a phrase with specific meaning for Veronica. Instinctively Veronica had thought of Therese and her father's maid. But she had already censored the word, servant, when she spoke. She hadn't done so to spare Eva's feelings; for she knew nothing about Eva, but she felt guilty towards the servant whose loyalty was the only permanent memory of her own childhood.

'If I get married,' Veronica said, 'my life will be different. If you got to spend a life time cooking and cleaning children, then why you let parents spend all that money on college and all that?'

Eva answered very quickly: 'You don't want to play second fiddle in your husband house.'

Veronica seemed a little rattled by her haste, but her memory had not yet awakened her to the fact that Eva was not at the college she had in mind. Eva had obscured the point very deftly; and Veronica had been returned without the slightest awareness of Eva's guile back to their wishes.

'It has nothing to do with fiddles,' Veronica said in a voice reminiscent of evenings at Lady Carol's house. 'If marriage is the be all and end all of a woman's ambition, what's goin' to happen to the country now they give us freedom?'

Eva was grinning like an old rogue feeling a sad admiration for her innocent ward.

'We two very different, my darling,' she said, and came close to share Veronica's view of her rash in the mirror. 'It have rules for goats and flies and even centipedes. And what man make for and what woman make for is total, complete different thing. You want a husband what can discuss politics, and have a little verse and so to go with what the two o' you doing at night. But not me, my darling. No quotation when the curtains come down and those lights go out. I want my man to think 'bout nothin' but what under him. He must have me and take me like it was a night-cap he know exactly why he take.'

Veronica wanted to rebuke the note of mockery in Eva's voice.

'I can see what you want,' she said very primly, 'you probably won't get the children, but you'll get stuck with the rheumatism and the old voice groaning all night long. And then you'll think which really more suitable: old men or young men.'

Eva seemed to lose her passion for the aged father of a husband who would finish her days. Then her logic was restored, and she turned to talk with Veronica, slowly, patiently, like a teacher with some good, yet backward child in class.

'You too green, Veronica, too green for this world,' said Eva, one hand akimbo, and the towel hanging like a cape across her bosom. 'Is what a full, ripe man understand, your young men never know. Is in bed I learn that; and whenever it come your bedtime, an' please make it soon or you go lose Squires, remember that. A full, ripe man like a full ripe horse know the ground he riding. Excitement can make a young man get so wild that he start behaving like a hose-pipe inside you, 'cause he green, he think is only on the inside that a woman make her music. And he never give himself a chance to find the little keyboards that waiting for the right fingers to play, all sort a little secret places that mean more than his big lamp-post business. Some women got it in the nose, an' I don't know where yours is, but mine is a little spot no bigger than your finger-nail just behind my ear.'

sexual performance

Veronica's rash seemed to show the first signs of her embarrassment. This was the way Veronica might have spoken with Fola; but Eva had begun to trespass on her sense of decorum. Eva was as grave and precise in speech as Lady Carol during the elocution hour in the Maraval hills; but now she had begun to laugh at Veronica's obsession with the rash. Avoiding further talk about men, Veronica turned the conversation back to her face.

'Think this rash will clear away soon?' she asked.

'Hurry, please, I want to use the mirror too,' Eva answered.

'But why you so selfish?' Veronica rebuked her, 'if your face all right you don't care about anybody else.'

'I was thinkin' 'bout it,' Eva said, as though begging her pardon.

Veronica had turned her face for Eva's inspection. Eva coaxed the sore left cheek up to her glance, and smiled to assure Veronica that nothing was wrong. Brushing her hand lightly over Veronica's bosom, she said:

'Had your things yet?'

Veronica was taken aback; then she smiled into the palm of her hand.

'They come last night,' she said, like a child making up lies.

'Is that,' said Eva, 'but you lucky yours don't make you swell. It had a time I used to swell up bad, bad, bad all under my eyes. But Ado put an end to all that.'

'Why do you have to talk like that?' Veronica fretted, but the smile was still a shadow over her mouth.

'Is natural truth what I say,' Eva assured her. 'Long time they used to bend me up with pain like it was a child I making. And was only after Ado and me start to get together that I notice the change. Now they come and pass like it was red rain, most natural three days in the world. Ask anybody "in the know" 'bout these things.'

Veronica was unnerved by Eva's insight into 'these things;' for the complaint Eva had in mind had started two days late, and stopped a day too soon. Veronica had no reason to worry, yet she felt insecure under Eva's scrutiny.

'You think a man is cure for everything,' she said, with an expression of boredom for popular knowledge.

'Not only me,' said Eva, arranging the towel into a dancing partner, 'it got plenty doctors what say the same thing, and even recommend what me an' Ado do. But you got to watch them, 'cause they want to use their own first aid.'

'I never knew any doctor who was that low,' Veronica said.

'It got plenty things you don't know,' said Eva. 'You just green, but I could call six in this same San Cristobal who turn their surgery in a regular whore-house. Is bacchanal like fire when those curtains come down. And I know the women too. Some o' them explain it as emergency operation, but they never name the knife.'

Eva was in triumph as she rolled the towel to the width of an

arm and stretched it across her bosom. She watched her shadow
dancing on the wall as she heard the absent call of the drums. The
snake movement crawled and twisted over her stomach, up to her
arms spread wide and shuddering with muscle. The sun sharpened
its rays, sawing her shadow in half; and Eva suddenly had a vision
of herself mauled by some maniac whose sex had been aroused by
the skill her dancing showed. The maniac soon changed in her mind
to Veronica's father. It was Raymond who, shelving the compulsory
requirements for republican clerks, had got Eva into the sanctuary
of this office.

'What's your view 'bout taking things,' she said, as though some
leap of imagination made her feel that the gift of a car was not
unreal.

'What and from whom?' Veronica asked.

'You know, like gifts and so on,' Eva explained. 'Sometimes a
person would like to give you something, sort of make things look
more solid between you.'

'It depends,' said Veronica. 'Is it your boy friend? A distant
relation? An old man who just admires you? It all depends.'

'But you can't always be sure,' said Eva, 'sometimes you going
steady with a man, but you not sure you got the snake where you
want him, or that you even want him there.'

'You ought to know,' Veronica said cagily.

'But you can't always know,' said Eva, 'except you be the type
to set all sort o' trap like he was a rat or a cat what steal.'

Veronica seemed unduly cautious as she reflected on the accuracy
and speed of rumour in San Cristobal. It was some time since
people had been waiting to hear that Squires and herself had
announced their engagement. Squires was a member of the most
lucrative profession in the republic, respectable and proud of his
origins. His father was Chief Justice. But there was some obstacle
to Veronica's decision. It had to do with the intricacies of complexion in San Cristobal. Lady Carol herself, whose husband was
black as tar, had warned Veronica during their secret confessions
in the Maraval hills to watch her step. For Veronica was what the
families would describe as very light, fair chestnut brown. Squires
was a very dark, heavy, brown chestnut.

'They're certain things people understand without talking,' Veronica said.

'Don't make joke,' Eva answered, and her voice rose to a shout which, swift as a breeze, had startled her back to a whisper, 'it got things you can't always mention, not that you can't call it by name, but is all a matter of circumstance and time.'

'It depends who the people are,' Veronica said sternly, 'some people just know by a feeling.'

'Like Miss Walkers in the treasury building,' Eva said acidly, 'is marriage she would have today if she'd just tell Henderson that it was the boil he burst open on her big backside. Stupid woman.'

Eva danced away again, laughing at Veronica's innocence and the legend of the boil. But Veronica didn't think the episode very funny. She was guarding her own secrets about Squires as she inspected the scarlet vein running through her rash. She had once felt outraged when Squires offered to buy her a pair of black lace nylon panties which she wanted to wear. Eva reflected on the gifts, trying to number the trivialities which could make speech impossible.

'Is really difficult, you know,' Eva said, turning serious again, 'just to mention some things. You could tell a man in fun that he too old. Even in serious, like if you think marriage won't work out, you might tell him he too old. In a nice way, if you see what I mean, he could even come to agree with you 'bout that. But tell me, Veronica, tell me from the most honest part o' your heart. Would you tell a man who was a nice kind person and care sufficient to want to marry you . . .'

The bowl of face cream had slipped from Veronica's hands into the sink. The noise set a chill over her rash, and its echo had started a freezing spasm in her ears: 'I hope to Jesus, O Jesus, don't let her start asking me 'bout Squires.'

Impatient to get it over she snapped at Eva: 'Tell a man what?'

'Don't panic 'cause I sure we feel the same way 'bout this,' Eva said in the most compassionate voice her words could achieve. 'Could you tell such a man you won't have him 'cause he was ugly? Whether he was white, black, brown, blue or whatever colour you prefer, it don't matter. Would you really tell him what he already know, that it was because he was too ugly?'

The rash seemed to sparkle on Veronica's face, and her mouth formed an answer that was no louder than a sigh of relief: 'No, Eva, I don't think I could.'

Veronica soothed her rash again before changing places with Eva who now stood before the mirror, thumping her hands against the sink and dancing the snake movement through and around her waist as she sang: 'Want a brand-new car, to drive afar . . .' Veronica put a small pocket mirror over the rung of glass, forgetful of Eva's existence, as she played with her rash and tried to remember what it was she had to do at six o'clock.

Then the simplest and the weirdest and the most profoundly moving event of Eva's day occurred. She was packaging her breasts into a black brassière, chewing the frayed ends which showed where a seam had split open in a coil of black thread. Eva chewed the ends off and rolled them like a seed between her lips. And then it happened: this simple moment of private experience which exploded all her fears. She had leaned forward to spit the seed of thread into the sink when she had to stop, literally had to stop, because she suddenly remembered that Veronica was standing there.

Eva straightened her back and felt her hand slink shamefully away from her throat. She counted three for luck in silence and swallowed the saliva along with the little seed of black thread. It was the most uncanny sensation: the way her saliva seemed to throttle her tongue. She stared at the sink and thought she saw it shrink and cower in shame for the desecration which her spit had almost done. Her failure to spit the thread into the sink was like a punishment which reminded Eva how Baden-Semper and her sister must have felt when words exposed their lack of breeding. She couldn't spit into the sink because Veronica was there. It was simply Veronica's presence which judged what she was going to do. Veronica hadn't seen, but her presence was an accusation which made Eva's confidence wilt. Eva was waging a private argument with herself, repeating a false conviction which she felt like sin: 'there's no difference between she an' me, there's a difference between herself and myself, no difference whatsoever; but it got a difference somewhere between she an' me.' Speech changed with every emergency in her hope and reason.

Instinctively Eva had begun to summon from some grave of promises in her consciousness the most incredible fantasy about the conduct of this liquid and that liquid, the rival claims of water and water. There was a difference between water gargled from her mouth into the sink, and water spilt from a kettle on the stove, and the frozen white foam of water secreted under her tongue. Eva weighed the relative propriety of each discharge of water, and every result increased her punishment when it reminded her who she was and how Veronica lived. Something had gone wrong, wrong and dead inside her. She turned her back so that Veronica might not guess the change which had come over her. She reached for her leopard-striped blouse which hung from the door. But Eva's energy had deserted every movement in her hands. It was a painful journey of moments which her fingers made while they hooked the buttons into each hole. The broken seam still showed where one of the buttons had come undone, as though the brassière too was determined to betray her.

The imagination which had suckled at the springs of her work in the federal building was now alive and ripe. It had persuaded her to accept that Veronica would never have thought of spitting into a public sink. Veronica's presence had sprung an awareness of difference in her mind which Eva's reason rejected and her heart could never deny. Turning to face Veronica, this difference made Eva nervous; and a natural pride had suddenly plunged her nervousness into spite. She felt she had to recover her self-esteem whose fall from grace had not even been noticed. She had to do it, as she had to censor her spit; and malice was the easiest way. It would give a certain edge of sharpness to her tone. She had settled the ends of the blouse inside the skirt, and chosen her target.

'Is five days Fola Piggott aint put in her appearance,' said Eva, 'an' nobody ask no questions.'

'She isn't well,' Veronica said, abruptly startled as she dismissed the sharpness in Eva's voice. For it had suddenly reminded Veronica of Fola's telephone call at half-past four.

'Was she who call?' Eva asked as though she doubted Veronica's excuse.

'She call from the hospital,' Veronica said, returning her gaze on the mirror. 'I'm meeting her round six on Bruton Lane.'

And even the sink now saw what had happened; for Veronica's innocent reply was the final thrust of difference which poisoned Eva's wound, and set the signature of death over her future self-importance. Bruton Lane had associations which had always made Eva conceal her address. No one in the office knew where she lived. It was beyond coincidence for Fola to choose Bruton Lane as a meeting place; and Eva promptly understood, for herself, what Veronica was trying to do. Eva's lips were curling in like a nostril retreating from stench, and Eva thought: 'I go get my own back on those two nasty bitches. Now you just wait Veronica Raymond, and you, Fola Piggott, wherever you is 'cause it aint no Bruton Lane, I go fix each o' you with one shot. You nasty bitches.'

In the pause which helped Eva to weigh her chances of assault, Veronica had grown very sceptical. Veronica had just recalled the legend of Bruton Lane, and Eva's eyes were reflecting her own doubt about Fola's choice. Veronica was sure it was Fola' svoice on the telephone. This was the first time it had ever crossed Veronica's mind that Eva must live somewhere; and again her question was entirely without guile. But where innocence is natural and a need, there is no end to its power for creating muddle of danger upon increasing danger.

'You ever hear about some place called Moon Glow?' Veronica asked, in a voice enquiring after Lady Carol, and turned her indifferent glance back to the mirror.

But Moon Glow was the brothel which had won Eva's street its fame!

Eva was parrying, sure and patient as a boxer who undermined his opponent but suggesting some new weakness.

'It aint my business,' Eva said, 'but the way people see you and Fola together, hand in hand wherever you go and never one without the other. It making them talk, and I myself hear things.'

Veronica had lost interest in her rash. Eyes shot through with disdain, and her voice now lathered with propriety, Veronica said: 'Now will you say what you mean?'

Eva had a voice which could suggest apology for what she really meant. Subtle as cloud, it had emerged.

'Well you know what people give,' she said. 'It don't always look natural the way you two treat one another. And nobody was ever sure 'bout Fola.'

Veronica bristled with the knowledge of who she was. Indifferent to Eva's source of rumour, Veronica wanted to know the reason for such impudence. She simply thought Eva impudent and out of place.

'Cats may look at a queen,' Veronica said, 'but it doesn't give them or you the right to mew about Fola. People like you envy Fola.'

'Envy her what?' Eva shouted.

There was hot anger and a familiar hurt in Eva's voice, as though she had been unjustly forced to use the weapons of dispute she had learnt in Bruton Lane.

'Envy her what?' Eva repeated, as though the next stage of her betrayal was not yet ready.

'Everything,' Veronica said, 'looks, training, everything that makes up what Fola is. A lady.'

Eva had stalled for a moment. This word would never have been used in the office except in jest. The broken seam of Eva's brassière still showed where the button had come undone. When Eva saw it through the mirror, she knew she was right to think that Veronica had seen her try to spit the seed of thread into the sink. 'Perhaps she saw me,' Eva kept thinking as though it would deny her right to a reply. But the pride of Bruton Lane now seemed to claim Eva as its daughter. She felt a crushing humiliation at the thought that Veronica had seen and ignored her attempt to spit the seed of thread into the sink. It seemed the same kind of forgiveness which her mother would use towards her sister. The never-to-be-forgotten judgement was: 'poor Sue, she don't know no better.'

The pride of Bruton Lane was pounding like a drum in Eva's head. Eva had to strike back, not for her pride alone, but for the whole instinct of a childhood that was no less worthy of life. From the scum of a class that could not be buried without the total death of the Republic itself, Eva had emerged to the summit of a federal office which Fola and Veronica instinctively regarded as their back-yard; visited only out of obedience to their parents' wish; a sanctuary which was taken wholly for granted as their own. Eva thought she had nothing to lose which heaven itself had not already denied her.

She had collected her soap, powder, and forgotten hairclips: a hurried mess of objects crowding her hands. And Veronica watched her, as though ordering this abrupt departure. But the drums had signed their revolt in Bruton Lane.

'I know plenty 'bout you,' Eva said, as she turned to go, 'and why and how I know would make your hair turn red.'

Eva was diving down, deeper and deeper into the blasphemy of her illicit meetings with Veronica's father; but the instinct of her pride warned, and warned Eva that it couldn't help her surface again if she dare utter this revenge.

'Bruton Lane,' Eva droned, as though her memory had returned its music, 'why the hell you think the two o' you meeting in Bruton Lane? I can tell you why.'

The idle drag of the sweepers' brooms was approaching, dumb and fearsome in their warning, but Eva was going to speak on their behalf.

'You can play great,' Eva said, and her whisper was like the message from an enemy not far away, 'you can walk like your heel on hot ash, can't open your crutch for fear your pride leak out. But below where everything hide, you not only like anybody else, you so and different 'cause you nasty, the two of you, plain, stinking nasty. You can't talk 'bout fucking, 'cause you choose to do it your own nasty way, you and she and the great queen mother who train you up in the Maraval hills in everything except what nature fashion you for. Society, my arse, is nothing but a hot bed o' nasty women. Committee, my backside, is the law the country need to finish off all you.'

Eva waited to catch her breath. In spite of Veronica's apparent calm, she was shaken to her roots, like the time someone fed a laxative to the donkey which the bishop had hired for Palm Sunday.

169

The animal's pollution of the church was like the filth which words had now secreted in Eva's mouth. Veronica returned her glance to the mirror, and Eva heard her instinct demand some final triumph.

'People 'fraid to talk,' Eva said, 'but ask Lady Carol where she get her money. Ask her who money build her mansion in the Maraval hills. Ask her that.'

And the door closed, decisive and irrevocable, like the gates of a prison behind Eva. Eva stood outside on the terrace, in need of her over-worked hands, incapable of raising them to wipe the heat which stuck like a scab burning her ears. Instinct had demanded her alliance against a common enemy; but it could promise nothing more. It couldn't prophesy the damage which her own triumph might later conspire against herself. Eva was afraid.

'She is common,' Veronica kept saying, 'of course she is common and nobody to bother about, common as dirt, of course she is.'

But it wasn't wholly true. She had no doubt Eva was common, dirt common and forgettable as dirt itself. Yet she feared Eva's insight into what was common like money and menstruation, and clinics and hospitals. It was Eva who now made her innocence swell like a crime. For Veronica could not conceive of any reason on earth how Fola came to make her telephone call from the hospital. People like Fola didn't go to the hospital except in the most ominous emergency. The hospital and Bruton Lane assumed impossible proportions in Veronica's mind, impossible because they were wholly outside any alphabet of words or thought which she and Fola had learnt at college, outside any meaning that could claim a corner in their lives, now or at any time in the future.

Veronica bundled her cosmetic, parcelled soap and powder into a leather kit, and hurried out of the bathroom to telephone Fola's mother. Half-way up the stairs Veronica stopped, sudden as a signal interrupting traffic, the way dogs do through some hidden and inscrutable nerve of codes which tell danger. In some nameless part of Veronica's body, words were pouring like blood, just pouring without any pause in the noise they made. And their most fearful paradox was that brief and simple question they now asked about Fola's secret.

The question was: 'Who knows why?'

From infancy to this moment, these were the only words that had ever opened Veronica's ears to a belief in the voice of God. . . .

Alone and unnoticed, the sun is closing its solitary eye. The huge blue head of sky now broods an early darkness into the evening. A false light has alarmed the hands of the clock outside; but something in nature is changed. This dark is a minute too soon. It enters the hospital through waiting-rooms; it breathes a cold future over the eyes of the sick; scribbles its premature warning on the visible ends of the sheets. The wicked are afraid; while the young try to understand this calm resignation which now soothes the dying.

A porter stands on the steps of the waiting-room, gazing indifferently over the wall. It is the colour of twilight, a dark, greasy wash of stone rising level with his head. It makes the greatest division seem so simple; for a cemetery is on the other side. In the republic, architectural relations have always been straightforward: Law courts adjoin the prisons as this cemetery waits beneath the hospital windows.

The porter is waiting to clean the maternity hall: a small, dark room of protective odours against the plague of unmarried mothers. The queue is slow, sometimes neglected, regarded as a nuisance by the porter. He knows the doctors pay little attention to this corner of the hospital, although it is never deserted. Like poverty that is natural and a crime, these mothers are common knowledge throughout the republic. More than half the population have passed this way at some time.

The porter grows impatient with the women who wait. He begs the nurse to call him when they are through. He can't wait much longer because the smell is bad for his cough. He gets no answer, yet knows it will be all right, and hurries towards the asphalt patio where a procession of fruit and flowers is on its way to the expensive wards of convalescence. Lovers and clerical faces and servants like Therese make their excursion to the sick.

Alone and like the sun which has closed down, Fola sits at the back of the maternity hall and tries to ignore the sharpness of these odours melting in the air. Her hair is cropped short and her eyes are like the wicked who watch in wonder at their failure to explain. She cleans her tongue with a handkerchief, but the bitter taste remains. It rubs

171

against her palate, clouds the roof of her mouth; yet she shows no sign of discomfort. She seems removed from all sensation as she trains her senses to resist the sickly intrusions of the air. The hospital smells become a necessary atmosphere, harmless to her touch. She is determined not to leave until the room confirms her fantasy of secrets. She wants to live through the whole kingdom of details which she imagines now crowd her past. Then it will be time to meet Veronica at the Moon Glow brothel on Bruton Lane.

The voice of the nurse accuses her again. Half turned to the queue, the face opens a thick, black hole which names the statistics of her calling: B 532, age 22, three months? A 151, age 19, five months? C 36, age 35, three months? You three can come in next.

The names fall like loose teeth from her mouth. The nurse doesn't register any face, but looks up to make sure that the answer has come from someone near. Tonight she hopes to dance with the doctor; but the list of human numbers now trembles with her impatience. She slips it into her pocket and goes on the other side of the screen.

Fola listens; feels an uncommon awareness of herself now burst into hatred for the nurse. The nurse and the women! It is the animal docility of the women which hurts. Cowed and dejected in their waiting, these mothers look strangled by the charity of this room. 'So they are like that!' Fola thinks, as she hears them answer to their numbers in the Maternity hall. They carry the weight of their pregnancy like ordinary food; take their places with the same servile sureness of animals trained to their stalls, and wait for a nurse to announce their numbers. Yet their numbers increase the impossible disapproval of the republic.

Fola tries to see herself there in the shape and skin of their recent disfigurement. She wants to feel in the natural pulse of her own bowels the life which has increased their size. Her hands travel slowly up and down, searching the corners of her skirt, reaching to span the curves of her stomach. She relaxes her muscles, expands her bosom, and opens her fingers to measure her waist. She considers the faces of the women and the stages of their pregnancy—in order to imagine the accident of pleasure or assault which has fertilised their wombs. Fola wants to know. She demands the secret of her mother's waiting, begs it to open and flood her with know-

172

sexual connotation.

ledge. Curiosity spreads like an illness inside her, until she notices the women's indifference. They lean against the wall, just waiting for attention, patient and casual as plants, as though there were no memory to glance this moment back to another time. Numbers are their only claim to recognition. The nurse has been trained to see their future as a matter of months.

Fola cannot recognise the sameness of her sex in their indifference. She aches to know the origin of the life which each contains. She forces herself to see without any evidence at all the history of each face; the details of uncertainty which each has lived before the truth grew to an actual shape inside her. Fola looks away, looks back again, hoping to rescue each woman from the anonymity of her number; she rehearses the line and complexion that distinguish each face, so that she may restore each waiting mother to the individual privacy of her past.

But the faces are blurred by Fola's own obsession. The time she wants to resurrect is her own life; the face which now reduces the importance of the queue is her mother's face, surprised by its waiting before Fola's eyes. Imagination answers Fola's demand, offers her mother's body against that wall, growing in silence every day with a knowledge Fola has always been deprived of sharing. It is this room where so many individual disasters have been heard and forgotten; it is here Fola sees her mother waiting. And she, Fola, like a worm diced with so much covering of dirt had been brought to this room, fatherless in name, secret and unseen as a germ. Fola notices the women move forward, but she has forgotten their faces. It is time to meet Veronica.

As Fola turned to go, unsure, it seemed, why she was still waiting, she felt the gradual emptiness of the room close like a cell around her. The queue had been shortened. She heard the nurse's voice, and thought that she owed it to these women and to herself to hit upon some outrage which would shatter that servant's complacency. Behind the screen Fola could hear a woman's sob; then an interval of male voices, and the woman's voice rose again, much louder now. The nurse was whispering details about the woman's record. She was a prostitute on Bruton Lane, and this was her ninth abortion. It seemed she had come too late.

173

'But is not my fault,' the woman cried, 'is not my fault.'

Some of the women in the queue were smiling until they heard the nurse's voice again.

'Whore if you can't help whoring,' the nurse said, 'but get the men to use something.'

'Is what I tell them,' the woman sobbed, 'but they won't pay unless you let them ride bare-back. It aint my fault.'

There was the sound of a chair falling back. The nurse walked to the door, then returned behind the screen.

'What you go do 'bout her, doctor?' the nurse asked.

The chair had fallen. It crashed against a spittoon, and the noise sent a tremor through the queue of women in the room.

'Well what, doctor, you can't keep her here all night,' the nurse pleaded.

'Let it rot in her guts,' the doctor's voice shouted, 'it'll teach them to have some kind of standards. They have no standards whatsoever, that's what.'

Fola recognised Camillon's voice, cold and aggressive in its authority. There was no warning of song in its sound; but the woman was still trying to make some kind of plea. A door banged in the distance, and the nurse started to swear. Camillon had left. The woman continued to make her sick noises, like a cat.

And Fola thought: 'so we are like that?' For the first time in her search for a father, the word bastard was born in Fola's mind. It existed in its own right, like stone or mineral; not as extension of another thing, but a category unto itself. As you might say: 'I am a man and other than man, meaning spirit.' Fola was thinking: 'I am Fola and other than Fola, meaning bastard and other than, and other than, outside and other than.' Fola's life contained all that Veronica was, plus that tiny acre of awareness which Fola now named: and other than, and other than. Suddenly her secrets had given way to some power of wild and delirious adventure, some sense which was alien and yet hers.

Fola glanced for the last time at the queue, and thought there was some connection between those women and herself; waiting as they did, ignorant and secure, while some terrible future stirred to life inside them. But she would be different after she had left this room.

The porter was standing at the hospital gate; but when Fola turned into the street, she didn't hear the man ask whether her 'lot' had finished. She walked under the dead eye of the sun, thinking, as her speed swept her towards Veronica, how she would be in future active and free in all her enquiries. It didn't matter what she asked or where her questions carried her.

Fola felt like a man who had chosen to ignore all assistance in trying to find his way. Assistance became an obstacle in her way. 'So people are like that,' she thought, colliding without notice past a constable, 'what they know becomes a germ hidden in their attitudes of acceptance.' Fola was a dead germ in their knowledge and acceptance. 'So they know me,' she thought, 'as they know my mother waiting in that room, and in the power of their knowledge I have moved like a bee round and round their own habit of knowing.'

But Fola was not now like Veronica; she was Fola, *and other than.* She was going to sabotage everything which made for their knowledge. She would be active and free from the outside, active and free over their knowledge which no one could deny her. People had moved about her, feeling no need to pay attention. But Fola was going to surprise their knowledge with another Fola; Fola *and other than.*

She would let her friends and the families keep the Fola they had known, while she summoned a Fola other than the self they knew. She would make her own history, give it life and motive which she herself might not understand. Where others had felt the need to hide, to rest untroubled in their habit of knowing, she was going to be eloquent and free. She would select the beginnings of a fact upon which she could build any fantasy that might cripple their recognition. For this was at the heart of what she had now recognised about Piggott and her mother, about the room of women who waited for a doctor's reluctant advice. They had all been deceived by their ignorant habit of knowing. Fola had seen with the criminal indifference of her youth that Piggott and her mother had taken refuge in a lie which had become their only claim to reality. Fola thought that truth would be irrelevant for her purpose, if she could make people respond with the same intensity of feeling to her distortion of any fact. That's how she would begin. She was determined to offer an image of herself that would work like disease on their certainty. She would discover the families and her friends through their attitude to the details of this history which she was going to bestow on the self that was Fola, *and other than*. This would be her way of knowing.

Fola was getting near the Moon Glow. The street lamps grew the same yellow light over the harbour to show that nothing had changed. Trivialities were beginning to claim her attention as she watched the ocean, and thought that she should have had a wash and tidy her hair. But it was too late. Veronica might have arrived in this area of the capital where no one could expect her to wait. It harboured sailors on leave, and the local women were rough. She had to think of Veronica. Fola had to make her choice seem appropriate to the way she felt. Veronica would be confused at first, but she would give Veronica time to find her way.

There were rival histories of tragedy now living side by side in Fola's mind. It made her nervous. She thought she was walking too fast. She needed to be calm, leisurely; urgent to break word of the tragedy she was going to describe, yet careful to avoid Veronica's suspicion. As Fola got nearer the Moon Glow, her thinking seemed more cautious; attitudes started to suggest themselves. She had to impose some order on their willingness. Everything depended on whether Veronica would arrive. Suppose Veronica refused to come! For a moment Fola paused and tried to consider some alternative. But the fear was too vague. She decided to deal with emergencies when they happened. If Veronica failed her, she would think of something else. But she had to start today. Postponement would have been like illness in its betrayal. It was tonight, or never. Fola was hounded by this impulse to prove that she was free: *beyond and other than*.

The lights were going on inside the Moon Glow. A group of fishermen were loitering in the bar below. Then Fola recognised the white, wooden statues she had seen before. She didn't see Veronica, but she had the feeling Veronica would not be far away. It seemed nothing could desert her now.

On the first floor where Veronica was waiting, the atmosphere was uneventful. A red light circled through a loop of Christmas bulbs to tell the price of hard-boiled eggs. A notice said in chalk: 'No chicken till the fleets come in.' The bar was deserted. A radiogram was grinding painfully to its end, coughing and wheezing as it cried:

> Sometimes I love you
> Sometimes I hate you
> But when I hate you
> It's 'cause, it's 'cause, it's 'cause . . .

The waitress went to its aid; switched it off and returned to ask Veronica about her friend.

'I'd give anything to be like her,' the waitress was saying. 'If is the same lady what I see come in here three, four times close ago, then you can wait. But what she doin' this for?'

Veronica had refused to sit. The waitress plugged her fingers into her ears against the sound of the radiogram, while Veronica stood, gazing into the derelict corners of the room. The walls were covered with obscene wishes; all the intimacies of sex had been declared in charcoal lettering.

'I keep tellin' them not to make those marks,' the waitress said, pondering Veronica's relation to the police. 'An' they can't even spell some things right.'

Veronica gazed towards the stairs, unhearing everything.

'Can't be right in her head,' the waitress said, 'nice-lookin' lady your frien' is, got everythin' a young woman can want, proper trainin' in how to talk, an' be with people who really matter. What she want to mix up in here for?'

The waitress suddenly stopped, looking rigid with attention, yet pretending not to see, like policemen acknowledging the arrival of the President of the Republic. Fola had climbed to the top of the stairs. Promptly she ordered two packs of cigarettes; and that order was the beginning of Veronica's dismay. Like hypnosis and rats, Fola had always had a poisonous fear of tobacco smoke.

'But Fola you sound so strange.'

'Sit down,' said Fola. 'It's me you're seeing all right."

'Since when you take up smoking?'

'A secret, Veronica, but I don't want any secrets between you and me.'

'I won't stay here, Fola. Why did you have to come here?'

'Because there are no secrets here. That's why.'

'But suppose anyone sees us, Fola?'

'Who is anyone?' Fola asked, waving to the woman behind the bar.

'You know what I mean,' Veronica wavered, 'what would my father say?'

Fola paused. It was a long and obstinate silence while she looked at Veronica.

'What would my father say?' Fola said.

Her meaning was too much for Veronica to dwell on.

'Fola!'

'Did you always know?' Fola asked.

She had made her plunge; not as Fola; but Fola *and other than*.

' Know what? '

Fola tried to smile as she watched Veronica. The shadows moved slowly over the table and mottled their hands.

'Know what?' Veronica asked again.

'I didn't think people could keep things so dark,' Fola said.

'What should I know?' Veronica asked, forgetting her protest against the room.

'Do you remember the wedding?' Fola said.

'What wedding?'

'When my mother got married?'

'But that was such a long time, Fola, What are you getting at?'

'You were there,' Fola said. 'I remember you like it was yesterday in a sailor blue dress with red ribbons and a rose in your hair. It was nearly night when they returned from the church.'

'But what about it?' Veronica said. 'I don't remember a thing.'

'Would it make any difference if you knew?'

'Knew what?' Veronica interrupted.

'I could see from your look,' said Fola, 'this is the first you've heard me mention my father.'

'But why you bringing up all this, Fola?'

178

'It's never too late to know,' said Fola.

Veronica's eyes retained their innocence; but Fola's voice had discovered a note of wounded pride. Now Fola was in trouble.

'Too late to know what?' Veronica insisted.

The rival claims of different tragedies were waging conflict in Fola's mind. Was it too late to retract the claim which ordered her to say that Veronica was her sister, that Raymond was her father?

'Know what, Fola, is what I don't know that I should?' Veronica begged.

Fola's evasive silence had grown in those moments like a natural deafness. She didn't want to hear questions which she had not chosen to answer. She had Raymond's scarf in her bag; but a fresh claim had already conquered its rival in Fola's mind. Veronica seemed to forget how their silence had come about until she noticed the change in Fola's eyes. Fola's voice had grown more intimate: now she seemed more dependent on Veronica's interest. They ignored the arrival of a couple who slipped under the bar and disappeared behind the curtains into the dark passage-way.

'You know what I really want to tell you?' Fola said.

She paused, bestowing on her reluctance all the weight of a recent distrust.

'Tell me, Fola'

'The trouble is you so green, Veronica,' she said.

And Veronica's role seemed to be made. Veronica was normal enough to take offence.

'But what happen?' she said, petulance creeping into her voice, 'always you keep telling me I green, and it got things I can't understand, but you don't tell me what happen.'

One certain tragedy had found its corner in Fola's mind. Hard and cold as war which knows no individual defeat, it seemed impervious to its rivals. Fola's head weighed heavily on her hand as she glanced at the traffic of feet outside. There was ripeness and certainty of feeling in her voice.

'You must talk free,' Fola said, 'like talking with yourself.'

Veronica didn't move. She was nervous and attentive as a child under difficult cross-examination.

'You happy?'

'I don' know, Fola.'

'Fair enough,' Fola said, and paused as though she wanted to make it plain that she wasn't dissatisfied. 'They have plenty questions you say that to. But they have some you can't.'

'What it is trouble you, Fola?'

'I comin' to that,' said Fola, 'but tell me, unless you want to keep it secret from me. About Squires.'

'What 'bout him?'

'Is a year you been goin' together,' Fola said, 'an' your father an' his father take it like natural you two go come together for good one day.'

'You can't tell with such things,' said Veronica.

'I know,' Fola said. 'But tell me. You ever do anything with him?'

Veronica was feeling for her answer. Ordinarily, she might have spoken without embarrassment, but Fola's attitude had given her the feeling that everything was difficult; her questions were a trap.

'We kiss an' things like that,' Veronica said, looking round for some distraction.

'Remember you don't have to tell what you want to hide,' Fola said.

Veronica felt brought to trial by the ease with which Fola would grant her a reprieve.

'There aint nothin' I have to hide,' she said.

'Then that's the truth,' Fola said, as though she admired chastity, 'I take it that after one whole year, you never go further than kissing with him.'

It was a charge, like being too healthy in a family where all had fallen with infirmity. Veronica thought that her age was enough to make her Fola's equal in experience. She seized upon Fola's intention. She saw derision in the approval of a cowardice which had limited her desires to a kiss. She would refuse to surrender herself to Fola's poser; yet she had been taken for a girl who still had to grow up.

'I take it that's all,' Fola repeated.

'We do other things too,' Veronica said, as though she couldn't afford to lose Fola's interest before she had dislodged the charge of cowardice.

'Don't tell me anything you prefer to hold secret,' Fola said.

There was a new authority in her voice; for she had suddenly remembered Charlot's calculated indifference to her panic in the *tonelle*. Her voice was cold, disinterested, a simple reminder that Veronica was still free to guard her secrets. It made Veronica feel cheated. A stir of insult was gradually aroused in her.

'Nothing really serious,' Veronica said, 'but I suppose it gives the same feeling.'

Veronica waited, but Fola didn't interrupt, and it made Veronica feel she had to continue. In the interest of hearing Fola's secret, she had to barter her own privacy. But Fola had changed roles again. There was innocence in her attention. It seemed to require an effort for Fola to understand the different stages of desire which sex could relieve without doing harm.

'Sometimes we come near to doin' it,' Veronica said, trying to be casual and adult about herself.

An old reservation about Squires seemed to give Veronica a new freedom.

'I feel so sorry for him sometimes,' she said, 'the way he will go through all the motions without putting it in. We lie like that plenty times, straight or sideways according to where it is and the space you got.'

And Fola, now cold and docile as an earnest student!

'But nothin' more?' she asked.

For a moment Veronica wondered what Squires would feel about this exposure of himself; then the reflection ripened in her mind. She had more in common with Fola.

'Only once in the Maraval hills,' Veronica said, 'we got lost and nobody was near, and while I was doing the usual thing, it seem I forget. I just forget what was happenin', like my head was swimming after you been turning round and round and round, and he take the chance to ease a little ways inside, but he was scared something might happen, and quick, quick so, he pull away. He say it would be better after we get marry, when you could relax cool and have it all your own way. And we didn't do nothing.'

181

She watched Fola as though she needed her to be part of the same experience.

'It never happen to you?' Veronica asked.

Fola was alive with the recollection of a lifetime: the afternoon she watched Charlot's head, and dreamt his skin under her lips, and heard the drums ordering her to claim the first and only love she had known. But she forgot Charlot; for tragedy had ripened in her mind.

'That an' more,' said Fola, 'but I'm not scared, whatever you and others think, I've never been scared.'

She could feel imagination like a stimulant in her blood: but she showed no delight in what she had to say.

'What it is you mean by not scared?' Veronica asked.

Veronica felt innocence like a traitor.

'What I got to tell more difficult,' Fola said.

Veronica had understood. She started to search her memory for names. She had found the reason for Fola's curiosity about her intimacy with Squires. Veronica told herself she was no longer in Fola's power. It was Fola who needed her attention.

'You can trust me, Fola, you know you can trust me,' she said, emerging from her deference.

'I think so too,' said Fola, 'is just why I choose you to tell.'

'You needn't worry 'bout that,' Veronica said, trying to console her. There was a look of tenderness and hurt which Fola had never seen in Veronica's face before.

'There's always something we can do,' Veronica promised.

And the claim of tragedy emerged from Fola's mind to ask for habitation and a name. Whom shall I choose? And where? Fola's mind was recording a dispute of details which had already chosen their end. There was no misgiving in her expression of quiet and decisive control. Her need had trained her for any emergency.

'It isn't any of the people you have in mind,' Fola said, twisting her mouth with regret.

'What happen?' Veronica asked, feeling a depth of pity she couldn't contain. Her hand had moved along the table to comfort Fola's.

'I wish my mother and me could talk like we do,' said Fola, 'not hiding, but like you bring everything into the light.'

Fola spoke slowly, pausing for emphasis, preparing her gestures according to the importance of each detail. She felt like a witness, certain of her evidence, yet burdened with the need to avoid mistakes.

'You know about the *tonelle?*' Fola asked.

Veronica nodded in haste, impatient of irrelevancies. What could the *tonelle* have to do with this?

'And you know Constance Spring?' Fola continued.

'Sure I know Constance Spring,' Veronica said, waiting sadly and greedily for confirmation of what she had foreseen.

But Fola would not allow any kind of collaboration. She would not trust her tragedy to any previous knowledge Veronica might have had. A simple grain of fact was enough. The rest should be entirely her doing. Like a guide ruled by his own routine of knowledge for eager tourists, Fola was creating Constance Spring. She made Veronica feel the sting of the wind as she rode with her drumming lover from the *tonelle* through miles of deserted night, feeling lust, expectation and the terror of delight as she recognised a madness in his limbs. What insanity of need had identified this Boy with the power of his motor bike. Was he angry? Was it an unheard of appetite for her body? She did not know. Nor did she know why the accident of memory should have made her choose Powell for her baptism in this fantasy. But the dead germ in Fola had come to life. It was Fola, *and other than;* Fola the bastard who was active and free, summoning the history of a right that had never happened.

Dizzy with speed, she could find no pause in her thinking to name this frenzy which had charged her lover's nerve. The roads unfolded and were quickly lost behind their flight. The neighbouring fields slipped by, empty and black, not a light to tell where the sky was waiting. She felt the course of her blood like an ocean sweeping into eternity every secret germ of desire that made his music in her bones. Then the wind had stopped, blown down from the sky like a dead hand; and her breathing quickened. But her lover didn't speak. He wouldn't say a word, as he leaned the motor bike like a drunk man on one side. She stood mute, a free slave to his silence, until she felt all of her sex tremble under his tireless need to crush her down, back, down and back into the earth.

'And there he lay me down,' said Fola, 'to batter me with all he had. I cry, and cry with pain all inside me, 'cause it wasn't love make him do it. I beg him to let go, let go, but my begging only add to the murder he was making inside me. I think I just pass out, just pass out when he raised himself up off the ground. He wasn't on me any more. And I couldn't talk, my throat won't let a word pass, not even to tell him come back. He was gone; without a word he went and left me there, just where he lay me down.'

Fola's voice had faded to a tired and natural sigh of anguish. Now she waited as though it was her turn to listen, exempt from pity, outside and free from the obvious weight of her distress. Fola *and other than!* She hadn't changed her look of resignation. It wore to perfection the wide, shadowed softness of her eyes, now remote and melancholy in their mood.

'But Fola, Fola . . .' Nothing else remained from the crowd of words which strangled Veronica's throat.

'It happened to me,' said Fola, patient, decisive and complete in her acceptance. Fola *and other than!*

'But suppose, Fola, suppose,' Veronica cried looking round for the first assurance of their privacy, 'suppose it put you in the family way.'

Veronica was rubbing the salt from her eyes as she nibbled her wrist.

'Suppose it happen?' she cried again, her voice grown desperate and defeated in its certainty of the worst.

But Fola was silent. The Moon Glow narrowed its walls and closed in on her like the maternity hall exhibiting the secret germ that was not only Fola, but Fola *and other than*.

The trees threw down a cry of leaves outside as Fola thought: 'first things first, and first is the worst: my old image makes her ask: not who *he* is, but suppose *it* happens.' But this was not Fola whom Veronica now saw, and she didn't know there was another Fola; Fola *and other than.* This Fola had started on a history of needs whose details she alone would be able to distinguish: a season of adventure which no man in the republic could predict.

Title - History of need

Work! For the night is coming
When man's work is done.

CHAPTER VIII

Today the streets are gentle, quiet and gentle as a carpet strewn with fresh leaves. The sun is soft with light. It enters through a window which opens behind Chiki's head. Its shadows stride across the room, nestle over his eyes; then measure his body on the bed, and settle like cloth in every crevice of this little cave he calls his home. Home is Chiki's name for any place where a man has found and where he does his work. The Forest Reserve is Gort's home; that tenor drum is the total horizon of Gort's doing, as paint and brush are voices of an instinct which talks in Chiki's hands.

But today he cannot work. He sees his life's doing on the walls, and is afraid something has gone wrong. He is afraid of looking back upon the past which will reside for ever on those canvasses. Chiki is afraid; for as he starts his journey back, tracing each memory imprisoned in that paint, he reflects on a saying he has heard somewhere: how the prayers which an old man remembers are always those the child in him first uttered. And Chiki thinks, 'I am not so old, I am still not so old.'

Chiki is afraid these paintings may become a crutch which will remind the world that there was once great strength, great energy and strength in the gift they carry, limping from eye to eye. He is afraid, afraid in every nerve. He is afraid his appetite is coming to an end; afraid that he may yet fall victim to this fear which tells him he has earned the right to rest; the fear which now tempts him to fast on the reminiscence of what is done. He is afraid that he may yield to the weight of these hands that drag him to embrace, admire and embrace what is now past. 'The prayers an old man remembers . . . the child first uttered.'

Chiki is afraid of what he sees; for these three massive canvasses which now partition his home: they are the days and nights of his

187

remembered childhood. Like the music of Gort's drum, they have grown from that blind soil and vision of the Forest Reserve where he was born. Born under the spell of gods he cannot call his own, baptised in a bible which has always ruled him from his Christian infancy; these divinities collide and fuse and contradict: in conflict at one point, breeding a harmony at the next. They are the paradox which feeds his life, the mystery his hand has sought in line and colour to unravel.

But Chiki is afraid today; for his childhood stares with even greater threat than ever. He lets his glance steal to and fro, away and back again to these three canvasses whose themes, extracted from a Christian text, are now transformed into an opposite vision that has grown like weather from the Forest Reserve. He sees where the sunlight makes the wine of Cana sparkle with a redder paint than he remembers. He looks away, but every glance is cornered by a memory; for there, to the left of his glance, the shadows melt like evening over the massive tomb from which Lazarus is climbing back to life.

These themes are simple as the wine that moody preacher once miracled from water. Men do not marry in Forest Reserve; but wedding is their word for rejoice. Nothing can be more willing and ready to be told than the knowledge his childhood knows. How to rejoice! Lazarus is not so easy, but his legend is familiar; for the ears of Chiki's childhood, the ears which innocence has taken from him to bestow on Liza's head; these ears have heard in terror and in joy the multiple voices of the dead in a ceremony that has raged from midnight until dawn over the *tonelle*. Long, long before Chiki could read, when his eyes were like Gort's before the accidental darkness of any word on paper, his vision had seen Lazarus climb back to life, heard that dead voice grow miracles of sound in order to deny the power and permanence of the grave.

The third canvas is the nearest to his state of mind today. The sun cracks into splinters over its blue surface. The leaves are black where a crippled hand emerges from a body of miraculous strength to bury them underground. Chiki has no faith in the Christian promise, no need for humility, propitiation or dialogue with the other gods. But the weight of his paradox is greatest when he looks at his parable of the talents. Like today, when he is afraid! If something does not happen; if seed refuses for too long to stir and push its shoot with blossom from his hands; Chiki will roll from this bed and do what he has never told any man. Chiki will kneel and pray like a child imprisoned in its faith. As Liza bargains in her prayers, or Flo Unice on the price of sugar, Chiki will pray. He will beg his Christian angels to intercede, open the ear of heaven that is eternal in its hearing: those ears that are complete authority in their knowledge of his need. Chiki will beg them to answer the wish that his hands, like crutches which support a crippled man, may find their way forward . . . forward, forward to a fact in paint, a vision his instinct has not named, but which he feels is there.

Chiki will stoop on those knees, servile as women in the *tonelle*, and cry out his desire, confess his appetite to those absent ears. Then, like an actor making his asides audible since they are no less forgotten than what is said aloud, Chiki will repeat his fears to the gods he cannot call his own. Reduced to this servile stoop, natural and allowed as any slave's, the pride of his rebellion whispers: 'shame, shame,' it shouts in mockery at his weakness. 'The origin and end of all work is in your hands,' it argues. It charges him with coward and traitor to what his hands have already done.

For a moment Chiki will shiver at the thought that he is wrong. Knees are not the height to which he should reduce his size. He doubts his stature as an honest man. He sees himself a prisoner condemned for life and beyond the grave to this eternal paradox. But instinct triumphs; for Chiki knows his love for Gort. He knows his relation to the entire Reserve; and Chiki says that traitor is not true; traitor has never been his name. And when America brutalised his body, disfigured his face beyond the recognition of his nearest friends like Crim and Powell and Gort; he was not afraid. When his blood was pouring like the river of Jordan itself, making the night a scarlet slate that showed the blind, and growing and maddening increase of his punishment under the very hands he had baptised, Chiki was not afraid.

Now instinct takes him into its share of triumph, persuades him where he kneels that coward is not his name; and Chiki hears its voice, he hears this instinct like the mystery which Gort sees come and go as a season in the children's eyes. This instinct sanctions his faith; for Chiki believes, as Liza the taste of her liquorice, that the instinct is greater than any gift which has brought dumb landscape and dead paint to life. There was a time he used to think that he was free, until he saw himself imprisoned here, condemned like a slave for life and beyond the grave to the service of this instinct. Chiki believes it; and he will often turn belief into a fact that is at once as childish and as true.

When days are good, unlike today, and the canvas waits with promise, Chiki will grow nervous, like an emissary who has forgotten his army's message. The text of his message is right, but the order of his delivery seems wrong; therefore he dare not speak until his certainty has come back; for the result may be betrayal. Chiki will sit before the canvas and stare like a blind man at the absent sky. He will stand before the canvas, rubbing his hands like a thief. Nervous to touch that brush, afraid it may betray the message his instinct has not yet disclosed; and his hands will stretch, exactly like a thief's towards that little cubicle of oils, towards the wide, brass board where his brushes lay idle. Chiki's hand will close and crumple like a paper ball, until instinct takes it forward again; and like a man experienced in the act of public theft, regarding each object as though his thief's eyes said they were his own goods which these necessary hands must now recover without attracting public gaze; so Chiki will feel his hand like a hood over that brush.

Then the brushes begin a rivalry for first choice, each arguing with perfect logic that it is in his touch the text of the message starts. Chiki will be confused, buried in paradox, struggling to justify postponement until tomorrow; but the instinct reminds him how art and nature compose a war; it is dangerous to ignore this moment, fatal to embrace the other until his message fits the text. But the hand is there, wavering, now in withdrawal, now rigid with readiness, now lost in the paradox of what it sees and what it cannot touch. And as he turns in search of his reprieve, like the thief deciding to give up, telling the public eye that he will leave, Chiki's brush will rise like Lazarus from his grave, and turn the painter's hand into its cage. It cleaves like glue to his nervous skin, refuses to desert his hand, and while he argues for escape, some signature has been made. His fate is sealed. This moment now choses its own corner in eternity; and Chiki, like a man ordered to sign a truce, will now say, talking the way children do to animals and plants, Chiki will tell his brush: 'all right, it's up to you, in the name of Jesus and all the other saints, don't let me down. I go hold my own, give all I can remember, but it's up to you, don't let me down, 'cause it's up to you.'

Sometimes Chiki is on his feet when this happens; sometimes in prayer to eternities he cannot honestly call his own; and then that instinct which he calls, 'you,' giving it no other name but 'you,' that instinct will lift Chiki from his knees, in triumph and unashamed of what has happened. But pride remains and he will never tell it to anyone except, perhaps, the author who beats his life out on that tenor drum.

Chiki will tell Gort; for Gort grows larger every day, larger and more ominous than the warning which Chiki reads in his parable of the talents. Like the night America happened. Prostrate with pain that had ceased to stir his body; eyes blinded by those black fists which punished his skin as though it were a blacker crime, some ancient blasphemy that had to be removed, a sign which had obscured their promise of forgiveness; blind and dazed as Chiki was, his eyes now stopped with blood, he could still see beyond each hammering hatred on his skull, beyond the necessary insanity of that negro need, Chiki could see Gort's face and Gort's great hands. And around Gort's neck the gleaming steel of the tenor drum was telling Chiki before he died (for Chiki was sure his death was near), Gort's drum was telling him the connection between his energy and his desire and this need; and how these are the source and end of all man's doing, of all man's real doing: the springs of life which Gort cannot pronounce, yet which his instinct calls the world's creative will.

Gort frightens Chiki as he reads his own parable of the talents; for Chiki has always seen, with greater logic, seen this will as the only faith that can justify his life. Whereas to Gort, condemned by lack of learning to a deeper truth, there is no justify. There is no justify, for Gort is that great will itself. Neither heaven nor hell need justify the ground of will where Great Gort stands: the will that springs each day from his miraculous hands.

The evening was beginning to achieve its mischief. The Moon Glow bar was getting ready for its business. Once a month it happened: an American ship with naval recruits dropped anchor at Moon Bay. The sailors got a holiday of shore leave, two days, sometimes three, which wrought more change than a century of active history near this harbour. The sailors were young and hungry for the land. They arrived like starved bulls ploughing their horns through marble and gauze.

Experience of America had made Chiki very fond of these boys. Some were from the Southern states like Virginia where Chiki and Crim had worked on the farms. But they were innocent of custom in San Cristobal; for the idiocy which smeared complexions here, great as it was, had never been an absolute prejudice. Chiki had sat side by side with an ex-Governor's son in the San Cristobal college for boys. Democracy, as this experiment would be called, was not a goal to be achieved where colour was concerned. It was the natural background which happened during his formal learning. Until the incident which caused his expulsion, Chiki was a prefect with power to order that governor's son as he pleased; and while the laws of college were at work there was nothing the Governor's son could do. His privilege outside the school was no more than a toy when Chiki ordered him to remain an hour or two after the end of their day.

The Headmaster, like any of his staff, lived in awe, and under the shadow of the Governor's esteem. But the rules of the college were free from the violation of any law outside. If the Governor's son made the error of forgetting who he was while Chiki gave his orders, the end of that error would be inevitable, inevitable and no different from what would have happened to some anonymous farmer's son.

This was a paradox, but it was true. And it confused these young Americans who would arrive, arrogant and blind with a wholly irrelevant notion of their privilege. Their only privilege here was money, which no one cared to deny. But Chiki was a part of both worlds, loyal to his own, yet grateful to the state which had paid for the land in Forest Reserve. Gratitude was an instinct that was deep in the Boys from Forest Reserve; so Chiki often intervened to avoid a fight between the sailors and the local regulars at Moon Glow.

From his room Chiki could see a few faces round the arc of the bar; but he stayed inside because the fleet had not yet come to shore. The women were waiting. The air was split everywhere with noise: radiograms turned on full blast, and natural song. Moon Glow was one of the places where volume competitions between the radiograms occurred, and this was happening now. A great wail from those three throats, which wept with love, telling the same confession. The third radiogram at the end of the room was gaining favour with its boisterous cry:

> Sometimes I love you
> Sometimes I hate you
> But when I hate you
> It's 'cause I love you.

It was the latest hit, and had lasted nearly six months before the Moon Glow's taste got tired. A short, thick woman with fuzzy hair and copper ear-rings as large as wheels was singing the chorus of love and hate. Her lips were scarlet as the signals that flashed danger outside the Moon Glow. She wore a flat, crimson hat that took up no more space than a bandage plastered five inches in diameter over her skull. ' 'Cause I love you,' she sang as the man beside her drew nearer, trying to encourage her gifts.

'I like your sort o' flame,' he said, creeping his hand near to her skirt, 'I like it 'cause it burn me here.'

Now he soothed his genitals with his thumb. But his offer was premature since he was a local and the women knew the fleet were near at hand. It was this kind of refusal which had led to one of the wittiest and most decisive calypsoes in the history of carnival:

> An' when I catch them broken
> I go get it all for nothin'
> Yankees gone away,
> An' Sparrow take over now.

The whores hated this calypso; but its prophesy was certain as the gospel they had all forgotten.

'But why you don' leave me,' Belinda was saying as her rhythm broke on the sound of hate.

' 'Cause I like your sort o' flame,' the man reminded her.

Belinda now looked like a judge in doubt.

'You can buy me a chicken?' she asked, as though she knew the challenge that would drive him off.

The man had become intense, responsible, unwilling to postpone the flame which burnt him *there*.

'How you want it?' he asked, weighing coins in his pocket, 'fried, barbecued, or stewed?'

'I don't want no feathers on it,' she said with devastating finality. Every coin shook in his pockets; and he ordered the most expensive kind of chicken, as though he wasn't sure what had happened. Belinda was no less astonished.

'At least it go help me pick up my strength,' she said, and ran towards the bar.

She was deep in consultation with the waitress whom she had asked to change the records seven minutes after she had gone. Belinda would tell the man his time was up when she heard the new record warn with a calypso!

> Last train to San Fernando
> Last train to San Fernando
> An' if you miss this one
> You'll never catch another one
> Last train to San Fernando.

When Belinda returned to the table, it seemed that the man wanted to change his mind. A police corporal had arrived. He stood by the top of the stairs and looked for new faces among the sailors and the whores.

'Look it don't have much time,' Belinda said, as though the policeman now reminded her of prison.

The man concentrated his attention on the policeman, so that Belinda believed he was in trouble. It was a creed among the Moon Glow whores not to traffic with men who broke the law;

except, of course, they were related by *marriage* or frequent custom to the men.

'Is what you do that you watch the corporal man so?' she asked.

'Boy, you know what I wish him?' the man said, reconsidering the price of the chicken.

'Is what you wish him?' she asked.

'Not murder nor death,' the man said, feeling his anger get beyond control, 'nor nothin' to do with his family. I don't wish his children no harm.'

'Is what you wish him?' Belinda asked impatiently.

'I just wish him a shot o' diarrhœa,' the man said, as he pushed himself up from the table.

Belinda stared as though she had seen the chairs walk. For a moment she thought the man was mad; and she grew nervous since she had noticed the waitress going to change the record.

'Is what you mean you wish him diarrhœa?' she said. 'Is what make you wish him that?'

The man could barely explain his anger as he glowered at the corporal. He tried to tell Belinda the briefest outline of his meeting with the corporal that morning. He had parked his taxi at the corner of Saragasso Lane and Petticoat Row, and when he came back the corporal was waiting for him with a ticket.

'An' you know my friend,' the man said, following Belinda into the bedroom, 'all I tell him it was a shit what catch me sudden so and I had to go, that crab of a corporal still won't listen. That country buck what couldn't wear boots if it didn't have criminals in this republic.'

Belinda had softened, as though some need within her responded to the man's loathing of the corporal.

'I plead with him, my flame,' the man said, seeing a vision of the chicken diminish in price. 'I ask him, not in quarrel an' so, but like it was a Sunday school class, I ask him if he never had the kind a rush how it come emergent as I explain. I say, "partner, you know what I mean, man. Is common experience I tellin' you, partner." But the crab just stare at me like he never know shit in all his W.C. days; an' on the back of everything start to warn me that if I don't move quick he go report me twice, as if it was a double shit he threatenin' me with. That moon face crab what would stop wearin' boots the day criminals disappear from San Cristobal.'

He had hardly recovered from his inconvenience when he noticed that Belinda's attention had given way to the change of the record outside. Her face wasn't soft any more; and her eyes looked greedy and militant. She had heard his story; there was genuine sympathy written on every line of her brow; yet she had changed, swift as the gears in his car.

Without any comment at all, Belinda said simply: 'Come drop your garments.'

And as his fingers released the buttons, trembling with the same involuntary haste which had trapped him into ordering the chicken, Belinda scratched herself where it burnt, and waited like the corporal beside the car.

'Is why you don't undress?" he asked; for Belinda had made no move.

'What you mean undress?' she frowned, and her voice frightened him, 'it don't have time now for no steeplechase.'

He sat up on the bed, naked and angry, and thought in his impotence with both: 'whores and cops, not even God would fart on them two.'

But his anger changed again; and he was astonished as he watched the woman bend over him, washing his naked genitals with half a bottle of local gin. He sat still and docile as a child on its first communion morning.

'I don't want to charge you with sickness,' she said, 'but you never pass my way before, an' I can't take no chances 'cause those young American boys soon here.'

Belinda was massaging his penis like an athlete's hard, and muscled thigh. But there was no pause in her voice.

'An' strange as those American boys may be,' she continued, 'rich an' better off than me, I say to myself they hardly come out the egg-shell. An' believe me, I won't like when they get back home that mother or aunt or whoever waiting' to greet, believe me I won't like no parent to hear their poor kids gone rotten inside.'

Belinda poured another generous potion of the gin into her hand; tamed the rising pulse of the man's hungry flesh, and doused his testicles with her medicine. The man could hardly feel any longer as he heard her voice and watched her hands; for Belinda spoke and worked on his bath at the same time, at the same rate of speed, and with the same intensity.

'The corporal can play he don't know what shit is,' she said, bringing her ablutions to an end, 'but I got a little boy just gone twelve, and I know how a mother's bowels can feel when that sort o' calamity come down on her own child. What drop out your own, own belly stay with you all life long; and that feeling stay right with me when those little sailor boys what don't know no better come to make war on top my business. That mother feelin' remain.'

The man saw her turn away. He glanced at Belinda, then down to his genitals, like a child marvelling at a brand-new pair of boots. She was about to rest the gin bottle on the broken frame of mirror when a voice shouted from outside.

'Belinda! Belinda!'

She dropped the bottle in fright. The record hadn't stopped playing Last Train, and she couldn't understand what had happened.

'The fleet come, Belinda,' the voice called out, 'an' the one what call himself Chuck askin' for you.'

Every nerve was alert in her body, as Belinda scraped the broken glass under the bed, and frowned at the man. She didn't speak, but her hands were working like signals as she asked him to get dressed and go out a way they hadn't entered. The man was uncertain what to do, but he was deeply hurt by her denial, and he remembered the price of the chicken. Belinda tried not to speak, but her hands were talking her anxiety for anyone to see. The man had stooped for his trousers, but his movement came so reluctant that Belinda could tell he was going to make trouble; and now she really looked worried.

Not a word was spoken; but her hands were talking like a Boy Scouts' flag: 'hurry and go.' Up the hands went for: 'hurry'; then forward and away for: 'go.'

'But my money got the same smell,' the man said, as he trampled the trousers under his feet.

Belinda knew there was going to be trouble. She had nursed some private vision which was about to disappear. The man saw her turn, and turn again. She stood rigid, intense; trapped by her need and the danger in what she thought she had to do. Then the man's glance faltered; his eyes grew fire where he watched. Belinda had drawn a knife out of her bosom; swift and sure as the plunge of a snake, it was there; while the fingers of the other hand were snapping her signal: 'go, go, go.'

The man had hidden his nakedness before there was time to judge her intention. The belt came willing as water round his waist, and closed its catch above his navel.

'What 'bout my money for the chicken?' he said.

And the fingers were at work, snapping: 'go'; then snapped again with the clarity of language: 'till later.' But the knife was still there, trembling with purpose in her hand as she heard the calypso record warn:

> An' if you miss this one,
> You'll never catch another one,
> Last train . . . last train . . . last train. . . .

Head down, Belinda returned the knife inside her bosom, and followed him to the door through which her hand had ordered his departure. He was seething with hatred. His belt came undone. He stood on the stairs, helping its catch to close. As he turned to go, Belinda held him gently by his shoulder, her manner changed again as though her face was worked by switches. Then she spoke,

'It have plenty time,' she said, 'an' you can come back, but listen, listen good.'

The man was reluctant, but he waited. Belinda held his chin up like a child who had sulked because some wish had been denied.

'The same little boy I tell you 'bout,' she said, her voice grown mellow with truth, 'the one what drop out my own belly. You hear what happen to him?'

The man jerked his chin free, and listened.

'Well he just win scholarship for the big college what Chiki been to,' she said, her eyes bright with triumph, 'he win it, but he can't go if the parents not able to pay for the books. Is the books what bother me. I can't spoil his chance all 'cause o' the books. An' I go get them tonight. With the help o' Jesus an' all the spirits

I go get six years o' books from Chuck tonight. Is why you got to go, is only why.'

The man stood dumb. He wanted to say something, but words were not easy to come by as he looked at Belinda.

'I don't know what all the new freedom mean,' she said, ' 'cause they all crooks the political lot, all crooks, but I see how things start to change. An' I decide to back my little boy future. I go back it, like a horse to win I go back it.'

The man saw her turn inside, and the door closed. You could have strangled him with an infant's breath.

Alone, sweeping the broken glass under the bed, Belinda paused and looked up at the ceiling.

'Jesus, an' all the saints,' she cried, 'I loyal as any to my own kind. But you know, you know I didn't send him 'way for fun. You know my purpose is clean. It clean, clean.'

And she was ready for the night: this night which was her faith in the little boy's future.

The waitress had changed the records again. The radiograms came on like street lamps, one after the other, very low, hardly audible until the third radiogram was ready. Then the noise grew steadily as the needles bored their latest sermon into everyone's ears:

> Sometimes I love you
> Sometimes I hate you.

The waitress joined in the chorus as she emptied the beer into two glasses. She paid no attention to her hands, guiding the neck of the bottle into the sparkling white froth that topped the glass. Her eyes were wedding bells as she looked up at Gort and sang her heart's confession. She had married her voice to the metal splendour of sound which grew louder near the radiograms:

> But when I hate you
> It's 'cause I love you.

Gort lifted the bottles up from the glasses to remind her why she was there. Her stare pointed like knives into Gort's throat; then she glanced across the dance floor where the old Englishman sat at the corner table, waiting for Gort.

'If you want child to look after,' she said, baring her teeth at Gort, 'is why you don't leave your drum one night an' plug some pussy. Is only pussy go help you get what you want.'

Gort passed her the money and left quickly, forgetting his change. The glasses were tottering in his hands as he joined the old man at the table. Gort had retreated because something was urging him to slash one glass across her eyes. Aroused in this way, he was a man of violent temper; but he was always protected by a fear which paralysed his hands whenever he was about to strike. He believed that his blow would be fatal. Something always prophesied that Gort's fist, harmless as its strength may have been, would surely stop the life of the person who had aroused his anger. His greatest protection was also his greatest fear: that he might murder in his rage.

The old man fumbled with the glass up to his lips and coughed when the beer chilled his throat. He was still coughing, and the froth spilt down his shirt. Gort took the glass from his hands and rested it on the table; then lit two cigarettes, and stuck one into the old man's mouth. Behind the thick, black lenses that swung from cheekbone to his brow, the old man's open eyes could see nothing.

'Cheers,' said Gort, helping him with the glass again, 'you know what I wish for?'

'Go on, wish,' the old man said in his sharp parrot's voice that was alive with sound, 'wish whatever you like except . . .'

'Hold it,' said Gort, 'an' let me wish. From me an' my drum I drink to the day you can see your home.'

Every wrinkle in the old man's face had turned to smiles. He was delighted with what Gort had said; delighted and amused that Gort, in the excitement of wishing well, had forgotten that he was blind. It was common evidence of their bond; for Gort, too, was now laughing.

'Never can tell,' the old man said, and hiccoughed as his hand found the table, 'no man knows how the pendulum will swing. But I'm sure, Great Gort, I'm sure it will swing my way. If it takes a miracle I'm going to see the old country again.'

He laughed all through the sharp, parrot-like stabbing of his words; and the way he said 'old country' as the light changed colour over his black lenses: it made Gort think he was talking of the Forest Reserve. Gort kept nodding his head as though the old man could see; and Gort thought, but dare not utter his feelings: 'it is wrong, Jesus an' all the spirits, it is wrong for a man to die old and alone, far, far from his wish for home, alone and with nothing more to do until his end.' For Gort believed the old man would soon die; and recalled the days when he had seen him vigorous and robust as the stevedores who worked on Lemon harbour.

The old man was the first Englishman who was also the only qualified engineer in San Cristobal. After forty-three years and sixteen days, for he now spent his leisure counting time, the old man would still repeat the first words he had uttered on his arrival: 'Cor blimey, how these poor bastards still alive with a bridge like that!' He was referring to the enormous and expensive Magdala bridge which swung across the Magdala river, dividing San Cristobal in almost equal halves. Those were the same words which had made him idle, and brought his pension before he had ever dreamt of going back to the 'old country.' For twenty-five years he had argued with his superiors that it was plain suicide not to pull down the Magdala bridge.

'And you see,' the old man said, laughing in triumph as he shook Gort's hands, 'look what your new Government do. Like infants in the school, Great Gort, they now obey that young American who arrived last week. Magdala is coming down, Great Gort. And who among those young upstarts, Raymond and all those little upstarts, who among them know that it was me, Bobby Chalk, who start that war to pull the Magdala down? From the day I arrive, from that very day till the next which I don't want to remember, but Magdala is coming down.'

Gort watched the light changing colour over the old man's head. His hair was white and soft as wool where it slipped like a chicken's wet feathers from under his beret. His brow was wide and high, receding like a mountain into his black beret. The thin shafts of his blind spectacles seemed to stretch like telegraph wires out the deep valley of his ears, now burnt near black from his long sojourn in the sun.

'You know, Great Gort,' he said, passing him the cigarette end, as he slipped into the vernacular which had come natural to his tongue, 'you know it aint so bad what you may think. Blind aint so bad when I hear my old ears pick up what the newspaper say: Magdala coming down.'

His wrinkles opened again, wide as a mouth while he laughed and shook Gort's hands. And Gort, watching him as though the spectacles grew natural eyes, kept thinking how he was no different from Liza now. This was the way Liza would rejoice when her rivals got a beating. How glad that old, blind man was to hear that Magdala bridge was coming down!

'An' I always tell you too,' he said, as the wrinkles closed into more serious lines, 'I always tell you, whatever we do, the English aren't bad, Great Gort. I know. I born there. Peace an' order come natural to our spirit. But they let pride turn them foolish, Great Gort, they're fools. I watch them come out here year in year out, and I wonder how pride can turn good men, good men; can turn such good men into fools.'

Gort saw his hands shake, and he leaned again to the old man's aid; but the old man had learnt where to rest his glass. Now he was trying to touch the yellow carnation in his buttonhole. Gort said, taking deep pleasure in the old man's neatness: 'Sharp, Bobby, sharp. It look real sharp that carnation comin' up from your hole.'

The old man didn't seem to hear as he fumbled his thumb over the burning petal.

'Seein' how that yellow weed spring from your black coat,' said Gort stooping his head forward to sniff the carnation, 'I say you could grow a whole garden 'pon your stomach.'

But the old man had grown less cheerful, He said as though he hadn't heard Gort's praise: 'The sun.'

But Gort hadn't heard. The radiograms now seemed to play a kind of double noise of the same tune. He looked towards the dials and saw the waitress fiddling with the second of the three radiograms. The sound came double again, and as the waitress turned away, Gort remembered what was happening. The two radiograms were playing the same song:

Sometimes I love you
Sometimes I hate you
But when I hate you
It's 'cause I love you.

The old man was still cuddling the carnation between his fingers, his head turned down to the lapel of his coat, as though his eyes had suddenly begun to see. Gort collected the empty glasses and hurried across the floor to the bar for more beer. It was their custom to count turns. But Gort paid for the drinks until it was time for them to go. Then the old man would give Gort his share of the bill when they got into the street.

While Gort waited for the waitress to arrive, the old man was talking to the carnation. When the woman arrived, Gort turned to avoid her eyes, because murder had started to knock in his fist. He gave his order, and turned his back to the bar, watching the old man; and Gort felt, holy and right as the judgement of God, why his murder would have been justified. Blindness like the season in the children's eyes was his bond to such men; but with this old man it was even greater. The blindness had long given way to the feel and sound of the old man's body. For Gort loved old Bobby Chalk. Old Bobby and little Liza were twin seeds, plants, or whatever you like, of any delight which Gort could remember in the Forest Reserve or here in the Moon Glow bar.

Gort would often wonder what happened to old Bobby Chalk at night when he left him at the door. Did his boots drop off all on their own? Would the buttons come undone without teasing his hands? How did Bobby's old head find the pillow? Gort's questions were only a way of telling his wishes which he dare not utter after they had laughed aloud: 'Good night, an' till the old Magdala pull down.' That was their bedtime noise each night they returned together from the Moon Glow bar to Bobby Chalk's house.

For Gort had never been inside the old man's house; and the old man had never invited Gort. But 'invite' is not the word to apply to old Bobby Chalk and Great Gort. It is the wrong word to use for their reservations at that moment of departure. Gort had always felt that his offer might have made old Bobby feel like a cripple if he had gone one step further. Gort felt this very deeply, and he could never bring himself to ask if it were true; just as he could never bring himself to ask Chiki about the mystery of the sugar. Gort would shake the old man's hand as they stood at the open door; then hurry off as though his absence was the surest evidence that he did not think his old friend was a cripple.

And Bobby had never ventured to ask Gort in. Sometimes the offer would stick out like his tongue; and suddenly he would postpone till another night. For the old man could never bring himself to risk that offer; since he believed that Gort might think this blindness was the only accident which could have allowed him into the intimacy of that house. As gardens were a natural joy to Bobby Chalk, so he believed that this suspicion would come natural to any man whose childhood had been what he called, colonial. Time and again Bobby would pause, as their hands fell away; and friendship ordered him to ask Great Gort if that were true. But the door had closed too soon. He dare not risk his need.

The waitress was shouting at Gort to take the beer away; for the noise was loud, and the radiograms had begun again to confuse Gort's hearing. The double sound had now turned treble as the three wet and absent voices cried in unison:

> Sometimes I love you
> Sometimes I hate you
> But when I hate you
> It's 'cause, it's 'cause, it's 'cause . . .

Gort took the beer but he didn't move; for he was startled when he saw the old man, his head still turned towards the carnation, and his lips moving quickly, and in anger. He was talking to himself. Then everything seemed natural; for Gort had suddenly remembered that this was an old habit of his own. Sometimes Liza, in mockery and love for Gort, would go down on her knees and crawl around the yard, whispering to herself: 'Not me an' sugar, O, not me, not me an' sugar, O not me.'

'Come wish me something now,' Gort said, as he passed the old man's glass. 'An' wish me good. Don't wish me no Magdala. Wish me good.'

But the old man hadn't looked up. He was still talking to the carnation, caressed under his hand: 'Sun, it's the sun, that bloody sun.'

'Bobby, I talking to you, man.'

'It's the sun, that bloody sun.'

'Bobby Magdala Chalk,' Gort cried out, 'I talking to you, man.'

'It's the sun,' said the old man, and raised his head as though he needed to see where Gort had gone.

Gort touched the old man's hand to remind him that the beer was there; but the old man didn't let his hand fall from its caress around the petal.

'Is the sun make it flame like that,' said Gort, 'you couldn't look so sharp if it didn't have no sun.'

Then the old man dropped his hand, as though in anger.

'Oh no, Great Gort,' he said, pushing the glass out of his way, 'it aint no sun.'

And Gort laughed like a happy clown; continued laughing until he noticed that the old man was grave and cautious as a judge.

'It aint no sun,' the old man said again.

'How you mean it aint no sun?'

' 'Cause I know.'

'Then what it is?'

'You like my rose?' the old man asked, not conscious of the change in name.

'A thousands times,' said Gort, 'a thousands times I tell you how it sharp, man. It come sharp, good, good sharp.'

'You see it there?' the old man said, hugging the petals again.

'How you mean if I see it there?' said Gort.

'You say it is the sun?'

'What else hell have to make it flame like that?'

'And you see it there?'

'Where else you think I see it, man?' Gort asked, now puzzled by the thickness which filled each line across the old man's brow. His skin looked heavy as tar.

'There's more than what you see there,' the old man said, leaning towards the sound which told him Gort's place in the opposite chair. 'I keep my frigidaire full of them. I keep a stock of what you see right here.'

'What? What you talking 'bout Magdala?'

'All colours,' the old man said, 'every colour my ears hear the servant call. I get her collect from that garden and stock them in the frigidaire. Full, full, Gort, I keep the frigidaire full of these roses.'

The radiograms charged their sound into Gort's ears; but he didn't hear the song. He was terrified of the look on the old man's face, sad, demented and cold, like the skin of a new corpse. Gort pushed his hand up and down his jaw as though he wanted to un-string the sound of the radiograms from his ears. He watched the old man's face, staring its blindness across the table.

'Why you have to keep them there?' Gort asked, as Liza might have done.

"The sun, it's the sun,' the old man screamed, 'can't trust the florist nor the sun. But it's the sun. The sun.'

His voice grew louder than the radiograms, and the waitress was about to laugh when she saw the look of panic on Gort's face.

'The sun? the sun?' Gort kept saying like a prisoner who had been tortured into confessing a word which had no meaning save its noise.

'You see, Great Gort,' the old man said, his voice much calmer now, 'it's the sun. You agree it's the sun.'

Gort shook his head as he saw the change in the old man's face grow slowly to its completion. The lines opened like a mouth across his brow, and the old man's laugh was like the sky, loud and crazy in its blue loneliness: his laugh and his voice sharing the dubious ecstasy of the radiograms:

> Sometimes I love you
> Sometimes I hate you.

And it was the old man in his original faith again; it was old Bobby Chalk saying that the Magdala had to come down. It was Gort's friend, gentle and cheerful and content, as though his blind-ness were a light that showed the 'old country' sailing like a ship into his arms. And Gort was on the verge of tears; Gort was crying into his sleeve.

'Perhaps he aint go die,' Gort cried, 'but he goin' mad. Good God, old Magdala goin' mad. Christ an' all the spirits, my own Bobby Magdala goin' mad, mad, mad . . .'

And the radiograms conquered Gort's weeping with those three voices, unanimous in their cry:

> Sometimes I love you
> Sometimes I hate you
> But when, but when, when, when . . .

The radiograms were loud, but no one could follow this paradox of love and hate; for the song had been suddenly swept out of hearing beyond the balustrade and into the street below. The music was drowned by a great torrent of sound which rose from the American voices. The naval recruits had arrived in a stampede of rejoicing, like cattle going home. They crowded round the bar, shouting a thousand different orders; their faces young and bright with hurry. The orders followed, strident, charged with a fearful urgency; and yet confused.

The waitress could not distinguish between the accent of voices, or the different needs which they were telling. The bottles bounced and rang with broken glass in her hands; the glasses changed places, danced from hand to hand, and disappeared before she could remember who had ordered what. Old man Magdala was now laughing. The blind spectacles jittered on his nose; his wrinkles opened wide across his brow; his hands looked greedy as they enslaved the glass, draining the dregs of froth down his throat. He wanted to hear the radiograms announce the cause of love and hate again; for he was happy, forgetful now of roses and the frigidaire as the naval voices rejoiced with youth in his nostalgic ears.

'Great Gort,' he shouted, feeling the excitement of those voices influence his own. 'You there, Great Gort? You hearing me, Great Gort?'

'I hear Magdala,' Gort said, 'You know well as the world I not moving till you ready.'

'Ready?' the old man said, delight increased with every syllable of praise in his voice. 'What nonsense you can talk sometimes, Great Gort. Ready? With a carnival like that?'

'They coming too abundant,' said Gort, feeling the push of the sailors behind his chair, 'soon they goin' send me an' you playing in the street.'

'I wish they could hear the tenor drum,' the old man said, feeling for Gort's hand, 'I'd like to see those young lads dancing to the tenor drum.'

'They don' understand my music,' Gort said, indifferent to the old man's suggestion that he should play. For Gort realised that this was what the old man had in mind.

'Don't understand?' the old man said, 'I tell you more than once, Great Gort, sometimes you talk such nonsense.'

'They dance different in their country,' Gort said, trying to sound his voice above the noise.

'Nonsense, Great Gort, I tell you a million times,' the old man said, 'sometimes you talk such nonsense.'

'Ask them,' said Gort, 'they'll tell you same thing. My music different.'

The old man was laughing, as Gort might have done when the children were gathered round, talking about things they didn't understand. And the old man's voice came strong and much clearer than Gort's whenever he raised it above the noise.

'If that was true,' the old man said, 'there'd be no Escapade in Blue, no Royal Navy Number Two, no Jordan Water, and no Name Like the Virgin Mary. There would be none of these if what you say was true.'

Gort turned his glance from the loop of Christmas bulbs which showed the price of hard-boiled eggs. And Gort was getting nervous, for he thought the old man was going off his head again; for Escapade in Blue, Royal Navy Number Two, Jordan Water, and Name like the Virgin Mary were the names of the Steel Drum bands. They were also the names which the Boys would use when the police raided the Forest Reserve. They were a secret code of messages which helped them to talk without disclosing evidence when the police asked their questions. Old Bobby Chalk was probably the only foreigner who knew these codes; for their bond of friendship was so deep that it refused any secret of this kind between old Magdala and Great Gort. Chiki had always hoped that the old man's knowledge would not get back to Powell, for Gort would have been in serious trouble. The madness of freedom which clouded Powell's mind was great enough to make him strangle Great Gort for such treachery. But no one knew but Chiki, old Magdala and Great Gort.

'I say you talk such nonsense sometimes,' the old man said. 'Those youthful legs, fresh up from their young, strong, American grass, and you come to tell me they won't understand your drum.'

'I don't see what they have to do with the Boys in Forest Reserve,' Gort said, relieved that the old man was not going off his head again.

'But you yourself relate the story,' the old man said, 'and I hear Crim and Chiki tell it more than once how you pay for the land in the Reserve.'

Gort smiled in sympathy; for it was not madness, he thought, but a lack of memory which had misled the old man. Gort collected their glasses, wondering how he could penetrate the crowd on his way to the bar.

'It wasn't that lot what give the money,' said Gort, and turned to go. 'Was not the white folks from the place with a name like the Virgin Mary. And don't let Powell ever hear you whisper that.'

'Hold it, Great Gort, hold it,' the old man said, seizing Gort's hand, 'what lot give the money?'

'Was the black folks from the place with the name like the Virgin Mary,' said Gort.

And the old man was laughing. Then his face changed, and he was serious, and sorry in the closing wrinkles of his brow; but not mad. It was the face which Gort had often seen when the old man talked about his work, and why the Magdala had to come down.

'Black folks my foot,' the old man said, 'white folks my blind eye. Listen to me, Great Gort, you listen. The human spine is the human spine. You understand spine, Great Gort? You know where is the spine? Well I'm telling you what I know. Your drum doesn't traffic in skin. It talks to the spine, the human spine. And that white spine in the Southern States has the same law as black. It's the same spine in my old country with the generation I don't know. Listen to me, Great Gort!'

Now the wrinkles were almost absent from his brow. Gort rested the glasses on the table, and watched the old man's mouth: the energy of movement in his lips, and the incredible strength of his voice. He was talking like a man condemned to death, a man who knows there is one chance which now remains to save his life; and the chance resides in what he has to say.

'Believe me when I say, Great Gort,' the old man said, and paused for a moment. 'Night after day I give God praise it is my eyes He took, and not my ears. However strong, no eye can see further than here or there; but ears, Great Gort, your ears can walk with the world however far. The ear doesn't know what distance is. It has no use for time. It only hears. So listen to me, you listen!'

The old man felt for the glass to take a sip, but it was empty. Gort was about to get more beer, but the old man had seized his arm.

'The drink can wait,' he said, and the wrinkles started to open again. 'Listen, listen, Great Gort, listen. I'm only giving some example, but the facts are the same. Take the men who rule China, or the men who rule India or the men who rule Africa. Miles and miles of distance separate them from our little home right here, I mean San Cristobal, but when each says what he intends to do, I hear. Sometimes he speaks today and I hear tomorrow or the next day. Sometimes I hear while he is even talking, because that box which brings me news is faster than any ship or plane. My ears don't understand distance of river or sea, mountain or sky. It only hears, Great Gort, like when I listen to your drum. And that's what I mean. Hearing is the law of the ear, and dancing is the ears of every human spine. That's so, Great Gort, that's so. Sometimes the ear doesn't follow very well and the spine is slow. But when the habit forms and the ear is hearing loud, you'll see what the spine can make a man's legs do. I'm telling you, Great Gort. It's tragic what happens in that place with a name like the Virgin Mary; but when the ears of the spine tune in, black legs and white legs forget their colour, and move, alike and equal in the craziness which catches those spines. And it's the same in the "old country" with the generation I don't know. Same spine, and the music in that Southern State talks the same message to the youth of my country I don't know. Night after day I hear them parading in that little box what brings the world into my ears. Germany, France everywhere in that old Europe you never been to, Great Gort, the young spines hear and the legs understand that same message from the place with a name like the Virgin Mary.'

The old man's voice was still clear and strong; and if his eyes were whole, he would have seen that he was right; for Gort, his ears vigilant as spies over the old man's words, was beating his fingers over the table as though it were his drum.

'Like how the Coca Cola makes Liza mad,' the old man said, 'tasting like honey on all the children's tongues. That music from the southern state, fresh as young farm grass, yet old as the sun, that music can forget all distance, move faster than sea and wind to command the young spines here and all over the world. And it's the same rhythm Great Gort, it's the same rhythm that rides all over your drum.'

But Gort didn't speak. He wanted to say something, but his silence came like a hand round his throat. It was like the night, only in reverse this time, the night Powell had explained about Little Boy Charlie and the champagne.

In such moments Gort found it difficult to look at the old man's face. Whenever the old man talked this way (for it wasn't often that talk of colour came up), two things would happen to Gort. First, the old man's name would change in Gort's memory from Bobby Chalk to Old Magdala; and Gort would catch himself christening the old man afresh, the way the Boys often changed their names in Forest Reserve. The second thing which happened to Gort was even stranger. Looking at old Magdala as he spoke, Gort would get the feeling that it was he who had caused the old man's blindness. Gort knew this wasn't true; yet he would have to look away, as he was doing now, his vacant stare abruptly turned on the loop of Christmas bulbs which showed the price of hard-boiled eggs.

'I go get some more beer,' said Gort, collecting the glasses as he rose.

'Hold it, Great Gort,' the old man said, 'hold it.'

Gort was a little unsure what would happen next; for the old man was pushing himself up from the chair. He stood full length, flagging his hand in search of Gort's.

'What happen, Magdala, you not ready to leave?' Gort asked.

And the wrinkles were shouting across the old man's brow.

'Sometimes you talk such nonsense, Great Gort,' he said, and the hand still flagged its signals for Gort's aid.

'Where you goin', Magdala?'

'Right over there,' the old man said, pointing towards the bar. 'I'm changing the table for a stool, right there where the youth making that noise.'

'But it too thick, Magdala,' Gort said, not sure what he ought to do.

'Come on, Great Gort,' the old man insisted. 'You go take me right over there, Great Gort, or else I call one of those naval boys. And you know, Great Gort, that will never do. Couldn't be the same either way.'

So Gort rose, leaving the glasses behind, and scrambled with old Magdala through the crowd and the settled rhythm of the voices which were giving way to the chorus of the three radiograms again:

> Sometimes I hate you
> But when I hate you
> It's 'cause I love you,
> It's 'cause I love you, I love . . . I love you.

The sailors moved back to make way for the old man; and it was clear from the look on their faces that their readiness had sprung from a double surprise. The old man's gaiety came as a shock when they noticed that he was blind. But his blindness was even less astonishing than the bond of hands which warned them what existed between Old Magdala and Great Gort. In less time than it took the waitress to pour a drink, Gort and the old man were seated on two stools, leaning like sailors over the bar. But their drink was slow in coming; for it seemed the waitress had forgotten where she was or what she ought to do. The sailor's boisterous orders had confused her; then Gort's concern for old Magdala as he sat him on the stool: confusion grew and spread like a fever in her head. But these were simple accidents compared to the disorder which had come full circle over her senses. Her hands trembled as she reached for the bottles, but her eyes were elsewhere. She was staring towards the top of the stairs as though her sight had deceived her. Fola had arrived.

The waitress had forgotten the old man and Gort. She left the bar without a word and hurried towards the stairs. Gort asked old Magdala to stop talking and wait a while until he was sure his eyes were seeing right. He saw the waitress, solicitous as a beggar, stand before Fola, blocking her way. But the waitress soon shifted to one side, as though the girl had insisted on her right to enter.

Remote and calm as the sky, Fola had said: 'I'll have a Coca Cola until he comes.'

'Till who come?' waitress asked, forgetful of her previous meetings with Fola.

'Mr Chiki,' said Fola, 'when he comes, I'd like you tell him I'm here.'

Fola pointed towards the corner where no one ever sat since it was too far away from the radiograms. The waitress looked round, like a policeman inspecting the bar, then scratched the palm of her hand for luck. She walked ahead of Fola towards the table, leading her gently by one hand as though she were blind. They looked exactly like Old Magdala and Great Gort, until Fola sat, fingered a lock of hair from her brow, and turned those amber jewels of fire that seemed to see every face before her eyes.

She recognised Gort from the visit she had made with Charlot to the *tonelle*. Gort turned once to see where she sat, but he didn't look again. For Gort was now consumed with argument. He and Old Magdala were talking like a radio that told bad news, news like invasion or destruction by flood. It had happened shortly after the waitress poured their drinks. The old man looked angry and determined as he waved a dollar note in front of Gort's face; and Gort grew sad, confused and sad as he regretted their change of place from the table to the bar.

Fola noticed the old man's anger. She saw the thick, black lenses and suddenly thought of an ancient, crippled hand, and the rat, and the half blind eyes that were a permanent memory of her childhood. She wondered whether the old man was blind; but she didn't think it likely, for he talked like a man who saw, emphasising his hurt as he waved the dollar note before Gort's face. The waitress was arriving with the Coca Cola.

'Is the old man blind?' Fola asked.

Glass and saucer were still making a rattle in the woman's hands. She set a paper napkin in Fola's hand, as Therese might have done; then spread a cloth over the table, talking as she judged her notions of the style to which Fola was accustomed.

'But he's old,' Fola said, 'why can't the other man let him have his way?'

'I not meddle in their business,' the waitress said, 'let them quarrel. They can even fight for all I care, 'cause when they get together again, not heaven nor hell can part them.'

The quarrel seemed to grow more violent between Magdala and Great Gort. The sailors at the bar had stopped drinking, curious and greedy for conviction that the friendship they had seen really concealed a flaw somewhere. Fola lifted the glass to her mouth, eyes glanced above its rim towards the bar. And suddenly the world was still, perplexed and still with the sight of horror. Fola gasped aloud. The glass fell from her hands, and all eyes were turned towards the noise of broken glass and the waste of Coca Cola swimming across the table and on to the floor.

'My God,' Fola cried, avoiding the sight of the bar.

'What happen, lady?'

'There, there,' Fola said, but she didn't look up.

The waitress turned to look at Old Magdala and Great Gort, but nothing had gone wrong. She looked again, and everything seemed the same until she saw the face which she had known so well; the face which had become so perfect and hallowed in her own memory. It was Chiki.

'Is Chiki,' the waitress said and understood what everyone had learnt to forget.

For no one would ever say; no one, it seemed, had ever had the nerve or need to mention in their talk about the Reserve this obvious and astonishing fact: Chiki was unjustly ugly.

Now his eyes sparkled with rage as he watched Magdala and Great Gort. He bit at his broken lips, and felt his ears grow numb with Old Magdala's words. He watched Gort leaning his head away, speechless and defeated as he tried to explain what Old Magdala should have understood.

'Forget it, Gort, forget it,' the old man said.

'But Magdala, man,' Gort begged, turning his head again in hope. 'I didn't mean it that way.'

'Forget it,' the old man said, 'forget it. There's a time and season for everything.'

'But Magdala, what wrong, Magdala?' Gort cried. 'What I was doing is what we always do. You know that, Magdala.'

'I say forget it,' the old man said, blunt and decisive as his hands clapped his meaning on the bar. 'We come into this world with a mother, Gort, but we don't leave with one. And so it goes with friends. We collect as we go along, but we must prepare to leave them behind.'

'But Magdala, man, Magdala,' Gort cried, hopeless to find the words that might have helped.

'I blind it's true,' the old man said, 'but money not foreign to my hand.'

Chiki stood like a tree shaking with ruin in the wind, impotent in every limb, a blind and tortured look of vacancy spread everywhere across his face. Then his eyes flashed across the room as though he had seen evil in every face, expending noise and valuable paper notes for a day. His body was ready to burst with hatred, like the time he spat on Hippolite's grave; Hippolite who was his friend and superior with paint.

He saw Fola, remembered who she was; and his hatred had now obscured the novelty of her presence in the Moon Glow bar. Glancing from Fola back to Old Magdala and Great Gort, Chiki seemed to feel the same cancer eating through his eyes. He had no time to reflect on the reasons that might have brought Fola here; for she grew with hatred in his head, like old Magdala's words. And hatred seemed to increase at the thought that Magdala could be forgiven, for he was old, and almost mad. But not her, not her, Chiki thought, not her and the curse which had produced her servile and benighted gang. 'Not her,' his lips were saying when the waitress touched him on his shoulder.

'Excuse me Chiki,' she said, nervous, almost terrified by the look in Chiki's eyes, 'is you the lady come to see.'

'What?' Chiki raved as though he hadn't heard.

'The lady there,' the waitress said, 'is you she come to see.'

And that word, lady, coming when it did, that word was like a noise, a signal which every country in its different way could recognise as the moment for its entry into war. Chiki had forgotten Old Magdala and Great Gort.

'Ladies first,' he said, 'if never before, it will be now. Ladies first.'

He was on his way.

Fola watched his head emerge from under the bar. He was naked to the waist, pink sore with marks where the bed had bruised his back. His nipples were ripe as a girl's; little sprigs of hair showed where his navel disappeared like a hole in his stomach. When he shook his head, two beads of water rolled out of his enormous eyes. His fingers were pygmy stubs of flesh exploring the great width of his nose.

Fola dared not turn her eyes away; for he had seen her. Chiki was watching while her eye noticed, in the gradual turn of his head, that he had lost an ear. A fly was climbing up the grooves of his shoulder; and soon got stuck in the fingerprint of wet paint behind his neck.

Chiki was cold, calm, subdued, all agression gone underground. He walked towards the table; a firm, deliberate step, as though he had to leave all evidence of his presence on the floor. He offered his hand in an elaborate gesture of welcome, not really holding hers, but feeling in her touch the weight and texture of his own intentions. His touch gave Fola a shock, and she saw that he had noticed the nervous clapping of her eyelids. Fola was unprepared; completely lost for a word which might have helped her through that wall of resentment in his eyes.

For Chiki could not control that look. Old man Magdala and Great Gort resided in every vein now swelling under his eyes. Fola had forgotten why she was there. She waited, speechless, and forgetful of her purpose, like the evening she was about to leave the maternity room. She had that feeling again as she watched Chiki: a new acre of awareness had grown inside her thinking. In the room of mothers dispossessed, the word, bastard, was born. Now a similar seed had been sown in the Moon Glow bar. She thought of Chiki's ugliness and her own bastard origin. And the two seemed equal halves of the same exposure. That's what she was thinking as she watched him stoop like an angry volcano over the chair.

'What does the lady want?' Chiki asked, and turned his head towards the puddle of Coca Cola that drained, slow and deliberate, across the table and on to the floor.

And Fola, embarrassed by his power, yet loyal to the purpose of her visit, heard her voice break free with words: 'I'm looking for my father.'

Now she had spoken, Fola seemed to lose all confidence. She had simply hoped to meet Chiki, talk with him as strangers might have done; recall her visit to the *tonelle*, disclosing all that had happened since; and then, confident of his sympathy, express the need which her words had now, in haste and fear, betrayed.

'Does he come here?' Chiki asked, and Fola knew that he didn't understand.

For Chiki never shifted his glance. He was tracing his finger over the table, which now reflected a company of clowns mocking their own portraits in the Coca Cola water. He was trying to achieve a likeness of Piggott in the puddle of water; hoping to postpone her attention until the image of Piggott was there.

'What did you say?' Chiki asked, as his finger-nail outlined what might have been a brow, made wide and fierce under the hood of a policeman's helmet. He was reducing Piggott to the rank of private.

'Looking for your father?' Chiki said.

A long and heavy silence followed: the silence of a man who is about to discover an answer for himself and all the world. Chiki didn't lift his head because the image of Piggott would not hold in the slipping line of water. His anger was growing beyond control. Hatred was coming out from underground, as he abandoned the portrait of the clown in water. He crushed a leaf of tobacco in his hands, and leaned his head back, scooping the flakes of tobacco into his mouth. To those who knew Chiki, this was always the ultimate signal for a war. He had to chew something. He chewed as he studied the image of a face turn dry over the table. And Fola watched his lips sag and splutter, like strips of leather hanging from his gums. She could see the saliva foam black with bubbles under his tongue.

Each glance seemed to discover a new deformity in his face. Fola knew it was wrong to stare; but it was fear, fear and the hopeless feeling that she had lost the chance of being his friend. She was near to losing her control. In a moment of innocence, in order to prove her sympathy, Fola wanted to tell him that he wasn't really ugly. But she had restrained herself, noticing again the lacerated roots of flesh from which his ear had fallen.

Now Fola felt a sudden stir of guilt at the thought that he was not her father. But she could go no further; for Chiki had deprived her of any fantasy which she might have decided to invent. She had forgotten her own method of discovery when she was most in need of surprising the man who had already judged her need, her presence in the Moon Glow; who had already judged her whole future. She was confronted only by what she saw and the thoughts which arose with each recognition of Chiki's ugliness. In the disfigured landscape of this man's face, she had seen her own bastard origin and the room where the women waited. But Fola wasn't hearing the numbers which were the women's names; or the numbers which measured their pregnancy. Fola was hearing her own words. As she watched Chiki, her phrase, *and other than* was reaching to extend its meaning. The phrase *and other than* had conquered fresh territory; and the territory was Chiki's ugliness. Like the birth of the word, bastard, in her mind; *ugliness* had acquired a conception that was divine. That man whose hatred she could almost touch was no longer the painter, Chiki. It was Chiki beyond any summit Fola could attain. He became Chiki, *beyond and other than*.

Chiki's silence was like a punishment; for it was Fola who had come to speak. Chiki was within his right while he waited. Fola wanted to speak. Like the night she said good-bye to Charlot, she needed to speak. Then old Magdala came to her rescue; but this rescue was even worse than denial. The old man was leaving the bar.

'It seems they've settled their quarrel,' said Fola, 'the old man is going.'

And Chiki looked suddenly relieved, until he turned and saw

that Old Magdala and Great Gort were not together. Gort remained on the stool, shaking his head, while one of the Americans helped the old man towards the stairs.

It was beyond belief: Old Magdala leaving the Moon Glow bar without Great Gort. Hell and all its devils grew poison in Chiki's eyes. He looked at Fola as though he would slit her throat.

'What happened?' Fola asked. 'I don't know what happened.'

Chiki was slow to speak. His hands made rats' noise against the table. But his body was steady. Hatred had gone underground once more, lurking to replenish its fury. His voice was calm: the calm which warns that madness is about to show its hand. He might have been talking to Liza now, his manner was so gentle, so gentle with spite for Fola.

'I'll tell you what they were quarrelling about,' Chiki said, glancing from Fola to the bar and back, 'I'll tell you.'

In the pause that followed, Fola ventured to say: 'I hope it's something they can make up.'

'I'll tell you,' said Chiki, chewing the tobacco like a hungry ox, 'the old man is blind. You've got that? The old man is blind. Old Magdala, that's the old man's name, and Great Gort, they are like that.'

Fola watched his fingers lock and tremble before her face.

'Not playing at being friends,' Chiki went on, 'you've got that? Old Magdala and Great Gort are simply Old Magdala and Great Gort. You've got that? They come here every day. Gort buys and pays for their drinks, and when they leave, Old Magdala pays back Great Gort. You've got that.'

Fola felt stupid as she nodded her head each time the question came; then Chiki turned his head away as though he had to avoid her face; for hatred was coming up from underground. His glance was devouring his hands which repeated the rats' noise against the table.

'But what you will understand,' said Chiki, his head still turned away, 'what you can understand about what happened just now between Magdala and Great Gort, I can't. I can't ever understand. Whatever madness caused it, I can't understand, for it's the first time Old Magdala ever thought of paying his own bill at the bar. He can't see. Yet when Gort said, "what happen, Magdala, hold on till we get home," Old Magdala behaved like he was mad, told Gort he had lost his eyes but money was never foreign to his hand. Is what he told Gort: "Cripple or blind, each man should still be able to pass money himself for what he takes, to pass it with his own hand." Old Magdala and Great Gort.'

The rats' noise grew like thunder on the table.

'Old Magdala and Great Gort,' Chiki said again, raising his head to stare at Fola. 'That Magdala should refuse to let Great Gort take him home 'cause Gort won't let him fumble to pay his own bill at the bar!'

Fola needed to avoid his glance, but she dare not turn her head away.

'But I don't, I don't,' she stammered.

'You don't know Magdala and Great Gort,' Chiki shouted at her, 'but you can understand why Magdala should be mad enough to want, even need to break the rule that is old as his friendship with Great Gort. You can understand that, you and your tribe. But I can't, I can't.'

The sailors were aware of Chiki's voice, and turned to hear what happened. Fola rubbed her heels together, and tried to make distance with her body between the table and the chair. The waitress was coming towards them. She stood beside the table, then stooped to ask what happened, when Chiki's voice hounded her away.

'You get to hell from here,' he yelled.

Fola knocked her knees against the table. She wanted to leave, but Chiki had turned the Moon Glow into her prison. Someone had switched off the radiogram to hear what had happened; and all eyes turned on those two: Chiki and Fola like man and woman at the jealous point of murder.

'You're looking for your father, you say?' Chiki said, and kicked the table from between them. 'I'll show you your father.'

Fola thought he had gone mad. Her mouth made a noise like funeral bells when her teeth knocked and slid away. Chiki rose from the chair, pushing himself up as though his strength would soon fail him. For a moment Fola thought of him as an old man. He held her hand and pointed to a door which showed on to the street. The crowd closed in on them, anxious to avoid a fight. They were sure Chiki would strike her. One of the sailors had thought to intervene when the whore Belinda crossed his path and warned him that he wouldn't leave alive.

Chiki stood in the door and watched the sun burn black on the distant hands that worked in the harbour. Fola followed him out to the balcony where small wooden statues of the saints were tinselled in robes of silver paper. There were Chiki's pets, the dolls of adoration, as he called them. He was staring towards the white wooden church in the middle of the town. There was something instinctive and habitual about the look of recognition in his eyes. He knew this town in every mood and weather: the uncomplicated landscape of cobbled streets where his hand now guided Fola's glance as though she were an idiot and half-blind. His hand moved towards the forest receding in a dark, green altitude of leaves beyond the harbour. Then Chiki's hand circled the wooden statues of the saints, and rested where it pointed at the sea. Fola watched the sea, still as grass in the windless afternoon. The labourers were moving about like mad automata, lifting huge crates of logs and fruit from the street. Their heads were crowned with cargo like a ship.

'There, there,' said Chiki, his voice grown soft and dull from exhaustion, 'there's your father. Look there by the ship, there's your father, and it's the end of everything. Everything, everything done, finish and done like with those men down there. They've found their father too.'

Fola glanced from the church to the wooden statue of the Saints, and thought that Chiki was talking about God. She thought she had detected some religious nostalgia in the mad directions of his hands sweeping across the landscape.

Ignorant of his meaning, and still confused, Fola asked: 'Is it God you mean?'

And her ears were shocked when Chiki answered.

'Yes, yes, you're right,' said Chiki, 'God is their father, is their money, is the reason Old Magdala leaves without Great Gort. You're right. God is their father, is their money, their money and their father.'

Chiki belched and spat over the balustrade into the street.

221

'And that benighted lot down there,' he said, slapping his hands near the wooden statues of the saints, 'that lot labouring like cattle. They're no different, no blasted f——g different from the lot who rob them o' their labour. I tell you no different, I know them. No different. I have no need to prop them up with virtues they don't have. I have no need to call them angels because they starve. They're the same as the swine who rob them. Their intentions are the same, and their lies are the same. Because it's money, money, money which father them both. It's God, yes, the God what is their father and their money.'

And Fola suddenly thought of Charlot. She thought of Piggott and her mother too. But it was Charlot who arrived like the echo of Chiki's words. What Charlot by implication had tried, time and again, to say, was loud as day on Chiki's tongue. Fola was steadier now; but different worlds were at war in her head. It reminded her of the rivalries which she had had to harmonise when she and Veronica met on this same floor. Her confidence was gradually coming back; but she spoke as though she were at college, and the argument had taken place between herself and Charlot.

'But they have to live,' said Fola, glancing from Chiki to the harbour, 'they have to eat.'

'That's always their excuse,' said Chiki, 'whenever you describe the hell they choose to occupy, they retreat like dumb cattle with the same excuse. Silent until Piggott slaughters them.'

'But it's true,' said Fola, almost afraid that she had lost her chance of ever getting to know the man whose eyes looked bayonets towards the harbour.

'Isn't it true,' she asked again, trying to let him know there was no challenge of argument in what she had said. 'Isn't it really true that they have to eat?'

And then Chiki's face had suddenly turned gentle. For Gort had pushed through the crowd and come to stand beside him. Gort held Chiki's hand and shared his view of the harbour, as though he had forgotten that Fola was there. And Fola watched the change come slowly to fruition in Chiki's face as though he had found his rescue. Now he looked much older and not so strong in the impact of his presence when he stood beside the other man. But she saw a light,

sharp and steady as the sun, sparkle his eyes, and the wounded
dimples deepened into his cheeks. The radiograms had started to
grind with their misery again:

> 'Sometimes I love you
> Sometimes I hate you
> But when I hate you
> It's 'cause I love you.

There was neither love nor hatred in Chiki's eyes as Fola watched
his face. It still retained its sadness and the look of impotent anger,
but his smile had softened the lines that ran like scars round his
mouth. Fola could tell by the sudden lustre of his smile that something of the earlier gravity had changed, and a little of the hatred
too. And as she glanced at Gort, resting her glance where their hands
still met, Fola started to wish herself in Gort's place. She would have
liked to be standing there; for Chiki's smile, like the secrets of her
own private fantasy, had become a kind of agreement between
their lives. Like the evening she left the hospital on her way to this
same bar, Fola felt that she had discovered a partner in some
unknown adventure. Nothing more was said until Chiki took his
hand away and looked at Gort.

'It says somewhere, Great Gort,' he said, 'man born of a woman
has to die. That's all it says. But if he must spend every day of all his
years collecting food and gathering wood for fire, he's not a man.
Find some other name for the beast you see there breaking his back
with timber. 'Cause food is a dog's excuse.'

But Gort didn't answer anything. He leaned over the balustrade,
searching the street, as though he hoped to see old man Magdala
coming back.

'But he is a man,' said Chiki, like the children repeating their
certainty for Gort's approval. 'We know they're men, Great Gort,
you and me know those beasts there can still be men, can prove what
you tenor drum won't ever argue 'bout: that they're men, Great
Gort, whatever happens they're still men.'

They walked away and left Fola standing in the balcony. Gort
looked back twice before they had reached the bar; but Chiki
never did. Fola waited until they had taken their places at the bar.

Then she went back to the table. She had never experienced such a feeling of rejection in all her life. The waitress came up to comfort her, but Fola was adamant about her wish to be alone. She ordered a second bottle of Coca Cola and studied the heads of the men who leaned towards the bar.

The waitress was astonished. She knew, as Gort and Chiki did, that there was only one decision left for Fola to make. She should have gone; and they were sure that any moment now her departure would take place. It was the sole thought in Chiki's head as he sipped a glass of local gin. But there was one force which no one in the Moon Glow had bargained for. Those who knew Fola were not acquainted with Fola *and other than*. In a way, it was Charlot who had now come to Fola's aid; for her visit to the *tonelle* had done one thing that was permanent in its effect on Fola's thinking. It had altered her whole relation to what she understood as error. She was afraid of Chiki; but she knew that Chiki was *in error*; and she knew that he was not aware of his error when he spoke to the woman who had made this day her special adventure for contact with the painter from Forest Reserve. It was Fola's certainty of Chiki's error which kept her in her chair. It was the last and only straw which now grew strong as an anchor in her hand; and she was determined not to let go. Fola would not let go.

Chiki never looked over his shoulder to see whether she had gone. From time to time Gort would whisper in his ear: 'she's still there, is like a mystery, Chick, the way she still stay there.' Chiki didn't look; but this was the beginning of his doubt. He played with the glass between his hands, drained its emptiness down his throat. But Chiki would not look. He saw Belinda and her sailor boy embrace and disappear into the passageway. The radiograms were grinding sadly to a close while the waitress tripped her fingers round the Coca Cola bottle. She was returning to the table, fresh paper napkins under her arm; but something had changed in her thinking, for she thought of Fola now as a woman. With each stride the waitress could feel how one word gave way to another. To her brief way of thinking, a woman had been born inside the lady since Fola had stayed. Like a whore who knew her wares, the lady in her remained. In spite of Chiki, the lady had remained. Only a won⸱ 1. could have stayed

'There you are,' the waitress said, arranging the napkins on the table, 'my own warrior blood run through your veins.'

Fola didn't answer. Her face was pale; but there was confidence in her eyes. She was searching her handbag for a slip of paper. She pulled her diary out from under Raymond's scarf which she always carried like a token of good luck. She tore a page from the little gilt-edged book and asked the waitress to remain a while. She had come to see Chiki, and only his decision could frustrate her plans.

In a large and legible hand Fola wrote: 'That you of all men should deny a woman the right to make her *own backward* glance!'

Fola watched the waitress stride across the floor. She listened to the radiograms, unsafe and insecure, scraping their melancholy rhythm to a close. But she did not look up from her glass to see what would happen at the bar.

As Gort looked at the lines, he could recognise that they were not Chiki's hand; but he read the same mystery that comes and goes like a season in the children's eyes. And Chiki bowed his head, reading; and read again and felt like a man who had made his first arrival somewhere; yet recognised a welcome given in his own voice; in his voice and with his own words. The pride of rebellion told him: stay; it mocked the weakness that was about to give way. He parried and wavered like a man betrayed; but instinct had conquered his knees again.

For the second time Chiki was on his way.

CHAPTER IX

Today the Moon Glow is quiet as the church not far away. The sailors have left, taking their custom out to sea. The radiograms have gone to sleep. The bar harbours flies and the idle voices of Belinda and the waitress. They sit in a mood of vacancy and prayer, waiting for the impossible to happen. The fleet will not return for months; their harvest is remote.

In such moments, as the darkness gathers, instinct will lead them back to the gospel rhythms of their childhood. The paradox of love and hate is wholly forgotten. They sit, watching the early clouds of night collect around the wooden church in the centre of the town; and together they sing like the radiograms, wholly ignorant of their unison or the text of their message.

And as they sing, the waitress and Belinda are taken forward to the ordinary details which fill a woman's day; the secret domesticities which the future will not let them see. The waitress tries to anticipate, forget and anticipate the dirt which labour has piled thick and high over every stitch of her husband's underwear. She sings as though the washing board is already under her hands; the lather gets black and solid as mud. But soap and the instinct of her hands will conquer a universe of dirt, provided it is her husband's dirt. She loves that man who is her life; yet neither love nor the labour which cleanses his workday uniform reminds her why she sings.

She sings as her grandmother used to sing while the old efficient hands were scrubbing an infant's excrement away. Filth falls, melting like stars over the wet, wringed clouds of diapers that remind the waitress of a time her memory cannot capture. Yet she sings; for the seed of the dead grandmother's will is still alive, alive and active in her own voice. The chorus of her chapel days is now nearer than the night that waits outside. She pauses for a while; hears Belinda's voice gain favour through the quiet of the room. Then she starts again in harmony like the radiograms, her eyes grown bright with promise, religion come natural as her loyalty to the man she loves. The voices rise and fall, mellow and sure as the hour they celebrate:

> Work! For the night is coming
> When man's work is done.

Now Belinda's voice emerges louder, more rapid, as though the future has suddenly quickened her rhythm. She has no husband but a boy not long gone twelve. His future is her journey too. She cannot read the freedom which has brought this change of ambition for her son. But it is there, menaced by the familiar lies of her own trade, perhaps; yet it is there, like the change of flag and anthem for San Cristobal. And nothing can reverse her need to back her only husband's future. She will back him like a horse whose triumph she cannot predict, yet whose capacity for speed she knows. She knows the stride her little boy has made; for he has done it without aid. Alone, without advantages like those who go to college as if it were their home. Her only husband just twelve years gone! Her only horse has triumphed with his stride over a foreign track, a world of custom that is so near and yet so far from all his childhood has bestowed.

Belinda knows that he will lose the common tongue in which they used to talk at night about tomorrow. Paradox enters her thought again; for she is troubled by the thought how a mother is about to saddle her own son, encourage the journey from which he will never return to the love which started in her womb's embrace. Her boy will never be the same again; and yet she sings, hears her own tongue startle the night with a future that is bound to be her loss. Her boy is on his way, forward and for ever gone; and yet she sings; farewell. And farewell seems to spring more willing, much louder and more willing in the chorus of her chapel days:

> Work! For the night is coming
> When man's work is done.

The voice of the waitress has found its volume; she gears it to a harmony with Belinda's cry; and the voices confirm a fact which grows more certain as they look from the bar towards the distant harbour that has turned dark. It is the hour which tells the truth of their son:

> Work! For the night is coming
> When man's work is done.'

As their thoughts of work and night combine, they think of Chiki. The waitress stops her singing, glances in query at Belinda, then hurries from the bar to switch on the lights. But Belinda does not relieve her voice. She thinks of Chiki too; for it is Chiki who reminds her of the future that awaits her boy. It is the same future which Chiki entered at much the same age as her little boy; but Chiki is strange, mad and strange, as the radiograms which bring

227

a live real voice from a universe of miles away; brings it unchanged to conquer the taste of their ears; until, with time, that song of love and hate has ripened like a cry from infancy in their years. They sing that paradox of love and hate as though it had been heard from the moment of its birth on Gort's tenor drum.

So Chiki and the radiograms come side by side in Belinda's mind; for Chiki has known, known and forgotten, it would seem, the future which is waiting for her little boy. She remembers the morning like her name, that morning Chiki walks out from Forest Reserve with a bag of books like a harness on his little back. Crim and Gort are there, laughing and clapping as though little Chiki is a horse which they have asked to back. She can remember Powell's face, and Powell's eyes as he stands with Gort and Crim, watching the saddle of books on Chiki's back. Everyone is gay that day, loud with farewell and praise as though Chiki is going away, going to America or the moon.

The college for boys is not so far away, and yet his friends from Forest Reserve come out to sing their luck, to sing farewell as little Chiki and his books begin to sail away into a different world, a different style of life. But Powell is still, watchful and still as the Forest when the police arrive. For Powell and Chiki are like fingers on one hand, together in everything they do. Belinda can remember that morning, and the moment Powell half-turns to see his friend; the moment Powell half-opens his mouth to speak to the saddle of books on little Chiki's back. For Powell won't look into Chiki's eyes; and not from jealousy or shame that he is left behind.

As Belinda recalls that day, she can remember Powell's pride, the pride and certainty of his words. She can hear Powell's voice ordering the silence of the crowd as he begins to speak with Chiki; not speak, but order and command, like a man who knows his horse from the earliest stages of its training, a trainer who now takes this chance to remind his future champion of its prize. So Powell's voice, with tears of joy streaming down his proud, black cheeks, Powell says: 'Now listen, Chick, don't think I can't talk to you no more, 'cause you still live here, is still Forest Reserve you got to call your home. So listen, Chick, you listen what I got to say. Is this Chick: no nonsense from today. From today all nonsense done, 'cause it aint you alone what goin' up, is all the Boys what have no scholarship, Chick. We can't al' go up there, but we with you, Chick, like those big books what on your back. Remember all the Boys waitin' to hear. Every question those powerful big folks put, Chick, you got to answer for yourself an' all the Boys back home, 'cause the Forest still here, an' is your home, even if you go stray, is still your home. An' the Forest waitin' to see you prove, prove an' prove again what the Forest can do. So no nonsense Chick. You do what Pow· would do if he get that chance. No nonsense Chick, is work you got to start work. From today, is only work.'

Belinda can still hear Powell's voice like a chorus to her chapel hymn. She wonders about that future which Chiki has learnt and swallowed like a pill. Belinda sees the waitress return; her eyes rest on the shaft of light which enters through the passageway, and she wonders what Chiki is doing now in his room where the voices are not even as loud as the whisper of the leaves. What is Chiki doing? Chiki and that lady who comes every day to talk with the painter from Forest Reserve? What are they doing? What are they talking? Those two, woman and man, only different in age, but alike in the way they treat that future which they have swallowed like a pill; swallowed, and, it seems, forgotten like the result of every pill. Belinda cannot measure this future which awaits her only husband just twelve years gone; yet she sings, for nothing is clear but the fact which the chorus of her chapel days now tells:

> 'Work! For the night is coming
> When man's work is done.'

Chiki's room is full of expensive aroma, but he pays no attention to the girl who walks like a miracle of promise. Fola begins to talk; then stops, interrupts her thought to see what progress her cooking has made. For Fola has promised Chiki a decent meal. It is days since she has made comments on his leanness, the careless hunger in his eyes; days since she has tried to bribe him with some charity.

Chiki has relented. It is his birthday, but Fola dare not ask how old. To keep her promise is enough! So from her federal wages she has purchased this extravagant meal. But her cooking is unsure; for she has never had to do this chore while Therese was there. Chiki helps. From time to time he stops his brush, inhales the turkey's roasted smell, and warns that the fire is too high. A moment later he says it is too low; but he doesn't stir from the canvas which grows a face he has never seen before.

He thinks of Fola as he glances from his work to be reminded of his parable of the talents. The crippled hand looks weaker in this light; but its body grows more massive with the coming of the dark. He cannot see the blackness of the leaves which seem to slip like water from his canvas. Chiki is pleased with the subtlety of movement which takes those leaves into their open grave. Fingers stir the earth away, and lower to the right the leaves are falling out of sight. But above the massive head that cannot see behind its burial, the paint shines bright. An incredible harvest of yellow paint sprouts like a field of corn. The blades are green as grass where they plunge like a river over the edge as though the canvas were not large enough. The little pods of corn hang fat with grains like the surface of a honeycomb. Again that subtlety of movement shows the yellow stalks shaking like hay under the wind.

'Movement,' he whispers to himself in triumph, 'movement is my greatest gift.' He can make the surface of a canvas crawl like any crab, or gallop with tons of colour like a horse. Movement and the blend of violent colours are his technical assurance. Natural as the forest leaves they come to life under his eyes. He hears Fola move about the odours which now thicken through the room. He makes one desperate stroke with his brush as though he had forgotten an item which is organic and inevitable to the face he paints. Then Chiki stops. He rests his brush on the brass-covered board where palette and paint accumulate a fearful mess. He rubs his hands, takes another glance at that face, then leans his body on the bed.

Like the emissary who has got the text of his message right, Chiki now pauses as he hugs his knees and looks towards the ceiling. But he is not afraid. Today his hands have strangled any waste which they encounter. He experiences something different in his body, now prostrate on the bed. It is a feeling like regret, or shame; but more like shame. For Fola seems to drive him back to his misgivings as a man. It is not the painter who now occupies his thought. It is the

230

man whose private history paint can never be a substitute for. For that's how Chiki has grown to see his life. It is the same and separate from his work.

When Camillon stops him on the street to ask about his paintings: that's what Chiki will tell him. A man is related to his work like fingers to a hand. He has always thought Camillon a fraud, the worst kind of fraud; for Camillon's lie, the lie that is Camillon's whole life, goes deeper than the evil power which money makes. Camillon is a doctor because his height does not allow him to be a lawyer. Law is nearer to his heart, but he thinks the court would require a greater altitude of gestures when he meets his match in argument. Chiki has always marvelled at the tiny accidents that can determine the future of a life, even the history of a place. Give Camillon six inches more in height, and he will be a lawyer; and Chiki wonders what would have happened then. Would the prisons become more crowded? Would the rate of infant mortality go down? He doesn't know; but he thinks of Camillon as he recalls the episode which Fola has described, and Camillon's poisonous attitude to life has forced Chiki to pay attention to his own infirmities.

Chiki is not without grave faults. Aunt Jane is sick. They fear the huge carbuncle to be a malignant sign of a disease which dams its victims in everyone's eyes. Yet Chiki has not gone to see his grandmother who may never leave the hospital bed. It is not fear; it is not shame which keeps him away. It is something which he thinks very near to Camillon's way of life. It is some kind of amnesia which has walled the old woman out of his mind. He forgets Aunt Jane as though her sickness were an old and forgotten death. Gort goes, and so do Crim and Powell; but Chiki stays where he is as though she were alive and well in the Reserve. And there is neither shame nor regret in his absence. He simply doesn't go; for Aunt Jane in her illness, in her dying absence, has been forgotten. This is a grave fault with Chiki: the need which makes him think first, and sometimes only of himself. This massive attention to himself and his own needs is sometimes painful to observe; painful because it contradicts his love for Gort which no power beyond the grave can question or deny.

His weakness has caused great hurt. Like the time Hippolite was buried. Hippolite, his dearest friend, his master in the art of paint. At the height of his power, when paint is making greater magic every day, Hippolite killed himself. Chiki can discover no reason for his friend's deliberate dying. Obsessed with the meaning of Hippolite's work, Chiki asks no questions, finds no excuse for an act that seems betrayal of all that work. 'To hell with what Hippolite has done with paint,' he shouts as he spits on his grave and turns away. Hippolite's wife is crying because she understands. But Chiki will not let her speak. Like the evening he came so near to losing the woman which Fola's talk has confirmed to be alive. And Hippolite's wife cries and cries, not only for her loss, but for the lack of sympathy which seems impossible in one so large and loyal as Chiki is to Hippolite. 'It wasn't his light,' Chiki still shouts whenever she tries to speak, 'Hippolite's brush could use the light which Hippolite was. But it wasn't his light. No man should put out the light he didn't give himself. To hell with the work he's done, I say, he had no right.' Now it is useless to regret what he had done. But Hippolite's wife has explained how much her man has suffered. Hippolite was dying of cancer.

Now prostrate on the bed, Aunt Jane and Hippolite come to mind. And Chiki reflects on the lack of interest he has taken in his brother who also has been dead some time. Yet when he was alive, that brother, much older than Chiki, provided for his needs at the college. Chiki doesn't really know his brother. He thinks of his college days; and wonders whether his ingratitude started there. Sometimes Aunt Jane has tried to give fragments of his brother's life; for Chiki was small when his brother went away. But his brother is dead; and it seems no different from the years when he was alive and generous in what he gave to help Chiki through his college days. His brother's death is like a date in foreign history which he has had to learn.

'And so it would have been again,' he says, as he hears Fola stir not far away. He is thinking with gratitude of the accident of luck which has brought her to his knowledge. But it's not the result of Chiki's doing. Today she might have been alive, yet dead to his concern. For Chiki's prejudice is like a wall when it has taken final shape. There is no way the damned like Fola was that afternoon, no

232

way without a miracle for them to enter into Chiki's heart. And hearing Fola rattle about with forks and spoons not far away, he sees his prejudice as his greatest loss. He recalls the second day she came. He can hear her voice again. It is the voice of innocence, solicitous and clean. It harbours no reservation in her appeal.

'I want you to help me,' Fola says, believing that she has earned the right to surrender secrets that can bring about her fall from the respect of the world of privilege she has known; secrets that may start great mockery in the world which she has now dared to meet in the painter from the Forest Reserve. 'I want you to help me find my father.'

'I can help you search,' says Chiki, twisting his thumbs as his advice takes shape, 'but I can't promise to help you find.'

'Where should I look?' she asks.

'Everywhere,' Chiki says, and glances at the canvas which exhibits his parable of the talents.

'But I have so little to go on,' Fola explains, as the painting offers its distraction. It is the canvas which celebrates the wedding at Cana. She watches it and waits in hope for Chiki's answer. But he is slow to speak, as though he has to choose new methods of deception.

'But whom should I ask?' she says.

'Everyone,' Chiki replies, and rests his hideous stubs of fingers on the table.

'But I have so little to go on,' says Fola, 'I've never seen him.'

'You know nothing at all?' he asks, and his urge to enter this adventure seems greater than her need to find.

'Then,' he says and pauses as he sees an empty canvas wait with promise, 'then we must invent.'

And Fola is stalled, at once embraced and equally estranged by his use of that word we. She is completely in his power as she ponders that light which comes into his eyes. She notices that his ugliness has disappeared.

Next day she is surprised when Therese calls her aside; whispers their secret with the confidence and gravity of private knowledge that only happens in a war, or after a relative's shameful disappearance from the land. Therese whispers Chiki's message; and Fola accepts the invitation which brings her to his little cave each day.

When the federal office closes, she telephones her mother; asks to remind Piggott that nothing has gone wrong; then tells Therese a time for supper. And Fola goes to the Moon Glow home which is Chiki's name for any place where a man has found and where he does his work. She nibbles at sandwiches which Chiki has refused; and while she talks, argues and talks as though the painter were Charlot, Chiki is in a fury with his brush. Chiki invents a face which Fola does not know, a face which he himself has never seen before. But Chiki does not know; neither Chiki nor Fola knows that the republic will never be the same after that face has made its first appearance for the public gaze.

Fola was radiant when she announced that their meal was ready. Chiki didn't move from the portrait which stared at him; but he was watching Fola. He saw her and tried to guess what she was thinking as she cleared the paints away and got the table ready. This was an enterprise in which Fola had become an extension of himself. They had met for a meal in his home. The occasion was solemn and contradictory at once. He inhaled the roasted smell of their meal again, and thought of the way some people lived each day, and the occasion was like some ruined memory in an old man's heart. This was the way Bobby Chalk might have felt as the fire roasted the winter evenings of his childhood.

Fola now looked like any wife, nervous in her frenzy of preparing food. Chiki recalled his college days, and watched her as though her face were a clock which ticked that time. Her face could now tell what his own cunning silence had concealed. Chiki watched her as though he wanted to find out, as though he had to see for himself the smallest reaction which their meal evoked in Fola. And his affection for Fola grew with each glance that caught something he ought to know. His glance was slow, deceptive, leaking from the corner of his eye until it had become part of the casual lift of his head towards Fola. This was an old gesture which told that Chiki was about to speak. But Fola had got in first.

'I wonder what Charlot would have done if he were teaching then,' she said, guiding a dish on the table.

'What could he do?' Chiki said, 'what's more I don't think your Charlot much different from the man who came to speak that day.'

Fola had a sudden twinge of regret as she heard him refer to Charlot as 'your Charlot.' She hadn't lost her affection for Charlot, but she thought the association in Chiki's mind was out of place. Yet she said nothing that would betray her feeling. She thought she understood why he had said 'your Charlot' as she tried to recall the words which the speaker had uttered, wholly ignorant of the effect they would have had on one boy.

'I suppose they had to kick me out,' said Chiki, 'with a Governor I wouldn't have got off, so what could I expect, considering it was a PRIME MINISTER.'

'Which Government did he lead?' Fola asked, searching her knowledge of history.

'I don't remember,' Chiki said, 'but he came out for his health, otherwise we wouldn't have seen him. Prime Ministers don't have time to waste on colonies which have served their purpose.'

'Yet you say San Cristobal still served some purpose when he was here,' she said, trying to test Chiki's logic.

'Of course, it did,' said Chiki, 'that's why I got mad.'

Chiki's body was now erect. He had forgotten the portrait as he sorted out his argument that followed the British Prime Minister's words. He looked down at Fola who now sat in the chair.

'I was so mad when the Bands went to the pier,' said Chiki, 'imagine Powell and Crim asking me to paint a message on the posters which they waved. . . .'

Chiki paused to look at the portrait as though he had recalled the day he had signed his own death warrant. For he had refused to paint the words which were to tell the island's gratitude for the Prime Minister's visit. It was Gort who suggested that he should give way, Gort and the irony he had suddenly noticed in the words which Powell had chosen. For the flags which waved the Prime Minister goodbye had said: 'THANKS FOR YOUR VISIT, SIR. HONOUR TO OUR KING BUT ALL HONOUR AND GREATER THANKS TO HIS TRADE UNIONS.' Chiki had painted the words in spite of what had happened. For it was that visit which caused his expulsion from the San Cristobal college for boys.

He could still see Sir Spencer Marlborough's great jowl like a shoulder of pork strung round his neck. He could still hear the eloquence of the great man's voice. It was more than a decade before San Cristobal became self-governing; but the Prime Minister must have known that it was bound to happen. Looking at those loyal faces assembled in the huge college hall, Sir Spencer had finished his speech with this reminder:

'It is not for me to say . . . what changes the future will bring. But the time will come . . . the time . . . in a way that time is already here considering the, the, the changes that have happened in this island . . . the time will come, I'm sure, when you will be called upon . . . to make decisions on your own . . . and it is right! . . . My life's work has been in the service of that right . . . it is right! . . . that a time should come when you must choose alone.'

Here Sir Spencer paused and glowered at the window where the sun was bursting like a furnace from the east, his voice now careful and repetitive as a code which the whole college should understand. Then he continued, returning the half-full glass of water to the table.

'You will be free to choose,' he said, 'and no one, no one I repeat, neither my country nor any other under that sun . . . no one should interfere in your decisions. But however you choose . . . and that I repeat is your right, however you choose I ask you to remember, remember . . . and I'm sure you will remember . . . the country which it is my honour and privilege to lead, and whose great history, from the beginning of this very island, is a fact for everyone to see . . . I am sure you will always remember that great country without whose guidance and whose great example . . . this very college where we now forgather . . . might not have been today . . . might not, perhaps, have ever happened . . . I ask you nothing more but to remember . . . in your choosing, remember!' No one was clear what happened then; but the stupendous applause had come abruptly to an end. The Headmaster's face was scarlet as blood, and the Prime Minister was smiling, half in apology and half in surprise, while a porter dragged Chiki from the hall. He was still using foul language when they heard his voice from the college yard.

Fola now thought of Charlot and the *tonelle* as she watched Chiki's hands conduct his argument that day. It seemed he had forgotten their meal. His brush was conducting the rhythms of his argument that day. From time to time he would glance at the portrait, then his free hand would snap and close into a fist with a solitary finger pointing erect. This finger ruled like a flag over the discovery of an insult he had detected in the Prime Minister's wish.

'And from that day,' said Chiki, coming towards the table, 'I made my way back to the Reserve, not only to live, but to be where I belong.'

Fola watched him throw the brush aside as he drew up a chair.

'I don't suppose he understood it that way,' said Fola, thinking of Charlot and their visit to the *tonelle*.

'Of course not,' said Chiki, 'he understood the very opposite. He was bestowing an honour on our memory. Like how athletes remember a record, and in the same moment think it was only possible because of some special trainer. That's what he was thinking. He was thinking that we would all go to our graves proud, damned proud to say and repeat for all the world to hear that his great country had taught San Cristobal how to choose. That's what he was saying. Take away the past when his great country ruled San Cristobal, and there'd be no republic, no college. We all would have been still in the bush. That's what he was thinking.'

Chiki was laughing; but Fola was already thinking beyond this moment. She was thinking of the parallel which Charlot, in spite of his age, became in the Prime Minister's words. She had grown tense until she realised that Chiki was determined to be gay. He was laughing like a child, hysterical and for no reason she could guess.

'When I was in America,' Chiki said, trying to restrain his laugh, 'a white cracker who paid our wages used to say whenever I arrive, you know what he used to tell me?'

Chiki had to stop again, because his laughter was beyond control. Fola had relaxed, urging him to hurry up and talk.

'He used to say,' said Chiki, 'looking me straight in the face, he used to say: "Chiki, it says somewhere how man come from the monkey, but whenever I see you I feel sure he gradually going back." Is what he used to say every week, how I remind him that man might still go back to the monkey.'

Fola had become austere. She wanted to rebuke Chiki for laughing; for she felt an impossible hatred towards the man who had thought of Chiki as a monkey. But Chiki was irrepressible. He was still laughing, until he suddenly wiped his eyes and looked at Fola.

'And I'll tell you something,' he said, pointing that same finger at Fola, 'that monkey talk isn't as bad as what the Prime Minister and your Charlot feel. Sir Spencer really believes nothing would have happened without him. And Charlot took you to the *tonelle* to remind you where you started, and to remind himself how far he has brought you. It is there, at that point, Charlot and the Prime Minister, however different in class or age, it is there the two meet like fist in glove.'

Suddenly Chiki rose from the chair as though he had just remembered his portrait. He reached for his brush again, stood before the canvas, and parried with his fingers in the air. Watching his eyes as they measured every detail of the portrait, Fola was sure he had forgotten about Charlot and the Prime Minister. His concentration was intense, but he made no further mark on the canvas.

'No good,' he said, 'this won't do.'

'You won't throw it away,' Fola said rising from the table.

'No, no, but a plain line drawing will be better,' he said, and came back to the table.

Chiki was ready to eat. Fola didn't speak; for there was no point in Chiki's argument that did not fit like brick in the shape of her own thinking. Chiki was ready to eat. Instinctively, Fola had returned to her chores like a wife drawn back to the domesticities of her life, a woman in her man-made role. Chiki didn't move. He sat still, his head bowed. But he felt an incredible wave of gratitude for her presence in this room. He had forgotten to notice her movements, for the atmosphere seemed a kind of perfection in which the simplest and most elemental functions were about to be performed.

And in that moment Chiki was startled by a wish he dare not utter. He wanted a home; that is, a room like this with his work to hand, a wife and children. Chiki wanted to possess the whole paraphernalia of what he had now come to think the most beautiful tribe man had made: the family. He wanted a family in that ordered sense; but suddenly he was struggling to change his wish because he

238

anti intellect

for the self satisfactio o make himself satissfied a rational for why he should (be worshipped (charlot) by her bc he brought her so far, felt it was not true. It was only the role which the occasion had made so real. But he couldn't keep his eyes off Fola as he paid homage with his attention to the need which had brought her here. Chiki continued to stare, a look of hurt surprise in his eyes, for he was sure that he had seen in Fola, seen with the terror and delight that was locked, incommunicably locked in the tomb of his private self; Chiki had seen the agile and unkillable spark of his own wilting spirit. And for no reason his mind could reach, the thought occurred to him: 'we are both going to die.'

The room was quiet, an interval of expectation which, it seemed, had suddenly summoned afresh the odours of Fola's cooking. He was afraid to speak, but his appetite was not ashamed to show its strength. It was howling within him for something to do. Fola made a signal to start. Chiki became athletic, precise, even a little apprehensive. Fola left again and soon returned, carrying an enormous turkey that looked like a headless human body massaged with oils. There was a new look in Chiki's eyes. An aspect of severity and caution now strained his face. The lines sharpened; his chin had come alive, pleated and quivering as he waited.

Fola passed rapidly to and fro, arranging knives and forks, spoons and plates, all of which she had got Therese to bring in secret from her kitchen. Chiki watched the cutlery like the implements of a battle which was about to begin. Fola was busy as a Boy Scout. Chiki looked at the turkey as though it were a wounded protagonist whose future he was going to decide. He paid no attention to the minor cast, necessary but unobtrusive in their appointed places: boiled rice, potatoes and red beans. The table had become an overcrowded stage. Fola picked up the carving knife while Chiki waited for the slabs of meat to fall away from the stuffed skeleton of this roasted bird.

Now the turkey looked alive, the amputated legs trussed with thick string, the large hole at one end leaking a green stuffing which had swollen the hollow of its stomach. The wings were pierced with wire. Crisp, and wet, they looked like sweating stubs of arms. There was an aspect of captivity and crucifixion in the turkey's posture. Fola coaxed the knife through the succulent white breast of the bird, and Chiki felt something strange happen inside him: something atavistic and compelling. A certain carnivorous delight was spreading over his face. His eyes had lost their moisture. Dry and fierce, they seemed to stare through an aura of quiet frenzy. And Fola had noticed, for she thought as she sawed the wings away: 'what marvellous control he has. He is a gentleman!' For only a gentleman could have censored the act of murder which Chiki's hunger was demanding. But his calm was magnificent. His hands rested innocently on the table: the disciplined stillness of his mouth, the total authority of manner which seemed to close like a lid over his passion.

And Chiki was wondering how it would be possible to record in paint that current of feeling which his stomach generated as he watched Fola's hands. His appetite was a naked fury, striving to assert itself. Chiki imagined his fingers like claws mauling the delicate white meat, his hands dripping with the brown juices that crashed against the dish. Then, in a backward glance to some forgotten time, he got a vision of himself and other men hacking the hides from enormous animals whose names they didn't know, animals which had burnt black over the midnight fires, roasting to a palatable toughness while he and the men were sweating happily with the rage of a whole week's hunger. He could feel his teeth grinding through an incredible and lasting depth of meat.

They started to eat. Chiki chewed with great care, pausing from time to time to listen to Fola's anecdotes about her college days. Sometimes he would interrupt to smile at her, a slow, grateful acknowledgement of what she had done. She could feel how he listened as though she were a pupil again, and he were a teacher curious to hear what had happened to his own creation. All concentration was situated in his ears as he heard her speak. Sometimes his memory would seize upon the slightest turn of phrase that was familiar. He would pause in his eating to consider what she had said about her attitude to history; then he would turn his gaze up to the ceiling like an actor cribbing his lines; for Fola's mind was sometimes more rapid, made more alert by its nearness to the things it analysed. Chiki would keep his gaze on the ceiling, and his eyes were eloquent with praise, as though they were asking heaven to hear what Fola had said.

Then his eyes, melancholy with some nostalgia he couldn't name, would swing towards Fola. Already he was trying to suggest her future.

'You have a real gift,' he said, resting his knife in order to conduct that rhythm of words with his hand.

'Gift?' Fola exclaimed, laughing at herself, 'for what?'

'I think you're a born teacher,' he said.

And Fola shuddered at the thought. But Chiki was adamant; for he was struck by the unity of thought and feeling in what she said. When she tried to emphasise some point, her speech seemed to become an act. She brought dead dates to life; she seemed to breathe the period she described.

'I'd like you to become a teacher,' Chiki said, 'to do exactly what Charlot was doing.'

'But why?' Fola said, forgetful of the name Charlot, but nervous as a schoolgirl surprised by praise.

' 'Cause there's a connection,' said Chiki, 'for me it is a clear connection between the artist and the teacher.'

Fola smiled, shy and secret as a kitten when she turned her head away. But Chiki was still thinking with a feeling which seemed regret, now joy that Fola might become a teacher. His mind was a soil of ambivalent wishes. He was seeing Fola's future and his own: Fola as a teacher because he believed she had the actor's gift as well. And that is how he had conceived of an excellent teacher. To fertilise a fact with life and not betray its precise importance! This was his requirement for a teacher as well as the connection which made artist and teacher alike in his mind.

But some new regret now seemed to darken his thought. He was about to quote that saying: how the prayers an old man remembers are always those the child in him first uttered! For Chiki thought he saw his own future darken. He was thinking about a strange limitation in the nature of his work. It had always haunted his imagination. Now Fola had revived it. He could surpass the movement of her hands if he transferred them to his canvas. He could make the texture of her skin rejoice with colour. But he could not capture the sound of her voice. No conspiracy of line and colour could record her voice. No artifice would help to transmute the sound of Fola's voice, or the magic of Great Gort's drum. But he didn't tell his regret.

Fola saw that change of melancholy in his brow. It had come the moment she was about to ask his age. But nothing could persuade her to speak while she watched the shadow which darkened over Chiki's face. And the wordless atmosphere remained, but it did not seem to trouble them. The room was calm, appropriate and complete. Like a prayer in silence.

Only the echo of Belinda's voice broke like an obvious truth through the dark of this little cave which Chiki had named his home: Belinda and the waitress like two radiograms together:

Work! For the night is coming,
When man's work is done.

CHAPTER X

When Fola left the room that night, something had changed within her. The Moon Glow bar was dead and still as nails. She saw Belinda fast asleep in the corner where her row with Chiki had taken place the week before. The waitress was propped like a skeleton against the bar. Work hadn't ceased, but she was weary. Her mouth made a slow, thick dribble which collected in her hands. The radiograms looked like dwarfs, squatting obscenely upon the dais. But the night was still, still and dumb.

Something had happened to the rhythm of Fola's senses; for the night was ordinary as any that had gone before. Yet her eyes seemed to impose some long and slumberous delay on everything that moved. Chiki had walked with her from the room across the Moon Glow floor and down the stairs. He was afraid for Fola, as he had once been afraid for Powell; for it was Chiki who had influenced Powell in his pride, the pride which made him recognise any foreign gift as a method of enslavement.

Chiki had noticed the change which had now matured to a fearful dumbness that would not let Fola speak. He tried to humour her with anecdotes about the families: Lady Carol, the Vice-President and even Piggott. But Fola would not respond. He offered to walk her home; but she had begged, with obvious regret, to be alone. This change was a kind of contradiction she could not name. She needed to be alone; and yet she needed someone to hear what was happening to her as she walked under the black awning of the trees.

She could barely distinguish the shapes which the landscape offered her glance. It seemed that everything rose from the night, slow, still, in agreement, like the radiogram repeating its human paradox of love and hate. But the street made no noise; and when some stir of movement happened, Fola did not hear. The night was an expanding grave awaiting every step she made. For a while she would think of Chiki's wish that she should teach; but her mind was no longer receptive to this kind of talk. There was no one left to teach. Every ear in the republic had been closed: closed and remote and sealed like the perfect vault of sky embracing its eternity over the painful struggle of a double moon.

Under the wide vault of sky, the old moon had lost half of its face where the new moon emerged into a dubious splendour of yellow light, hard and clear. There was no subtlety of difference as the moons exchanged their vigilance. The new moon was thrusting up through little clots of blood which mottled half of the old moon's face. It was the only sign of movement in the sky. The new moon looked like bone, exact and without any of the shadows which were closing over the old moon's retreat. But the street was still there, immobile as a tomb under her gaze: dumb and interminable as the republic's dirt. Her memory had to resurrect something; and Chiki's canvases soon came to life before her eyes. She saw his room emerge against the ceaseless background of the night; and for one moment the Moon Glow had achieved an atmosphere of propriety in her mind. The canvases blossomed with light and colour. The bible had been redeemed from the monotonous routine of a prophecy which seemed to burden the street with a future of defeat.

The recollection of their meal now seemed to quicken Fola's step, as though the future was offering itself for her possession. Yet there was nothing to possess as there was nothing to instruct. A solitary day's experience had doubled her age; and as she reflected on the families and her own past, Fola's anger increased. She thought of Charlot, and heard his voice like a waste of words that didn't connect. Lectures and dates, the intervals of pleasure on the Morant beach: everything had acquired the same throttled pulse and breathing as the street which guided her towards the grave of this night. She thought of her mother and Piggott; and suddenly her anger had increased.

But Fola could not name the exact target of her anger. Her anger seemed to be without specific origin. It was imprecise, devoid of any future. Anger was simply there, almost tangible in its weight. It was not the memory of Piggott and her mother which angered her. For she thought of them now as victims of some general lie, some universal conspiracy against the source of life. Ignorant, self-deceived, Piggott and her mother had exploited what they called experience in order to frustrate her desire. Their love was a prison especially built to secure her loyalty. A prison which was securely guarded by the families' arrangements for her future.

Fola understood this with a blinding clarity; understood and accepted. But her acceptance had turned like a dagger against herself. She despised their folly and her own weakness in submitting to their authority. She felt weakness and shame like crutches under her crippled arms. Yet some unfamiliar need was taking shape inside her: the need to cut herself off from their possessive concern. She had never felt so intensely this need to be deprived of their affection; to return, untouched and without abuse, all the rewards of their ambition. She started to feel sorry for Piggott. She couldn't bear the thought of wounding him. But sympathy was the only reward which she could now offer for his attentiveness. She would not let her sympathy grow soft; she would not allow her attitude to slip into some compromise with what they had achieved on her behalf. For she was convinced in every memory of her past that they had used her as a way to exalt themselves.

From tonight Fola was going to act with the greatest severity. She was going to sever all loyalties from the past which this night had disclosed, thick and dumb as dirt. If anything of a future still remained, she was going to protect it against the hoax of success which they had bribed her into. She would confound their expectations by everything she did. She was going to fight Piggott, her mother and the families; and not in argument, not with words in defence of Chiki and the Forest Reserve. She was going to fight them with the details of her life from day to day, and on their own ground. She was going to wage her war in the sanctuary of the Maraval hills, and in the sacred residences which freedom had lately named Federal Drive.

She could hear Charlot's voice again, swallowed by the rage which Chiki had turned against her on their first meeting. She glanced up at the vault of sky, and saw the new moon like a rare and expensive alphabet that spelt one word: Lie. Then Chiki's voice returned, like the accusing echoes of the dead in the *tonelle*, ordering her to see where the lie resided. Money was the answer which grew loud and more menacing than the nightmare blackness of the sky. Those ordinary, decorative bits of metal and paper which could not appease any hunger, make adequate shelter for any head; yet punished every appetite with the enormous power which a vain and incredible hunger had bestowed upon it. Those simple digits of spending which men had invented and which men could no longer order to behave like the metal and paper on which they were inscribed! Ordinary fragments, like used Christmas paper, which changed their size and smile from hand to hand like a magician's trick!

Fola had seen the stages of its transformation in her own home. Lady Carol and Vice-President Raymond were rich. Piggott and her mother were not; but they had pawned their future to possessions that worked like an armour against the spiteful forgiveness of those who were much better off. She had seen the magic work, delicate and rare with the splendour which distinguished her mother's cocktail parties. Lady Carol would celebrate something or other this week-end; the Vice President would follow a fortnight later; and finally her mother would crown the season with her unique example. From home to home, from promise to promise, generosity revolved like an epidemic which knew the infirmities that qualified for dying. Spending was a contagion that travelled like the gracious noises of approval from mouth to secretive mouth and crooked ear.

This night had returned Fola's image among those families. Thick as the night itself, she could see that waste: first nights in some tropical substitute for furs at the republic's freedom theatre, for culture like freedom had arrived to share its own legacy; the intellectual seances that increased with each new federal committee, artists' salons, and the smart, sophisticated circles that had started, with logic and some learning, to demand the restoration of an active faith in the Christian certainty of each man's temporal defeat.

Week after fortnight and month from the year of Independence, they met for circle and seance: the whole man-fabricated tomb of getting together when words came plentiful as dirt. The young and the old, according to their fashions of hope or despair; they were *there*, simply *there*, a self-propelled circus of talking animals deprived of their original voices: a frozen weight that could not stir without the touch of money, without the miraculous grace of metal and common Christmas paper.

Nothing could embarrass Fola now the search for her father had changed its meaning. Indeed, she was no longer so eager to know who he was or what had happened to him. Her enthusiasm had taken a new turn. She wanted to find him in order to see what would happen to those who had deprived her of this knowledge.

She walked towards the light that spread thinly over the streets; and Charlot seemed to follow like a shadow at her heels: Charlot and the *tonelle*. It seemed that all her years had been gathered up like the improbable ceremony of corpses telling their past, faceless and absent, yet familiar in their scrutiny of what had gone before. Fola could hear a confession of voices in the night; and suddenly she had stopped, as though startled by the thought which had occurred to her.

She had begun to realise what was the ultimate punishment of the dead. She thought she saw the limitation in each corpse which had returned to tell its history. It was this obvious and overwhelming fact: *they had no future they could choose.* Memory was their last and only privilege. They could not leap beyond themselves, beyond the moment their own story had ended. Their angry strictures on the living, like old people rebuking the young, was only their way of bribing the present into a state of neutrality. They had to stabilise the present, even discredit its passions, in order to exalt their own achievement in the past. Death was a weight which fixed them for ever in one attitude. They could not now destroy any part of what had gone before; they could no longer hope to alter the size of any neighbour who had shared that past with them. They could not break from the futureless spell of the tomb. They could not now be rescued from the corpse's embrace. Because they were dead; dead and deprived of a freedom which breathed: a freedom which breathed error and remorse, perhaps, but which, nevertheless, still breathed.

But those who survived were still free to breathe. And Fola was alive. She was talking to herself in a frenzy of conviction. 'I'm alive, alive, I'm alive.' Fola wasn't aware how loud she had spoken. Something had happened to shake her disenchantment with the future. Like the afternoon the word, bastard, was born; like the night she saw herself *beyond, beyond*; some fresh awareness had arrived. She felt it like a wound which denied all pain, a soil of some immeasurable promise. She was young and *alive.* She was alive to the change which was taking shape within her; alive to the passion which would let her give new meanings to the past; alive to the power which ordered her to choose some future for herself.

This was her privilege over the dead; this was the sole advantage which gave her a leap *beyond* the decrepit skeletons residing near the Federal Drive, polluting the live air with wave upon wave of their corpse breathing. To be *alive*! To breathe and be *alive*! She felt it in every pulse of the voice talking to herself under the street lamp. Its urgency was equal to the need for food.

Fola had forgotten Piggott and her mother. She had deposited the families like sediment somewhere in her past. She did not even think of Charlot or Chiki. She was alone; yet knowing no terrors in this solitude. She was alone as she watched the grave night of faces approaching from all directions. She seemed to expect the town to recognise her change, to be part of this live promise which had grown abundant as the dirt under her feet. But nothing was changed beyond her private vision. The sea burnt dully: a quiet, yellow haze that fell from the lamps and trickled towards the pier.

The public clock struck loud, telling the lethargy of the town to ears that had thrived on not hearing the waste which time implied.

Fola remained under the street lamp, shocked by the fixed, black stare of the night. Things showed her their meaning as she brooded on the ancient and rigid habit that refused to stir their waiting. She saw the buildings climb like tombs, obedient in their wish to touch the sky. She heard the usual noises of this hour. She saw a girl her own age crouching behind a tray of peppermint and fruit, gazing at the pavement, beseeching the dancing shadows of the light to send her custom before her eyes closed down. A man was polishing the windscreen of his car, waiting for hire.

Fola could not move as she heard her own voice making obvious comment on the slumber of the town. An incredible stupor strangled the night. Everything was stuck in its place. Dead and stuck there. The vile architecture of commerce dominated the street. It stood erect, monstrous with greed at the end of the day. Something inside her was screaming: *just for a move on.* Anywhere, *but just for a move on.* After the treachery of this sleep, it could not matter where the town moved. It did not matter what danger its action would produce. *But move, just a move on*!

Fola too was stuck, waiting. She heard a voice, and saw the corporal walk out from under the awning of the trees. His voice had given her a shock. At least he had a voice which made some noise, she thought, as she watched him approach. He stood before her: and Fola was startled again when his voice made another noise. But she hadn't paid any attention to his questions. She was trying to imagine what kind of noise the very first man had made. She grew furious, enraged, because she knew how he would interpret her waiting. People shouldn't just wait the way she was standing here under the light, looking like a thief who was about to be caught. 'Or he thinks I'm just a girl,' she thought, seeing the corporal slip a small black book from his pocket, 'he thinks I'm just a part of the traffic he can regulate. I'm traffic, but more dangerous because I'm *alive.*'

'Where are you coming from?' the corporal asked again.

'The Moon Glow bar,' Fola said in triumph.

The corporal started to memorise her face under the light. He was alert.

'And where you going?' he asked, noticing the nervous twitch of her skin.

'What's that?' Fola said. She was playing for time. She was going to invent some fantasy for him to feed on. It would have been treachery to satisfy his sense of duty by an ordinary reply. She knew that any mention of Piggott's name would have evoked an apology from that servile face that looked at her, waiting for answer.

'Where you goin' little miss?' the corporal said again, searching her bosom with his eyes.

'*There, there,*' said Fola. She was panting with excitement.

'There where?' the corporal asked, his voice now sharp and alert with caution.

'You didn't hear?' Fola asked, and her voice rose to a shout, 'it's going to happen soon.'

'What's going to happen?' the corporal asked, reflecting on the trouble he had always had with the Moon Glow bar.

'It's going to happen,' Fola repeated.

'What's going to happen?' the corporal shouted, angry and impatient.

'Soon, very soon,' Fola screamed, and ran like a fugitive through the night.

The corporal stood, stupefied, waiting as though the boots had stuck his legs to the street. For a moment her face was all he could remember. The corporal knew nothing else about her. Nor did he know that their brief meeting was evidence which would soon confirm the first and gravest tragedy to befall the republic.

CHAPTER XI

There was nothing dramatic about the days which passed; yet they were different from any other period of Fola's life. She had hoped to bring about some violent change in herself; she was determined to wage the kind of war which would reveal her as a stranger in her mother's eyes. She had thought that Piggott and the families would

249

be confounded by what they had to argue with. But it didn't work that way. Her friendship with Chiki seemed to make for the opposite result.

Fola had become, instead, the natural product of a change. Everyone seemed to adjust without effort to the difference they had noticed in Fola's manner. Even her mother, who allowed nothing to pass without comment, behaved as though this change was really no part of Fola's decision. They saw the same person in a slightly unfamiliar context of habits. The nearest parallel would be a child whose clothes denote that it has grown without making any special claim for the obvious difference in its height. And Fola's sense of order helped to encourage this attitude towards her change.

She had become more attentive to her mother's need for her affection. Now and again Fola would try to talk with Piggott, implying that things were not the same. But Piggott's response hadn't suffered any change since the evening she had wounded his pride by the reminder that he was sterile. Only Therese grew more alert each day; for neither Piggott nor her mother knew where Fola spent her evenings. Veronica would ask, and then apologise.

The day Chiki finished the portrait of the unknown father, Fola decided that she would celebrate the occasion with Piggott and her mother. She had become expert at this kind of duplicity. But it was not a joke. Fola was thinking that a time would come when she would be able to assemble all these experiments which Piggott and her mother and the families shared in. And that would be the moment to prepare for their conversion. Chiki had a strange superstition about showing his work even after it was complete. The harvest wasn't ripe, he would say, until the crops had settled where they belonged. He had refused to let Fola see the portrait; but he had agreed to celebrate. She drank her first glass of local gin which almost made her sick.

That night Fola was punctual for supper. Piggott was delighted. Her mother was quick to express surprise. Therese said nothing. But a shock had swallowed their words when Fola declared that she had brought gifts for the family. She had crowned Therese's ambition by buying her a fan. The temperature hadn't changed; but fans had become a fashion throughout San Cristobal. And Therese had often expressed her agreement on the fan as a fitting item of *style.* On her way home Fola had stopped at the florists to get her mother a huge bouquet of gardenias. Among them were two chrysanthemums, and a stalk with one scarlet rose. Piggott's gift was a quart bottle of brandy which she had bought at the Moon Glow bar. Fola thought of it as a souvenir which marked her discovery of Chiki and the Forest Reserve.

Piggott played his part with an astonishing lack of candour. He hugged Fola to him, kissed her on both cheeks and ordered Therese to lay the table. The family were truly together on that day. But Agnes had suffered an unusual defeat. When she recovered from the shock of Fola's gesture, she made to speak. Fola had anticipated what would happen. Very quickly, and without causing her offence, Fola had smothered her mother's disbelief by pretending that she too had been surprised by what she had done. Agnes agreed, and there was silence. Yet Fola managed to conduct these relationships with remarkable frankness. There was nothing in her attitude to make them think that she was getting soft. She was precise and firm about the things she wasn't going to share. Her refusals often evoked apology; her acceptance crowned everyone's delight. Agnes had become almost docile during that harmony which Fola seemed willing to preserve. Piggott had begun to feel that Fola had restored his claim of being a natural father.

But Fola wasn't altogether free. She had begun to realise how complicated any change could be; for it was Chiki, more than anyone else, who made her aware of this lack of freedom. Their first encounter was still fresh in her memory. She had seen him then in a certain way; a way which their friendship could not easily overcome. The Forest Reserve was always there, like shadow and eclipse over their affection for each other. Sometimes she would have great difficulty in choosing gifts for Chiki. She was afraid of the effect her choice would have. Would he think that she had done it because he was poor? His ugliness never bothered Fola; yet she had a strange suspicion that Chiki might attribute pity to her gestures. It was odd how these simple details helped to confuse the whole meaning of change.

This caution had made Fola very conscious of her age and her own

251

lack of needs. But it was greater than ever this afternoon; for she was making her first visit in daylight to the Reserve.

From a distance the forest rose in a splendid harmony of colour and sound: a quiet profusion of noises she could not identify. Was it the cry of parakeet or kingfisher or the brief, erratic buzz of the humming bird borne leisurely through the last red bars of sunlight which imprisoned the hills? The light worked like a juggler in its subtle manipulation of shade on shade. An even crop of leaves now shook like hair above the mottled, black brow of the hills. Fola had never felt such satisfaction among the soothing domesticities of her mother's garden. There, the roses looked like startled puppets imitating her mother's taste. Sometimes she wished the plants would refuse attention, leap from their soft, moist beds of dirt and horse manure. Passive as slaves in their allotments of earth, they had for-gotten how to grow. She wished that garden could pursue its natural roots and be the stature of this forest, remote, free and intangible in its strength.

As Fola approached the boundary of the Reserve she could see the flat, wooden roof of each hut, the ragged tiers of black shingle which seemed to stagger under pressure from the wind: a seedy repetition of decay. It seemed incredible that nature could weave so perfect a deception over the stranger's eyes. The trees hadn't lost their splendour, but the noises changed where she stood looking across a pond at a communal yard. The body of a lignum vitae grew tall and solid above her head; but the human heart of the forest was utterly disfigured. She knew that Chiki was in the yard, but couldn't see beyond that rough disorder of foreign faces which grinned and yelled and grew silent in turn. She traced the slope of leafy track which crawled out of the pond, stepping tiptoe, nervous and careful to avoid detection.

Then Fola paused, shocked by the obscene chorus of abuse which rose from beyond the huts. Mathilda and Flo were engaged in the worst kind of war.

'You can talk till your tongue drop tired,' Flo shouted, 'I done say what I go do. I go break your ribs if you touch what belong to me.'

'Your senses must be gone mad,' Mathilda answered. 'Is a man you go let push you 'pon the gallows? Men cheap, my dear, it aint have no price when a real thirst catch them lonely.'

'I aint give two farts 'bout men, once you don't touch my own.'

'It have plenty you call your own,' Mathilda returned, 'is a regiment you want to recruit, or what?'

'If my regiment grow is 'cause you can't serve what come.'

'Is just why poor Jack O' Lantern dead,' Mathilda said. 'You wrap round an' squeeze poor Lantern till he aint even had what make a man. Then you go tell everybody how he can't make the grade. You self, Flo, you walk 'bout tellin' everybody how poor Lantern weak. After two rabbit shake how he start to blow like a bugle all over what you got. Is what you say, an' everybody in Moon Bay know what you do him, 'cause Lantern was once a man with a commandin' prick. The whole o' Moon Bay know that. But you wicked, Flo. You work underhand and dirty, too.'

'You real brass face,' Flo screamed, and the voices seemed to narrow the distance between the women. 'Real brass face, you can be, real brass face. . . .'

And gradually the voices died, as though the law had arrived to warn them what would happen. There was a coarseness of impact in the atmosphere of the yard which frightened Fola. Suddenly she heard a noise, a soft, nervous whisper of a voice like the throttled cry of a bird caught in a snare. It stopped for a moment, then came again, painful and sharp like a rat. Fola was still terrified of rats. She stood still, feeling a gradual stiffness tighten her fingers, wondering whether she should stoop and pick up a stone. But she couldn't bring herself to look. She didn't want to see what was behind her. Then the noise returned, a piercing yell which made her shiver. Fola heard the rustle in the grass and turned. She went stiff in every nerve. She wanted to shout at the animal, but she couldn't summon her strength to speak.

The spectacle was gruesome beyond anything she could imagine. The black bitch was chewing lazily, one eye half closed against the hungry stammer of a fly. The fly buzzed over a little pool of fresh blood, and the bitch shook its head. The fangs leaned from its jaws like broken nails through a scarlet treacle of breathing skull. Fola felt a hard fist of vomit stick in her throat. She closed her eyes and stooped, scratching round her feet for a stone. The bitch heard the rustle in the leaves and trotted off, leaving the torn carcass of its infant pup behind.

Fola had lost all sense of direction. She felt her heart like a galloping hoof under her breast. She was running down the track towards the yard where the voices rose louder and more fretful. For some reason she could never understand, the bestiality of this episode had assumed human reality. Leaning against a tree, her eyes insanely fixed on a dumb curve of sky, she could see Camillon's face, smooth and perfect as these trees brooding over the Reserve.

The grass rose and turned like the mouth of a cave around her. She had a perfect view of the yard. Chiki was standing near an iron pot which swung white bridges of steam over a woman's head. The woman bent low on her knees, pumping her breath into the sporadic flame of burnt charcoal. It would require a miracle, Fola thought, to bring that fire alive. Chiki passed his hand through the cloud of smoke, spreading thinly across the yard. Another woman sat in the door of the hut, scrubbing her child with a bunch of pawpaw leaves. She dipped the leaves in a basin of suds and scrubbed the crease of his ears. The boy screamed and kicked whenever she bruised his skin. There must have been a shortage of water, Fola thought, because she could see a thick cap of lather covering his head; yet the bath was over. The woman lifted him up from the basin and passed him to the tall slim girl who was waiting beside her. The girl had taken off a faded blue cotton dress to dry the boy's skin.

'Come along you,' the woman shouted.

'I comin',' a child's voice answered.

'Stop comin' an' come,' the woman said, pouring a kettle of tepid water into the basin of lather.

Fola recognised the child whom she had seen dancing in the *tonelle*. The lather settled like honeycomb round Liza's ankles. The woman was disentangling the short, stiff coils of plaits that looked like roots sticking out of Liza's head.

'Who send you with my hairpins?' the woman shouted.

'It aint yours,' Liza said.

'Lies, is lies you comin' with?' her mother said. 'For that I go clean behind your ears.'

'I beg no, Ma, I beg leave the ears for next time,' Liza pleaded.

'Lies, lies,' the woman fretted, 'for lies I go wash your ears.'

Liza stamped in the basin, and the lather splashed over her mother's dress. The woman buckled her forward like a fish and slapped her bottom. The yard was crowded with faces, but no one paid attention to Liza's scream. Chiki had walked away from the iron pot towards the cactus fence. Three boys took turns, trying to blow up a pig's bladder. Once a week, on Saturday mornings, they went to the market to buy a fresh pig's bladder from the butcher. Cutting a branch from the pawpaw tree, they fitted the hollow stem through one end of the bladder and pumped it with air to the size of a football.

'Head it here,' one of the boys said, 'head it if you say you can head.'

'I go head it,' the boy said.

'Don't hands it after it leave your head.'

'An' don't face it either,' the other boy said, ' 'cause facin' aint heading'.'

'If it touch my face that aint no foul.'

'But you too ugly,' the boy said.

Chiki was laughing as he watched the ball drift from head to head. The wind carried the bladder beyond the reach of the boys, and a man emerged from the cactus fence to return it with his forehead. It soared past a woman's face. The wind pushed it further towards the huts where a group of girls were searching each other's head for lice. One girl put out her hand to help it back to the middle of the yard, but the boys screamed at her. It had to be kept aloft by heads. The girl stood still, closing her eyes, and the bladder wobbled for a moment above her head, then tottered down, and bounced softly off her nose. The boys were in control, but the men remained like soldiers expecting an emergency. In a matter of minutes the entire yard seemed occupied with keeping this bladder aloft.

'Look out,' said Chiki, 'don't move.'

'Turn round let it drop on your neck,' one of the boys shouted.

'You can't save it that way,' the other boy said.

But the man was eager to prove his skill. He continued to move, his hands spread wide, his head hung low between his shoulders. And the bladder guided him mischievously on to his disaster.

'Oh Jesus Christ,' the woman yelled, 'everything done break up.'

He had stumbled over the iron pot and fell heavily against the woman. The water ran cold over the woman's hands. The fire had gone out, and the crabs were fully alive. There was panic in every face. The woman screamed and shook the claw which clung severely to her thumb. The man felt the crush of shells under his bottom. A claw punctured his arm. The bladder exploded and quickly shrank into a little heap of raw innards. It moved slowly over the dust, drawn like a wet rag behind the labouring crawl of a huge blue crab. The pot was safe, but it was a long time before they could capture that silent regiment of claws. Fola had never seen so many crabs. It must have been food for the entire yard escaping from the iron pot.

'You go all eat them raw tonight,' the woman said. 'Be Jesus, if you eat tonight, you go eat them livin'.'

All the women had flocked to her defence.

'Big, big men behavin' like infants,' Liza's mother said.

The woman sucked her thumb, and wiped her eyes, and swore obscenities at the man. Her tears were no more than a sign of complete exasperation.

'An' he don't even work,' the woman said, 'if he work it would have some godly excuse for him. Look, look at the son-ov-a-bitch how he wastin' my life.'

The man stood near the huts, shaking dust from his trousers. The boys groped out of sight, hoping not to be seen. They knew what would happen if anyone dared to laugh while the woman was talking. Each would have paid a brutal price for what had happened. Now they hoped the woman would concentrate all her fury on the man. He looked terribly ashamed as he propped against the hut, pretending to be occupied with his trousers, pretending not to hear what the woman was saying.

'When the crab season over what you go eat?' she shouted.

'Grass,' the man said, feeling the need to defend his pride.

'Spinach all right if you got something to go with it,' she said, 'but all that marrow vine paint the children's guts like a regular forest. They shittin' nothin' but green all day long.'

'Is better than the market meat lyin' three days dead with flies,' he said.

'There aint nothin' fire can't kill. Is only excuse you make for not findin' a work.'

'Find? You ever know me lose a work?' the man shouted.

' 'Cause you never had one,' she said.

'Then what it is you sendin' me to find?'

'You too damn lazy.'

'An' look at your guts,' the man said, moving towards her, 'how it swell if I wasn't workin' 'pon it.'

'Is all you good for,' she cried, 'but I aint here to make litter like a pig all year long. My pussy can find somethin' else to do.'

The man stiffened and glowered at her from where he stood. There was threat in the woman's eyes as she watched him stand, rigid with warning.

'Woman, is time your tongue close down,' he said, and his voice had changed to regret. 'Don't give me no more talkin' to like you is Jesus sister holdin' forth on Mount Sermon Number Two.'

'Find a work,' the woman repeated, as she watched the crabs escape. 'Is all I say. Find a work or I go have to see 'bout myself some other way.'

Now the man moved closer, warning with his hands as he spoke.

'Look here, Queenie,' he said, 'puttin' big people business one side, is bad to talk like that when children present. Is bad, bad, that.'

Then he held her by the arm and dragged her like a mule into the hut.

Not far away, Fola could see the men collecting firewood to tune new drums. A dry steeple of bramble was smoking slowly into the evening. The wind raised blue wreaths of paper ash, and trickles of soot, weightless and more minute than any dust, spotted the leaves. There were traces everywhere on Powell's vest which was already heavy and grey with sweat. He wore it outside his trousers with the front end gathered and screwed into a knot that lapped against his navel. His muscles moved like fish when he heaved and plunged the axe into the tree. The intervals between the lift and thrust of his axe were measured. Crim and Gort who worked opposite him made swifter strokes. One followed the other, repeated their strokes, and waited for the descent of Powell's axe. It came like a pause into their haste; but it was a more calculated act than any they could achieve. Powell felt a greater intimacy to what he was doing. The smokng bramble and the tree, the red blaze that would scare the forest later, the sizzled tuning of the 'drum', the abortive melody that would grow painfully under his hands into a passionate statement of sound: everything was part of his attention in this moment. The future was concentrated in his hands driving the axe with such grave delibera-tion into the hard, white rib of the lignum vitae. He was a small man, tight and intense with a fearful precision of movement and gesture. From time to time his lips made a twitch like the action of the skin when a fly alights. His hands were neat, the fingers splayed, nervous and alert as claws. And no word passed from him to the other men.

But this quiet couldn't last. Fola was suddenly startled by the furious protest of the dogs. Lured by a foreign scent, they had come out to the middle of the yard, whining at the tiers of smoke which lifted above their heads. Tails taut as wire and erect, they searched the far corners of the cactus fence, watchful and sure as they sniffed their way through a muddle of pots and pans. The huts were awake, staring from the windows which opened on a crowd of worried faces. Children were hurrying through the torn partition of blinds to see who had arrived.

The dogs rushed forward, shivering with rage. Heads down, they clapped wet fangs at a pair of black boots. The corporal kept calling for silence as though the animals were a school of ruffians in revolt. Now the corporal turned, inviting someone to restrain the dogs. He had felt a row of teeth like the points of a saw piercing his boots. He kicked out at the dogs as they retreated noisily into the cactus barri-cade around the yard.

'Let loose the Geyser,' a man's voice begged, 'let the Geyser go for him.'

'Where Geyser? Open up Geyser quick,' some of the bigger boys shouted in chorus to the man's appeal.

The corporal was fencing with his helmet, his rear strenuously guarded with a waving cane. The black bitch leapt chest high, spraying his sleeve with her tongue.

'Leave the stripes an' take off his arse,' the man's voice begged again.

He seemed to rebuke the animal for wasting its chance. The bitch grovelled and fretted, flexing its tail like a whip. Some of the children were screaming for mercy, tears boiling in their eyes. They had learnt to fear from infancy whenever the police arrived. The bigger boys rolled over the pile of broken crab shells, helpless with laughter.

'Pandemonium in the yard.'

'Is long, long time I don't see a bacchanal so,' the young voices rejoiced.

'Let loose the Geyser,' the man's voice begged again, 'long time the Geyser aint try his jaws on the law.'

The corporal held his ground, hoping to smother a dribble of sweat that rambled into his eyes. The cane slipped from his hand, and the dogs, dangerously encouraged, now dashed at his knuckles. He stooped on to one knee, making dog friendship with his mouth, whistling meal-time noises to distract them away. He offered the helmet like a kettle of bones; but the dogs were reluctant to be bribed.

'Who own these beasts?' the corporal demanded, swearing his oaths at the persistent black bitch.

'They free,' a woman's voice said, 'you can take them home.'

'Let loose the Geyser,' the man shouted, 'it aint fair 'pon the Geyser to keep him in chains with a feast like that goin'.'

'Who own these beasts?' the corporal begged again, as they charged together. 'Who own these beasts, I ask?'

'They born wild,' the woman answered.

'Is where your licence?' the corporal demanded in his confusion, 'is where your licence?'

'We don't sell liquor,' the woman answered again.

The corporal was in reverse, the cane raised level with his brow. Then the dogs relented, as though in doubt. They heard the familiar voice call again, and they clapped their tails in the wind, offering their backsides to the corporal's cane. But he was afraid to strike. Powell was sauntering down the track, dragging the axe behind him. The dogs frisked about, answering his call with their tails. The corporal fitted the helmet over his fist to polish the silver crest which sparkled on the hood. Then he balanced the helmet on his head, and saddled his face with its leather strap. He flogged his trousers with the cane, and watched the dust settle back over the yard. There was a fearful severity in his eyes. He knew it wouldn't be long before he got his turn.

Powell had reached the yard. Not far from the nearest hut, he cleared his throat and spat with amazing accuracy into a hole. Two paces further, Powell shoved the axe into the ground, and covered his spittle with a lump of earth. He looked at the policeman, waved his axe in a gesture of welcome; then bowed in modest acclamation of the law and walked into the hut. The corporal flexed the cane under his arm and probed the large flaps of his pocket for the little book. That book was a notorious, black register in the Reserve. The men were unsure of the reason for the corporal's visit. Gort saw the little black book, and decided to remind everyone why the corporal had come.

'Roll call,' said Gort, thrusting his chin out in military command, 'name, age an' favourite prison.'

'Crim as short for Criminal,' said Crim, 'arrive at a port call mother's guts. Last heard of in his grave.'

'Corporal say behave,' said Gort, 'but he not say how.'

'Too far east is west,' Crim answered, 'too far order end up in rank disorder.'

'Crim!'

'General Gort,' Crim answered.

'Corporal say?'

'Order!' said Crim.

'An' Gort reply?'

'Too far order end in rank disorder,' Crim answered.

The boys clapped at their retorts. The corporal waited as though he were deaf. And soon, like a change in the light, the yard was quiet. Gort noticed that the women did not contribute to the men's horseplay; and that was a dangerous sign. The women had an uncanny way of predicting trouble. Gort turned away, hoping that Crim had read the code of messages in his glance. He snatched a branch of leaves from the fence, and chose a stem to clean his teeth. The sky had become a target for Gort's attention. Chiki was returning from the hut where he had gone to speak with Powell. Crim was alert to Gort's messages. He shared a similar interest in the evening as he walked towards the fence, contriving a false reluctance in every limb. They sat together on a stump of tree.

'Position?' Crim whispered.

'Not clear,' said Gort, retrieving the stem from a crevice of tooth.

'Things lookin' strange,' said Crim.

'Real bad is what I guess,' Gort said.

They began to check on the whereabouts of their friends during that week.

'Expedition Number One?' Crim asked.

'All clear,' said Gort.

'You sure?'

'Dead sure,' Gort said again.

'Escapade in Blue?'

'The Navy say nothin' happen,' Gort answered.

'That leave Stone Wall Junction.'

'An' Constance Spring,' Gort added.

Gort was counting names and faces as he tried to guess the reason for the corporal's visit. He felt a growing sense of insecurity.

'Place with name like the Virgin Mary?'

'The Jordan roll all right,' said Crim.

'Only the Spring I can't swear for,' said Gort.

'I din't have no plans,' said Crim.

'And Wednesday night?'

'Nothing,' said Crim, 'Brigadier One Foot hide his crutch an shout "thief, thief," like he was the biggest loser o' the lot.'

'Then somebody tryin' to frame up the Forest,' said Gort.

'I don't know,' said Crim, 'I got no answer why that constable man come here.'

'The Forest in real trouble,' said Gort.

'You think it bad?' Crim parried.

'Bad, bad,' said Gort, and looked to Chiki for advice.

The women had seen it. They couldn't say what had happened, but they had learnt the strategy of the Law in search of the Forest

261

Boys. In ordinary times, when the theft was something you could hide, the police moved fast. They would surprise the huts by the violence of their demands. They entered like soldiers, swift and certain, action and order identified. Chairs were thrown out, beds dismantled. The children raised shoulder high, swept all the ledges clean. The police knew what they were after. When it was over they would walk out with evil in their eyes for everyone, making a filthy prophecy of the things that would happen on their return. In the very last stages of their defeat, the questions came, always the same questions, and the men would answer in order to cut short their stay.

'But this is different trouble,' the woman said.

'Stealin' may be all right if they keep it simple.'

'Is what I tell Gort.'

'Now they do it on some criminal scale,' Liza's mother said, 'an' what goin' happen now?'

'You think they had a fight?'

'They don't have fight without blood,' she said, 'an' I aint see no blood in what Crim wearin'.'

'Nor Gort. Nothin' 'bout him stain.'

The corporal was still there, scrawling his pencil through forgotten names. He heard the voices whispering negotiations through the yard; but he paid no attention to what they were saying. He had recovered his self-esteem because he knew they were afraid. At least the women could be relied upon to make him sure of that. But he would not make too great a show of confidence. There was nothing to report. According to the orders he had received it was still too soon to press for the information which he had been sent to get. He had restrained himself from asking questions; and now the dogs were quiet, sprawled lazily under the huts. He wanted to make sure that nothing would arouse their spleen again.

But he distrusted the men, Crim and Gort whose silence was a habit of making plans. You could never predict their mood. They were accustomed to extremes of punishment. It was a matter of pride for them to evade the law; but if the case was clear, and all escape appeared impossible, they were resigned to any extremity of punishment. Crime had to be impressive in its effect on those whom they despised. The police were prominent among their enemies. The corporal knew what they thought of him; for he had lived, as a boy, among men whose loyalty to crime was similar. The police were a separate race of spies, despicable pimps and hired slaves whose lives were a dedicated act of treachery to the poor.

Like a child who can't articulate the lie in what is not wholly false, the corporal said simply, to himself, it was not true. He looked up at the sky where everything seemed more bearable seen from below. He pretended to be at peace, and chose for his wonder that massive slush of cloud pelted like cakes of mud by the bleeding fist of sun back of the hills. His waiting worried the women. Silence for them had two extremes of meaning; a calm of the heart which knew the pulse of what had not been said. Sometimes it was like that with Crim and Powell and Gort. Pleased as a breasted infant, the Boys would bend their heads, marking out segments of music on the drums while the women sat beside them, all speech surrendered to their hands that needled tomorrow's underwear. Or silence was like this waiting, an evil intention which no word would risk to touch.

The women's voices shouted for Liza; but she had gone outside. The silence was now thick as leaves. First they had heard an echo of sirens overhead; then the sharp, brief drag of tyres, scraping to a halt. The corporal had suddenly found his courage. The police had arrived: a dozen or more in two cars. They were armed with bayoneted rifles. One of them broke the news; and Liza ran in, terrified by the burning points of the bayonets in the sun. She stumbled and fell flat on her stomach, as she reached the yard. Chiki grew tense. Gort was nervous.

'What happen?' Crim asked, hurrying to pick Liza up.

She couldn't talk, and she was too scared to cry.

'What happen?'

It seemed everyone spoke at the same time. Their questions were like the opposite of praise greeting her in the *tonelle*.

'What happen?' Crim shouted at her.

'Vice-President Raymond,' Liza stammered.

'What happen 'bout Raymond?' Chiki cried.

'They find him dead,' said Liza, 'the police find him dead.'

263

For a moment there was no stir throughout the yard. The forest too had died. Every ear was possessed by the fear which Liza had disclosed. And then disorder followed, like a violent burst of floods. There was complete disorder everywhere. No one could hear the other's voice as the women shouted in terror to the neighbouring huts: 'Raymond, they find him dead. Somebody kill Raymond.'

Liza's mother was shouting the news when she felt a large fist of bone like a hammer pummelling her neck. Piggott had pushed her aside. Powell ran out from one of the huts seething with rage. He had lifted his hand to strike Piggott on the head, when suddenly he felt the point of a bayonet probing his arm. He let his arm fall slowly down, seeing for the first time how many bayonets surrounded them. The dogs frisked up and down, growling in spasms at the police, nervous and resigned as though they understood their defeat. The black bitch circled the stump of tree where Gort had sat, came nearer as though preparing for attack when the corporal drew his cane and struck with fatal accuracy over its head. The animal fell sideways; then rose making blind circles round the yard until it staggered through the fence. The howling seemed to last for ever where the blood traced a tortuous track of paws that showed a thick red path through the forest.

No one had spoken. They could hear the howling of the animal drift further away. Beside the iron pot, a small boy stood rigid with fright, struggling to conceal the shudder of his body as he felt his filth drag slowly down the back of his legs. Secret. . . . Secret and silent as the night, all the women had withdrawn. It was impossible to tell whether they had left together or at safely measured intervals. A minute ago they were all there, sobbing aloud. Now they were gone. And no one seemed to notice. The police were busy binding the men's hands behind their backs. Piggott strode round the yard, peering over the fence, round the sharp corners of the huts, signalling one of his men to search the huts. He seemed calm as a farmer inspecting his cattle. But there was a look of aggressive hatred in his eyes. His eyes burnt black and steady under the sombre blue peak of his cap: a man indisputably in command, committed to revenge, sure of the torture his enemy would have to endure.

Neither Crim nor Gort had softened in their habit of resentment. They had surrendered their hands to the cold cuffs of steel that locked blue-black over each wrist, but their silence was strong as their habit of indifference. Powell stared at the ground, determined and assured as though he saw fresh plans taking shape in the dust. Chiki rubbed his hands behind his back and followed Piggott with his eyes wherever he walked. He tried to imagine what would happen an hour from now. Whenever Chiki was caught in a similar crisis, escape impossible, all aid denied; he would try to imagine the future: whether it was an hour, a year, a decade from now. He would deny the moment its truth. He would see himself in another place, at another time, living a new set of emotions which were independent of what he felt. He would rescue himself from fear by dreaming. But dream and certainty became identical in that future his imagination had made.

Chiki saw Piggott return from one of the huts, dragging a sack behind him. The corporal ran forward to relieve Piggott. They ripped the sack open and emptied its contents on the ground. It was Gort's tenor drum and three pairs of batons. Gort tightened his muscles and looked away when he saw the rifle butts puncture the navel of the drum. The corporal threw it over the mound of stones. It was a kind of blasphemy to every eye which saw. Gort felt a sudden sweat freezing the ends of his ears as he heard the crash of the drum against the stones. Crim and Powell had a similar emotion. It was like waiting for news of the dying. They tried not to see Gort's face. But Chiki became suddenly aggressive. He was waiting for Piggott to turn again.

'Now what the hell you do that for?' he shouted.

Chiki had stepped forward. Crim was shouting at him to stop, but the policeman had intervened. Chiki straightened his body and gasped. The policeman had struck the butt of the rifle into his ribs. The blow cut Chiki's wind. Chiki was trying to free his hands. He felt another stab of pain racing like blood down to his groins. Crim spat, and the corporal drew his cane.

'All right,' Piggott said, raising his hand. 'You'll have him later.'

Crim spat again, and the corporal shifted his body to avoid the spittle.

'It will be blood next time,' Piggott said, moving towards him.

A bayonet emerged close under his chin. Light broke from the edge like splinters dancing before his eyes.

'You, yes you,' Piggott said, pointing at Gort.

Gort's eyes were vacant. He seemed to hear nothing but the echoing death of his tenor drum.

'Where were you last night?' Piggott asked, 'or the night before, or the one before that?'

Gort couldn't answer. He held his head down, staring at the ground like a deaf-mute. His drum had died.

'He was where he always is,' Crim said. Crim's voice was militant; his eyes flashed like daggers.

'An' where that?' the corporal asked, choosing the naked curve of shoulder bone where he would strike Crim next. 'Where that?' he asked again.

'Where he always is,' said Chiki, 'that's where.'

Piggott lifted his cap to mop his brow. He asked the corporal to move back. He stepped nearer, an arm's quivering length from Chiki. A sudden wheel of his body had brought him round face to face with Powell. But his elbow had found its target. It had finished in a jerk against Chiki's navel. Chiki felt a sudden tautness under his skin. His groan had died in the lingering echo of Piggott's voice.

'If it's how you want it,' Piggott said, 'it's how you'll get it. Only one of you will swing for Raymond's death, an' he will be better off dead than you who stay behind.'

Inside the hut the women stopped close, straining to see through the crevices of the window, still as a wasp's dead wing. Under a bed the children clung to each other like flies stuck where they had died. No sound rose from their waiting in the huts.

'It better be me who dead,' said Crim, ' 'cause if I stay alive, be Jesus Christ if I can stay alive, only one purpose go serve my breathin'.'

He felt the bayonet prick at the back of his thigh, and suddenly Crim had a terrible fright. If they cut off his leg he would be helpless to avenge himself. The thought started a shudder down his spine. 'Not now,' he thought, 'not now. Perhaps after, but not now!' He couldn't afford to lose his leg.

'So you think one o' we here kill Raymond,' he said, 'you got no evidence at all, yet you think is one o' we.'

They noticed the change in Crim's voice. Powell wondered what had come over him. Crim spoke very quietly. Piggott noticed the tone of compromise. Their secrecy couldn't last much longer.

'Is you kill Raymond?' Crim asked, thrusting his chin out at Gort.

Gort couldn't answer. His face retained its look of permanent stupefaction.

'Is you Powell who kill him?' Crim asked again. He spoke as though he had decided to change places with the police. He was the law.

'All right answer an' get it over,' he said, looking at Powell.

Powell turned his head and spat over his shoulder.

'So you see,' Crim said, looking regretfully at Piggott, 'you see for yourself nobody aint know nothing 'bout it.'

Piggott mopped his brow again. The heat had increased. He was becoming impatient, irritable, overwhelmed by the need to avenge Raymond's death.

'Nobody was near Four Square recently?' he asked.

A rasping note came into his voice. He felt the pulse of a muscle swelling his temple. He began to lose control.

'Which of you drag the body to Four Square?' he shouted, ' 'cause it wasn't there you kill him. You know what you've done?'

The police sensed his hatred. On such occasions they, too, became slightly afraid of Piggott.

'Say something,' the corporal shouted. He was nervous, but he was playing fierce. 'The Commissioner want to give you a chance to explain what you do.' He was pushing his cane into Chiki's back.

'A proper way to rule,' said Chiki, ignoring the cane, 'the poor outside the law, and if you outside the law you get priority attention when the law in search o' some criminal.'

He was addressing himself to Piggott. The police were nervous of the orders they might soon receive. For a moment the youngest constable felt he ought to restrain Chiki. 'He's asking for it,' he said to himself, 'the fool is asking for it.'

'It ever had a time you remember this Reserve except like now?'

Chiki asked. 'Look round this yard, an' what you see? What you see, Piggott? Nothing here is foreign to you. Whorin', hunger, the whole lot. You start from scratch like any o' these men here. Now you got power, an' you feel you can put out your memory like a fire. But you can't Piggott. You know how a poor man feels who got to answer a murder he knows nothin' of. You know it 'cause your own life start here. Like any o' these Boys you start from scratch.'

The women had heard Chiki's voice. It was a miracle that Piggott hadn't stopped his mouth before. The children had heard Chiki's voice. They didn't understand what he was saying; but if Chiki could speak while Piggott stood silent, it meant that Chiki was boss. The Reserve was taking over from the police. The police couldn't guess what Piggott was thinking. His face was set. His hands grew stiff and slippery with sweat. But he was brief.

'Take them,' Piggott said, turning away, 'everyone.'

The police had signalled the men to step forward; but Powell refused to stir. Chiki started and stopped when he noticed Powell. Then Crim collapsed on his back. He lay like a dead weight on his hands. Gort was making to stoop when the corporal yanked him up by the waist. Two of the policemen were dragging Crim across the yard. They dragged him to where Powell was standing. Crim got up very slowly. The stones had opened a dead scar on his knee. The wound burnt and bled freely through his trousers. Then he thought he saw the sky open. The sky was raining blood down his eyes. The police had stood him next to Powell. They knocked their heads together several times. Powell fell on his knees. He felt his skull divide as the pain passed through his eyes. Gort tried to run, but the corporal had tripped him from behind. Chiki moved sideways towards the corporal. For some reason he saw the stunt which threw Gort flat on his stomach as though it were murder. It was worse than the assault on Powell's head. The corporal's presence assumed an odour which filled him with disgust. The corporal noticed the look in Chiki's eyes. He came towards Chiki. He came closer. Chiki watched him, waiting for the distance to diminish. Then he was near enough, and Chiki spat loudly into his face. This was the moment the young constable had dreaded. The corporal did not retaliate because Piggott was going to take over. This was the moment Piggott himself had dreaded. 'It's the bayonets now,' he kept saying to himself, 'from now on it's the bayonets.'

Fola's eyes were seeing mad. In the stagnant shadows of the pond she could recognise three faces: Veronica's, the face of Raymond's corpse, and her own. The silence which introduced the bayonets had riveted her gaze to those reflections which argued from the dead water. They were telling her what to do. This was more terrible than the silence she had noticed when the old moon gave way to the cruel thrust of the new moon arriving under that black vault of sky. For a moment her ears had refused to hear what was happening in the yard. She was imprisoned in a deafness that was deeper than the death which had opened like a grave to swallow up the town and the impudent voice of the corporal whom she had recognised among the policemen in the yard.

Veronica was wishing her not to move. The face of Raymond's corpse lay neutral under its casket of stale water. But the other face, the face she saw as Fola *and other than* was swelling to the size of a sea. It reflected Chiki's blood which was screaming its first accusation into Fola's ears: 'If you don't go before they've taken him away, it means you have refused.' The water had stayed her progress down the slope. Then the wind passed like a chill across Fola's eyes. Now she could hear Chiki's voice in a lonely altercation with the police: the voice, which had grown familiar as the canvases which made the reserve Rejoice with the wedding at Cana.

The voice had erased Veronica's reflection from the water. Charged with revolt, Chiki's voice was bleeding its last refusal to give way to Piggott and the law.

'I'm me,' she heard Chiki scream, 'I'm what I do, but murder is not my trade, Piggott, not murder and not money. That aint my trade.'

The corpse still lay under its lid of stale water, making Veronica's grief more real. From either side, Fola had been accused. Chiki's voice grew loud and large as her own face reflected in the water. And Raymond's corpse remained. Like Lazarus rising from his grave, the corpse was reminding her who Raymond was. She couldn't accept postponement as a chance to save herself. She had been accused; for she had already taken sides within herself. Fola hadn't refused to move, but it was only by her consent that she had stayed. Each moment compelled her to an action; then warned her that she had already chosen; for waiting was a kind of action. She had chosen to be restored to the treacherous safety of her past. She had chosen to stay with Raymond's corpse.

Now Fola saw herself no different from her mother and Piggott, except that she would be ruined for ever in her own eyes. Like the dead souls that could not trespass beyond their recorded lives, she had cut herself off from her own future. Her faith was false, more poisonous than the power of metal and Christmas paper with which the families had purchased their privilege in San Cristobal. She had renounced her right to be a part of that live promise which had made her feel alive. Alive and other than a corpse. Integrity was the word which now stirred in Fola's ears. It pushed her like a hand into the light where she could see herself, less honest than her mother, more derelict than the dead, more dumb than Raymond's corpse. Chiki was a gift bestowed upon her by mistake. If, in this moment, the bayonets had punctured his live heart to death, that would be the end of her adventure. His absence would be the end of live promises, the end of her need to invent and leap beyond her past. Every moment of her life would remind her of a future that had died at birth, like the rotting foetus in that woman's womb: the woman whose cry could never reach Camillon's dignity.

Alone, unseen, Fola had actually crossed the pond. She felt the grass knee high, searching her thighs. She couldn't deny that the way was clear. Obstacles avoided her attention. She had to move on. The naked branch of the lignum vitae tree showed itself a foot above her head. The track was waiting to guide her to the yard where Piggott and his squad were ready to take the men away. The cactus fence drew her attention to the passage through which Powell and the others had walked. Fola could see the iron pot and the crushed flakes of crab shells in the middle of the yard. She knew she couldn't continue to inspect the earth. That was the privilege of the men who stood, heads bowed, feeling the clods of blood manacled in their hands. Fola raised her head. She saw Piggott, determined as stone, waiting for a confession he had chosen to hear. Without any evidence against the men, Piggott had decided to confront them with a fact. In the name of duty, Piggott had usurped the roles which she and Chiki were agreed belonged to them. And it seemed, in that moment, that Fola's pride had been wounded. It seemed that Piggott's sense of duty had returned Fola's future.

Fola had been restored to that freedom which now ordered her to put an end to Piggott's authority. Her future was safe as the blue scarf which she held in her hands. She put the scarf in her bosom, and walked out from the grass towards the middle of the yard. It was the corporal who recognised her first.

'Sir, who is that girl?' he said, and withdrew his hand from Piggott's shoulder.

There was an embarrassed look of privilege in the corporal's eyes. It seemed to say that the girl's arrival was a clue. He had detected something which Piggott himself could not guess. Piggott didn't move. He stood aghast, making excuses to himself for Fola's presence in the yard. It was the novelty of it that shook him first. Perhaps something had gone wrong at home. He thought that it was not unlike Fola to find him wherever he was. She had dared the crime and squalor of this yard to speak with him. Piggott glanced around at everyone, the police and the Boys, as though he wanted to chastise their wonder. Contempt was obvious in his look. He had made it clear that this was none of their business.

Powell became full of hate as he watched Fola stand silent and wait for Piggott to speak. Chiki pretended to ignore what he had seen. He rubbed his heels in the dust and stared at Piggott as though the privilege of a lifetime had been accorded him. It didn't really matter why Fola had intervened. Chiki wanted to see which way his influence would work in her encounter here with Piggott. Piggott noticed the women assemble in the yard. Fola's arrival had brought them out from every hut.

'What are you doing here?' Piggott asked, trying to smile at Fola.

'Piggy,' she heard her voice say.

'What's happened at home?' Piggott asked.

Her fists were clenched. An early nervousness had made her face more rigid than usual. Piggott became uneasy. His mind worked fast to discover the domestic tragedy which had occurred to Agnes.

Fola was slow to speak. She turned her head away, wondering what the man would make of her presence in the yard. Gort and Crim were trying to sort their emotions. They hated Piggott. Fola was not very difficult to assess. Fola could tell what she was worth in Powell's eyes. His hatred grew and stretched like a hand towards Fola's throat. But Fola's discovery of error came once more to her rescue. She wouldn't let go. They were perplexed by the silent and sustained defiance which now swelled her lip.

'What is it, Fola?' Piggott said, his voice caressed to a whisper by his misgiving. 'What you doing here?'

In a split second of reflection, Piggott had recalled Aunt Jane's visit to the house. Perhaps Aunt Jane had divined with her evil eye this dreadful afternoon. He looked round the yard in search of Aunt Jane's face; then gave all his attention to Fola standing an arm's embrace away.

'You know what happen to Uncle Ray?' he asked.

Fola didn't seem to hear. Her eyes rested their glance briefly on Chiki. Abruptly she turned her head away, and focused Piggott with her stare as though she wanted to say that this was her own affair. She hadn't come to rescue Chiki. She had come to redeem herself from what Piggott was doing.

'Fola, doo-doo!'

'Piggy!'

'What happen to upset you so?' he asked, as though he had forgotten Raymond's death.

'Let the men go,' said Fola.

Piggott's ears had begun to sting him.

'What it is you say, Fola?'

'I know who killed Uncle Ray' Fola said, the voice now firm and melancholy as it was the afternoon she was about to claim Veronica as her sister.

'You know what?' Piggott gasped. He was shaking his head like a startled bull.

'I say I know,' said Fola, 'so let them go if you want to hear.'

Piggott glanced idly round the yard. He thought Fola was speaking under threat from someone hidden in the Reserve.

'You know what you're saying, Fola?' he asked.

Everyone saw how the wrinkles opened under his eyes. The skin sagged a little where his chin had begun to tremble.

'But where were you three nights ago?' Piggott asked, disclosing the first item of evidence. He didn't mean it as a question. It was a way of calling Fola to her senses.

'Tell me, Fola, where were you that night?'

'In the Moon Glow bar,' said Fola. 'Ask him.'

Everyone turned to look at Chiki. Again, Piggott found himself recalling Aunt Jane's visit to the house. He looked at Fola and Chiki, changing his glance quickly from one face to the other. Gort was scared. He saw Crim staring at Chiki, and he knew they were all thinking alike. They thought Chiki had murdered Raymond.

'What do you know about it?' Piggott asked, glancing again at Chiki.

It was too soon for Chiki to connect. Any utterance might have betrayed what Fola was doing. He wavered, and thought, and tried to anticipate what would happen.

'Ask her,' said Chiki, 'she knows everything.'

The words rolled slowly from Chiki's mouth. He spoke like a man who felt that his crime would be more easily explained by someone else. Now they all watched Fola. Slowly, nervously, as though she had no influence over her hands, Fola was pulling the scarf from her bosom.

'This belongs to Uncle Ray,' she said, holding it out, not caring, it seemed, whose business it was to receive it. 'It was in the Moon Glow room.'

Chiki turned his head away. He was afraid for her. At what point, he wondered, would Fola ask him to complete what she had started. Chiki had to steady his nerve. He noticed Piggott's confused misgiving, and he felt much better. Then the obvious revelation came. But Chiki was not expecting it.

'It was my father,' said Fola in a voice that mourned the dead of all time, 'it was my father who killed Uncle Ray.'

She spoke directly to Piggott who could barely feel the scarf drop from his hands. Fola repeated her evidence again and again. Piggott didn't stir. He wanted to move towards her, take her head in his hands, and ask her to consider what she was saying. But Chiki had spoken. Like a brush making its signature without his effort, Chiki's voice had made her evidence conclusive.

'There's a picture of him in my place,' said Chiki.

The police looked like cattle that had forgotten where they were. Piggott glanced at Chiki, then back to Fola, as though his eyes were about to tell the truth of their agreement. He reflected on Aunt Jane's visit again; and every nerve of his body had grown rigid with caution. He ordered the police to remove the handcuffs. He ordered the corporal to remain. He ordered the others to return at once to their station; then called the sergeant aside and whispered in his ear. No word of this evidence was to be repeated to relatives, colleagues, or the national press. The sergeant saluted, and led the squad away. His sole duty was to guard their silence.

The women watched Fola as though they had seen Guru's soul recover its flesh and stand in the *tonelle*, shouting what he knew about the diamonds which had disappeared again. Fola stood there, her eyes now closed, fists knotted like Aunt Jane's in her possession. They thought the girl was a corpse until the corporal disturbed her sleep.

'Sir, sir,' the corporal stammered as he tried to attract the Commissioner's attention. He was moved almost to tears by the change in Piggott's face. The wrinkles had quartered the skin under Piggott's neck. His throat looked like dead meat.

'What is it, Corporal?' he asked, but scarcely hearing.

'It's the same lady I mention, sir,' the corporal said. 'An' it was Bruton Lane she was makin' from that night.'

There was still that embarrassed look of privilege in his eye, as though he felt ashamed of having said what he knew.

CHAPTER XII

The crowd had grown thick outside the huts. The rumour of Raymond's death had already acquired the status of an old event. The details multiplied, made room for every speculation which would help the understanding of the crowd. The wildest contradictions now found an equal place in some forgotten crevice of the past; so that the murder lost its original power to surprise. The past arranged itself like the scattered fragments of a puzzle, assisting everyone in its completion. The secrets of a life which could no longer deny the truth had been discovered afresh.

Some started to surmise that Piggott was really Fola's father; but the girl had developed a grudge against her parents and used her knowledge to expose the lie which had deceived San Cristobal. There was a rumour that Raymond had been conducting an illicit relation with the mother all these years. Humiliation had driven the daughter mad. Her presence in Forest Reserve had brought the evidence nearer home. She had obviously sought help from one of the Boys.

Since evidence was scarce it seemed easier to explain the facts. Each detail of rumour contained a truth. Each truth gave birth to a logic that was free to choose its end.

A general hush descended on the crowd when Fola and Chiki emerged into the street. The corporal walked ahead, and Piggott followed close behind Chiki and Fola. The heat was unusually intense for this time of day. The iron lids were wet with steam spurting up like water from beneath the earth. The car rumbled and coughed, then cruised tentatively down the street, crushing the little clouds of heat. The voices grew louder as the car raced out of sight. Piggott saw the faces melt slowly into the distance. He tried to think what should happen next; but he had already lost his power to order events. He might have been able to shape the future of the approaching night, but he could not choose its end.

The heat had sprung a heavy moisture all over his body. Sweat trickled in and out of his body, covered his eyes, made a sour taste of brine at the back of his throat. He was not alone under this singeing stupor. Heat showed on Chiki's face and the corporal's neck. Perhaps it was making the same bright patterns on Fola's face; but Piggott dare not look at her now. The heat was everywhere, yet he could feel a chill spread inside him. He heard the corporal saying something. Piggott didn't catch the words, but he recognised the servitude in the man's voice. It gave him strength. He started to think that things were drifting; he couldn't let things drift this way.

'Is it Headquarters first?' the corporal was asking, 'or the other place?'

'The other place is nearer from here,' Fola stammered.

'All right, that's enough,' Piggott said quickly, 'we'll hear from you later.'

Fola had spoken to break the spell of her own fantasy. She had to say something to prove it was her body occupying this seat; to prove the car was real, others were listening, that Piggott would recognise her voice. But her voice had brought Piggott back to his sense of duty. He was afraid that anything she said might undermine him further. He wanted to be alone with Fola, although he couldn't tell how that was going to help.

'The other place first,' he said.

'Moon Glow,' said Chiki, 'Moon Glow Hotel, corner Bruton Lane and Independence Square.'

Chiki's voice sent a shudder through Piggott. He felt unbearably exposed in Chiki's presence. Chiki's knowledge of the man, his relation to Fola. It was like a final judgement on everything that had been kept secret from him. Piggott tried not to think of Agnes; but it was impossible to separate her from the face which was waiting in the squalid little hotel in Bruton Lane. That face became more urgent than any evidence it could offer about Raymond's death. Piggott hardly thought of Raymond now. He thought only of that face which Fola had resurrected. He tried to imagine what it looked like; tried to imagine how Agnes would explain its death away. Why did she have to hide that Fola's father was alive? This secrecy was outside the meaning of a lie. He would have sworn that Agnes had never lied to him; until he heard Fola admit the existence of a man whose death had promised him the right to claim her as his daughter. It was a sudden stab of jealousy which made him wonder whether Agnes had even seen the man during their marriage. But he couldn't allow this speculation to take hold of his reason. He looked out of the corner of his eye at Fola. Would this portrait show any resemblance to her face? Already Piggott was beginning to create the stranger's face from his recollection of Fola's in all its variety of moods. Would the portrait really prove what he was looking for? It seemed that he needed to find it there.

Aunt Jane was in his mind again; Aunt Jane who must have known that this would happen. He couldn't compromise with the primitive source of Aunt Jane's power; but Fola's evidence was like a faith which melted his doubt away. Perhaps Agnes would deny it. What then? The complications now increased with every thought of Fola and her mother in open conflict as they gave their different evidence to the republic. Now the conflict gave rise to some secrecy which Fola and her mother shared; some secrecy in which he, too, would soon appear suspect. He thought of his job and his wife's disgrace. Then he thought of Fola's health; for madness was the only abnormality which could produce such a fabrication in her mind. But he quickly dismissed this fear. Fola was not mad. Indeed, it was her sanity which he feared. He didn't want to risk a public statement from her; but he would have to start with what he could believe. And he believed that Fola had discovered who her father was.

Chiki memorised the distance by the familiar landmarks which they passed. These were his own charts for measuring time: the unfinished architecture of a church which rose behind an orchard of citrus trees, the small tenement of houses racing backwards like the carriages of a train in the yellowing twilight. The smell of the town was creeping towards them. A flock of pigeons swooped down on the corrugated iron roof of the rum shop called Last Lap. Three streets away the car would turn left, and the wooden white steeple of the cathedral would spring into view. This was the landscape he had chosen for his night vagrancy.

But the faces were blurred. Houses and streets came vividly alive, yet the faces played tricks with Chiki's eyes. The car dipped and turned again, and he saw a woman's hands twist and meet like cork-screws above her head. He recognised a male voice chanting the price of nuts. The car swept dust over the brazier where nuts were roasting. The man waved, and his mouth stayed open like a door, his tongue thrust out into the air like a knife thrown from the back of his throat.

The car grazed a kerb and the driver started to brake. All traffic had slowed down. Everything seemed to prepare for a long pause. You could tell from the dumb agitation of the faces that the town had heard bad news. Everything was still except the pulse that

277

hammered in Chiki's brain. He held his head down to avoid Piggott's eyes. Yet he gave little thought to Piggott at this moment. It was his greatest enterprise. That's what he was thinking as he invented the details of his evidence. If Fola could sustain her part, there was no need for her to speak in public. His portrait would be the perfect substitute for everything that had to be revealed. He would let Piggott have a history of Fola's visits to the hotel. He would describe the details of their first encounter, the reason for her return each night. He was going to use the facts as Fola knew them. He would use them as the basis of evidence which no one could deny.

When this was done, he would go on to organise the raw materials which had made the portrait whose destiny would also be that of San Cristobal. 'Where nothing is known,' he thought, 'it is easy to make invention credible. In art as in the multiple intercourse of human life this is true!' If the man was dead, as Fola's mother had said, then his death would increase the power of his influence upon the living. For the time being, these simple facts would fertilize the public imagination. Chiki began to organise the facts. Fola had found her father. Fascinated by the nature of her search, he had made the portrait as a souvenir of their discovery. Fola's father was the face which he had immortalised. Neither he nor Fola knew the reason for the man's bitterness against Raymond, but Fola's father had made it known that Raymond's death would be his crime. The scarf could be identified by Veronica or her mother. Fola's father had come several times to the painter's rooms after he had made that threat. They didn't believe him since there was nothing about him to suggest he was a homicide. Chiki and he had talked about everything except the past which trespassed on his memory of Fola's mother. Chiki had found the scarf in his room. Uncertain of her father's guilt, feeling some impulse to protect her own discovery, Fola had taken it away. Perhaps they should have spoken to the police; but they had not. This was as far as Chiki could go to involve himself. If Fola could sustain her role of the bewildered girl! For her memory was still fresh with the shock that her father was alive! Now her reason had been suddenly crippled by the discovery of his crime!

'I never thought he would have done it,' Chiki said, dropping his head, a huge and weary block of bone, into his hands.

'Is here it is,' the corporal said.

A crowd had gathered under the awning of the Moon Glow. The light had changed, and the faces looked dull and formless in the early dark. If it were rumoured that the police were going to search the Moon Glow, the crowd would soon swell into a tumult which Piggott cou⁻ l not control. He wanted to speak with Chiki alone; but duty became less urgent in its demands. He didn't want to leave Fola to the scrutiny of the crowd. But it would have been an open violation of his privilege if he had allowed her to go home. He got out of the car and signalled her to follow. The corporal had run ahead, ordering the dispersal of the crowd. They parted in separate rows, limping indolently away; then quickly closed again and pressed towards the awning of the hotel.

When Fola stepped down from the car and looked towards the awning, she could barely distinguish the faces of the crowd. She was dazed by the heat. The temperature had dropped, but her head felt light as paper. Shadows formed under her eyes spinning black circles up from the street. She thought she would collapse. She rested for a while on the corporal's arm. She heard a vague buzz of voices gathering sound as she approached the hotel. Fola walked as though it were the greatest effort to remember where she was. She noticed the statues on the balustrade above her head; and saw Chiki's shoulders disappearing through the tasselled curtains of the hotel.

But everything seemed foreign to her understanding. For the first time Raymond's death became real. She felt an impulse to ask Piggott if it was really true. She had rushed to Chiki's rescue in the Forest Reserve. Now she felt utterly naked before the crowd. They had brought Fola to her senses. She realised that Chiki was acting on her initiative. Chiki was going to carry this act of invention to its logical conclusion. She didn't know what he was expecting her to do. It might not be difficult to hold her tongue; pretend that her memory had failed; refuse to let herself be trapped into answers whose truth she could not prove. This was possible, but she was terrified by the weight of her responsibility for what was about to

279

happen. It was she who had started Piggott on this enquiry. The moment they were suspected, Fola knew that Chiki would be lost. Perhaps it would have been better to let the police proceed with the arrest of the men in Forest Reserve. Chiki could have proved his innocence. She wanted to withdraw from this fatal enterprise. It was not too late to take Piggott into her confidence. But she could not act alone without exposing Chiki to the consequences of their deception. If Piggott knew, he would find ways of fixing the guilt wholly on Chiki's side. This would have been a greater treachery than her refusal to intervene in the Forest Reserve. She was climbing the stairs which led up to the bar. The corporal noticed her agitation. She wanted to attract Chiki's attention, but the corporal had come between them. He was asking whether she felt all right, but Fola paid no attention.

'You all right?' the corporal asked again.

Piggott had stopped in the passage which led to Chiki's room. He noticed the corporal's delay and came back to see what they were doing.

'You want me call the Commissioner, miss?' the corporal asked.

Fola was staring over his shoulder towards the bar. She saw the waitress making some signal with her hands. The woman's face froze all expression when Piggott appeared.

'What is it, corporal?' Piggott shouted.

'The lady not lookin' well,' the corporal said.

'I'm all right, I'm all right,' Fola said, her voice was quick, nervous, almost inaudible in its gargle of syllables.

'Give her some water,' Piggott shouted to the woman at the bar.

He avoided any direct exchange with Fola. She was still looking towards the bar, trying to read some meaning into the woman's face. Piggott returned to the door where Chiki was waiting. He was impatient to have Chiki on his own. The corporal pulled up a chair. Fola sat down, keeping her glance on the woman's face as she approached with the glass of water. The corporal noticed the way Fola's hand shook when she lifted the glass to her mouth. He could learn nothing from the mute expression on the other woman's face. He left them together; and hurried across the floor down the passage to Chiki's room. He needed to be given fresh orders.

'Is what trouble you get yourself in?' the waitress asked. 'Time an' again I tell you keep out o' this place, 'cause I know it would 'ave bring trouble.'

'What is it?' Fola asked, 'what is it? What it is you want to say?'

The woman was glancing over her shoulder towards the bar.

'What it is you have to say?' Fola asked.

'I don't know what trouble I go get myself in,' the waitress said, 'but is the *Houngan* priest I hiding under the bar. He won't say what it is he know, but he was waiting to see you personal.'

There was a sudden clatter of glass over the floor. Fola's hand rattled like dead bones across the table. A sweat broke over her forehead, twisting a cold, wide trickle of water down her face. The woman thought she was crying.

'Is what it is the *Houngan* know,' the woman asked. 'When he hear the police comin' up the stairs he went cold all over. Is what happen?'

The *Houngan* had raised his head above the bar. Fola caught the look of terror in his eyes. The woman tried to steady her hands. She was shaking all over. The *Houngan* had crept towards the stairs, keeping his head level with the bar. The corporal emerged from the passage. He saw the *Houngan's* head dive out of sight. The corporal stumbled past the chairs and leapt full length across the passage that opened on the door. But it was too late. The *Houngan* had escaped as the corporal pushed himself up slowly from the floor.

'Is what it is happenin' here?' the woman shouted, 'is what you all go do with this girl here? Look at her.'

Fola was shaking all over. She saw the gradual death of the light darken the room. The night was coming down like a hand over her face. She was going to be sick. The woman ran from the chair to the bar and back, asking what to do. She wanted to scream; but she was afraid they would suspect her of some crime. Fola had leaned her head over her hands. Her sobs made a frightful swelling at the base of her skull. The skin ran a constant shudder down her neck. She suffered a total lapse of recognition. The corporal's voice was an alien noise stabbing forgotten names into her ears. With relief she heard Piggott say: 'Tell the driver to take her home.'

Fola was walking on paper, soft, crisp, noiseless. The strong male arm was a pillow of cloud smothering the weight of her back. The stairs slid her softly down into the streets. The gravel broke and melted like icicles under her feet. She was sliding down, down, down; but an unfamiliar darkness guarded her privacy. The crowd had contracted into a solitary face. The leaves dissolved in the wind like ash covering everything. Slowly her consciousness of place and time returned. The car was cruising gently up the Maraval hill. She had abandoned thought of everyone except her mother. When she saw the *Houngan's* shadow slip beneath the bar, the image of her mother had emerged into the room. It was her first recollection that her mother was alive somewhere. It had obliterated every aspect of the day from her memory. She had forgotten Chiki. Piggott became obscure, then wholly hidden under the mask of his duty. The corporal was a shadow making improbable noises. Only her mother remained. Fola had never felt this need before.

For the time being Fola had ceased to care about what had happened. It didn't matter if her father came to life; if Chiki's perjury had been revealed by Piggott's questions. She cared for no one but her mother. Some old and dormant bond of blood had come alive. The darkness showed everywhere some promise of her return to her mother. The past had contracted into a single moment. She hoped that by some miracle of speech, some magic of recognition in their eyes, Agnes would understand this moment and her daughter's need. She had no other prayer but to be with Agnes. She wanted to coil herself to an infant's size, and nestle calm and forgetful in her mother's arms. The street lamps were going on. In the cracked angle of the mirror, the corporal could see her face. Her lips were moving, but the sound soon died. She was whispering through a salt, white froth of spit and tears: 'Aggie . . . Aggie . . . Aggie . . .'

The car circled the lawn. The corporal saluted to the shadows slipping over the porch and into the house. The corporal sat quiet beside the junior constable who drove, afraid to repeat what he was thinking. They were committed to the same order of silence; but rumour was tempting them to speak. They would have spoken. They would have liked to measure and exchange the rumours which had followed Fola's departure from the yard. But they were both cautious: cautious and afraid that neither could entrust his future to the other. The junior constable could rise to stripes if the corporal uttered one error which he could relay to Piggott's ears. They couldn't trust each other; but a natural need was urging them to speak; for tragedy was like a flood that day.

'When it rain it pour,' the corporal said, as though he were talking to himself.

'Telling me?' his junior agreed, 'is that I know.'

'An' when it pour near Bruton Lane,' the corporal said, 'it always bound to flood.'

The junior constable had agreed. He seemed to feel some sympathy for the corporal whose regular beat was Bruton Lane.

'What you see, corporal, on that round,' he said, 'not even half the police force ever know.'

'Time comin' I won't believe my eyes nor ears,' the corporal said, watching his junior through the mirror. 'Tonight it is a girl saying that she know what nobody else don't know. This mornin' it was a man sayin' that he don't know what everybody else done know.'

'You mean the doctor?' the junior constable asked.

The corporal scratched his ears as though he didn't trust them to relay what he had heard.

'Eva any better?' the junior constable asked.

'I aint hear nothing since midday,' the corporal said, 'but whether she alive or dead, she had no right wantin' to reach beyond her station. Is doctor she want to marry. Now doctor even refuse to say he ever see her face before.'

'So many go in that place with abortion trouble,' the junior constable said, 'poor Camillon might be right.'

The corporal frowned and pressed his thumb into his ears.

'Forget my arse,' he said, and his voice startled the man beside him, 'Camillon been sleepin' with that girl ever since she get that job in the federal buildings. Is a common secret all over Bruton Lane.'

The corporal wiped the crease of his ears, and watched his junior in the mirror.

'But why she wait so late?' the junior constable asked.

' 'Cause Camillon is a liar,' the corporal shouted, as though Eva's misfortune was his own, 'Camillon tell her in the very mother's presence that he was going to marry her. All Bruton Lane was waiting to see Eva get what she want. Was lies, just lies that go kill her.'

They seemed to be agreed upon one fact: neither male nor female should desert their proper station.

'I hope she live,' the junior constable said, 'will teach her a lesson for the future.'

But the corporal did not answer. He had decided to close the subject of Eva who now lay dying in the hospital ward which Camillon was ashamed to visit.

'Swing right,' he said, 'an' make it fast.'

'Reserve again?' the junior asked.

'Till a sentry come,' the corporal said, 'Piggott want constant watch keep on the Forest.'

The driver braked suddenly; yelled his oaths at a black cat which had plunged through the headlights across the street. He was afraid of killing animals; but the corporal urged him again to hurry.

'Make it fast,' he said, elbowing his junior's ribs, 'step on it, man.'

The car was making its return journey to the Forest Reserve. But there were no sirens to announce their coming. The night was fearful as the children who struggled to keep awake, wondering what would happen to Chiki.

'Light the lamp,' said Crim, 'I want to see my face.'

'It too early,' Liza's mother said, 'the oil won't last till sleepin' time.'

'Light it all the same,' said Crim, 'I want to see my face.'

Liza's mother had not yet overcome the shock of Piggott's fist against her neck. The look on her face suggested that the yard was not yet free from danger. Sooner or later the police would come back. She could still hear the name, Raymond, fatal and loud like the howl of the black bitch bleeding her ears. She searched for the box in her bosom. It fell from her hand, and the matches scattered over the floor. Crim scooped them up, selecting one which he scratched several times over the worn sulphur of the box. The rest were piled on her lap.

'There,' said Crim, watching the blue flame spread slowly over the wick, 'is better now.'

In his elation, he seemed to forget the importance of what had happened. Some of the women sat on the bed, talking in whispers about Raymond's death. They wanted to know when it had happened. They could talk freely now because they were relieved by Fola's admission about her father. And the police had gone. But Crim looked happy. The women were almost scared by the wicked grin which lit his face as he raised his head up from the lamp.

'Could have been me,' said Crim, caressing Liza with his knees. 'The bastard dead. Once an' for all done dead.'

'When they go bury him?' Liza asked.

Her mother pulled her away, threatening to make her kneel in the dark if she spoke again.

'Is not buryin' fit for the swine,' said Crim, 'I'd drag his dead carcass through the streets for all the Boys to see. Is what I could do if I had the law in my hands.'

Crim rubbed his heels together. His feet made enormous shadows that stretched over the floor and finished on Powell's face. Powell sat silent in the corner, head bowed, wringing his hands like wet clothes.

'Everywhere it have people like me,' Crim said, 'Gonavieve Bay, Half Moon, Petion Square, Dead Ville an' the Saragasso Lane. Everywhere it have people like me. I'd drag him for all to see.'

'You sound as though you would have like to kill him yourself,' one of the women said.

She didn't like the way Crim spoke about the dead. There was no evil which could not be forgotten by the death of their greatest enemy. But Crim was deaf to their pity.

'If only it was me who do it,' he said, 'tonight would have been my night o' glory. I could go out in that street where they searchin' even now for the killer an' clap for joy. Clap, I tell you, clap! But is sufficient to know he done dead, whoever do it.'

'He left wife an' child behind, Crim,' Liza's mother shouted. 'They have a guts like yours an' mine. Is the same grief go rip them open, same, same grief as if death take me from Liza. You hard, Crim, you too hard.'

Crim rose from the chair. He paced round the room to make sure Powell would pay attention to what he was saying. He knew Powell would join him in celebrating the justice which had brought Raymond to his end.

'Is hard you say Crim is,' he said, moving backwards to the chair. 'Is what hard mean you don't understan'. You have pity for Raymon' wife an' chil'. Is them you have pity for. Well let Powell tell you what the bastard do to Little Boy Charlie. For a week he make Little Boy Charlie wife an' chil' starve. An' for what? For what he do that? All 'cause a drop o' champagne stain his jacket. Raymond could buy all the jackets in town. He could buy all the champagne that ships ever bring in this islan'. But he make Little Boy Charlie pay for a simple mistake that couldn't cause harm to a lice in Liza's head. Is what you mean hard?'

'Don't talk so loud,' Liza's mother said. 'People outside.'

'I don't give a rass who outside,' said Crim.

He was breathing hard and fast, wiping one arm across his mouth as he spoke. The women were afraid he might want to repeat what had happened to Raymond. Perhaps he was thinking that Piggott too should go.

'You too excited, Crim,' one of the women said. 'Steady your nerves before they get you in trouble.'

'It won't make sense to bring a fresh murder on your head just so,' Liza's mother said. 'That don't make sense at all.'

Crim wiped his mouth again, and sat down. Powell did not speak; but he had raised his head to see the women's faces. They knew that he agreed with Crim, and suddenly the women felt treacherous and ashamed. They were taking sides with Raymond and Piggott. They were asking mercy for the enemies of the Reserve, for men who never gave a thought whether Liza and the children of Forest Reserve were left to starve.

'My mood that night was ripe for murderin' him,' Crim said. 'But the nearest I get was to slip some crush glass bottle in his pocket. Was the best I could do for Little Boy Charlie.'

'But he dead now,' Liza's mother said. 'Since he done dead you can let him rest.'

The room was quiet but for the fall of leaves over the huts, and the hot, white whisper of the flame frying the air inside the chimney. A moth swooped round the lamp and fell softly down the oval brass belly of the lamp. Liza was dozing where she stood, her body safely cradled between her mother's thighs. The woman could feel a gradual heaviness sink the breast which pillowed Liza's head. There was an odour of peppermint in the slow warm intervals of breath which filtered down her arm.

'We ought to give thanks for what that girl do,' Liza's mother said, 'nobody know what would have happen to all you inside that cell.'

'Would have been different from any ordinary arrest,' the other woman said. 'Even when the Bands fight in Dead-Ville an' slash the constable 'cross his neck, it was a sight what they do to young Jack o' Lantern an' his Boys. Smash in their face with kick an' butt. Some o' them couldn't talk for days. An' he was just a ordinary constable what get slash.'

Crim seemed to agree. For the first time he was trying to think what might have happened if Piggott's men had taken them away. The thought had started a hot, quick palpitation under his left eye as though his own wounds came fresh with the memory of previous battles he had had with the police. Once they had broken Powell's ribs.

'Whatever you feel 'bout Piggott,' the woman said, 'is the girl save all you from a terrible bashin' up.'

'They couldn't hold you for the murder,' Liza's mother said, 'but they would have use the chance to spring a next charge 'pon the lot o' you.'

Crim was pitiless in revenge; but the women's talk had calmed his mood. Gratitude was his sole weakness. Aroused by the full meaning of Raymond's death, he started to feel that Fola had earned his thanks. He felt no less hostile towards Piggott; but a miracle had happened when he started to think of Fola in her own right. The image of Piggott had receded from his mind, and he thought of Fola strictly in terms of what she had done. For the time being, she became what she had done, independent in her action, elevated by Crim's gratitude beyond any relation she might have had with people like Raymond and Piggott. No obstacle of motive

287

had entered his mind to cast doubt on what he felt. The girl had saved their skins. He was reluctant to make concessions to the women, but the force of gratitude had reduced his pride. He believed he ought to admit that the women were right. But he remembered their talk about Raymond, and suddenly changed his mind. He was going to wait until he and Powell were alone.

'That girl, Fola,' Crim said, and stopped.

Powell had leapt up from the floor at the sound of Crim's voice. The girl's name was like a poison in Powell's ears. He made to speak; then changed his mind and walked outside. Liza's mother prised the window up to see where he had gone; but the light showed nothing but his shadow hugging the curve beyond Mathilda's shop. She wanted Crim to forget the girl.

'What 'bout some food?' she asked.

Crim shook his head, and pondered Powell's hatred of people like Fola. Generosity was like the very stench of the enemy from whom Powell had to receive.

'What 'bout you?' the woman asked, offering the food to the tall boy who squatted in the corner.

But the boy shook his head, and answered from the dark that he wasn't hungry. No one wanted to eat. The shock of Raymond's death had robbed them of hunger. It made Crim wonder about the greed men called their appetite. No kind or quantity of food could have tempted them to eat. Even Karl, whom the dogs had learnt to hate for his gluttony, had refused. It was as though his greed had waited for this tragedy in order to abandon him. Crim tried to recall some evening when a similar disaster had shocked them out of their normal habits. But he could think of nothing equal to this atmosphere which choked the light in everyone's eyes. The darkness was pushing up from the floor like a mangrove swamp, flooding the corners of the hut. And suddenly they realised that something was missing. Powell had gone out. They knew where Chiki was. But Gort's absence was like the weight of what had happened to Raymond.

'Where Gort?' Liza's mother asked.

And Crim replied: 'Where Gort?' as though question and answer were identical.

Gort was alone; alone with a mystery that collected only evil in his head. He lay on the mound of stones beyond the yard, and blew his nose, feeling the slime of mucus fall down his sleeves. The thin partition of gristle shook and dripped red inside his nostrils. He blew his nose again, and a noise like the sea burst in his ears. It made him hear the chime of bells telling a funeral in the Saragasso cemetery. The noise made new echoes when he blew his nose again. It seemed there was nothing he could do but punish his nose.

He lay on the mound of stones. Gort wept for his loss; he wept because he could not understand. He had looked for the last time at his drum where a segment of the steel had been torn open by the stones. He had seen the paint of Chiki's navel ripped wide apart. The hole opened on a darkness which shut him out from everything. He was blowing his nose as he watched his hands, all skill denied them by the fatal disfigurement of his drum. That smooth, polished basin of steel was the only source of delight he had found reliable. Women might betray him; children turn rude against him; but his hands had taught that steel to talk. His will resided in that drum.

He was a simple man, sparing of speech; and so his sadness turned on simple questions: simple and deep, for mystery now seemed to cover everything with evil. There was no need to remind himself of his relation to the drum. It was their bond which had given Gort the name everyone had chosen for him. When you said a man was great in Forest Reserve, it meant that his faults were a privilege which he had earned. There was nothing he could do to lose your admiration. Chiki was simply Chiki to everyone. But Gort was Great Gort in their admiration. He was unique in his relation to that tenor drum.

Gort's whims were often treated like a natural impediment. In some ways, his deficiencies had a force which no one tried to resist. They could compel attention like a child's. Like a child, his fears had the same sharpness of impact as his delight. One example was his refusal to have sugar in his tea. Sometimes the slightest doubt would make Gort feel some terrible evil was lurking where he could not see. Gort avoided sugar like a poison; he avoided it as he now did the shape of his dead drum which lay not far away.

language & contrasted w/
drum literacy – privillege/agency

And he thought of the children and the blind; for the death of the drum reminded him that he could not read or write. He had grown to feel this like an impediment which he knew he was too old to correct. Gort always thought he was too old to learn what came to children like their natural breathing. And it made him slow to ask questions. Perhaps the questions were simple; but he was sure the answer would be part of that way of knowing which he had failed to learn as a child. It was this darkness that gave him a special kinship with the blind. And it made him cautious in talking with the blind. Such talk made Gort feel guilty about the tremendous advantage of his sight. It seemed unjust that Bobby Chalk could not see. And as he would feel the unjust advantage of his own sight; so he would watch Liza read, and feel his lack of learning increase its weight. But he was reluctant to ask too many questions because he didn't want to impose the weight of his impediment on others. Perhaps, he thought, it was the way old Bobby Chalk might feel from time to time. It was this blindness which had poisoned his taste for sugar.

Gort had suddenly discovered something which must have been obvious to everyone. Yet he found it difficult to ask Powell, or Crim, or even Chiki. Gort found it difficult to ask why they had never bothered about the mystery which he had discovered. For it was a mystery to Gort that his discovery had not produced a similar effect in Chiki or Powell or Crim. Perhaps they understood. He could not ask, because the answer would have been simple, and yet beyond his understanding. For it belonged to a world from which he had been excluded by his lack of learning.

As he watched his dead drum not far away, this mystery of the sugar had returned to plague his lack of understanding. For he could never accept the day his drum would die. Yet it was there, dead, and mysterious as his fear of sugar. Ordinary as it seemed, how could he explain his mysterious fear of the sugar. For years he had bought his sugar from those three women: Flo, Unice and Mathilda. He chose according to his need. But one morning something happened, like the season he had seen come and go in the children's eyes.

Gort had bought a pound of sugar from Mathilda's shop. Half-way on his return, the sugar dropped from his hands. He cursed his luck, but kept straight to Flo's shop where he bought another pound. And then it happened: that fateful pause which started the mystery in his mind. Gort couldn't understand why he should have been so shaken by what he had realised. Suddenly he hurried away to check his memory. That day, Gort bought three pounds of sugar; one from each woman. His memory had served him right, and from that moment the mystery grew like an evil over his lack of understanding.

The mystery was there, dark and sinister in those three shops; it was there behind those women's eyes. 'Witches,' he said to himself, 'they are witches.' Witch was the word he used; and sugar became for him the source of all witchcraft. He started to live again the nights and days which told a history of hatred that was larger than any San Cristobal had known. Flo hated Unice, and Mathilda hated both no less than she was hated by them. And yet, Gort thought, and yet, and yet! It was mysterious as the death of his drum. These witches were agreed upon one thing:

Mathilda sold her sugar at five cents a pound!

Flo sold her sugar at five cents a pound!

Unice sold her sugar at five cents a pound!

The power of evil behind that agreement had completely shattered Gort's mind. But how could he ask Powell or Crim if they had noticed it? How could he explain this lack of understanding to Chiki? Perhaps they understood: but their way of knowing was a world from which he had been shut out because he could not read or write. He would not ask.

As Gort watched the drum, he felt a similar impediment of speech. The tears were running down his cheeks. No one but Bobby Chalk had ever made him cry this way. Tougher than Crim or Powell if he had to be, Gort now felt his weakness spread to every limb of his body: a child shut out in the night as he blew his nose to attract attention. The darkness crawled slowly out of the forest and covered the yard. He could no longer see the drum. But how? But how? It was like the mystery of the sugar all over again. How? How? How could he explain to Piggott what he had done? What law in all San Cristobal would agree that a murder more terrible than Raymond's death had been committed on his drum? How? How? The women heard Gort's noise, and came out. They thought it was the dog. But they found Gort prostrate on the mound of stones. He was too weak to blow his nose. And he was crying.

The Forest could understand why no one ate. And the republic too! For Piggott's appetite was no greater at this hour. The light that blazed near Federal Drive was like the darkness in this yard. The Boys from Forest Reserve, the original and forgotten bastards of the new republic, were now remembered by everyone. For the night had made them equal with the law. They shared in the same new faith throughout San Cristobal. They had to start with what they could believe; and they believed that Fola had discovered who her father was.

CHAPTER XIII

And so Black Fortnight had begun. The republic was in pursuit of a man whose sole identity was Chiki's portrait, a man whose name had become Fola's father. The nights were haunted by a face which always eluded memory. In the uneasy intervals of sleep, some fugitive step was often heard, pacing the muffled stillness of the hour, leaving no trace of crime. But the republic's faith grew stronger in its sleep; for everyone had dreams; and each dream seemed to confirm the accuracy of the painter's eye. Each morning awoke with fresh promise of evidence to prove that Fola was right. Memory shone like a torch on her mother's secret which everyone had known and forgotten; the class war this crisis had resurrected.

The darkness was always a nervous change from daylight. It arrived and settled in all its size, filling the trees with a regiment of faces no vigilance could yet identify. By day, the children would play a game of telling what everyone wanted to know. They would watch the mirrored half of a face through broken bits of bottle, and sing:

'Who kill Raymond?' one voice began.

And the chorus answered: 'He!'

'He' was the face which looked down from the wall where their fingers pointed. The bigger boys collected into squads as though they were police, conducting an independent search; for the republic had offered a reward for Raymond's assassin: a reward which seemed as large as America or the moon.

But the portrait gave no evidence of complexion, height or size of the body which finished where the republic's posters were stuck on every wall. The painter's hand had preserved the naked outline of a murder and a man: a face which had been caught in every line and movement of its features. A narrow precipice of forehead was sliding softly into the hollow arches of two curious and tormented eyes. The eyes looked suspicious and alert in different ways. The left eye seemed more nervous, more reluctant to open up as though it were afraid of what it saw, glancing backward from the corner of its socket. But the right eye was wide and fierce, a triumphant glare of certainty dazzling its surface. The eyes seemed to compete for an exclusive vision of what confronted them; fixed, hard and determined, as though they were in private agreement about two different ways of seeing. Shadows came natural over the face which seemed to change its glance according to the direction of the sun. The children were astonished by the movement which brought each line alive before their eyes. Sometimes it seemed that the whole head had lifted itself up from the poster, crawling like a snail or crab over the wall. It played curious tricks on their staring. But the game continued.

'Who kill Raymond?' the boy's voice cried.

And the chorus answered again: 'He!'

They had pointed casually at the wall behind them; but their fingers were accusing a man who had paused to check his likeness to the portrait. The man turned, staring anxiously at the children. They had noticed his terror. His face started to shrink, and his hands grew cold. He was about to speak, when the children burst into song again, chasing after him as they shouted: 'He! He! He kill Raymond!' Their voices went with the wind, attracting notice from every window. People rushed into the street, asking: 'Who? who?' And the children, aroused by their triumph, quickened their pace behind the man, shouting: 'He, he, he kill Raymond.'

Through lanes the width of a hand, up the sharp, dry bramble

293

of a track, the man ran like a hare, leaping through puddles of mud and broken bottles towards his home. The children's voices had ended in a hush far, far in the distance where the echoes continued their chase after the man. There was no trace of him in the street. He had plunged through the foliage of the trees, slicing his skin against a nettle vine as he fell noisily into the pond. He struggled to surface, clutching at the red shadows over the near bark of a lignum vitæ tree. He used his hands like spades, ploughing his nails into the soft wet earth. His mouth made bubbles with the mud as he kneaded his forehead into the ground, trying to raise his legs on to the grass. He heard a child's voice crying for help. He stretched and rolled over on his back.

Liza began to scream when she recognised his face. She stood where she was, convulsed with fear; scratching her fingers into her eyes. The women ran out from the huts, snatching bramble out of their way as they ran in search of Liza. Her mother was terrified. She lifted Liza with one arm, and wrapped the skirt around her with the other. Liza was still making a violent shiver in the skirt. She hid her eyes with both hands as the women moved towards the pond where the *Houngan* sat. He had pushed himself up, letting his back rest against the branch of the lignum vitæ tree. He wiped the mud off his chin, and raised his head to see the women.

'Jesus an' all the Saints,' Liza's mother cried, 'is what happen to you, *Houngan*?'

'Is what happen?' the women repeated.

'Is how I hear the child scream.' Liza's mother said, 'make me think the criminal man let loose 'pon she.'

The *Houngan* braced his body and tried to stand.

'Is what happen to you, *Houngan*?'

'Is what happen we ask,' Liza's mother said, 'You lookin' like you commit some crime.'

The *Houngan* thrust his arm out as though he had given an order for silence. But the women saw his arm fail to keep its balance in the air. It trembled and fell weakly down his side.

'Is what happen to you, *Houngan*, is why you can't talk?'

'Is what you do?'

294

'All right, all right,' Liza's mother said, growing impatient with the others, 'let him catch breath. Is how you expect him to talk in that state?'

The *Houngan* continued to wipe the mud from his chin. Liza's head emerged from the skirt. She saw the *Houngan* slowly grinding his teeth, and she started to scream again. The women were agitated, and the *Houngan* lost nerve again.

'Is what you keepin' Liza with you for?' a woman shouted.

' 'Cause she scared,' the mother cried.

'All right she scared, then take her inside.'

'But the child scared,' the mother cried, 'the child scared.'

'Great Jesus,' the woman shouted, 'I see she scared. Is why I say take her inside.'

'But she scared,' the mother insisted.

The women grew irritable and obscene as they argued about Liza. The *Houngan* wanted to call for order; but he wasn't sure of his strength. He seemed more scared than Liza as he tried to raise his arm, calling the women to his aid.

'Tell it, *Houngan*, is what you think happen?'

'Is what you see, *Houngan*,' Liza's mother begged, 'is what make your vision tighten up your tongue so?'

'He movin' like it was a ceremony,' the other woman said. 'Is the spirit go ride him.'

'Tell it, *Houngan*, tell it now you can.'

But the *Houngan* couldn't speak. The glare burnt his eyes sore and set a momentary darkness over the women's faces. He had felt his power slip, and he was afraid. The gods had chosen this moment to punish him. Perhaps he had betrayed his authority. He had gone beyond his proper sphere as a servant of the gods. Perhaps he had been given warning the night that soul challenged his power; and the dead boy, wailing for his unknown mother, threatened to free himself from the sacred water in which the gods had locked his soul. He had been made speechless that night by the turbulent passion of the dead boy telling his loss in the tent. Only a miracle had saved his dignity, rescued his power from disgrace; and when the dead soul withdrew, changed suddenly to a calm of spirit until its final release into the night, he knew the gods had intervened.

Yet he had come out of the tent assuming all the powers of his command. Nothing had changed his pride. But that night was a warning. He shouldn't have taken the girl into the secret chambers of the *tonelle*. Perhaps it was this blasphemy which had angered the gods. He had given way to the conceit of his privilege by granting the white man's request. It was Charlot whom he wanted to please. He had used his pride in order to feel some equal status which the stranger represented; and the girl had trespassed upon the secrecies of his calling.

But the gods were vigilant. Patient in their knowledge, they had worked out his punishment. They had arranged a public crime which would be his burden. He was pursued by their revenge; for the voices he had heard last night were clear and familiar as the dead boy's cry in the *tonelle*. The gods had refused to name his sin; but they had instructed him in the nature of his punishment. Sooner or later San Cristobal would agree that he was the man who had killed Raymond. No plea could soften the gods' revenge.

He had been absent from the *tonelle* for the second night, chased by his fear of the gods' judgment. He knew it would happen soon. The end was near. Beyond the gods, there was no power to intervene in his behalf. He saw his future like the end of his hand. He had seen it in the children's hands, pointing their accusation when he fled. He had seen it in the faces of the women who waited, innocent and terrified by the silence which locked his tongue. It was the power of the gods which had chosen their questions. It was the power of the gods which worked that cruel and accusing chant in the children's voices. He hadn't committed this crime; yet he knew it was his responsibility. He couldn't claim the girl as his daughter; but he was sure it was that night which had fathered the part she played in Raymond's death.

That night rehearsed each stage of worship in his head. The drums were exploding as he felt his eyes swinging about his ears, swelling into a cataract of flames which lit the women's faces. They froze and melted into dust. The pond contracted to a circle which the women entered, dancing the *ververs* into dust. But the gods would not arrive. The light of the flambeaux grew dim. The tent had collapsed over his head, but his power failed. The *Houngan* could hear his own bones rattle and dissolve in the ceremonial jars which fell and spilt ashes over the secret chamber. The girl who trespassed on these secrecies was kneeling before him, but he had lost his power to convert. The gods had returned his frailties. He was helpless as the girl panting with fear for the change which now paralysed his mind. He was changed for ever by the wave of desecration which swept that night. There was a feel of chaos everywhere. The wind stifled his breathing. He had put out his hand, trying to disfigure the fugitive gaze of the face which reflected his own image in the pond. The women had come under the spell of his possession. Liza climbed out of her mother's skirt and stood before him, pointing at the dry cakes of mud which hung from his chin.

'Is what happen, *Houngan?*' her mother asked again.

'Is what put you in a fright, *Houngan?*'

But he did not answer. He had stumbled past Liza, staring at his reflection in the water. A wide shadow of smoke passed over the trees making a dull blur over the water. He was haunted by his knowledge of what must happen. His end was near. He could hear it in the echo of voices gathering their echoes on the other side of the Reserve: 'Who kill Raymond?'

'Is what happen, *Houngan?*' Liza's mother asked. But he was not there. He had leapt across the pond, galloping up the track of crisp dead leaves. They saw his body disappear behind a thin haze of smoke which travelled slowly into the pond.

'Is what you think he see?'

'I don't know,' Liza's mother said.

'Where Gort an' Crim?' one of the women asked.

'I don't know,' said Liza's mother, 'they been to look for Powell.'

'An' Chiki?'

'No word come yet from Chiki,' Liza's mother answered.

An odour of burnt leaves followed them back to the yard. Liza sheltered under her mother's skirt while the women watched the slow, thick movement of sandflies that circled above their heads. They stood still and watched the sandflies, bright black and nervous as leaves sailing in circles with the wind. The smoke had chased more sandflies from the forest into the yard. The women searched their memories for omens of the day. The sandflies grew thicker, a sure warning of some personal tragedy which would befall the Reserve. This tragedy would be near and more personal than Raymond's death, because it was still unknown. But they were all reminded of a night the sandflies had collected in similar numbers. It was the time the police raided the Reserve, and Titon disappeared with the casket which contained nothing but Guru's false teeth. They were sure the sandflies were warning that something had happened to Powell.

'Exact like the mornin' his uncle left we all for good,' Liza's mother said.

'You think the police kill Powell in sceret?'

'I don't know,' said Liza's mother. 'If Gort an' Crim don't know, how you expect poor me to know.'

'He go come soon,' the other woman said, consoling her, 'Powell go walk back this very day self.'

Now the dogs started to whine as though they understood the omens which the *Houngan's* visit had prepared them for. Liza slipped between her mother's legs and ran towards the hut where the black bitch lay. Its head had fallen sideways against its paws. A lid of skin grew tight, quivering with sound over its teeth. The animal's cry had distracted the women's attention from the sand-flies. They watched Liza caress the animal's head.

'Since mornin' the dog make that noise,' Liza's mother said. 'Like do know what go happen here.'

'Tell Liza take her outside. I can't stand that groanin'.'

'It don' make no difference,' the mother said, 'what go happen will happen. I only wonder where Powell get to.'

'He go come soon,' the woman said, 'you know how Powell is sometimes, strange an' quiet in his ways.'

'But is since morning',' Liza's mother said, 'breakfast an' his midday meal still there, not touch.'

'Is what you worryin' so for? Powell all right.'

The bitch continued to whine; but they noticed that the sand-flies had suddenly broken their flight. They seemed to struggle with their wings, trying to keep their balance. But the wings would not take flight again. They were tottering down to the yard.

'Don't touch it,' someone said, 'let them dead jus' so.'

The women moved back a little, watching the sandflies wriggle. They gazed in a fearful wonder at the flies as though they were a human corpse struggling to come back to life. Then they were surprised by Liza's voice. She was making a bed of cardboard and leaves under the cellar when she saw the men's feet coming towards the yard. Gort and Crim had just turned the passage which led between the huts into the yard. Liza's mother ran forward, impatient for news.

'He not anywhere,' said Crim. His voice was low, almost inaudible, and cold beyond feeling as he stared at the sandflies.

'I been Half Way Tree, Gonavieve Bay, Saragasso, Petionville, Church Row, everywhere within reasonable walkin'. Wherever there's bands livin' I been, an' he aint nowhere.'

Gort walked past the women. Liza's mother was silent. She was going to cry any minute; and the women drew near.

'Is only one place left,' said Crim. He paused, staring at the sandflies which stuck against his heel. 'Is a chance they got him in the Jamestown gaol,' said Crim.

'But what Powell do?' Liza's mother shouted. 'Powell aint do nothin'. W'at they hold him for?'

'Who say so?' one of the women asked.

'How come you hear that happen?'

'But what Powell do?' Liza's mother continued.

The women were getting hysterical.

'Nobody aint do nothin',' Crim shouted, 'but it don't make no difference.' His voice was sharp, irritable, and full of censure. He was looking at Gort who remained silent.

'Is only a chance,' said Crim. 'I don' know for sure. But is a chance he with all the rest. It start this mornin'. Squash, Bugles, Pips, the whole lot get collect this mornin'. Every man of age if he fit the same description of the criminal who kill Raymond. The police collect twenty-five from round the *tonelle*. Women an' children howlin' like it was a new murder for the numbers they collect. An' all 'cause the police couldn't find the *Houngan*. Is two nights they been wantin' him to help with some questions, an' when he didn't show up this mornin', the arrest begin. Some say twenty-five, some say fifty. You can't tell for sure. But is a chance Powell get collect with them too."

'But Powell don' look like that man.'

'He don't look nothin' like him,' the women repeated.

'It don't matter,' Crim said.

'But Powell don' look like him,' Liza's mother insisted.

'Jesus Christ, woman, it don' matter,' Crim shouted. 'Look or no look, if the police collect you, then you done collect. It happenin' everywhere, an' specially where the Bands live. Some people already start to forget how they look. It have a man in the Belle View pull out all his teeth to make sure his face change. An' a next done cut off one o' his ears. It got men doin' terrible things to themselves for the sake o' disguise. Every place it happenin' soon as the posters put up that face in the open air.'

'Powell in the Jamestown gaol,' Liza's mother was crying.

But she didn't continue. Crim looked at Gort, deciding what he should do about the noise which rose from the street. He bit his teeth and swore. Liza's mother was sobbing, and the women waited round her, listening as though they would never escape that noise from the street. The children were chanting again: 'Who kill Raymond? Who kill Raymond?'

The men left the yard again to go in search of Chiki. Ever since the search began, Powell had become more reticent. He would leave the yard without telling anyone his whereabouts. When he returned, he would behave as though his movements had nothing to do with anyone else. It was exactly the way his uncle, Titon, had behaved when they heard the police were going to raid the Reserve for the diamonds which had disappeared.

The search for Raymond's assassin had put an end to the Boys' raids at night. No one expected to be given orders; but the gangs were still waiting: Escapade in Blue, Royal Navy Number Two, and Name Like the Virgin Mary. They continued to meet in the yard, exchanging news about Raymond's death. Crim had an idea which might have helped them to continue their raids at night. Since they were familiar with the ways of criminals, he thought they might offer their services to the police. They would work as a voluntary patrol in search of Fola's father. It would have given them legal access to places where they dared not trespass in ordinary times.

But nothing could be decided because Powell was not there, and Gort had ceased to think about anything but the death of his tenor drum. He walked behind Crim everywhere like a small dog on a leash. When Crim tried to explain his plan to Powell, he showed no interest. Then he said he was tired. Powell had become cold, sullen towards everyone. But Crim didn't press him. He thought Powell was in one of his moods, only much worse since Raymond's death. Crim had decided to wait; but Powell had now disappeared.

'I don't feel he in gaol,' said Crim. 'I was only tryin' to pacify the yard, knowin' how them women can go wild when they scared.'

'But where he get to then?' Gort asked.

'I can' say,' said Crim, 'but I feel he stay away to show his feelin'. Powell got a bad grudge 'gainst that girl gettin' mixed up with the Boys. He done don't like her, an' he want to let Chiki know.'

'But she save we skin that evening Piggott an' his gang come in,' said Gort, 'they would 'ave beat the hell out everyone down in the cell. Guilty or not guilty they would have make we pay for that bastard, Raymond.'

'Powell didn't show no feelin' then,' said Crim. 'Was only Powell who never look thanks or anything. Like he was vex' 'cause she do what she do.'

'Ever since that evening he make a change,' said Gort, 'I didn't say nothin', 'cause it didn't make sense.'

'Powell was always strange,' Crim said.

'And proud,' said Gort. 'Strange an' proud. He always treat the police like they was his special paid servants.'

'Was the reason he quarrel with Chiki soon after,' said Crim. 'He didn't like that Chiki offer up any portrait. An' he didn't like how the girl an' Chiki was gettin' on.'

'He always had a bad hatred for them people,' said Gort, 'but it don't have no reason he should go on like this, takin' it out on the Boys.'

'Crim.'

'W'at happen?'

Gort paused, and looked over his shoulder.

'You don' think Powell do it?'

'Do what?' Crim asked, and his mouth hadn't closed after he had spoken.

They hopped the bus that drove towards Bruton Lane. It was almost empty; for people had grown suspicious of anything named public. They seemed to think that public transport and the public posters were part of the same intention.

'You got sandflies up your way?' the conductor asked.

But Crim didn't answer. Gort shook his head as though he had forgotten where he lived. The street passed like foreign boundaries before his eyes. Crim fumbled in his pocket for change, but the conductor stopped his hand and made signal with his eyes. Pity had urged him to give them a free ride.

'It not true they go close down the Bands?' the conductor asked. 'I hear it rumour 'bout town.'

Gort showed no interest in the news. The police could have closed his ears, or sealed a blindness on his eyes like old Bobby Chalk's. He had abandoned his claim to anything that mattered.

'But the sandflies aint leave out nobody,' said the conductor, trying to console them, 'they rompin' wild all round the Federal Drive, Maraval hills an' wherever the big powers be.'

Crim looked up as though he needed confirmation about the spread of the sandflies; but he didn't speak. He was thinking of Powell and the time his uncle disappeared.

'But the good God know why he send them,' the conductor said, taking sides with the boys, 'no hosepipe, an' no flit will ever wipe out what the good God send to afflict who sin.'

The bus shook and grumbled as it came to a halt near Independence Square. Crim stepped down, and Gort followed close behind, his head turned towards the street. They walked away, trying to avoid the crowd which were collecting round the Independence statue.

A formal mourning had been imposed on the town. Flags flew half-mast over the public buildings. There was a special Mass in the Catholic cathedral. But the public grief hadn't stirred anyone to eloquence about Raymond's virtues. Fola's confession had started a scandalous division in certain well-known homes. Women who had formerly drawn on her charm as a model for their daughter now referred to her as the girl. She was the girl who made them wonder about the fraudulent secrecy of men. Respectable fathers left meals untouched, outraged by suggestions that their propriety was now in question. Others who had met by chance in forbidden houses of the town shared confidences in the hope that they might be convinced that Fola's mother was never among their list of half-remembered pleasures.

There was no consolation in the thought that Fola's mother had kept her secret all these years. Her status had made such a reluctance seem perfectly natural. But she might have postponed her secret until she thought the girl was old enough to know. There were men for whom the least substantial rumour could become a permanent stain on their ambition. Content to be in the public eye, they had a dread of ever being in public doubt. This panic had started when two anonymous women from the Bloomfield sugar estates arrived at the President's office. They were chased away. But they found his house and insisted that his wife should hear the respect their hearts had honoured him with. They wanted her to be free from any suspicion that the man who had fathered their own children and was by right her husband would have arranged the murder of his closest colleague. Scandal and the charge of murder became identical extremes. The families couldn't agree which was the graver of the two. Political murder had become a grave domestic urgency.

Crim heard the voices exchanging rumour. Someone was saying that the assassin had given himself up. Then the rumour changed. The crowd were waiting to form a patrol which would go in search of Fola's father. Then Crim felt a hand pull him gently from behind. He was relieved to think that Powell had returned.

'You see Chiki anywhere?' Therese asked.

For a moment he tried to think how he could avoid her. But Therese was dressed in mourning for some loss.

'We lookin' for him,' said Gort, as though he were talking to the servant's black dress.

'You think he in Moon Glow?' Therese asked.

'We don't know,' said Crim.

'Jesus an' all the Saints,' Therese cried.

Crim felt a sudden resentment towards her as though it was she who had caused Powell to desert the Boys.

'What happen?' Gort asked.

Therese wiped her eyes dry and looked towards the Moon Glow bar.

'Tell me it happen anywhere else,' she said, 'an' I would believe. But this pass all what possible. Not possible, I tell you, if I didn't see an' hear right where it happen.'

'What happen?' Gort asked her again.

'Is Piggott,' said Therese, glancing towards the Moon Glow bar, 'he send the wife away in secret, and throw Miss Fola out the house. Throw her right out with not a stitch o' clothes.'

Therese wiped her eyes as she spoke, glancing from the men to the Moon Glow bar.

'An' if you know how he used to idolise Miss Fola,' she said. 'Miss Fola was his all in all. Nothing she could ever do to set his back 'gainst her. Miss Fola was a queen in Piggott eye till the night he throw her out. Good God, it seem like the whole world come to a stop.'

Gort was silent. Crim hadn't relaxed in his resentment towards her; but he couldn't control his urge to hear what had happened to Fola.

'An' where she is?' he asked.

'I don't know,' said Therese, 'she not with any o' the families, but perhaps Chiki might know. I say to myself Chiki might know.'

'Is why he throw her out?' Gort asked, coming nearer to Therese.

She was careful not to disclose anything which might betray her loyalty to Fola. In no circumstances would she have exposed Fola to Gort or Crim. But she had to find her, and she believed that Chiki and his friends could help. Nothing else would have forced her to share the secrets of Piggott's house with these men.

'I don't think she left with a friend in all this world,' Therese cried, 'not after how I see how they treat her that night.'

'Is what happen?' Gort asked again, feeling that the assassin had been found.

'Is why he throw her out I can't say for sure,' Therese said. 'Believe me I can't say for sure. But it was after Miss Veronica what lose her father break the news. Was Miss Veronica what cause it.'

Piggott had been broken completely by the strain of Raymond's death. Already he had been torn between his friendship with Raymond, and the need to protect his wife from any involvement which was bound to embarrass her. The authorities had tried to console him by paying tributes to his record of public service. But they could not conceal their doubt about the motives which might force Piggott to avoid any unpleasant evidence in the search for Raymond's killer. No one could have expected him to be impartial on this occasion. He had refused to promise that Agnes would, at any time, help to identify the man whom Fola had declared to be her father. He had arranged for Agnes to leave the house in secret. No one knew where she had gone. She was not there when Piggott's assistant came to ask whether she had anything to say about her daughter's evidence, so the case had been taken out of Piggott's hands. He had retained his status as Commissioner; but he was not allowed to exercise any powers in this search for the man who had murdered Raymond. And finally there was Veronica's arrival.

This was the episode which Therese was trying to keep secret from Gort and Crim. She could get no further than telling them the fury which Veronica's news had aroused in Piggott. Fola and Veronica had sat at opposite ends of the table, staring at each other, charged with a hatred they could not control, enemies for ever. Veronica had come to avenge her father's death. There was malice and spite in every line of her face as she told the disgrace which Fola had brought on all the families. Fola hadn't yet lost her nerve. She was ready for anything which Veronica had to say. But Veronica had chosen her knowledge with malicious care. She never raised the question of her father's death, except to explain for Piggott why Fola was trying to protect the men in Forest Reserve.

Piggott listened like a man in a trance. Veronica could recognise in his face the same terror she had felt the evening Fola had spoken of her fantastic desire for the Boy from the Reserve. Piggott watched Veronica as she repeated the history of that night, and he could not judge which was a deeper grief: his wife's humiliation or Fola's unspeakable disgrace. To have been made pregnant by a ruffian from the Forest Reserve! All his achievements had crumbled. Fola had dragged him back to the forgotten squalor of his past. Something had rocketed inside as Veronica brought the news to an end. Therese had never seen such a coarse and primitive violence before, not even among men in the Reserve. Piggott had gone berserk.

It was this change of temper which had made Fola utterly defenceless in his presence. She had no strength to explain how Veronica had come by her information. And Piggott gave her no chance to speak. Alone and denied, Fola was paying for the dumb power which could not explain Fola, *and other than*. Everything seemed to go suddenly dry inside her. There was a taste of dust on her tongue. Her blood was like gravel. Her eyes had grown hot and hard with staring at the insane contortions of Piggott's face. He looked like an animal in pain as he lifted Fola up from the chair. Then the last vestige of restraint gave way; and a cruel violence came into everything he did.

Therese and Agnes watched, their eyes made impotent by the thunder of his fists on Fola's body. Piggott had plunged across the table, seizing her by the throat to bring her into line with the steady hammering of his knee against her ribs. His hands fell like iron on her skin, as though he thought it his duty to murder the seed which that ruffian from the Reserve had planted in Fola's body. Her mouth split open at the side, and a pool of blood ran down her chin. Agnes had fainted; but Piggott was too blind with rage to notice her collapse. Veronica went to her aid; while Therese could not be severed from her loyalty. She sat on the porch, putting one leg under Fola's head. She arched the body up so that her hands could make a bed under Fola's back. Then Piggott closed the door, as though he had forgotten what he had done. Therese could not see, but she kept her hands like a coffin round the corpse which Fola had become as she lay there. She had taken Fola to her house that night; but when day broke over the Reserve, Fola had gone.

[handwritten marginal note: Piggott beats Fola]

'I want her know my house free,' Therese said, as she glanced from the Moon Glow back to Gort and Crim.

Gort looked at her as though he could see nothing but the mourning black dress which she wore.

'Is what I want her know,' said Therese, 'my house aint got the style she used to, but it free anytime she want. Is all I want her know.'

Crim had softened towards her. He leaned his head sideways as though he wanted to suggest that he would have done the same.

'But don't behave like she dead,' said Crim, ' 'cause I aint think she dead.'

'Never mourn before it is time,' said Gort, slapping his hand on her back.

'I not mournin' for Miss Fola,' she said, ' 'cause I know she alive somewhere.'

'Then change out o' that frock,' Crim said, and turned to go.

'Is the other one I mournin' for,' Therese said, waving her hand towards Bruton Lane. 'Is poor Eva what lyin' now like Miss Fola look that night.'

'The Bartok girl?' Gort asked.

'She dead, this morning,' said Crim, 'I hear it when we was lookin' for Powell.'

Now the men understood her mourning, but they couldn't guess the depth of Therese's loyalty to those two girls. Eva and Fola were twin griefs in her mind, twin loyalties which were different, and yet equal. For only death could free the secret which she had kept from Fola and all the girls who worked in the federal buildings. Therese was Eva's aunt.

The town was in a state of siege; but the search had reached the remotest corners of the land. At Half Moon Bay where news was rare, and people had lived without asking questions about the politics of the new republic, several posters with the assassin's face had appeared. They were stuck on walls and trees, made prominent on the back of every bus. Children copied the face in pencil on their slates; and old people searched their memories for a resemblance which they were certain could be identified. There were so many rumours about the man, that no one finally knew what to believe.

He had been seen in a field of cane armed with an axe. The fishermen saw him leave the land one night. It was an hour or so before the half moon set but the light was good, and the nervous brow which the posters showed was the same that turned to avoid their glance. They had missed the chance of a reward.

Men who had a criminal record went into hiding because they had seen the portrait and were confused. The slightest resemblance was sufficient justification for arrest. They could easily prove their innocence of this crime; but they were not sure about questions that might have trapped them into a confession of some other crime. Some people described how they would notice a change in the shape of a mouth or eyes, and got the feeling that their faces had started to take on the shape and expression of the assassin's.

'But why would she want to surrender her own father?' the fisherman asked.

'A hatred,' the woman explained. 'Is a hatred the mother impart. Like the time Sunny Boy kill his father. Was the mother who put it in his head to take that step. Moreso the girl was great, an' since people believe the Piggott man was her Pa, was better to get rid o' this one.'

'Could be so,' the fisherman said, 'no father is bad, but having two is a terrible business.'

The fisherman was reflective. There was a look of melancholy in his eyes. He seemed to think of everything at the same time: that face which haunted his recollection, disturbing the routine of his life, for his men were losing interest in their work. Preoccupied with ways of finding a man they did not know, the fishermen had begun to neglect the boats which kept their families alive. The price of fish had risen because the catch from Half Moon Bay was dropping every day. The fisherman thought of the girl's discovery of her father and the subsequent destruction of the *tonelle* near Forest Reserve. The news had reached Half Moon Bay the following day. Thank heaven, he had no children!

'You remember the story Gort tell when Forest Band visit Half Moon Bay?' he asked. 'Young boy who make such sensation for *Houngan*?'

The farmer began to rehearse the details of Gort's story. The fisherman wrapped his fingers round like wire. In moments of crisis he was always prone to meditation.

'He never did find his mother,' the farmer said, 'but look what happen now this girl fin' she father.'

'Is what I been thinkin',' the fisherman said. 'He die all alone with his madness which didn't touch nobody else. She find, an' findin' set confusion all over the place. Might have been your own father missin' the way that face haunt every man with lookin' an' searchin'.'

'Is bad I always say, is bad findin' out.'

'Bad an' good,' the fisherman said. 'It got two sides to findin', only we can't choose which favour what you fin'.'

The fisherman stared past a group of boys assembled round the poster on the tree. And the thought occurred that you couldn't predict what would happen to those boys. Perhaps they were staring at their own future. Any one of those boys could become president of the Republic. Any other could become the president's murderer. Ignorant of the future, they were yet trained to expect it. They were here and in the knowledge of their future at the same time. The future was there like that face stuck on the tree, and yet not seen anywhere.

'Is like your work an' mine,' he said, staring from his aged eyes into the farmer's face. 'Is a farmer what you is. You hold the land right there under your hand, plain for any eye to see, but no harvest can come till those crops show their face in all its fullness. Is the same with my trade only in reverse. I sit an' wait not knowin' if anythin' dead or alive under my boat, but I train to expect what I can't see. You didn't put that face there any more than I put fish in the sea, but you know it got a owner somewhere. I see that face there like you see your young plants, but I don't know him more than you know your harvest till your crops show up.'

'What I can't tell,' the farmer said, 'is if I ever see it before. Is hours I spen' takin' it in, an' sometimes it feel I never see it ever. An' sometimes I feel it is a face I see hundreds o' times before.'

They saw young Jack o' Lantern coming down the street. He carried a small tenor drum strung by a loop of wire round his neck.

The drum bounced against his chest as he walked. Then he turned into the school which served as a church on Sundays.

'I hear police attack them bad in Forest Reserve,' the woman said.

She was afraid for her son who often called on the Boys in Forest Reserve.

The farmer didn't answer. He had seen one of his cows in the distance. A girl was leading the cow on a rope down the track which separated the fishermen's huts from a blossoming field of corn. The cow's tail lashed the ears of corn which fell like hay over the track. The sun went under cloud throwing wide shadows over the huts; then surfaced in a great blaze of light against the face of the village clock.

'Is only the girl herself can say,' the farmer said in answer to a question the woman had asked.

'But why the mother won't talk,' the woman asked, 'why she won't say yes or no, only go silent in hidin' like the mother who drive her boy mad.'

'Who it is say she hidin'?' the farmer asked.

'Corporal Cuttin' come home last night,' she said, 'he was givin' news 'bout what happen after the girl confess.'

They heard a noise like wheels rolling across the sky. Without any visible change in the air, a burst of thunder had surprised them. The sound grew dim, coming gradually to an end. Then the rain came like spray lifting off the sea. And the fisherman started to think about the weather. The weather was often a chance for bringing things to an end. It could reduce passions during a public quarrel; sometimes it helped to postpone a fight. The fisherman recalled a time when the weather had saved Half Moon Bay from a terrible murder. A fight had started on the beach. The man lifted his woman up by her plaits; then dropped her like a sack of sugar on the sand. He had leapt on her, burying his thumbs in the sink of her throat. She was good as dead when the clouds burst, and the man pushed himself up in fear and ran for shelter. What dominated his mind more than the thought of murder was his fear of catching cold.

The rain came faster, and they ran into the school. But nothing had changed except a look of momentary surprise in their eyes. It had taken them a little time to recognise the corporal. He wasn't wearing uniform, and his ordinary clothes, brown khaki trousers and a navy blue shirt, had produced some confusion in their minds. They couldn't tell whether the absence of the uniform had detracted from his worth as a man, or added to his stature as a constable.

The corporal was talking to young Jack. He could tell at a glance what effect his presence had produced on them. It was exactly what he had hoped for. He had come back for a day to his native village, and he felt like a man whom success had given a chance to do as he pleases. The corporal was free to do as he pleased, and he had chosen the most patronising form of personal freedom: the freedom to be ordinary. He was free to encourage the fisherman and young Jack in the feeling that the importance which Half Moon Bay accorded the state of corporal could not affect one of her sons. And it increased their admiration when they reflected on his special knowledge.

They drew nearer. The fisherman sat beside young Jack. The woman made a noise with the bench which produced a burst of indignation from the farmer. She seemed to agree that she was not worthy of their company as they listened to the corporal's account of what had happened in Forest Reserve.

The corporal spoke in a very confidential tone of voice. From time to time he would remind them that his hesitation was only part of his responsibility to the law. After all, this issue had to do with the gravest of all crimes: and not just murder, but murder of the Vice-President of San Cristobal. He gave them knowledge which, in similar circumstances, they would have known. But he wasn't going to risk secrets or advice. Except it was advice on ways of finding the assassin.

'You know where that girl been to school?' young Jack asked.

'Yes, I know all that,' the corporal said. His silence was a way of letting the man continue, like a lawyer using the familiar trap of acknowledging his opponent's point.

'She wasn't goin' get mix up with that sort o' murder,' young Jack said. 'An' talk 'bout her father. Nobody ever hear 'bout her havin' any father but Piggott.' He paused as though he wanted to call the corporal to his senses. 'An' I don't have to tell you who Piggott is.'

'What it is the corporal say?' the farmer asked.

Jack glanced at the corporal who nodded his head and continued to look through the window at the tree with a portrait of the assassin's face.

'Corporal say he identify the girl two nights before the murder happen,' Jack said, 'an' she say the murder was goin' to happen.'

'Oh, no,' the corporal interrupted.

He raised one hand, but didn't speak. Jack had already started to correct his error.

'She didn't say what it was,' Jack said, 'but she say something was goin' to happen.'

The corporal stroked his knees and watched the farmer's face. The fisherman sat still, grinding his teeth like an ox chewing its cud. The muscles moved like hard lumps of gristle going in and out of his jaws. He paid no attention to what his face was doing. He had a way of being so still that his slightest whisper had the violence of sudden explosion. This was soon forgotten after he had spoken; but what startled them now was the fisherman's presence of mind. The corporal had drawn their attention to it before he answered.

'Two things I want to know,' the fisherman had said. 'Why she feel she had to give this information? An' where it was she an' the police meet?'

'Before we were only smokin',' the corporal said, 'but now we actually in the fire.'

In Half Moon Bay this was a way of saying you were about to discover something. The fisherman went on grinding his teeth. It seemed that he had never really stopped during his questions.

'She was there,' the corporal said, 'right there in Forest Reserve.'

'The papers didn't say that,' Jack said.

'We didn't let them make any mention,' the corporal said, 'but I tell you she was there. An' further information tell us why.'

Jack could feel his ears grow heavy with waiting. He restrained himself from asking questions because his questions always seemed to lead to an answer which embarrassed him. He didn't mind not knowing something; but he felt ashamed when an answer made him aware of things he had never suspected.

'But what bring her there?' Jack asked.

He was trying to play the corporal's game. The way Jack asked his question suggested that he would discover an alternative answer which would confound them by its obvious truth. He had reverted to the original suspicion he expressed before the others arrived. He believed that Piggott was using the girl to frame one of the Boys in the Forest Reserve.

'What happen at night the day can't see,' the corporal said. 'She been carryin' on with one o' the Boys in Forest Reserve. Is why she was there.' He could feel the weight of their astonishment. It was the first time he had resisted the temptation to play with their feelings. Their disbelief now seemed so pathetic, the corporal couldn't wait for questions.

'Is Chiki, Aunt Jane grandson,' he said.

'Painter Chiki?' Jack asked, still trying to retain what the corporal had said.

'Wonders never cease,' the woman said, pumping the end of a breast that hung, long as a shoe, inside her dress.

'Piggott adopted daughter an' Chiki!' the farmer cried.

Their response showed a similar sense of having no clues. It was the fisherman who caused a shift of emphasis when he spoke.

'What wrong with Chiki?' he asked.

The corporal hadn't expected this; but the other voices had followed too soon.

'It don' make sense,' Jack kept saying. He repeated it several times before anyone else got a chance to speak.

'People can do all sort o' things for love,' the farmer said.

'Especially when you young,' the woman agreed. 'Then your feelin' come fresh. You can kill or save from killin' cause o' that feelin' what light you up like a Chris'mas tree. It lift you high as a cloud.'

'Is how poor people who got nothin' to hide can feel,' Jack argued, 'but people o' that girl class don' expose themself that way. Never.'

'Under any class you call,' the woman said, 'people is people.

313

Like sickness, I tell you, love can strip any woman bare. Leave she naked, naked so!'

The woman broke off her reminiscence. Everyone noticed the change which had come over Jack. His face grew tight and nervous. The woman looked up at the men, then glanced past the door, trying to catch the outlines of the portrait on the tree. Even the corporal seemed to forget his privilege, as though he regretted what he had done. The others couldn't understand why news of Chiki and the girl should have produced this effect on Jack. They hadn't really seen the meaning of the corporal's visit. But Jack understood. Until a moment ago, he felt easy in argument with the corporal. Now he understood. He was thinking of his brother, Jack o' Lantern, wondering whether there was some law in heaven which had arranged that he should share his brother's fate. His brother had murdered a constable for the same reasons. Cutting was explaining before the others arrived.

'So I tellin' you, Jack,' the corporal said, 'get rid o' your drums. Tell your Boys not to provoke or play hard, 'cause the law goin' treat it like the crime that man do.'

'For how long they want to do that?' Jack asked. He looked at his drum as though it had already been confiscated.

'I don't know,' the corporal said, 'but I think it will be a general clean-up for good. They want to clean all what belong to behin' the times like drums an' ceremony for the dead an' all that.'

'The Bands don't cause no trouble,' Jack said. 'Sometimes the Boys fight an' things like that, but the Bands don't cause no trouble.'

The corporal became very cautious.

'Look at it good,' he said. 'You go see there's more to the Bands than you think.'

'But is all we got,' Jack said. 'Come rain or sun, is all we poor people got to make glad with.'

'Is true,' the woman whispered.

'People in Piggott class don' need the Bands,' Jack said, 'except for special celebration an' so, 'cause it have radio an' all class o' music box in their house. But the Bands is all we got.'

The corporal cracked his fingers.

'They say it make a bad impression on the outside world,' he said.

'But the outside worl' won't know we if it wasn't for the Bands,' Jack said.

'But is what they say,' the corporal replied. 'Now San Cristobal is a republic an' we free, we got to keep in step with nations as such. Music must be music. Frenchman, German, any kind o' man can play piano or violin once he know how to play. It aint make no difference where the instrument made. Piano is piano an' violin is violin. But no musician but the Boys can beat those steel drums. Not so? Tell me if it aint so?'

'An' what wrong with that?' Jack asked. 'You see anythin' wrong with dat?'

The corporal didn't answer. He didn't know whether anything was really wrong with what he had said; but he had done his duty to the village. Now he was going to complete it in the name of the law. The authorities had chosen him, as a native of Half Moon Bay, to explain their case. It was too soon to show them the proclamation which would become law from midnight. There was no clause which stated how long this law would last, no hint of a regulation in emergency. The proclamation meant a permanent break with the past.

The corporal saw the fisherman watching him, silent, inscrutable, his eyes empty of meaning. That glance had returned the corporal to his past. He had eaten out of that old man's hands. They had all gone speechless with memory under the spell of the old fisherman's silence. And the corporal, like the frightened child he was in their memory, forgot his office. He pulled the envelope from his pocket, and revealed the official proclamation in print. It was the only time in living memory that news had come first to Half Moon Bay.

'. . . from this day forward, day forward, this day forward . . . and ever as long as ever . . . as ever . , . the playing . . . playing . . . instruments herein referred to . . . herein referred to as Steel Drums . . . as instruments shall end . . . as from this day . . . forward forward forward. . . .'

The words crashed under their eyes, swift and unseen like the last drops of rain shaken from the trees. The corporal had left. They watched him past the door. He paused under the trees, then slipped like the shadow of the face on the poster out of sight.

'Was that he really come to say,' the fisherman said, 'something tell me he was only waitin' a chance to come with some news 'bout the Bands.'

'Is what time it is?' the young Jack asked.

The woman rose from the bench and went outside to look at the village clock. A boy ran up the steps and pushed past the women into the school. He was looking for the fisherman.

'Sharkie say the boats ready,' he said, 'is half-past five gone.'

The fisherman didn't hear. He was watching the light which sparkled in Jack's eyes. The light broke, and tears rolled down Jack's cheeks. The farmer drew nearer, rubbing his wide, cracked hand down the young man's head.

'Don' cry, Lantern, don' cry,' he said.

'What you mean don't cry,' Jack said, 'what . . . what you mean . . .' He couldn't finish his sentence. He was stuffing the cuff of his shirt into his mouth.

'Don't cry,' the farmer repeated, 'whatever happen we go stand beside you.'

The woman had returned from the street. She saw Jack's tears, and felt a sudden flush of saliva swimming round her tongue. She felt an intense hostility against the corporal, as though he had ordered the proclamation which would put an end to the Bands. She wanted to hug Jack to her. He wasn't much older than her own son who played bass drum in the Moon Bay band. The fisherman sat beside him: he and the farmer filling the space on the bench with Jack bending forward between them. There was an awful silence in the school, like a moment's pause in mourning. It lasted until the boy spoke.

'The boats waitin',' he said.

The fisherman looked up and shook his head.

'Not tonight,' he said, 'go tell Sharkie we aint goin' out tonight.'

The boy walked slowly towards the door, looking over his shoulder all the way. The woman came forward and sat on the floor opposite young Jack.

'He take after his brother,' she said, glancing up from the fisherman to the farmer. She spoke as though the young Jack o' Lantern was dead or absent.

'I remember his brother weddin' good, good,' she said. 'Buckets o' people gone wild that he get it in his head to marry Flo. After all those years livin' with her in sin, that he should want to marry.'

She paused to wipe a froth of saliva from her mouth.

'An' what commotion it cause all 'cause o' his feelin' for his drum,' she said. 'They couldn' get him to repeat what the preacher was sayin'. "Say after me," the preacher man would say, an' Jack o' Lantern just shake his head yes like he agree. "All my things," the preacher say, an "all my things" Jack o' Lantern repeat! Then trouble start. Nobody could understand it at all, with bride an' everybody waitin' hours in the church for Jack o' Lantern just to repeat what the preacher man say next. "All my things," the preacher man say an' pass on. "I thee endow," the preacher man add, an' Lantern won't budge. Everybody believe is that he don't understan' foreign word like endow. Poor preacher man in panic, an' Flo wettin' up she bloomers all over, so 'fraid Lantern go shame her in public. So the preacher man change his tune an' join up with the devil there an' then, all to get the weddin' over. "Say it," he tell Lantern, "it aint make no difference if it happen or not, is only formality everybody accept." An' he repeat again: "I thee endow." But Jack o' Lantern just shake his head like he was Judge Benedict passin' judgement. "Not my tenor drum," he say, "to you, Flo or Jesus Chris', not my tenor drum".'

'I remember it like yesterday,' the fisherman said, 'Lantern had bad, bad faults but he couldn't understan' make-believe in any form or fashion when it come to his music on the drums.'

They spoke as people do at a wake, but they made it seem that young Jack was the recent corpse. They were transferring to his presence all the virtues of his dead brother.

'I know how it feel,' the farmer said. 'I got cows. I watch them from the minute they drop out the mother' belly. Is me help pull them out sometimes. I teach them to walk. I feed them with bottle like real human infant, an' I watch them learn to graze. I know what it mean when some wild-time gangster enter an' take them off. Carry them off without reason or warnin', all the labour my two hands build. I know that feelin', only this worse. I can get a next cow, but you can' get a next music.'

Young Jack raised his head. His face was creased like a pillow all over, and his eyes were red.

'My brother always say he would die rather than surrender the Bands,' he cried, 'an' like his word, it was the Bands what make him murder that constable. Was the only thing he ever teach me to own, the only thing here, in heaven or in hell, I can call mine, this Steel Drum music those vagabonds in the capital go order to stop.'

His head fell forward as he blew his nose. They all watched him and thought of the morning his brother was sentenced to death. The school had become the courtroom, as the wind carried the sound of dead Jack o' Lantern's voice into every ear.

'I don't care who make the country's laws,' the fisherman repeated, 'if they let me make the country's music.'

He could still see old Jack o' Lantern's face and hear his voice accepting the punishment for his crime, as he asked the law to grant his last wish. And Chief Justice Squires relented to give the order that Jack o' Lantern's tenor drum should be buried with him. All the bands met at Half Moon Bay. The names were fresh in the fisherman's memory: HALF MOON BAY, SARAGASSO AND CHACA-CHACARE, BELLE VIEW, CHRIST CHURCH ROW AND THE COCKPIT COUNTRY, SULPHUR SPRINGS, MAGDALA POTARO AND FOREST RESERVE. Powell and Crim and Chiki were there. But it was Gort whom they chose to play Jack o' Lantern's drum. The bands played together all the calypsoes and digging songs which had made Jack o' Lantern famous. Then Gort alone played the hymn which every childhood in San Cristobal had learnt from infancy:

> Work! for the night is coming
> When man's work is done.

It was the last time they had heard Jack o' Lantern's drum, as Gort opened up the lid of the coffin, made the sign of the cross, and laid the drum gently beside the dead body of his master; for as Chiki had always acknowledged Hippolite to be his superior in paint, so Gort never failed to name who was his master on the tenor drum.

The fisherman looked towards the tree where a crowd had collected. The boy had spread the news that young Jack was crying; and everyone came to hear what had happened. Sharkie and the fisherman had left their boats. A huge crowd followed them up the streets, converging on the school. When Sharkie entered, he saw the farmer nodding his head.

'I agree,' said the fisherman.

'Me too,' the woman said, 'is a proper way to end if we got to end.' The woman was shaking her head like an enraged bull. You couldn't distinguish grief from the look of militant revenge in her eyes.

'If is the last time it happen,' young Jack said, 'the Half Moon Bay band go beat over my brother grave tonight.'

They got up, and the crowd started to disperse. For a moment they looked like the ragged, derelict squad of an army whose survivers could not understand their defeat. The fisherman put his arm in Sharkie's and walked towards the bay.

'I want you tell all the boats,' he said, 'I want every man meet tonight where they bury Jack o' Lantern. If is the last time the Bands go play, his grave is the only place.'

CHAPTER XIV

Fola was the last person to see Powell. Chiki had arrived to save her life. When he heard Fola scream, he had run down the passage and burst through the door in time to see Powell's body making its plunge through the window and down the back stairs which the waitress and Belinda often used for departures that were confidential or illicit. Powell had escaped.

But it was Fola, alone, who saw him for the last time. For what Fola saw that night was not the strong and handsome face which she had invented for Veronica one evening in the Moon Glow bar. Abandoned by Piggott and the families, alone and without aid,

Fola had been confronted by a fury which was more consuming than her desire to be alive; a force whose history was older and more powerful than the triumph of her own freedom from the families.

She had seen in the force of Powell's presence the fury of hatred which was old as Powell himself. She had seen the urgency of murder in a man who could not allow his chosen enemies to stay alive. Her memory was still fresh with the rage which had driven Piggott to go berserk on her body; but this had been reduced to childish petulance by the weight and meaning of what Powell had intended to inflict on her. As the *tonelle* had started her on a journey back in time, a journey which had helped her to see her place in Charlot's world; so Powell now worked a transformation in reverse. His presence had consumed that world, catapulted her out of all reminiscence of the past. Swift, timeless, like the achievement of death itself, Powell had dictated her arrival in this moment which contained them both. She was now other than a woman who had lived in error; she was now other than the girl who had tried to make her own backward glance. She was beyond redemption in the eyes which focused Powell's hatred on her life.

The episode had come about after the following events.

Fola had left Therese's house to take her refuge in Chiki's home. There was pain in every muscle of her body. Her brain had sprung a furnace more blinding than any fever she had known. Her mouth still dripped with blood. Chiki had washed her wounds while Belinda and the waitress went in search of medicine.

'Are you afraid?' Chiki asked.

'I wasn't until that night,' said Fola, 'the night Therese took me away.'

Chiki grew more nervous as he watched her mouth tremble. Her skin seemed to shudder and crack with fever.

'What about your mother?' he asked, hoping to keep her alive by talking.

'I don't know,' said Fola.

She grew more weary with talking. Chiki signalled her to be

still, and cleaned her armpits with a wet handkerchief. He paced round the room; then filled a glass with local gin, and gulped it at one thrust of his elbow up. It burnt his teeth, and started a trickle of water down his nose. Fola noticed that he was nervous. She tried to swing her head towards him.

'It's more than we had bargained for,' she said, striving to be cheerful, 'the town doesn't feel the same.'

'How you think it will end?' Chiki asked.

'I don't know,' said Fola.

'You still want to find your father?'

'I'm not sure,' she cried.

'You're not giving up,' Chiki said, trying to give her confidence.

'It's not me,' she said, 'it's the crowd I'm thinking of. What's going to happen?'

Chiki didn't answer, because she had turned her head again. He saw her hair like wet feathers sticking to her neck. He was afraid there was nothing he could do but call the ambulance and have her taken to the hospital. Yet he waited as though the future would arrive with some alternative.

Some hours later there was still no change in Fola's condition. Chiki was nervous. He had heard of Eva's death that morning and got the fear that a similar future was now awaiting Fola. But he was reluctant to expose her to the rumours that would happen in the general hospital ward.

Then he remembered an old friend whom he had known during his college days. Dr Kofi James-Williams Baako had lived near the Reserve; but he was never one of the Forest Boys. He had always avoided Chiki at college until the event which caused Chiki's expulsion. He had felt great admiration for Chiki that morning, but he had no time to bring this to fruition; for Baako won the science scholarship that year. In obedience to his father, he went to Cambridge where he studied medicine. Eight years later he got a Fellowship to travel in America. But the medical profession did not attract Baako, and he settled in America for almost a decade. He had returned to the study of Science and Technology which was his original wish.

His career was varied and astonishing in its range. He had returned to San Cristobal to fill the chair of Science and Technology at the republic's new university. Baako had never practised as a doctor; but he had become well known, and even loved, for his work in extra-mural classes. Like old Bobby Chalk and the Magdala bridge, young Baako was always saying that the university should be pulled down. It reminded him too much of the secluded leisure he had absorbed during his Cambridge days. Time and again he would insist that a new republic like San Cristobal, made backward by a large illiterate peasantry, and weaned into complacency by a commercial middle-class that had no power in the world which organised its money; such places were in a state of emergency, an emergency which was no less exacting and no less dangerous than emergencies caused by war.

Like Lady Carol and her phrase about the First World War, Kofi James-Williams Baako would end every public lecture by saying that the universities in a post-colonial country could serve no purpose unless they deserted the ancient notions of an élite; for the twentieth century had destroyed once and for all time the active concept of that privilege. James-Williams Baako wanted the new republic's university to forsake the ritual of cap and gown, to desert the lunacy of mumbling its thanks for food in an ancient and irrelevant Latin tongue; forsake the quiet and obsolete splendour of academy, and assume the burden of the bush.

Chiki had enough equipment for arguing with Baako; but they felt alike, for Baako was the only educated native in the whole republic who bought Chiki's paintings because he knew what they were about.

Baako was in a violent temper when he arrived at the Moon Glow bar. The sandflies had grown to the size of an army near the college halls. They had crowded over his ceiling the night before, and he hadn't slept.

They had polluted his food the following day. But it was the spectacle of Fola which brought about his recovery from this anger. He had been enraged by the proclamation against the drums, and now he seemed to see in Fola's illness the moment he was waiting for.

'Should we send her to the hospital?' Chiki asked.

'It depends,' said Baako, as he put the stethoscope away and patted and wrapped his fingers over Fola's pulse.

'I can't do much for her here,' said Chiki, nervous as a child, 'depends on what, Kofi?'

'If you think there's a good reason she should die,' said Baako, 'my answer is yes: send her to the hospital.'

And Chiki was relieved. Baako said he was returning to the university hospital right away and would expect Chiki to send a messenger for the medicine which the university-college hospital would have dispensed. Chiki had invited him to a drink, but he refused. So Belinda and the waitress offered to join Baako in the car back to his sanctuary. As he turned to go, he put his hand on Chiki's shoulder, and looked towards the crowd which had collected round the Independence statue.

'You know, Chiki,' he said, 'we've never talked about what's happening to us here in San Cristobal.'

'No,' said Chiki, recalling their journey from Forest Reserve to the world of Cambridge and America.

'You use those people for your work,' said Baako, 'but that's not good enough.'

Chiki glanced from the crowd and back to Baako.

'I do what I can,' said Chiki.

'And you do it well,' said Baako, 'but your relation to that crowd cannot be that of any artist to a similar crowd elsewhere.'

'The question is to discover one's work,' said Chiki, 'and having found that work, my business is to get on with it.'

Baako watched the crowd as he spoke. He was a short man, clean-shaven, neat and intense. His legs were slightly arched, and his hands were inclined to shake in moments of excitement. He watched the crowd, considering what Chiki had said. His hands began to shake as he fitted a hearing aid in his left ear.

'Say that again,' said Baako, turning an ear to Chiki, and his eyes towards the crowd.

'I've found my work,' said Chiki, 'and my business is to do it.'

It was difficult to tell whether Baako had heard. He seemed to have a special relation to his hearing aid. Sometimes he could hear

323

the whisper of a leaf. At other times the noise of volcanic thunder could evade Baako's hearing aid. People had come to wonder whether Baako's deafness was deliberate when he did not care to hear. But he had heard Chiki this time.

'The work will always be as clean as the atmosphere in which it's done,' Baako said, as he glanced at the small wooden statues on the balustrade, 'if the air is rotten you'll survive because you are a little stronger, but you can't get much further than surviving. And it's not good enough.'

'Politics is not my business,' said Chiki.

'Nor mine,' said Baako, 'but we're both the business of politics whatever else we choose to believe, and especially in a place like this where a voice can be heard if it chooses to make itself heard.'

'So?' Chiki said, alert and cautious as he waited for Baako to answer.

'My point is this,' said Baako, 'if Government is rotten, then every activity under its authority will be polluted too. And I don't mean parties. It makes no difference whether they are to the right or left if the actual way of governing is rotten.'

'Things change and they remain the same,' said Chiki.

'Because we do not try to choose their destiny,' said Baako. 'Leaves blossom and die and blossom again, but the tree remains, because it cannot chose to be other than that tree. But if politics is the art of the possible, then your work should be an attempt to show the individual situation illuminated by all the possibilities which keep pushing it always towards a destiny, a destiny which remains open. But you close it, Chiki, if you get bogged down by thinking how things change and yet remain the same.'

Chiki's attention was divided. Nervous about the future, he was now thinking of Fola.

'I am not satisfied with what political freedom has done here,' said Chiki.

'Not satisfied?' said Baako, 'I am positively scared, man. The freedom to make your own laws is absolutely necessary before you can move on, but the moment you embrace it as a goal which you have achieved, you're finished. And that's what those men in

Federal Drive have done. Their innocence and their ambition don't let them see what's under their very nose.'

Baako's hearing aid seemed to tremble with sound as his voice drilled its meaning into Chiki's ears. Chiki was still nervous, almost defensive as he listened to Baako.

'Independence is only a freedom to clear the air,' said Baako, 'to make the abortive life you've known more liveable; but it's then the problem of being alive, and trying to be alive in a state of freedom, it's only then the problem begins. And we mustn't postpone the time, Chiki, or the next generation will have to start by first wiping the muck we've left behind out of their eyes: the whole muck of suspicion and distrust, and even hatred, 'cause there's a world of dormant hatred in that crowd you see there!'

'I know,' said Chiki, as the spectacle of the crowd distracted his mind from Fola's illness.

But Baako didn't seem to hear. If he heard, then it seemed that he was not satisfied with the weight of Chiki's agreement.

'They are quiet,' said Baako looking at the crowd, 'because they are not sure what would happen if they made a move. They know that bottles and stones and knives can't cope with the republic's weapons. But there's a limit even to fear; and I tell you, Chiki, one day they will give way to the opposite of that fear. They'll go berserk, and the result of their madness will last a long time.'

Chiki seemed afraid for Baako; for his hands were shaking beyond control. It seemed that the small bag would drop from his hands any moment as he spoke.

'You can change constitutions overnight,' said Baako, anger growing dark and heavy over his small, bright eyes, 'you can bribe people with more wages overnight. But freedom or no freedom, if that crowd ever give way and go berserk, you can't clean up the result of that madness overnight. That's what those complacent imbeciles in Whitehall don't seem or care to understand about their African problem. That madness will linger, freedom or no freedom, like the memory of slavery in San Cristobal. And it's bad, Chiki, it's bad to pass on dead memories to the generation coming after us. It's not fair on them, Chiki.'

He hadn't finished, but a constable had come up the stairs and surveyed the room. He was looking for the owner of the car parked at the corner of Bruton Lane and Freedom Square.

'What's happenin'?' Chiki asked.

'That car outside,' the corporal said, 'the driver anywhere here?'

Chiki glanced at Baako, but they didn't speak.

'Is it yours Dr Baako?' the constable asked.

'What number?' Baako asked.

'S C 1 000.'

'That's mine, all right,' said Baako.

'So sorry, doc,' the constable said and bowed as he retreated down the stairs.

They watched his head slip below the level of the floor. Then Baako shook Chiki's hand and walked towards the stairs.

'We've got to make the leap that son-of-a-bitch dare not make,' said Baako, as he walked down the stairs. 'We've got to report on what's out of place, and attempt what must be done. The result can be left to God or the Devil or whatever agent chooses the contingencies of our life. Good night.'

Chiki had waited in the street as Baako drove away. He stood there trying to see the faces of the crowd in the dark. It was the first time he had spoken with Baako about the new republic; for they seldom met since Baako's return from America. Baako would come to Chiki's room to choose a painting, but he never spoke. His silence was that of a man who seemed to feel it might be rude to say what was in his mind. He admired Chiki's return to the Reserve; but he seemed to think that this kind of integration was bad for Chiki and the Reserve. It was the kind of power which cushioned Chiki from further shock; for it was a power which helped to make Chiki's peace with what he had surpassed. Chiki had caught his meaning, and he reflected on it as he watched the crowd.

The street lamps were on, but the night was thick, and soon the faces and the town were swallowed up by the dark. It was then Powell made his move. He must have been hiding somewhere near the Moon Glow bar, waiting his chance to get Fola on her own. He had come up the back stairs and entered by the window. At first Fola thought it was Chiki making his escape from the police;

but there was no reason Chiki should have been in danger; except, perhaps, her real father had announced himself and brought the search for Raymond's assassin to an end. In spite of her fears, she could barely feel the urge to turn her body. She called out for Chiki; and when Powell's voice came in reply, every trace of pain had deserted Fola's body. She had leapt from the bed; but Powell's eyes now paralysed her thinking. She couldn't move, and she couldn't manage the weight of her tongue. Powell seemed calm, even harmless, except for that look which came like lightning from his head. Powell had gone insane.

'No noise,' he said, rubbing his hand inside his shirt, 'no more than a sandfly can make, I warn you, no noise.'

'But . . . but . . . but . . . what have I done?' Fola stammered.

'Enough,' said Powell, 'you an' your lot done do enough.'

'Why? Why?' Fola's voice dribbled.

'It too late,' said Powell, rubbing the hand inside his shirt, 'it too late to explain, just as it too late for you an' your lot to make your peace with me.'

'But what have I done?' Fola cried again. She was hoping to persuade him into some kind of argument.

'You come into the Reserve that evening,' said Powell, now the hand rubbed more vigorously inside his shirt, 'an' I know why you come.'

'I only tried to help,' Fola started.

'Exact, exact,' said Powell, 'but what I do I want to do all by myself an' with my kind.'

Fola watched the hand and wondered what would happen next. She was afraid to scream, lest her panic should force Powell into some act of violence.

'I was only helpin',' said Fola, 'not helpin' you, but helping myself too.'

'Exact, exact,' said Powell, 'helping yourself, like when the police raid Forest Reserve for ol' Guru diamonds, an' my uncle Titon had to disappear. You was helpin' yourself.'

Fola tried to turn, but Powell's movement forward had brought her hands to a halt.

'You don't understand,' she cried. 'You don't understand.'

327

'Exact, exact,' said Powell. 'I don't understand. An' what's more, I don't want to. Where you an' your lot concern, I hope I never live to understand.'

Now Powell's hand emerged slowly from inside his shirt; but his fist was still hidden, as it rubbed against his chest.

'What I do I do alone,' said Powell, 'no help from you an' your lot, 'cause I learn, I learn how any playing 'bout with your lot bound to end. You know the rules too good, an' it too late, it too late for me to learn what rules you have for murderin' me. So is me go murder first. Otherwise is you what will murder me, or make me murder myself.'

Fola didn't stir. She felt nothing but the insanity of that stare which fixed her to the bed. The fist was emerging from Powell's shirt, and she saw the edge of the knife gleam like diamonds under his hand.

'Please, please,' Fola cried. 'Please, please. I can explain. You don't understand, but I can explain. I want to explain!'

'An' make me murder myself,' said Powell, as he prowled sideways, moving closer to the bed. 'One time I murder myself, but no again.'

He was coming towards her. Fola had strength enough to retreat further along the bed. She thought to jump through the window, but it was too far away, and Powell had suddenly held his knife out, poised and ready for its work.

'You won't know Little Boy Charlie,' he said, as he crouched towards Fola, 'but that night I murder myself. One bottle o' champagne make me murder myself, just as I say.'

'What are you talking about?' Fola cried, and her voice was louder, its sound increased by her panic and the certainty of what would happen.

'Make me murder myself,' said Powell, thrusting his free hand out to seize her throat. ' 'Cause champagne is a rule I don't understand, was not my rules, champagne is why I murder myself, so for that, for that, if nothing else, for that, Raymond an' you, beginnin' with Raymond an' you . . .'

And Fola's eyes closed on the scream which grew from her body like a noise unheard before. It was not only her voice, but her body, and the body of every living creature which saw its end in her own death: a noise which grew beyond the cry for rescue.

And that was all she could remember: the point of the knife about to take her throat and Chiki standing like a cripple over her, asking what had happened; asking and again asking why and what had happened. Like the time her grandmother had put her consciousness to sleep with that rat, she awoke to Chiki and his words as though they had travelled from abroad, nameless and unremembered landmarks in her life.

The sandflies were beginning to enter from the open window. They settled like specks of dirt on Chiki's hand; but he didn't seem to feel. His presence of mind had deserted him. He drained the bottle of local gin down his throat; but it was water, or blood or rain making a clot under his tongue. He couldn't tell. The door was open where he had burst into the room. Some women had collected in the passage way, but he didn't seem to see them there. His mind was vacant, finished and sealed. His memory was empty, except for the open window which he had ceased to recognise, and Fola collapsed upon the bed, and the feel of water, or blood, or rain making a slow drizzle down his throat.

Then the women dispersed along the passage; for they could make no sense of what they saw, and neither Chiki nor Fola tried to explain. It was the empty night space in the door which returned Chiki's sight and his sense of touch. It was that emptiness which brought Chiki back to his senses; and gradually he recognised the face which now filled the empty space. Gort was standing in the doorway, oblivious to Fola or the startled look of recognition in Chiki's eyes.

Gort was standing there like a man whose eyes were blinded by the simple light which they had seen. Gort alone was there, enveloped in that cloud of mystery which shut him out from the world which reading would never open to his eyes.

'You see Powell?' Chiki asked.

Gort shook his head as though he had forgotten who Powell was. He hadn't seen Powell; and he was too startled by the simple light which blinded his eyes, too charged with mystery to remember Powell.

'I want to ask you something,' Gort said, as though the answer would determine all his life in the future.

'Come in,' said Chiki.

'No,' said Gort, 'it too private. You come out here.'

Fola turned and watched them disappearing into the dark of the passageway. 'Even Gort,' she was thinking, 'even Gort is against me.'

'Good God, Lord, why?' she cried as the tears burnt her mouth, 'why do they hate me so? What have I done but try to help? Why? Why?'

*   *   *

AUTHOR'S NOTE

Self-judgement, offered from the best intentions, can often be misleading. But I don't think I should be far off the mark in describing myself as a peasant by birth, a colonial by education, and a traitor by instinct. As an adult, my instinctive treachery has always been directed against the Lie as it distorts the image of my neighbour in his enemy's eyes. These characteristics occur in different ways throughout this narrative which I have tried to keep as close as possible to the facts as I know them.

But there is one episode in our history of the time which remains obscure. The present author doubts whether any writer, foreign or native to San Cristobal, historian or otherwise, is likely, at this time, to recover the truth. I am speaking of Powell's disappearance from the land. Is he still alive, or did he die, as rumour says, at Half Moon Bay?

But this is known. Exactly two months and four days after the episode which brings this book to a close, enough evidence was found to prove beyond doubt who murdered Vice-President Raymond. It was Powell. His tenor drum was unearthed on the very site where Raymond's body had been found.

Powell has never appeared since the night he tried to finish his work on Fola. But his life has provided the literature of San Cristobal with two important themes. By historians and analysts, he is presented as a man who saw freedom as an absolute, and pure. It was this purity which crippled his mind until he could no longer see

330

authentic.

Freedom – theme

the act of giving and receiving as other than a conspiracy against himself and his most urgent need. A considerable body of critical writing has taken that line.

To the novelists and poets he appears in a slightly different, a slightly more melancholy light. Powell has become in their work the purest example of a man for whom nostalgia was an absolute. But his nostalgia had been trained by habit and the force of need to thrive on a memory which had never happened. Powell's life was dedicated to one impossible achievement. He had striven throughout to embrace that absence which was the seed of his nostalgia. He leaned towards that absence as though it were an ordinary object within the reach of his arms.

I describe these two themes as important because they are taken seriously by the men, some gifted and possessed of great learning, who have built their work upon the tragedy of Powell's life. I do not share either of these speculations; but the themes are important because I have read some of the books and found that, different as my mind works, I cannot discredit the energy of the men who made those books. That literature is their work; and the best among them have clearly made that work their life.

I have no equipment for logical analysis; and although I am not so old, I feel it is too late to try. There must be another way to the truth of Powell's defeat. To those who go different roads I can offer one piece of intimate evidence. Historians and analysts may be interested to find a connection between Powell's feeling and the fact that his real name, entered in a Pentecostal registry at Half Moon Bay, was Jesus Napoleon Flowers. Foreigners may laugh, but this is nothing extraordinary to people who know San Cristobal. For Jesus Napoleon were the names, like many others, which his mother had chosen from the titles of a picture on a Christmas calendar. This habit of naming had started as early as the emancipation of the San Cristobal slaves.

But I cannot see Powell this way; for I am nearer to what happened; nearer and more involved, perhaps, than any living person who shared in that Drum Boy's tragedy. Believe it or not: Powell was my brother; my half brother by a different mother.

Until the age of ten Powell and I had lived together, equal in the

affection of two mothers. Powell had made my dreams; and I had
lived his passions. Identical in years, and stage by stage, Powell and
I were taught in the same primary school.

And then the division came. I got a public scholarship which
started my migration into another world, a world whose roots were
the same, but whose style of living was entirely different from what
my childhood knew. It had earned me a privilege which now shut
Powell and the whole *tonelle* right out of my future. I had lived as
near to Powell as my skin to the hand it darkens. And yet! Yet I
forgot the *tonelle* as men forget a war, and attached myself to this
new world which was so recent and so slight beside the weight of
what had gone before. Instinctively I attached myself to that new
privilege; and in spite of all my effort, I am not free of its embrace
even to this day.

I believe deep in my bones that the mad impulse which drove
Powell to his criminal defeat was largely my doing. I will not have
this explained away by talk about environment; nor can I allow
my own moral infirmity to be transferred to a foreign conscience,
labelled imperialist. I shall go beyond my grave in the knowledge
that I am responsible for what happened to my brother.

Powell still resides somewhere in my heart, with a dubious love,
some strange, nameless shadow of regret; and yet with the deepest,
deepest nostalgia. For I have never felt myself to be an honest part
of anything since the world of his childhood deserted me.

* * *

CHAPTER XV

Tonight the new republic is on the eve of some terrible revelation:
the drums are still, all music surrendered to the ominous silence of
the sandflies, crowding each ceiling in San Cristobal. No one can
tell the age of the moon which lies buried behind the vault of black
cloud moving nearer and nearer towards Half Moon Bay. The
capital is solemn, like a wake that has refused to celebrate the
departure of the dead with farewell music. The Federal Drive keeps
watch. They think of the drums, now sinister and unforgettable in
their absence, like teeth that have fallen out; dead and removed,

transporting the roots of pain elsewhere, yet lingering with the memory of a loss which opens in each gum.

For the drums, like old teeth which had found their ultimate root, cannot be replaced. No substitute will take their place, and the superstitions of the republic are aroused by the conquest which these sandflies have brought about in every home. The families and the Boys from Forest Reserve are equal under their spell. The Reserve is afraid.

There are rumours that Powell is dead, that Powell has been seen going out to drown at his own request at Half Moon Bay. But the Reserve is afraid because this rumour is like the night, a part of the unknown which warns, but does not offer its reason for the steady increase of sandflies which populate the Forest.

Poor irrigation, and obsolete methods of drainage are reasons offered by the knowledge of science; but science is inadequate since it does not speak the language of popular belief. Here, science is like a radio whose wires and switches are already part of the noises which they announce. Science can only prove, select and prove, the details of an order which it has assumed; a method of discovery that works in collusion with the very world of things it sets out to discover. Bad drainage is the seed which gives birth to sandflies. That's what science says, and begins its journey, step by logical step; origin and end, cause and effect working in collusion with the very method of investigation which science has chosen in order to reveal what it now sees.

But the sandflies are there like the rumour of Powell's death; and science cannot conquer the Forest's fear; for science is no substitute for the faith which reaches towards that nightmare warning which the sandflies insist are there: absent and real as the hand of God. The sandflies are there: dumb yet eloquent as the voice of God. Tonight the Reserve and Half Moon Bay are troubled by their faith.

In the capital, men breathe under the same black vault of cloud. The families near Federal Drive have forgotten what they learnt, for science has lost its hold, dismissed like a servant whose work is limited to minor chores; science has been deserted by its latest allies; excluded by that necessary habit of not knowing what lies beyond

333

the nightmare movement that shows the sandflies like a signature of doom on every ceiling. These sandflies are a fortress that reminds each memory of a war, defeat and war and a triumph that seems no longer safe.

Lady Carol is terrified as her hand tries to kill a memory that crawls with wings over her galloping heart. Weary with trying, she breathes and slumps down on a chair and watches the sandflies conquer the furniture that reminds her how her fortune started. Mrs Raymond has forgotten her husband's death; thinks only of the punishment which will pursue her widowed days. Veronica is envious and full of hatred for herself as she reflects, and in reflection comes to admit that Fola's secret and disgrace will never be equal to the scandal which these sandflies now bear witness to.

The Reserve knows why the sandflies are here. The drums are detained like prisoners who cannot ask questions of their future. The *tonelle* is no more than an acre of burnt ash where Guru's spirit, fresh from its sacred water, now rides with messages that tell of Titon's fate. The sandflies are Guru's voice rehearsing that day when the police arrived to question diamonds that were not there; when Titon escaped with a fortune that was false. And so the sandflies have come, like the dead who do their duty; the sandflies are here to plant a monument to Powell's disappearance. Powell and his Uncle Titon, pursued from infancy till now by gods which had already chosen their end. Alike those two, infant and uncle are now made equal by their absence. Poor Powell, remembered and admired, loved and remembered when he was well! Poor Powell, remembered while his conscience was clean, loved while his pride was whole! Like the morning his young voice was begging little Chiki, ordering the achievement of his own childhood to work, work, work and prove what the Forest can do. Poor Powell, grieved now he is gone like the freedom his madness has betrayed! A freedom which his pride in its disease will never know. Poor Powell! Once forgotten and ignored by those who make the law, and now expelled by the same ambition which his uncle's greed pursued and could not reach. The sandflies are there like the night itself, and the Forest knows why.

But the families are more afraid because they cannot tell what evidence this witness will disclose. Lady Carol and Mrs Raymond and Veronica. Forgetful in their triumph, and alike in crisis; for they are asking the past, as they have always done, to stay entombed. They are scared to breathe until the past has promised like a corpse to hold its tongue. Near the capital, the families along the Federal Drive are vigilant and nervous as they wait, begging the past to hold its tongue; begging the present to disperse the weight of that evidence which crawls and collects like the nightmare clouds moving under and beyond each ceiling.

All the families, all but one! Only one woman is exempt from fear; strides up and down from end to end of a room which hides her freedom; purifies her secret as she summons the past to her aid. She gazes at the ceiling as though the sandflies are not there. Only one woman is untroubled by the judgement of the past; she alone hears rumour like the common wind that comes, investigates and goes. No rumour can now disgrace the knowledge which her heart alone has known. No rumour from the past, no judgement of her neighbours still alive, no prophecy which the future hides: nothing and no power here or beyond the grave can alter what she has felt from the moment her greatest, her beautiful and most cherished burden was born. No voice alive will deny; no corpse returning can discredit the love which her misfortune grew: the love which has remained, troubled, it's true, but larger and more real than the sky of sandflies which cower from her gaze. She is puzzled, but not afraid as she paces this room, pauses to watch a movement of hands in the near-by graves beyond her window; then looks up at the black vault of cloud; looks up and hears her voice astonish the nightmare sky with a faith which cries that justice must still be there.

Rich with memories of the past, and not alone in what she knows, Agnes now sits and waits as though her ears have been promised an answer from the sky she cannot see: justice must still be there since love has never deserted the sole and cherished beauty she has borne. She thinks of Lady Carol, yet sees no face but Fola's; sees only her daughter grow like the altitude of the Maraval hills. She thinks of Veronica and Mrs Raymond, yet hears no voice but Fola's; hears only her daughter like a promise which no price of

335

diamonds can ever purchase. 'And yet,' Agnes cries, 'and yet, and yet,' she cries again in a vision that is real but cannot grasp what it has seen. Fola has gone, but justice must still be there; for love has never deserted the beauty and burden of her mothering days.

Two items of the past now occupy her memory; for Agnes is too deaf with wonder to care what happens when everything is known. Her heart is ignorant of any compromise with what has gone or what will soon arrive. She can hardly feel the nearness of the chair; for Fola is a noise that lives inside her skull. Her daughter and her love are like the weight of an anchor in her hand. Two items of the past arrive to prove what she has always known. She has always been loyal to Piggott. Arriving with ambition, Piggott has never made a step which Agnes has not confirmed, known and confirmed, in the interest of his future. But Piggott is a minor loyalty compared to the size of her earliest wish for her daughter's future.

Agnes thinks of the families, and recalls the afternoon years ago, when a rumour of diamonds in the Forest Reserve came near as sin to tempt her pride. Agnes can see where the sandflies crawl that very afternoon when money shows all over Piggott's face: a promise like discovery in his hands. But no step is ever made till Agnes asks and orders why. She watches her hands as though they are still alive with argument and the risk that may ruin her recent marriage. That's why they are not rich.

She can see Piggott's face grow heavy and heavier with disenchantment. She recalls the look in his eyes; sees Piggott, her recent and only husband, come urgent with rebellion, arguing his case like a man who will not be dispossessed. Loud with ambition Piggott repeats what has happened; swears he will be loyal to his luck. And Agnes can hear her own voice, loud as the price of diamonds; Agnes can hear her voice refuse his offer. Agnes repeats with lunatic pride that she will risk any poverty while Fola is alive. She will not yield; will not and never yield to Piggott's luck while her beauty and cherished burden is alive.

'Listen, Aggie, listen,' Piggott cries, 'no one knows except . . .'

'Don't matter who know or won't ever know,' she answers.

'Just listen, Agnes, for God's sake, listen,' says Piggott, and tries again to bribe her with what he knows. 'Old Guru never find no diamonds. Is diamonds he use as his trick. From Commissioner down, the police every one still believe the raid come to a stop 'cause Guru never had no diamonds. An' I keep thinkin' 'bout diamonds too till Carol Baden-Semper find out the old jeweller's trick. Is money, Agnes, real money the old jeweller learn how to make. Is money, Agnes, I say real money like what I earn an' you collect to spen' on me, yourself an' Fola too. An' no one knows what Carol find, no one but me, Baden-Semper, an' Raymon', my second in command on the Forest beat.'

Piggott watches her like a child who sees its toys about to be destroyed. He repeats again, as though Agnes has just arrived, how Carol Baden-Semper has stumbled on the place where Guru hides the money his skill has made.

'We believe the Titon man what disappear,' Piggott cries, 'we believe is he what murder Guru an' run wherever he run, believing is diamonds he find. But no one knows, I tell you, Agnes, no one but me an' my second in command know where Carol Baden-Semper take us; take us an' show us Agnes, show us I say real money, I say money, Agnes, real money what I earn an' you spend on yourself an' me an' Fola too.'

Agnes watches her hands, yet sees no shape but the child's face which stirs her love; closes her need to wealth that is sure, abundant and sure. Agnes glances from Piggott to the hand that is her daughter's face. Piggott interrupts her brooding; repeats his luck, multiplying the promise that will build a castle, plough the future like a farm whose certain harvest is wealth.

Piggott argues for his ambition's sake; he argues for the sake of her own enrichment, for the sake of Agnes; and then he feeds his voice with the weight of all he knows to crush the only obstacle in their way. He argues for Fola's sake; he argues how Fola can become as large as the future his luck has found.

Agnes doesn't stir; she glances from her hands to Piggott's face; watches the movement of his mouth at war, yet hears no sound. Agnes is deaf to any reason in her husband's logic; for she will not yield, will not and never yield for the sake of the beauty and cherished burden she has borne. She stares at Piggott; challenges the look of rebellion in his eyes; she hears the threat of ruin to her recent marriage. But nothing will change her faith. She signals Piggott with her hands; orders him to relieve his knees and stand erect like a man; for she is going to speak now, and for ever hold her tongue.

'Enough is enough,' she says, as she hears her small daughter's snore in the neighbouring room, 'you've done your duty, Piggy, you do well to let me know. But listen, once an' for all, listen! Whatever heaven intend, I don't know; but I believe justice is there. An' sad as I was when Fola happen, I say no luck is bad if justice is there. So listen! Little Fola start life with misfortune not having no father as she should; but while I got strength to work an' eyes to see, I say this, Piggy, nothing go happen to put more strain on what I bring into this world. Let Carol Baden-Semper an' Raymond share what they find, an' good luck I wish them. But you can choose right here an' now. Take your share o' what you three find, an' finish this marriage which I will explain when my child is old enough to hear. Do that, Piggy, you can do that. Or if you want to stay with me, choose Fola an' tell the others they can have your share. Don't argue, Piggy, don't talk no more, 'cause I hearin' only with Fola's ears, an' she fast sleep. You can hear for yourself, Piggy, she fast asleep.'

And Agnes has won. Poverty has managed with the crutches which make her equal in stride with Lady Carol and Veronica's mother; the crutches made by no other than the burden she has borne; the beauty which has deserted her tonight. 'But justice must be there,' she cries, as she sees her daughter grown tall and more beautiful, but wild as a fugitive whose stride disperses the sandflies that cannot tell what will happen behind the nightmare sky. Justice must be there. Fola has gone, leaving her no other faith than the justice which heaven hears Agnes cry must surely be still there.

Agnes rises from the chair. She paces the room, wonders whether Piggott is still awake in the capital where his vigilance is not allowed to work. She thinks of Therese as she stands by the window and watches the neighbouring graves in Half Moon Bay. There is a movement which makes no noise; but it is there, ploughing the earth as though some corpse is being taken from its remembered cubicle of rest. She thinks of the fire in which the *tonelle* died; and wonders whether these ignorant peasants in Half Moon Bay are trying to resurrect a relative. She remembers she is alone, and wonders, in a moment of fear, whether these people are mad enough to bring the ceremony to life with an actual skeleton of the dead. But the night is thick. Like the sky, it will not let her see beyond the vague darkness of that movement over the graves.

What are they plotting with the dead? What monster will arrive to surprise her waiting? And she thinks of Fola, wonders where Fola has gone. She tries to see what journey her daughter has made from the moment now eighteen years behind, when the seed of that burden was planted against her wish. Agnes reflects on the horror and delight which had combined to open her body; open and make it grow with a future which has deserted her tonight.

Agnes can see herself cradled in that moment: no older and no less beautiful than the burden which has unjustly punished her by its absence. A difference of three months in age. Is it three or four? She isn't sure. For a girl's freedom divides time into years with weeks and months as unimportant intervals. Like any girl, she marks time by the events which have made a difference to herself and the people she knows. At twelve, for example, she remembers Ashton surprising the bishop and everyone else by his madness.

Once a gentleman, gentle and to order. Poor Ashton! On Sundays her mother, then housekeeper to the bishop's palace, her mother used to set the clock according to Ashton's arrival in the street. He is on his way to church; and all Petion Ville knows it is not a minute later than seven minutes to eleven. Ashton is poor, a carpenter and sometimes butler in the bishop's palace; yet everyone goes in search of Ashton for advice about money; any misfortune which can be solved is offered for his wisdom. For Ashton is honest; poor, but honest, gentle and orderly. And yet that afternoon which has become part of the island's history, Ashton comes out of his house, sits on the step, and smiles, harmless as an infant, as he watches his own nakedness. He carries an awl in his

339

hand; but it is an instrument of his trade. The street is horrified, but Ashton doesn't seem to recognise the neighbours who plead with him to cover his nakedness. His wife arrives; takes his head into her arms, and begs him to say what is wrong. He stares at her; but there is nothing like anger in Ashton's eyes. Then he lifts his hand, like a man offering his welcome to a friend, Ashton lifts his hand and stabs his wife fatally in her chest. Up and down, the way he would use his chisel, Ashton pierces his awl into her heart. During the trial, and long after his imprisonment and release, no one could get him to explain what happened. Each question will hear his voice reply: 'She was so good to me, so good she was to me.' Poor Ashton! Mad and free, he died like a dog.

And then at eighteen. Three months before or two months later, Agnes can't remember. But a similar thing has happened: similar in its lack of reason. Except, perhaps, that she has always felt something stir inside her when the bishop's nephew appears. He is a boy no older than herself. She hardly knows him, for he has not long arrived from England, carefree as any student on holiday abroad. Tomorrow he will be gone; but something always shakes inside her when he appears. He has the face which she would like one day to call her husband's. Is it the blond difference which makes for its magic? Or his carefree manner? For he keeps company with the local boys much older than himself. But she thinks of him that afternoon as she lies on the floor of her mother's cottage.

Her mother has just come home; begins again to plague Agnes with precautions. Agnes has heard it all before; but now she doesn't hear. Agnes is restless. It's not the bishop's nephew who calls her from the cottage. No one has called her. Nothing interests her now but the empty solitude of the orchard. Agnes walks alone. She envies the leaves their freedom. She looks up at the sky and wonders what happens there. She stops at the still heart of the orchard. She sprawls flat; imagines her body cradled like an infant's on the grass.

She wants to do something; but she doesn't know what. It is the largeness of the sky, the freedom of the leaves, the wild and careless frolic of the clouds. They make her feel like a cripple until she tries to exercise her legs. She tries to memorise the clouds, and

340

feels some foreign power assail her legs. She jerks them up and away. The skirt falls to her waist, and now her naked thighs are stiff with an effort to stay erect. That foreign power grows more familiar under her skin. It feels like some part of what she has not known before as hers.

Like steel, her thighs become two points of tension quivering for support. She raises her head; tries to rescue them with her hands, but her fingers won't bend. Her legs are swollen with the same tension she has felt in her thighs. She thinks they will burst, but she can't relax. She doesn't want to see her body loose its tautness. It has become an exercise in pain, spreading up her spine and across her eyes. The grass is a gymnasium which encourages her in this impossible exercise. She thinks of her body going through the rules of a slimming class. But this is not so. It is an age since she has forgotten why she is there, caught in the spell of that force that drives like an engine through her thighs.

She has forgotten everything except the still, turbulent energy of her legs suspended in air. She feels some huge and reliable force of energy holding her up until she loses all recollection of her body on the grass. She is a part of the orchard, a cloud that travels with the freedom of the leaves. She is just there, ruled and overwhelmed by this strenuous conflict of muscle which she has started in her own body. She is sweating, but her skin has lost its feel. The moisture is only a way of knowing that she is holding on, a sign of endurance. She will not rest her legs on the grass. She will not give in because she must not fail her body in the demands which it is making on her strength. She will keep her legs in the air for ever.

That's all she thinks. She wants her legs to see how strong they are. To avoid exhaustion, she thinks of the things she has seen holding on. She thinks of telegraph wires in the wind. While every-one waits, guessing the moment they will snap and fall; the wires stretch, tremble and stay. A morning after the hurricane has struck, the wires are still there, steady as the distance between the poles which they connect. She feels the same strength and certainty in her legs. She has to hold on. That power must last. She feels it in her thighs and in her hands. Everything is now transformed by her will. Her feeling has grown from a simple exercise of legs and arms straining upwards, grown with her whole body into an overwhelming passion to keep them there, suspended in the air.

And then it seems the sky has crumbled. The orchard covers her with surprise. For there, like a guardian angel over her head, she sees the face which always makes a stir inside her nerves. Soft as cloud, swift as a breeze, the bishops's nephew has arrived from the treacherous foliage of the trees. His smile is like a wound in her heart, hot and wide open. The blond face breathes like snow over her body: but her eyes are startled by the power passing upwards from her legs. She sees that face and marvels at the colour which blinds her eyes. The sun has turned his head into a farm of gold. It is not her wish to help him in this enterprise; but she cannot stir. His hands, though gentle as the clouds, now swing like a chain around her throat. His sweat comes fast, makes jewels on her brow. Her mouth opens like a hole under his lips. Her tongue begins an exercise in sex which it has never known before. She hears his body chime a future which his face has always promised might be her own.

She is afraid, resistant and afraid, until the power of her legs allows his weight. Flesh moves like cloud inside her flesh; flesh upon flesh, hardens and starts a wound that does not last after her mind forgets the body it has opened to this alien thrust. Soon, gradual and soon like the subtle change of cloud, her fear transforms itself into a freedom that outstrips the wind, dismantles the orchard from its leaves, and crowns her body with a silence like the sky. Eternity has happened under her skin.

Then she feels him leap, quick, light as a feather from her bosom. The bishop's nephew is afraid. Panic is like a warrior's mask over his face. He stares in the distance. His mouth trembles with a wish he cannot utter. He glances at her; then stares across the grass as though he were a partner in some crime he wants to share alone. He moves his hands, appeals to what he has recognised. He begs, beseeches and begs with his eyes. But his partner will not postpone his right to their equal enterprise. Then the bishop's nephew runs, alone and terrified of what he sees. He runs like a fugitive who cannot escape the trouble he is asking to postpone.

The orchard wails as Agnes stirs from the grass and sees, with horror, the reason for her blond boy's flight. This other face is not familiar. She has never seen it before, except in the legend which colour has identified with crime. Black as the bible night which taught her childhood to recognise a sin, she sees this other face approach. A face she has never met before, yet knows it to be a native of the soil that trembles with horror under her hands. Lust is like a murder in his eyes. It is her only chance to scream; but the orchard shivers with a terror that strikes her dumb. Sin would be easier to bear than the savage hand that throttles her cry. No cloud here, but a storm in every bestial plunge that rapes her body. No husband on her now, but a bandit whom madness and pride have driven to snatch some portion of the pleasure he has seen distributed before his eyes. Devoid of love, bestial in his act of robbery, his lust goes mad as it orders him to make one claim: that savage right to devour his share in what has just happened before his eyes.

And so Fola became that beauty and cherished burden which Agnes has always borne! Fola, now fugitive as the double fatherhood no certainty can separate. And Agnes reflects, in anguish and horror and delight, she reflects that her conscience is clean. Her secret is a truth which she has never known. Only justice can say what happened that afternoon; and love will agree that it were better Fola did not see the darkness which her rebellion has so nobly sought to bring into the light.

The night is like a wall outside. Agnes begins to feel her early fears. She stands at the window, waiting for some stir of light over that movement which she hears not far way. The sandflies are still there above her head. But the night hides something she cannot name outside. That movement is there, ripe and near as the graves: some terrible burden which the new republic will awake and find it has to bear.

CHAPTER XVI

When Powell was old enough to be a father: that is, eighteen or nineteen in the Forest Reserve; he was consumed by a passion for reading. He might have been trying to do on his own what he had

343

ordered Chiki to perfect under the tutelage of experts from abroad. Or he might have been preparing himself for argument with Chiki when an opportunity allowed them to meet. For Chiki had now left the Reserve.

A year after Chiki went to college, his brother had written to say that it would be better if he moved out of the Reserve. Aunt Jane couldn't think where on earth Chiki should go. Children didn't live in hotels; and the whole idea of leaving the Reserve to live elsewhere in the same island confused her. But Chiki's brother, now qualified as a dentist in Chicago, knew the solution. And Chiki became a boarder at the same college. He made new friends, in particular a German called Von Glatz whose parents, foreseeing the nightmare which was approaching Europe, had sent him out to San Cristobal as a boarding student at Chiki's college.

For the next seven years, Chiki was hardly ever seen near the Reserve. Once a month he would go on Saturday night to eat cooked crab backs with Aunt Jane. The Reserve was proud of him. They hugged him and kissed him when he arrived. The children would stare in wonder at their legendary Crown Prince. When Chiki was leaving, the women would give him small parcels of food. Peppermint and liquorice he would keep; but the more greasy contributions were passed on to Gort. Gort used to say, sometimes in jest and sometimes, it seemed, in earnest, that his own education would be solved if he could only split open Chiki's head and see what his brain was doing.

Chiki never spoke to them about the Reserve; and they never asked him about his new friends who boarded at college. One topic filled their time; for it was a sport to which they were all profoundly linked. It was the one activity which cut right through every gradation of class or fortune in San Cristobal. They spoke about cricket. Chiki had started to make a name throughout the island as a promising wicket-keeper and opening batsman. The Reserve had already begun to see him on the turf at Lords against an English Test Eleven.

At that time, Crim was a bloodthirsty fast bowler and, therefore, the best challenge for Chiki. The college would sometimes hire Boys like Crim to give the college team practice; so Crim went to the grounds where Chiki played and lived. Crim was extremely dangerous with a new ball, and the college authorities thought it better that he should not be hired after he had broken two of Von Glatz's ribs with a ball that rose like lightning no more than a yard from Von Glatz's batting crease.

Chiki was the only player who was not afraid of Crim; but the college boys did not know that, excellent a player as Chiki might have been, it was the Reserve which saved his life.

In no circumstances would Crim have tried to damage little Chiki from the Forest Reserve. Crim bowled at such speed and with such savage intensity, that it seemed, sometimes, he was using cricket as the only arena in which he could wage his war against people who were more fortunate than himself. Dr Speigel the Oxford graduate who taught history at the college once remarked that Crim reminded him of similar situations in England. The finest and most dangerous English fast bowlers, he was suggesting, had always come from the country's working-class. Speed was their weapon.

But Crim had it fixed in his mind that a blow to Chiki was a deeper blow to the Reserve; for the day Chiki became a famous man, and that was certain, the Reserve was going to make it known to the world what they had done. Crim would bowl to Chiki at the same speed and with the same intention of challenging him. But he would never pitch the faster balls in line with Chiki's body. Instead, he would make them turn, at the same lightning speed, just a fraction of an inch outside the off stump. Chiki was being taught by Crim when to avoid edging those outswingers into the hands of the wicket-keeper or the three men crouching in the slip field. As a result, Chiki became expert at a stroke which no one could surpass. Swift as a bullet, he would shuffle across and steer the ball along the ground between the three men waiting behind him.

The Reserve was divided in its loyalties, perhaps; but cricket, an activity which meant much more than sport in San Cristobal, cricket had proved that the division between Chiki and Crim was real, but the roots of the Reserve had remained.

But Powell gave all his time to reading. Every afternoon, at half-past three, he could be seen on his way to the library. He had taken over Chiki's place in Aunt Jane's heart; and every other day she washed the same shirt which Powell wore on his way to the library. This was the same time of day when Chiki and his friends were coming out from college. So Powell and Chiki often saw each other in the reading-room of the public free library.

Powell read every newspaper he could put his hands on: the local dailies as well as the papers from England and America. It was an indication of Powell's state of mind at the time that the *Manchester Guardian* was his favourite paper from abroad. He liked the *Guardian*, he would say, because it managed, in spite of any crisis, to breathe between the devil and the deep blue sea. A newspaper, Powell would add, was not unlike a man. They both needed breathing space in order to see where the wind was blowing.

So Powell bestowed on the world's news the attention which Crim had given to cricket. He saw Chiki every day; and each day the paradox of their life was repeated. Chiki would arrive with Von Glatz and others. Powell would be sitting in the reading-room; and it seemed that they could smell each other's presence before their eyes had met. But they did not speak. And yet their greeting was clear to each. For Chiki, however remote from the Reserve, could never have brought himself to ignore Powell completely. He could not. And Powell, whatever he thought about Von Glatz and the college, would never have done anything which might have embarrassed Chiki. Each acknowledged the other's world, with Chiki living a precarious balance between the two. Yet something had to be done when their eyes met. Their mouths did not move; their hands showed no sign of movement, but they knew the welcome had happened; for the index finger of Powell's hand, subtle as the snake-like movement in the index finger of Chiki's hand, had worked a signal of welcome which no other eyes in the library could have recognised. It was perfect as espionage in time of war: some Fifth Column activity against and on behalf of what they did not really know. But it worked; and they were agreed on the result.

Powell memorised everything he read, and in particular those events which might have been taking place in England or America at the time. He was preparing himself for that test of intellect which might happen some day between Chiki and himself. But Powell never guessed that such a day would have proved him to be Chiki's master; for it was against the codes of the college to pay too much attention to current affairs. Any college boy who became a journalist with the local dailies would have been considered a pathetic failure. The day never came for Powell; but it made no difference to his application. He would finish his reading; return the papers to their shelves; stride through the long corridors of books which made him giddy; and walk out into the street. He did this every day from half-past three until the library closed at six o'clock.

But Powell had never borrowed a book; and no argument would ever persuade him to ask that favour. Chiki had noticed this; for he noticed everything that Powell did in the afternoon. Powell haunted his sleep each night, until he could no longer contain this conspiracy of silence against himself. One afternoon, it was shortly before his expulsion from the college, Chiki decided to speak with Powell. He was standing on the library steps with Von Glatz and his friends. Dr Speigel drove up and offered to take them back to the college. Powell was leaving the library when the boys began to crowd the car, and immediately Chiki asked to be excused. He stood alone until the car was out of sight; then chased after Powell who was walking up the street.

'Hello, how?' the college voice said.

'Hello, so so,' the voice from the Reserve replied.

And each realised that neither had said: Chick, or Pow. But it did not matter. They regarded that loss of memory as an arrangement agreed upon by their different worlds. Powell knew that Chiki must have had something which he needed to get off his chest. Powell was calm, walking leisurely beside his friend as he begged the *Guardian* not to betray his memory. But Chiki was nervous. His silence was like a thief's, hoping that there might still remain one chance to deny his guilt. Then Chiki spoke.

'You know, Pow,' he said, feeling the name in conflict with his tongue, 'I see you in the reading-room every day.'

'Nothing else to do,' said Powell.

'But I notice,' Chiki said, 'that you never borrow any books.'

Powell smiled, but he did not answer.

'The papers may be all right,' said Chiki, 'but they can't take the place of books.'

Powell smiled again as he promised the *Manchester Guardian* that he did not care what it had failed to say.

'The library is free,' said Chiki, 'the books are there for you and me and anybody who care to take them away.'

Powell didn't smile this time. He turned his head away as though he was seeing his reason confirmed on the windows that opened beyond the street. Then he glanced at Chiki and quickly back to the street.

'You know how things go back home,' he said.

'But I don't understand it,' said Chiki, 'you read more papers than any man in that reading-room. It's plain contradiction not to make use of the books as well. They cost you nothing, Pow.'

But Powell would not be drawn into argument; and the *Manchester Guardian* could never have any idea what was happening here. Powell glanced up and down; then said again: 'You know how things go back home.'

But Chiki insisted that it was mad of Powell to hunger for the papers while he shut the books right out of his mind. This paradox was more fantastic than the signal of welcome with the index fingers. For Chiki knew; he knew and accepted the answer which had already taken shape in Powell's mind. Yet Chiki persisted with his questions as though the memory of an entire childhood had been put to sleep. It was weird, but true and perfectly allowed: the way Chiki's memory worked as though it could come alive, then go to sleep, according to the situation which confronted him. And there was no lack of integrity in this switch from temporary amnesia to the accurate power of Chiki's memory to hold what it had taken in. This was the paradox which Chiki had become; the paradox which all his future to the grave would probably remain. Chiki understood, and yet could not control this new and alien need to ask why.

There were two reasons Powell would not borrow a book. He had it fixed from infancy in his mind that if he took this piece of property into the Reserve, someone would steal it. Even Gort who could not read. Transported to the hooligan atmosphere of the

Reserve, that book had one future which was theft. That was the first seed of Powell's understanding. The second conviction in Powell's mind (and here he was absolutely correct) was this: there is no country in the world where public theft is dealt with by librarians. When the book had disappeared, and Aunt Jane asked what would happen next, the answer was clear. Powell, Aunt Jane and Chiki knew that answer: the police! the police! the police! Liza's big sister had not yet learnt to talk; but her infant tongue would have found a noise which answered a thousand times: 'Is police what catch thief. Is police what catch thief.'

This afternoon, in the new republic of San Cristobal, the police were out on an assignment that reduced all the libraries in the world to a derelict museum of old-fashioned toys, abandoned, useless and ignored.

At Saragasso they were seven hundred strong, one-third mounted on horses, and half with orders and bayonets that pointed from black cars. Few people had known until this day the formidable numbers of men who were paid to guard the law. The cemetery lay not far away, waiting for the day's result. The Federal Drive was made excessively secure; a squad of thirty to each cabinet residence. The capital was armed tooth and nail from prosperous suburb to derelict tenement and stretching wide and far across the open fields. The children's parks had been beseiged. The blind went home, and simply waited.

Every heart under that indifferent sun was waiting in fear and terror of the rumour they had heard. Every house in the Maraval hills was closed. Lady Carol and her husband waited. Forgetful of their recent loss, Veronica and her mother waited. Agnes had forgotten the possible justice which she trusted; forgotten the terrible moment her beauty and cherished burden had happened. Agnes was waiting. Piggott could not seek Fola in the hope of her forgiveness; for Piggott was waiting. Liza was waiting on her knees, making a child's unblemished bargain with God, as though Gort's life was an eternity of peppermint and liquorice which would become all hers. The entire republic waited; watched and waited for the sound and future of that rumour which they had heard. Every heart was a clock; but no heart in all San Cristobal could now match the gravity of Fola's heart and Chiki's heart, as they heard their own waiting like a clock, ticking their terror and their wish that Jesus and all the Saints would not desert Great Gort in this hour.

Throughout San Cristobal, Gort had become the name of leper or angel according to each wish. Lady Carol saw him dead, and had no doubt that the republic, more vigilant than ever, would make her wish come true. Fola's ears were like spies waiting to hear a miracle come alive; Chiki's magnet like, waiting to attract the impossible. It was too late to unwish what had happened now; for Gort had already arrived in Half Moon Bay.

Immediately he had spoken his secret mystery to Chiki in the Moon Glow bar, Gort took a train. And no one saw him in the Reserve again. That was four days ago. His journey was less painful, but no less arduous than the historic journey which that other man had chosen for his death on a public cross. The Bands in Half Moon Bay received him in secret that night. He slept in the fisherman's hut; and three days later it was clear why he had come.

Gort could not bear the death of his drum any longer. He had started to walk about like a lunatic who could still recognise the order of the world which his madness saw. So he spoke with Chiki that night, explained what it was he could not understand, and decided that his death was the only answer which would make sense. Gort said that he was going to violate the law which had proclaimed against the Bands. But he would do it on one condition only; and that condition would depend on the Boys in Half Moon Bay. He said that he would do it alone in the face of tank or gun, provided they dug up dead Jack o' Lantern's drum. He would play on no other drum; and if he could not play, then he would drown himself.

That was the rumour which the new republic of San Cristobal was waiting for. And it was true; for every village where Bands had thrived before the proclamation ordered their death, was challenged with this decision: Would they let Gort go alone? Or would they follow him, and pay once more that unforgettable homage to dead Jack o' Lantern's grave. News of Gort's decision had multiplied like the posters of the portrait which answered to the face of the man who had murdered Raymond. For Gort had asked one favour of Chiki. He had begged Chiki to tell everyone in the Reserve why he had refused to risk his conscience with the taste of sugar; and to tell them also why he had gone to Half Moon Bay. He spoke about the mystery of the sugar and the new mystery which had come from Jack o' Lantern's grave. His last words were: 'Kiss little Liza good-bye just in case. An' please, Chiki, please go see Aunt Jane before she die.' And he was gone, committed now and for all time to the need which was his fatal enterprise.

But Gort might have died alone the morning he awoke in Half Moon Bay. No one can predict what would have happened to him if Fola were not alive in Chiki's Moon Glow home. It was Fola's suggestion which turned Gort's private wish into a national rumour. When Chiki explained what Gort had said, Fola seemed shaken from the memory of her episode with Powell. She looked at Chiki as though she had heard in Gort's words the very opposite of what she had seen in Powell's hateful eyes. Her mind was a fever more active than the terrors of the night in the *tonelle*. And Chiki, watching his hands as though he could not understand what they were doing, obeyed what she had ordered. They got Belinda and the waitress to collect every gin box they could find in every street within walking distance from Bruton Lane. Fola cut them into squares no larger than a book; and Chiki painted in a firm, red oil the exact words which Gort had used to help his lack of understanding. These were Gort's exact words:

> Flo sell her sugar at five cents a pound
> Mathilda sell her sugar at five cents a pound
> Unice sell her sugar at five cents a pound.

'Drum Boys everywhere! Consider those three vipers what the devil himself won't fart 'pon! Consider what you know 'bout Flo, Unice and Mathilda!

'Now answer yourself 'cause Gort won't be alive to hear! Answer yourself this mystery:

'If those vipers what hate so bad, and what never plant cane shoots in all their life. If those vipers can reach common agreement 'bout the price of sugar, answer this mystery:

Call to rebellion — rebellion against law that was past not allow them to play the drums (Agenc

'Why can't the Boys what make the music that is San Cristobal only joy, why can't Half Moon Bay an' the rest harmonise to keep the drums alive? Answer for yourself, Drum Boys, 'cause Gort won't be alive to hear!'

Chiki and Fola worked like plantation slaves all night: Fola with a pair of scissors, and Chiki with his pencil and brush. From the night of Gort's departure until this afternoon, some four days later, no less than two thousand copies of Gort's words, painted by Chiki on Fola's cards, had been circulated in every village where drums once thrived north and south of the Madgala bridge.

The Boys from Half Moon Bay had dug up dead Jack o' Lantern's drum; but they were silenced by the fear that the law would force them to betray Great Gort. For none of them could say for sure whether they would follow Gort as he played Jack o' Lantern's drum through the streets of Half Moon Bay. It was the arrival of Fola's cards which made each man identical with his wish. The Boys from the Bay said, yes; dead or alive they would follow Gort as he played the drum which had once christened every tongue with praise.

As Fola's suggestion turned Gort's wish into a national rumour; so Gort and the Boys from Half Moon Bay might have been left on their own if the oddest and most historic accident did not occur. America had happened again; America that was the price which the Reserve had paid for their Forest land; America that was a miracle of money and bread! It was the accidental touch of an American hand which pushed the new republic into this afternoon of hysterical self-defence.

Jim Aswell was a white businessman from Virginia. He had made a fortune out of women's vanity in his cosmetic days. He came to San Cristobal the year before Independence, and decided to remain. It was he who started and encouraged the craze for radiograms. But Coca-Cola was the kingdom where his name made magic with lights that behaved like kites before the children's eyes. There was no village in San Cristobal where the word, Aswell, was not raised like a flag above the trees.

In Half Moon Bay and Forest Reserve, Chaca-Chacare, and the

Cockpit country, his name could be seen like a rainbow of lights over that legendary bottle of gaseous fluid. Old women and children sometimes believed that the name Aswell and the title Coca-Cola belonged to the president of the new Republic. It was a name to fear; but no one, among his vast regiment of workers, feared Jim Aswell. They liked him in a way they could not feel about the distinguished and hereditary planter, Sir Patrick Bloomfield.

Until Aswell's arrival, the name Bloomfield was sacred. A third of the republic's arable land was used entirely for sugar cane; and Bloomfield was hereditary governor of the local sugar syndicate. The Boys did not dislike him; nor would it be true to say that they liked him. For they never saw him. Sir Patrick Bloomfield, buried in his hereditary prestige, had become like God. He was absent and yet everywhere. But Aswell was there for everyone to see. A short, rugged man with a red brow where the sun had scorched his skin like leather. He knew what was happening in every village where his name was like a law on each palate. He visited the workers' homes as though he were a farmer who could not afford to ignore his livestock. He knew their names; and the older workers had begun instinctively to call him, Jim. The younger men said: Mr Jim, but the name Aswell seemed to have no meaning except in the lights over that magic bottle.

Aswell seemed to like this arrangement, and there was no question how his workers felt. He was a man of very fierce temper, loud in speech, but splendid in his humour. In Forest Reserve he would ask to have a try at cricket which he would have called black magic if it were not also England's national game. He would hold the bat like a spoon, and swing it like an axe; the way Crim had seen the baseball players do. But Crim never bowled at Aswell, and his reason was part of the workers' feeling. A ball was like a dagger in Crim's hand; and he always said that he was not sure whether he should murder Virginia Jim. He didn't want to burst Jim's heart with that diabolical in-swinger. The Boys liked Jim Aswell, and it was this nameless affection which got him involved with Gort's decision.

On the second day of Gort's departure, a young worker named Kem Barrett had been arrested by the foreman and taken to Jim

Aswell. Kem was the courier who stole time to circulate Fola's cards throughout the villages. He had distributed more than half the cards himself. He didn't play in any of the Bands, and he had no great love for the drums. But he had such a passion for changing San Cristobal, that his colleagues had given him the name Kem Radical Barrett. Barrett liked it as Aswell liked to hear himself called Jim. Different in age, race and fortunes, Kem Barrett and Jim Aswell were alike in one thing: they were honest and blunt about what they felt.

When the foreman took Kem into the office, Aswell noticed before a word was said that the young man was meticulous in his dress. He did manual work; yet he wore a tie to the factory. The seams of Kem Barrett's trousers stood erect as knives. His shoes were making a black fire under Aswell's eyes. The tips looked like polished teeth bursting out of his toes. Aswell sent the foreman away, and indicated the chair in which Kem sat. And Kem was afraid, not of Aswell, but of his own failure. He felt that it was careless of him to be caught. He had betrayed the cards which the villages would have to answer. It was Aswell who broke the ice.

'How come you look so tidy on a job like this?' Aswell said, and smiled. He was amused by the young man's erectness of manner.

Kem didn't answer. He lowered his glance, feeling shame for his failure.

'How come?' Aswell asked again, 'you look like a lawyer.'

Then Kem raised his head as though he had to let Aswell know that lawyer was no part of his ambition.

' Lawyer clothes an' my clothes hold different meanin', Mr Jim,' Kem said. 'Lawyers use tidy wear to hide something else. But I tidy 'cause a man with my radical views can't afford to look like a hooligan.'

Aswell sat up and watched the young man as though he had spoken in a foreign language. He had always been perplexed by the fluency of the most ordinary Boys in San Cristobal.

'That rough wear is bad,' said Kem, determined to crown his failure with an honest statement. 'A worker in untidy wear cannot lead, Mr Jim, 'cause he will always confuse the confidence of the workers what want to follow him. A workin' man, Mr Jim, is

354

more careful an' fussy 'bout clean clothes than any model from back where you come, sir.'

Aswell was no longer amused about Kem's clothes. He admired Kem, and it was the weight and meaning of this admiration which he was now considering. He felt no threat from the Bands; but if the cards really brought them out in conflict with the police, it would certainly disturb the work in his factories for three or four days. And there was nothing Aswell valued more deeply than time. Time and money were synonymous in his enterprise. He was not going to dismiss Kem, that was clear in his mind; but he was doubtful whether he should allow him to go on distributing the cards. It was the risk which his mind was urging him to take as a token of his admiration for young Kem Barrett.

'I put it to you,' said Aswell, as his eyes measured Kem's nervous, black face, 'I put it to you, Kem Barrett, you know what those cards could mean.'

'Could,' said Kem, 'I can't say what they will mean. But sure I know what they could mean.'

'Good,' said Aswell, growing more serious with each syllable, 'we agree on what they could mean. So I'll put it to you, Kem Barrett, tell me what you would do if I were in your place and you in mine.'

And Kem lifted his eyebrows like a schoolboy who was waiting for a question to pass along the row of ignorant answers which preceded his.

'Considerin' what the cards could mean,' said Kem, 'could, Mr Jim, could! If I believe that could might happen, as a man with interests to protect, I would not only dismiss you, I would arrange for you to get lost in prison.'

'In other words,' said Aswell.

'But Mr Jim,' Kem interrupted, believing he had already lost his job, 'before I silence you for good, I would get you to tell me why you do what it is you plottin' to do.'

Aswell rose abruptly from the table. He walked across the room and waited by the window as he studied the faces of the men in the factory yard. He creased the red wrinkles on his cheekbone, and chewed his teeth like an ox, considering a forbidden enclosure of

355

fresh hay. It would be impossible to say what happened then in Aswell's mind; impossible to hear from his own lips, for he died of a heart attack the following week. But when he left the window and returned to speak to the young man, Gort's moment of mystery had found its perfect sanction. Aswell watched Kem as though he wanted to be through with the whole business; and his voice came like an order.

'Listen, Kem Barrett,' he said, 'I'm going to give you this afternoon off, and tomorrow until lunch. No pay while you're away. But be back in this factory at two o'clock sharp tomorrow afternoon. That is, if you want to stay in this work.'

Suddenly Aswell turned away and walked back to the window. Kem stood like a man completely paralysed, a look of dumb stupefaction spreading over his face. He tried to speak, but Aswell's hand shook like a flag before his face.

'Get going, Kem Barrett,' he said, 'and don't let me hear any more talk 'bout Drum Boys or whatever the hell else concern republic or police.'

Aswell had turned back to the window before Kem could utter a word of thanks. Kem closed the office door behind him. He was still confused as he walked down the stairs and across the yard, astonished and suspicious, and afraid of that unknown element which had produced Aswell's offer. He was wasting time until he noticed the foreman grinning his triumph at the gate. Then Kem found his legs, and raced towards the street. The foreman saw him stop and could not understand whether Kem Barrett was going to strike.

'You son-of-a-bitch what born blind,' Kem shouted, 'whatever happen I go live to see the day you eat grass.'

And Kem Barrett moved like an engine that backfired everywhere with the name his colleagues had given him: Kem Radical, Radical Barrett.

It was half-past two when Kem left Jim Aswell's office. It was the moment which had produced in the new republic this massive need for self-defence. For six hours after Kem's departure, rumour had begun to work like a witch, changing face with each variation, but remaining solid and invulnerable on one point. From village to village throughout the republic, rumour declared that Jim Aswell, king of Coca-Cola, had taken sides with the Drum Boys against the proclamation of the new Republic. Gort's moment of mystery had found its loudest sanction, made perfect and complete by that name which dazzled every face like a rainbow in the sky.

The public clock struck five, and Fola's ears trembled like a cat's; for she had heard the dead come to life.

An arm's length away; yet Fola screamed, 'Chiki! Chiki! Chiki! Chiki!'

And Chiki's voice like thunder through the Moon Glow bar burst with the wind towards Half Moon Bay.

'Hold on, hold on, Great Gort, hold on, hold on, Great Gort!'

And not Great Gort alone. They came like a heaven of music after judgement day from every village where the rhythms of the drums were born. East of Magdala and north of Potaro, up from the mangrove swamps of Essequebo, through the open plains of the Cockpit country; and the villages followed them as they would on the day before Ash Wednesday. Carnival had come for once before its season, as the Bands converged upon the federal capital where Forest Reserve now marched with banners that spelt Jack o' Lantern's name. *[handwritten margin note: way of acting in rebellion]*

Two at a time and sometimes three according to distance and time, Band and Village like the forest and its leaves were making their way towards the monument lately named Freedom Square. The Half Moon Bay was still far away: three hours to go before they would arrive, for Gort, caught in that mystery like a season in the children's eyes, had begged the Half Moon Bay to obey little Liza's wish.

Liza had sent a message by Kem Barrett, begging Gort not to play; but if neither she, God nor Aunt Jane could stop him, then he must play; but do not travel on the road. He should come back with the Half Moon Bay by boat. Liza believed that the police would shoot, but not to kill. Gort might run, and when the police shot a second time, he would be killed. But if they came by boat, the police would not shoot a second time, because the river would not let them run. The police might even be prepared to let them drown. But Liza did not care what happened to Half Moon Bay; because Gort could swim. And Liza believed, like the taste of liquorice on her tongue, that if Great Gort was not yet dead, no fish in all Potaro could tell where he had gone.

And the Boys obeyed Gort's order to play from the fishing fleet that sailed from Half Moon Bay. The capital had waited; watched and waited, panic like a cancer in every eye. But when the villages started to multiply, fresh orders came from Federal Drive. And not a shot was fired. From end to end of that enormous bridge, the rifles shone like toys. The bayonets blinked and cried with a noise that shook the sun.

For Half Moon Bay, trailing the echoes of dead Jack o' Lantern's drum, were on their way; beating their faith upon that fishing fleet of drums, sailing to the capital town. Gort led in solo with the calypsoes and digging songs that had first christened his master's name: Never, Never me again; Glory, Glory, King Coca-Cola; Doctor Say you Pay to Earn But Lantern say you Pay to Learn; The Queen's Canary Fly Away; River Ben' Come Down; Goin' to see Aunt Jane; and not the native folk-songs alone. The paradox of their double culture was no less honoured with rhythm. For they changed as the mood assailed them; and a mood had soon taken them back to childhood and the hymns of their chapel days: Hold the Fort For I am Coming; I Got a Sword in My Hand, Help me to Use it Lord; and back again the music would swing as though their moods were magnet which the rhythms had waited for. Now it was a noise of: Never, Never Me Again, and Daylight Come and I Wanna Go Home. And each time the change came, the bass drums would wait to hear from Gort who led in solo, and on no other than his dead master's drum.

The sky rejoiced with colour that could not match the magic of these drums, as Band and Village like a forest and its leaves, moved and nearer moved to the place that was lately named Freedom Square. Each song was a message taken by the wind; locked for ever in its echo that could not move and yet was everywhere under that screaming chorus of sky.

And not Gort alone: no praise exclusive for Half Moon Bay; for the island entirely cuddled in song was there. East of Magdala, and north of Potaro; across the open plains of the Cockpit country; from the mangrove swamps of Essequebo and up the hills of

358

Chaca-Chacare. These were the giants of sound; the Bands whose names were old and always honoured for the work they had done. But when Half Moon Bay was getting near; the smaller bands found their nerve and argued to come out. Forgetful of their lack of skill they entered that arena of sound: Village and Band like the forest and its leaves marching from Sulphur Springs, Belle View and Carlysle Bay, Barnadoes Pride and St Johns Silk; Vigie and the Valley of Ascencion; Spanish Town and Mont Sauteurs; Curepe and Couva, Sam Lord's Castle and Point Cumana By The Sea.

And the children, like amateurs who could understand each other, trailed behind the small village Bands. The children made the rhythms talk as though their tongues were tied; for they had no drums. They had plundered every object that looked like metal and could make a sound. Frying pans disappeared; kettles soon lost their criminal face of soot as the spoons scraped them clean with sound. Near Forest Reserve, an old woman was crying and laughing as though her eyes couldn't decide what water they should use. Crying and shouting, that poor old woman as she begged them to return her most intimate loss.

'Liza, Liza, where Liza?' the old woman cried, 'anybody see Liza? Jesus an' all the Saints, Liza gone off with my chamber pot. Good God, is my only chamber pot what Liza gone off with. Liza, where you, Liza? Beat if you got to beat, but don't bore hole in my chamber pot. O Lord, my only chamber pot!'

But the amateurs were too loud to hear; yet the old woman cried and laughed as she saw the tree open its roots to receive the slow, wet labour of her lost chamber pot.

The dark was coming; but it seemed the light had refused to die until the Boys were safely home from Half Moon Bay. They spread like a navy across the river that churned and carried them slowly towards the Moon Glow harbour. The fishing fleet from Half Moon Bay had arrived; and all the Bands assembled near Freedom Square were suddenly still. They were silenced by the spectacle of the fishing fleet, sails clapping in the wind, as Gort, once more in solo, led with a message from his master.

No one could see Gort, for he was too short to show his head above the Bass drums that waited around him for the Half Moon message. His eyes were closed like old Bobby Chalk's against the sun; but his hands were like a crusade of armies as the bass drums joined him in the hymn which honoured his chapel days. Freedom Square was waiting, happy and yet stupefied, like a girl that cannot tell the miracle she has seen. They had seen the *tonelle* transformed into a real, familiar tomb; and the corpses like Lazarus climbed back to life, denying the power and the permanence of the grave. That hymn had been learnt from a foreign tongue; but it had found cradle in the rhythm of the drums which were always there. For the Boys from Half Moon Bay now played as though delight was the only note their drums had learnt. A clean delight! No other sound or phrase could match the meaning which their drums declared.

The sky rejoiced; the worms must have wept for joy as they heard that rhythm of their chapel days; a rhythm which Gort had wrung from dead Jack o' Lantern's bones, awake and clean in his singing grave. Chiki stood at the window, collapsed with tears as he saw his canvases come to life; heard with his own ears the sound which no conspiracy of colour and line could ever catch. The tears ran like a river from Chiki's eyes, as the wind crippled his voice and sailed its echo into the drums: 'Hold on, Great Gort, hold on, hold on, Great Gort!'

But Gort was elsewhere. The drum had returned him to the free and open residence of his master. And the bass drums paused and waited as Gort led again in solo. Like the afternoon he buried Jack o' Lantern, Gort had now chosen the hymn that would pay homage to a life beyond the grave. The bass drums heard his meaning, and rolled with the wind towards Freedom Square where every drum now joined in praise: every drum and every village, like a forest and its leaves, striding with the sound of their chapel days:

> Glory, glory, Halleluja
> Glory, glory, Halleluja
> Glory, Glory, Halleluja
> Jack o' Lantern sailing home.
> Jack o' Lantern
> Jack o' Lantern

Jack o' Lantern sailing home.
Lantern! Jack o' Lantern
Lantern! Jack o' Lantern
Lantern sailing home.
Lantern, Lantern,
Jack o' Lantern sailing home.'

And so the night arrived, a skeleton of stars dancing to the rhythms of their journey home: a simple myth of man's invention transformed by the music of his hands into the miracle of Cana's wine, the living parable of America's bread. The day had obeyed no artifice of politics or crime, but the old and ultimate order of the drums. Then night came and carried with it the echo of their praise:

Lantern, Lantern,
Jack o' Lantern sailing home.

November 6.

It is two months today since San Cristobal returned Jack o' Lantern to his grave. But this morning the First Republic gave way officially to the Second. The drums did not play; there were no fireworks. The ceremony happened like a wedding that has never been announced. It was nervous, quiet, briefly reported in the national press. Dr Kofi James-Williams Baako, the latest president, arrived an hour late. He refused to leave the college halls until the police had cleared the streets.

In the shortest and most arrogant speech the radio has ever allowed, he said at noon that no mob had followed him to his job at the College of Science and Technology. Their absence was the rule which they themselves had made and which, therefore, he would maintain. But he was courteous to everyone who witnessed his signature in the Federal buildings. Later he spoke informally to the new Parliament. He spoke again about the republic being in a state of emergency; and made it absolutely clear that the university will not be the same during his term of office. He begged the opposition, and in particular the Shadow Cabinet, not to regard their small numbers as a sign of martyrdom. He agreed that

361

the republic had inherited the freedom to oppose. He emphasised that it was a method which he himself admired and would strive to preserve; but he begged each of his adversaries in turn to consider his meaning of emergency; consider the statistics for tropical diseases, consider the massive size of illiteracy which had forced him to say that the country's needs were in the nature of an emergency.

But he warned that he would not be gagged by a word which named the way things ought to be done. Democracy, he said, was not their monopoly. It was no less his passion, hence his reason for deserting the college halls to give attention to the extra-mural classes at night. But he repeated that he would not allow them or any other Opposition to sacrifice his country's needs because of their loyalty to a method of debate. When people cannot read, he said, they have no way of discovering the truth of arguments in a parliament which they seldom attend. Rumour quickly becomes an absolute; and the press, impatient to be first with the news, can turn that absolute into a commonplace.

It would be wasteful to regret that their failure had happened through an obvious lack of vigilance. He would undertake no risk without bringing his reasons to the attention of his adversaries in debate. But if they opposed his reasons merely because they thought their sacred function was to oppose, then his conscience to the country would assume a greater importance than their loyalty to a form. The laws of emergency would compel him to crush the living Shadow of their Cabinet into a forgotten ghost.

The country had inherited two difficulties from its past history. Illiteracy was the burden of the poor. It was a great danger, but not greater than the danger of a derivative middle-class which, by the peculiar curriculum of their education, could easily become an active enemy to the country. In their college days, the prefect system had already perfected their gifts for Fifth Column work. Baako said he knew what he was talking about because he, too, was a product of that education. Even to this day, he would still ponder the miraculous change which had come about in his relations to the College headmaster and his staff. He had betrayed his closest friends out of loyalty to that status which the honour of prefect had bestowed upon him. These experiences of childhood and adolescence were not to be dismissed as dead with the days when they happened. In San Cristobal, as elsewhere, a man was the sum of the experience he had been or refused to become from stage to stage of his development.

He wanted San Cristobal to forget that they were free, and work towards enlarging, in their way, the horizon of that vision which the present century had exposed them to. They should not be afraid of taking; for no gift, whatever its size, could dislodge the springs of life which made them who they were. He said he would ask the citizens of the Reserve and all like them to think again about their relation to the *tonelle*. He would not order them to change, but he would try to find a language which might explain that the magic of medical science was no less real than the previous magic of prayer. The difference was one of speed. Injections worked faster than a bribe for knowledge they could not guarantee.

But the main problem was language. It was language which caused the First Republic to fall. And the Second would suffer the same fate; the Second and the Third, unless they tried to find a language which was no less immediate than the language of the drums. He did not care to be president, and he was sure that he would not stay in office a day longer than the state of emergency warranted; for he had other work to do. But remember the order of the drums, he finished, for it is the language which every nation needs if its promises and its myths are to become a fact.

Baako has come to power in a constitutional way. The night the villages assembled round Freedom Square, he was there. It was Chiki's idea that Baako should address the crowd. Baako declined because he thought he had no right to share in the triumph of the Bands; but his attitude changed when Chiki put his suggestion to Great Gort, and Gort agreed that it would be a proper way to end the day if Baako was an honest man. Gort had never met Baako before, and he had no way of judging for himself. But college or no college, he thought, there was one man in the republic into whose hands he would entrust his life. Gort trusted Chiki's word, as he would have trusted Liza's guidance if he went blind. So Baako spoke. He was simple, precise and urgent in everything he had to say. Gort understood; but his religious impulse is so great, that he begged to follow Baako's speech with a hymn. Alone, and on Jack o' Lantern's tenor drum, Gort played:

> Lead kindly Light
> Amid the encircling gloom
> Lead Thou me on.
> The night is dark
> And I am far from home
> Lead Thou me on.

The night was dark, but no one seemed to notice the contrast between this home and the harbour in which Jack o' Lantern had not long arrived.

The fishing fleet is back in Half Moon Bay. Throughout the Reserve the children are asleep. The street lamps will soon fade and close for the night. The temperature of talk and silence is the same. Nothing is changed, except the drums. Both here and at Half Moon Bay, the drums are different.

Under a street lamp, close by Mathilda's shop, Therese is recalling the afternoon Band and Village joined like a forest and its leaves. The women stand around, waiting for her to disclose what happened in one house near Federal Drive.

Therese is grim as the Chief Justice himself. Her hands tremble with the memory of that afternoon as she recalls her stay with Chief Justice Squires' wife.

'Honest is honest,' says Therese, as she swings her head up to the light, 'an' Jesus know I never traffic with those Drum Boys, and what make me join them hooligans in the street, if I say you don't believe.'

She pauses and stares through the light that plays like fingers where Liza's mother stands. Therese seems apologetic and restrained. She turns to take Belinda's hand before she can begin.

'I wasn't go dance no dance,' she says, ''cause I wasn't goin' leave Chief Justice Squires wife in her crying state. If you see how she cry that afternoon, waters o' tears drop like snowball out the mistress eyes. Just cryin' an' crying where she peep behind the blinds to see if the police go shoot. Is how she cry I tell you, Bel, is how she cry 'cause the police won't shoot. Waters o' tears what make me not want to leave the mistress in that state. An' is how I come to leave, believe me, Bel, I only leave 'cause I notice that all the time she cryin', although she cry, madam big backside was shaking like a mountain from the tremors o' Jack o' Lantern drum in Great Gort hand. Is only how I come to leave. It say somewhere how faith can move a mountain, but no mountain, Bel, no mountain ever move so fast as the mistress backside ridin' under the window where she hearin' Jack o' Lantern drum in Great Gort hands. Believe me, Bel, is only how I come to leave.'

The women laugh; but it is not the old, loud sparkle of delight. It is nervous and insecure, like the new rhythms of the drums. Everyone wonders about this change in the drums. In a moment of doubt they seem to think that the drums will never be the same again. Perhaps the fire which finished the *tonelle* has also killed the ardour of the steel which used to burn with sound over the night. Perhaps it is the *Houngan's* loss of command. He is still alive, but like a corpse which has refused its chance to speak. Or is it Aunt Jane who carried the magic of the drums into her grave. For Aunt Jane has not survived the triumph of the Bands. She died in a coma, her head fallen like a black box of bones against Fola's arms. Chiki was there and also heard, seven minutes before the coma stopped her voice, that the man who partnered the bishop's nephew in that orchard afternoon was his own brother, Aunt Jane's grandson. Chiki has never heard before why his absent brother, his senior by eight years, should have had to leave the land.

Chiki is not the same. Sometimes the children wonder whether he is going mad. He hardly speaks, but sits alone and broods, his face grown more melancholy, like the drums. He sits and thinks and asks himself what is his future and the future of Fola. Then he will feel his loss, glance at the sky, as though astonished by the thought that a man like Camillon is still free to walk abroad. But he thinks little of what has happened since his meeting with Fola. No marriage can happen here. And yet, and yet, he broods, like the drums.

The drums have not ceased to play; but their call is not the same.

Their stride is less assured as though they have forgotten the speed and splendour with which they used to race their rhythms to the sky. Sometimes they seem to pause half-way; pause and stammer like a child or a woman who cannot restrain her tears. Sometimes they are heard to stop as though Aunt Jane is begging them to wait. They just wait, pause and wait as though for death or for some noise unknown, some noise which neither tongue nor steel can utter. The music has not stopped, neither here nor in Half Moon Bay; but everyone knows and says that the drums are not the same.

Is it Chiki's mood which has tamed the energy of the drums? He does not go any longer to the little cave he used to call his home. The canvases wait, empty and idle as his brush which begs him to come back; shouts aloud how that gift for movement in colour and line is still alive. The little cave begs him not to forget; answer and not forget the oldest need his life has known. But he never goes as though he were finished with canvas, brush and all. Sometimes he sits and cries like a child, forgetful that everyone is seeing. He cries because he is convinced that he will never paint again. Chiki will not paint because he thinks he is a man imprisoned in his paradox for all time: the paradox of what he is and what he cannot do. For Chiki is still obsessed with the failure of his hands to tell in paint the magic of that sound when the drums came sailing home. No conspiracy of line or colour, he thinks, will ever fix that sound on the canvases which beg him to come back; beg him answer and not forget the oldest need his life has known. But he will not go. Chiki! loving and most lovable Chiki throughout the entire Forest Reserve! Chiki, only thirty-one years old! Chiki's despair has become a habit like making love.

And Gort! Like the day his drum died, Great Gort grows weak and weaker under the weight of his comrade's despair. No moment of that painful journey to Half Moon Bay, no triumph of Jack o' Lantern sailing home, can match what Gort now feels as he watches Chiki dying from day to day. Gort alone tries to argue that neither Chiki nor the drums will die. Gort says he agrees that Jack o' Lantern's drum does not feel quite the same as his own; but he tries to forget this difference. He can't say what will happen. He does not know Baako; so he thinks there may be trouble. But he believes the worse is past.

In the evenings he will assemble the children and teach them how to play. It is the only way of proving what he argues. He admits he is no prophet. He cannot name tomorrow; but hoisting Liza as example on his knees he begs simply to say, Gort will say: as a child treads soft in new school shoes, and a man is nervous who knows his first night watch may be among thieves; so the rhythms are not sure, but their hands must be attentive: and so recent is the season of adventure, so fresh from the miracle of their triumph, the drums are guarding the day: the drums must guard the day.

Ann Arbor Paperbacks

Waddell, *The Desert Fathers*
Erasmus, *The Praise of Folly*
Donne, *Devotions*
Malthus, *Population: The First Essay*
Berdyaev, *The Origin of Russian Communism*
Einhard, *The Life of Charlemagne*
Edwards, *The Nature of True Virtue*
Gilson, *Héloïse and Abélard*
Aristotle, *Metaphysics*
Kant, *Education*
Boulding, *The Image*
Duckett, *The Gateway to the Middle Ages*
  (3 vols.): *Italy; France and Britain;*
  Monasticism
Bowditch and Ramsland, *Voices of the*
  Industrial Revolution
Luxemburg, *The Russian Revolution* and
  Leninism or Marxism?
Rexroth, *Poems from the Greek Anthology*
Zoshchenko, *Scenes from the Bathhouse*
Thrupp, *The Merchant Class of Medieval*
  London
Procopius, *Secret History*
Adcock, *Roman Political Ideas and Practice*
Swanson, *The Birth of the Gods*
Xenophon, *The March Up Country*
Trotsky, *The New Course*
Buchanan and Tullock, *The Calculus of*
  Consent
Hobson, *Imperialism*
Pobedonostsev, *Reflections of a Russian*
  Statesman
Kinietz, *The Indians of the Western Great*
  Lakes 1615–1760
Bromage, *Writing for Business*
Lurie, *Mountain Wolf Woman, Sister of*
  Crashing Thunder
Leonard, *Baroque Times in Old Mexico*
Meier, *Negro Thought in America,*
  1880–1915
Burke, *The Philosophy of Edmund Burke*
Michelet, *Joan of Arc*
Conze, *Buddhist Thought in India*
Arberry, *Aspects of Islamic Civilization*
Chesnutt, *The Wife of His Youth and*
  Other Stories
Gross, *Sound and Form in Modern Poetry*
Zola, *The Masterpiece*
Chesnutt, *The Marrow of Tradition*
Aristophanes, *Four Comedies*
Aristophanes, *Three Comedies*
Chesnutt, *The Conjure Woman*
Duckett, *Carolingian Portraits*
Rapoport and Chammah, *Prisoner's Dilemma*
Aristotle, *Poetics*

Peattie, *The View from the Barrio*
Duckett, *Death and Life in the Tenth Century*
Langford, *Galileo, Science and the Church*
McNaughton, *The Taoist Vision*
Anderson, *Matthew Arnold and the Classical*
  Tradition
Milio, *9226 Kercheval*
Weisheipl, *The Development of Physical*
  Theory in the Middle Ages
Breton, *Manifestoes of Surrealism*
Gershman, *The Surrealist Revolution in*
  France
Burt, *Mammals of the Great Lakes Region*
Lester, *Theravada Buddhism in Southeast Asia*
Scholz, *Carolingian Chronicles*
Wik, *Henry Ford and Grass-roots America*
Sahlins and Service, *Evolution and Culture*
Wickham, *Early Medieval Italy*
Waddell, *The Wandering Scholars*
Rosenberg, *Bolshevik Visions* (2 parts in 2
  vols.)
Mannoni, *Prospero and Caliban*
Aron, *Democracy and Totalitarianism*
Shy, *A People Numerous and Armed*
Taylor, *Roman Voting Assemblies*
Goodfield, *An Imagined World*
Hesiod, *The Works and Days; Theogony; The*
  Shield of Herakles
Raverat, *Period Piece*
Lamming, *In the Castle of My Skin*
Fisher, *The Conjure-Man Dies*
Strayer, *The Albigensian Crusades*
Lamming, *The Pleasures of Exile*
Lamming, *Natives of My Person*
Glaspell, *Lifted Masks and Other Works*
Wolff, *Aesthetics and the Sociology of Art*
Grand, *The Heavenly Twins*
Cornford, *The Origin of Attic Comedy*
Allen, *Wolves of Minong*
Brathwaite, *Roots*
Fisher, *The Walls of Jericho*
Lamming, *The Emigrants*
Loudon, *The Mummy!*
Kemble and Butler Leigh, *Principles and*
  Privilege
Thomas, *Out of Time*
Flanagan, *You Alone Are Dancing*
Kotre and Hall, *Seasons of Life*
Shen, *Almost a Revolution*
Meckel, *Save the Babies*
Laver and Schofield, *Multiparty Government*
Rutt, *The Bamboo Grove*
Endelman, *The Jews of Georgian England,*
  1714–1830
Lamming, *Season of Adventure*